A PRECARI...

Phoebe looked down, and ...... the first law of tree climbing: going up was relatively easy; retracing one's path was another matter. Her feet in their old boots began to slip. She flung herself against the trunk, clinging to it for dear life. "Why, oh why, can't mistletoe grow in more convenient spots?"

From beneath her came the crunch of snow.

"Because that would take all the sport from gathering it."

Phoebe froze. "Who's there?" she demanded with more aplomb than she felt.

"I'm the godlet of the grove," said the stranger with a hint of ghostly menace, "come to spy on mortals and punish them for desecrating my holy place."

Phoebe giggled involuntarily. "How shocked you must be by our modern garb."

"Not very fetching. Much preferred those flimsy things my priestesses used to wear," he said, appearing from the opposite side of Phoebe's tree.

"Dear heaven," she murmured. Her rescuer was a giant, bigger even than Papa. His hair shone like mahogany, even in the thin winter light. He had twinkling hazel eyes, a ready, good-natured grin.

"I believe I prefer to remain where I am," she said warily . . .

Praise for the novels of Monique Ellis

"Brilliant and exciting, this adventure of the heart will cast a mesmerizing spell over your heart."
—*Romantic Times* on *DeLacey's Angel*

"Just the right blend of romance, humor and suspense [and] a sparkling conclusion . . . a confection to savor."
—*Affaire de Coeur* on *The Fortescue Diamond*

THE MARQUESS LENDS A HAND

Monique Ellis

Zebra Books
Kensington Publishing Corp.

http://www.zebrabooks.com

ZEBRA BOOKS are published by

Kensington Publishing Corp.
850 Third Avenue
New York, NY 10022

First Printing: December, 1996
10 9 8 7 6 5 4 3 2 1

Printed in the United States of America

For my professional family:
Tracy Bernstein and Richard Curtis,
with deepest affection and gratitude;

And for my readers:
Thank you for your loyalty and support;

May you all have the happiest of holidays,
this year, and every year.

Enjoy!

Prologue

Philip Fordyce sat slightly apart at the reading of Portius Parmenter's will, repressing his chuckles with difficulty as the freezing December rain assaulted the tall windows of Parmenter's drafty office.

From behind the closed door leading to the rest of the inconvenient old house came soft whispers: the runny-nosed infantry and Peg Short, the cook who'd spent most of her life feeding the Parmenters. Much good their female curiosity would do them. Hezekiah Hatch, the sly solicitor Parmenter had employed most of his life, was explicit: not even a ha'penny to drink Parmenter's health had been left the servants.

Insulted gasps and more hurried whispers came from behind the office door, and then the hissed words, *"Cheese-paring old sod! Wouldn't drink 'is health nohow."*

" 'I forbid any expenditure for the purchase of mourning,' " Hatch droned on, shifting to the next page with a palsied hand, " 'especially for my useless widow and even more useless offspring, to wit: Mabel Parmenter, Phoebe Parmenter, and Priscilla and Prudence Parmenter. As for my sister, Emma Trask, I'm not about to pay for clothes she can well afford herself.' "

Hatch's eyes sought the widow's downcast ones, hidden behind the heavy veil she'd worn since she first appeared at the door of her connubial chamber upon learning of her husband's death three days before.

To Mabel, his second wife and new widow, Parmenter had left only pin money. It was all she deserved, according to her deceased husband, having failed in her duty to produce a male heir.

Fordyce froze, watching as Mabel Parmenter glanced nervously at the gentlemen flanking her—Hotspur Soames, the Earl of Penwillow, and his uncle, Justin Ware. What, by damn, had the old fellow been about?

To his daughters by Mabel, the solicitor continued, fifteen-year-old Priscilla and thirteen-year-old Prudence, Parmenter had left nothing.

There was an uneasy rustling as the mourners reviewed their positions given the terms of the will so far. Fordyce came close to snarling as he reassessed his own.

Hatch frowned the angry whisperings down, wheezed on. To his only child by his first wife, twenty-six-year-old Phoebe, Parmenter had left lands, house and contents, and heavy coffers. Perhaps she—Parmenter's malevolence rang clear through the insulting words—would be capable of producing a male heir.

Fordyce glanced at his timorous and confused cousin Mabel. Soames was scowling with disgust; Ware, patting the plump woman's mittened hand and murmuring low. Parmenter's widow, now all but penniless, had just become her stepdaughter's dependent, and her children with her.

As for the country heiress, she appeared caught between fury and shock. He wondered why. It wasn't a bad inheritance. Of course with the whey-faced, angular Phoebe Parmenter rather than his well-cushioned older cousin inheriting, Fordyce would have to change his plans slightly. But, only slightly.

His deep blue eyes snapped with appreciative humor at Emma Trask's shriek of rage as Hezekiah Hatch stuffed the will in his case. The venomous look old Porty's sister was throwing her eldest niece was a paradigm of the art. The farce of mourning Portius Parmenter was over that quickly.

Clarence Dorning stepped from the shadows where he'd been hovering, face mirroring the disappointment of almost everyone in Parmenter's dingy office.

"I believe," the vicar said, throwing a nervous glance at his distant cousin, the earl, "it is incumbent on us to find refuge in the Lord following these stunning pronouncements. If you will bow your heads, I shall implore God's guidance for all here present, and above all for she who has become supremely wealthy, that she may humbly proceed according to His will."

"Only will that counts here is old Porty's, clodpole," Hatch snickered. "Your God ain't got nothing to say in the matter."

"Just so was Our Lord sold for twenty pieces of silver," young Dorning slogged on, wavering but determined. " 'V-vanity, vanity, all is vanity,' 'And therefore never send to know for whom the bell tolls; it t-tolls for thee.' ' "

"Stubble it, Clare, and go back to your corner," Ware hissed. "This is neither the time nor the place for pontificating."

Phoebe rose from where she'd perched on a hard settee and threw the mortified young vicar an apologetic glance. Then, as Fordyce watched, she knelt before her stepmother, her dull umber gown sending eddies of dust to swirl over the creaking floorboards, and gripped the widow's trembling fingers.

"Don't worry, Mabel," she said. "Papa's will is unconscionable. We'll make adjustments."

"And just what adjustments d'you think you'll be making?" Hatch snorted from behind Parmenter's scarred worktable. "Tell me that, hmm?"

Phoebe stood and turned to face her father's old crony.

"I want you to draw papers immediately for my signature," she said, "with remembrances for the servants and tenants, and a hundred pounds for Aunt Trask. And when I say immediately, Mr. Hatch, I do mean right now."

"Cheapskate," Emma Trask muttered.

"Beyond that, dowries of five hundred pounds for each of my sisters," Phoebe continued, "and twenty-five pounds to Mr. Dorning to distribute among the poor in my father's memory, and two thirds of all that remains after that to my stepmother."

"Guess you want the Crown to get everything, then," Hatch cackled. "Farmer George'll be pleased, I can tell you. Tidy sum, between the land and the brass."

"I beg your pardon?"

"Your hands're tied," Hatch gloated. "It's in a clause I wasn't to read 'less you took a notion to play lady bountiful. Underhill's yours, but only in trust for your husband, and eventually your eldest son, and I'm the trustee. Y'can't give away so much as a farthing, or everything goes to the old king."

"But I haven't got a husband or an eldest son," Phoebe protested. "I do have a stepmother and two sisters whom my father has all but cast out naked on the highroad."

"You can house and feed 'em if you want," Hatch grinned, overriding the incensed murmurs, "but you'll do it from your allowance—and that's sufficient for a frugal one, not a frivolous four—until you've wed and produced a male heir, for until then not an extra penny will you see that I don't hand you myself, and I'll not be handing you many. I'll be advertising for a bailiff, but he'll be reporting to me."

"Dear heaven," Phoebe murmured, staring from the chuckling superannuated solicitor to her stepmother.

Emma Trask whispered rapid-fire in her son's ear, gave him a pinch and a swift kick in the shins. Cobber blanched, wavered, stubbornly held his ground. Across the way Nick Gusset, Mabel's elder brother, was showering similar encouragements on his younger son. Emma Trask grabbed Cobber's arm and slung him toward Phoebe.

"Now you listen well, my girl," she snapped. "My Cobber's the one for you. Keep everything in the family. Cobber, say your piece."

Cobber glanced nervously at his mother, then dropped to his knees, seizing Phoebe's trembling fingers in his huge paws.

"You see how it is, Cousin Phoebe," he blurted. "Best marry me right off, or the mother'll make all our lives a misery. I won't beat you nor shut you in the attics nor starve you, and I won't keep you in rags, neither. There'll be fires in every room, and a chicken in the pot Sundays and mutton the rest of the week. Jellies too, if you want 'em. We'll be merry as mice in a hayrick, word of a Trask."

"How kind of you, Cousin Cobber," Phoebe quavered. "That's a most generous offer, especially the mutton and chicken, but I'm not certain—"

"See here," Nick Gusset spluttered, dragging his younger son forward as Mabel shrank against the earl, "if anyone's to marry

Phoebe, it should be her stepmother's own nephew by blood. Alfie'll do fine by her. Better'n you, Cobber, that's certain. Energetic young rooster, that's the ticket, especially with an old stew hen, if you want some chicks pecking about the place. Alfie, now *you* say your piece."

Alfie, at seventeen barely more than a gawky boy, glanced about miserably. Then, with a martyr's air, he sank to his knees and pulled Phoebe's hands from Cobber's damp grasp.

"I won't beat you and I won't starve you and I won't make you sleep in the attics and you can have as many bonnets and gowns as you like, and some fripperies as well, and we'll have *two* chickens and a turkey every Sunday," he babbled. "That'd be even better, wouldn't it, Cousin Phoebe?"

"Maybe I should marry you both," Phoebe muttered, throwing a despairing glance at the pale, dandified vicar, who was once more hiding in the shadows. She gently freed her hands as she retreated in the direction of her stepmother and the earl. "Then you can divide the place between you, and everyone will be happy."

"Can't do it that way," Alfie protested, bouncing up and dusting off his knees. "Marry both of us, I mean. It's got to be one or t'other, doesn't it? Never heard tell of a woman having two husbands—not at the same time. Leastways not in Chedleigh Minor. Don't do things that way in London, do they?" he asked, turning to the earl, whose pale blue eyes were twinkling merrily.

"No," Soames choked, "we don't do things that way in London. At least, not at last report."

"Thought not. So you see, Cousin Phoebe, you've got to choose," Alfie insisted, first pulling Cobber to his feet and then turning back to the heiress. "Otherwise m'father'll make me come courting, and Cobber'll come courting too, and I don't know the least thing about how to go about it, and I doubt Cobber does either. I wouldn't be much trouble, I promise, and I did say we'd have turkey every Sunday as well. And," he concluded triumphantly, "goose and all sorts of puddings and I don't know what all for Christmas."

"Well, I—"

"Should be Cobber," Emma Trask snarled. "Place's mine by rights."

"I do believe such considerations should be postponed temporarily," Fordyce interjected, coming to stand beside his cousin's stepdaughter, "don't you agree, your lordship?"

"Indeed I do." Soames rose, turned with a slight bow to assist the Widow Parmenter to her feet.

The plump little woman hesitated a moment, casting an uncertain glance from Fordyce to her brother and Parmenter's sister, then to Justin Ware. Then she placed her dimpled hand on the earl's extended arm and rose stiffly.

"Don't worry, Mabel," Phoebe murmured, easing her stepmother aside and giving her a gentle hug, "we'll muddle through somehow."

"I know we will," Mabel whispered back, their voices reaching Fordyce faintly. "After all, haven't we always? But you mustn't consider marrying Cobber or Alfie."

"Despite the assurance of goose and puddings of all sorts? And fripperies? Just think—fripperies at last! I'm ready to consider just about anything."

Then, eyes clouding, Phoebe cast a wistful glance at the bumbling young vicar still lurking in his corner, fingers twiddling anxiously among his multitude of watch fobs. Fordyce frowned, following her eyes from where he waited with the earl.

"Poor Mr. Dorning," Phoebe sighed. "He's quite beside himself for fear he's encroached. There was no need for Mr. Ware to be so ferocious."

"Mr. Ware wasn't the least ferocious. Mr. Dorning was merely being silly as usual, and Mr. Ware very properly put him in his place."

"Mr. Dorning isn't silly, merely very earnest. How're your cheek and shoulder?"

"Still painful. It'll pass with time—and it'll never happen again."

"You should be lying down, with cool cloths to take away the ache. Oh, Mabel—how you've borne it all these years I'll never know."

"We hadn't much choice, either of us, had we, the laws being what they are. But at least we've had each other."

"And always will."

"Cousin Mabel!"

The two young women turned at Fordyce's peremptory summons, Phoebe's face stripped of emotion, her eyes overly bright.

"Yes, Cousin Philip?" Mabel Parmenter said.

"The others have gone on to the dining room," Fordyce snapped. "You should be joining 'em."

"If you'll permit me to escort you?" the earl said courteously, frowning Fordyce down, and again offering the new widow his arm.

She glanced at her stepdaughter and nodded, saying, "So kind of you, my lord." She placed her hand on the earl's arm and accompanied him into the corridor, only the slightest limp betraying her painful injuries.

"A moment of your time, if you please," Fordyce murmured, fingers curling around Phoebe Parmenter's elbow as she made to follow the earl and her stepmother.

Phoebe whirled to face her stepmother's cousin.

"Keep your hands to yourself, if you please, Mr. Fordyce," she snapped.

"As you will." He closed the office door, locked it and pocketed the key. "If you'll have a seat, Cousin Phoebe."

"I'm not your cousin, Mr. Fordyce—merely a distant connection by marriage."

"Why d'you dislike me so? I've always wondered."

Phoebe's eyes swept him contemptuously. "You stood by and watched my father abuse your cousin, and lifted not so much as a finger to put a stop to it."

"And precisely what good d'you think my interference would've done, beyond assuring I'd never be welcome here again? I couldn't afford that." He pulled a dilapidated chair over to the table Portius Parmenter had used as a desk and gestured to it. "We've a few matters to discuss, and it may require some time if you're going to take this attitude."

"We've nothing to discuss," Phoebe sighed. "You'll have to

make your departure by tonight. Your continued presence is unsuitable, as this is now a house of mourning consisting entirely of females."

"Your stepmother's dearest cousin and closest friend?" he countered, hands tightening on the chair's back until his knuckles showed white. "Sent into a cold December night? Told never to darken your door again, I presume? Come now, Miss Parmenter, isn't that a bit excessive?"

"You're hardly Mabel's dearest cousin," Phoebe insisted, reluctantly accepting the chair Fordyce was again offering. "Neither are you her closest friend."

"I'm most definitely both, as even you shall admit in a moment. What more natural than for me to remain as gentlemanly protector and kindly counselor to the entire household? Consanguinity renders my presence entirely proper."

"Given this is now my house, my opinions carry more weight than yours." Phoebe shot irritably to her feet, head high. "Now, if you've nothing more to say, I must join the others, and you must prepare your departure. Our being closeted like this isn't the least seemly."

"What a little prude you are." Fordyce chuckled, eyeing the pencil-slim figure with distaste as he placed strong hands on her shoulders and shoved her back in the chair. The dull brown hair in its severe knot, the pale face smudged by exhaustion—those would have to suffer a metamorphosis or his stomach would revolt when it came time to bed her, and his soul as well. Though many might not believe it, he did have a soul. "But, all that will change, I promise you."

"And you shall make it so?"

"I shall indeed," he said agreeably, placing the table between them as he gained her father's chair. He sat studying her until her eyes dropped. "I mean you no harm," he said more gently, "now or ever, so long as you're agreeable to my plans for Mabel and the girls. And for yourself, of course. Given Mabel's lack of funds, her position won't be an enviable one when you marry."

"I'll always take care of Mabel, just as she'll always take care of me."

"What if your husband says differently?"

"No honest man would."

"Oh, I think many might," Fordyce returned equably, leaning back in the chair. "Even Cobber and Alfie, once they realize the cost of having three unproductive females hanging on their sleeves, whereas if you were to consider my poor self—"

"So that's what this is about? Another offer of marriage tendered Underhill's fertile acres and heavy coffers? No, I'm afraid it's out of the question."

"You'll have to wed or the lot of you'll starve. Hatch has every intention of keeping you on short rations until you produce that heir your father wanted."

"You're presumptuous, sir."

"Not really. Merely a gentleman with far better ideas than you appear to have concerning how best to see to everyone's welfare, my own included."

"Oh, that I'll grant you—your own above all, and the rest of us can go hang."

"Don't tell me you're actually considering the good vicar? Because if you are, it won't wash. Dorning aspires to the dandy, lusts after the carefree elegancies of life, and only pretends at preaching to keep a roof over his head. An expert sail-trimmer. I know the sort well, being one myself, only while he plays at holiness I play at being the perfect guest—much preferable on a daily basis."

"You're despicable!"

"Not in the least—merely of an infinitely practical bent."

"Besides," she tossed over her shoulder as she rose and headed for the door, "how I choose to proceed concerns you not in the least."

"Dorning would run you off your legs in a month," Fordyce snapped. "Stop behaving like a jack-in-the-box and sit down. I have the key, and you're not leaving until we've settled things between us."

"I'm not marrying you, or anyone."

"Yes, you are. You're marrying me in two weeks' time. There's the license to get, or it would be a week."

"Over my dead body." Phoebe wrenched at the door handle, gave it up and whirled furiously to face her would-be husband. "Give me the blasted key!"

"Over darling Mabel's dead body, more like," Fordyce said, voice silky, "if you refuse me. I don't like to put undue pressure on you, but most convenient, wouldn't you say? Your father, one of the best horsemen I've ever known, suffering a fatal accident immediately after giving his wife yet another vicious beating?"

Phoebe shrank against the door, the blood draining from her already ashen face. "Dear God, what're you implying?" she said haltingly.

"I'm not implying it. I'm saying it."

"You're unconscionable!"

"No, Miss Parmenter—merely destitute, and possessed of certain valuable information. I was out riding the afternoon your father met his untimely end, you see. In Soames's game preserve, to be precise. Shall we say I witnessed certain events, and am aware of the identity of the participants?"

"You're lying. Papa fell from his horse and struck his head, and that's all there was to it."

"Hardly. A worm turned, and now a man is about to be devoured by worms. Oh, yes, my dear," Fordyce smiled with immense satisfaction, "I do believe you wish to marry me very much indeed. Only your father's refusal of all offers for your hand has kept us apart. Now, my love, we can make our fondest dreams come true."

"No," she muttered. "No!"

"Of course were you to wed another you'd be spared the expense of maintaining your stepmother, for in that event I'd be honor-bound to have a conversation with his lordship. Justice must always be served, mustn't she? Unless, of course, I'm sworn to protect those whom Justice should seek out."

Phoebe Parmenter remained where she was as the handsome, golden-haired man rose and came toward her.

"Say you'll marry me, dearest Miss Parmenter, and make me the happiest of men," he pleaded with an insulting parody of humility.

"I've no choice, do I," she whispered huskily.

"None, my dear, if you bear Mabel the affection you've always claimed. Otherwise I'll see she swings at the crossroads. Come, it won't be so dreadful." Fordyce seized her hands and brought them to his lips, nose wrinkling as he saluted first one chapped knuckle and then the other through her much-mended black mitts. "I'm a most peaceable fellow, I promise you, and merely require a comfortable home and a conformable wife to go with it."

Phoebe snatched her hands away and wiped them on her gown. "I don't like being nibbled," she snapped.

"But you must pretend to like it, don't you see? We must convince them all, my dear, that our sole reason for tarrying was to determine when we would make our joyful announcement. I believe it should be made instantly, don't you? For dear Mabel's sake?"

She closed her eyes, shuddered. When she opened them, Fordyce saw only the determination of martyrdom in their muddy brown depths.

"Yes," she said, "immediately. 'If it were done when 'tis done, then 'twere well it were done quickly.' "

"What a little scholar you are. I'd no idea. And humor, with all the rest? We'll rub on well together, you'll see. Very well indeed," he said with a smile as false as it was fond, pulling the key from his pocket and unlocking the door.

"No one will believe this, you know," she cautioned. "I've detested you for years. Everyone knows that."

"Just be careful to throw me the occasional adoring glance, and remember to call me Philip and blush and simper when I pay you compliments or place a chaste kiss on your brow, and we'll pull it off without the least trouble. And now for our big announcement," he said gaily as he opened the door. "I wonder who'll show the greater fury: Nick Gusset or Emma Trask."

One

It lacked but a week 'til Christmas.

The woods nestled beneath their burden of snow, black against white, scattered dimples telling of a midnight marauder's search for food. A few moon-kissed flakes danced in the air—great fat things filtering through the lacy branches like the spangles of a conjurer's trick, unshadowed by their parent cloud.

The solitary traveler pulled his mount to a halt, gazing at the purity of the winter scene. Before him the narrow lane meandered through a glen, a twisting, diamond-touched ribbon unsullied by human foot or horse's hoof.

The gelding, a massive, raw-boned creature well up to his rider's weight, jingled bridle and bit as steam rose from his flanks.

"Steady, old fellow," the bull-necked traveler murmured, deep voice soothing in the still night. "No need to read me verse, chapter and book. I'm well aware there're probably potholes under that innocent blanket, not to mention the usual ruts. Only a bit more, and we'll be at Penwillow's gates. A mile or two after that, and it's a warm stable for you and a soft bed for me."

The gelding whickered. From high on the opposite slope's flank came an answering bray.

"And precisely what might that be, d'you suppose, Bacchus," the traveler said, eyes narrowing as he reassessed the peaceful lane.

"That's torn it!" an immature male voice complained, rendered as distinct as if the youth stood next to him by a trick of topography. "Told you not to move around so much, Prissy. Now he's sure to know we're here."

The traveler's lips twitched at the answering petulant, "Well, I'm stiff, Alfie. This isn't near so exciting as I thought it'd be, merely dreadfully uncomfortable."

"Might as well give it up," the Alfie-voice grumbled. "Never thought it was a good idea to begin with. We'll go to Lord Soames tomorrow, lay the whole thing before him, and then—"

"No!"

"I doubt there'll be any more, and he's the first of his lordship's guests who's traveled alone in three nights," a new voice piped, also clearly youthful, definitely female. "It's this one or give it up, and we won't give it up, will we, Prissy?"

"No, we won't. You can turn craven if you wish, Alfie."

"And just how'll you manage without Sukey and me?"

"Gussets've never been known for gumption. Parmenters have it in plenty," the youngest voice returned. "We'll do swimmingly."

"Well!" the traveler murmured as the gelding tossed his head and sidled in an unusual fit of nerves. "It seems we're about to have an adventure, my lad. Certainly we could do with one after the past month, don't you think? A wager or a scrape, that's the only question. Steady on, now—no bolting. Wouldn't be fair to the infantry waiting on yon hill, now would it? Not after waiting three entire nights for just such a one as I, traveling with none who'd render their task difficult, not to say impossible."

He glanced about him as if noticing both the glen and its burden of snow for the first time—a broad pantomime more in keeping with a mummers' show than a man's interest in his surroundings.

"Best we make it easy for them and safe for us all," he murmured, genuinely assessing the terrain under cover of his playacting. "Wouldn't do to spoil their fun." Then, "I don't like the looks of the drifts down there," he proclaimed in a deep rumble. "Think I'll lead you, old fellow. Last thing either of us needs is for you to come up lame."

With that the stranger swung his leg over the low cantle and dropped to the ground, twisting so his back was to the young people lurking on the other side of the hollow. He pulled a double-barreled pistol from the saddle holster, removed the percussion caps and slipped them in the pocket of his old greatcoat. His hunting rifles in their worn cases he didn't disturb, nor the portmanteaux strapped on either side of the cantle.

Then he set off across the virgin snow, sinking to his ankles and then his knees as he led the uneasy gelding through thick white powder that squeaked and crunched, proclaiming his progress.

And then, in a flurry of scrambling mule and churning legs, the little band was upon him: a trio of tatterdemalion thieves in boys' garb, their faces hidden behind thick woolen scarves and low-pulled caps, the tallest astride a rawboned jenny. The traveler eyed the ancient pistol trained on him with extreme disfavor.

"Stand and deliver!" the voice he'd identified as belonging to Prissy commanded.

"And precisely what d'you want me to deliver?"

"Nothing whatsoever," the smallest one said. "That's the wrong phrase, Prissy."

"Well, it's in all the books," Prissy protested. "What would you've said?"

"We're not highwaymen—we're kidnappers. This is how you should've done it. Stand still or Alfie'll put a bullet through you," the youngest informed the traveler with the air of a determined governess. "I'll have your scarf, if I may. Then lower your head, sir, and put your hands behind your back, if you please. We have a need of you."

"Going to hold me for ransom, eh?" The traveler leaned against his horse's shoulder, eyes glinting merrily in the moonlight, hand gripping the bridle's cheek strap. "Sorry to disappoint you, poppet, but there's none would be interested enough in my fate to cough up so much as a farthing."

"Not money, silly—you! We need assistance only a gentleman unknown in Chedleigh Minor can render, and I've definitely never seen you before. A man the size of a small mountain? You'd've been most memorable, sir."

"Yes, I suppose I would at that," the traveler agreed easily.

"Now, will you give me your scarf and lower your head so I

may blindfold you? We must be in our beds before they miss us, and we must get you to the cottage first and see you comfortably settled and explain what's to do. That's a great deal to accomplish in a very short time, especially as Alfie must ride all the way back to Market Stoking, and that's miles! And, if you'll be so kind as to place your hands behind your back, I've a need to bind them as well."

"I don't mind the blindfold," the traveler said, smiling down at his diminutive captor. "After all, I must have no notion of where you're taking me, must I, if it's to be a proper kidnapping? Let's make an exchange, shall we? I lower my head, and the lad over yonder lowers his pistol. A shame if one of us were injured in the midst of such a grand adventure. Would turn it sour, don't you see?"

"I have your word you'll not try to escape?"

"You have my word."

"Alfie," she called softly over her shoulder, "I don't believe we'll need the pistol anymore."

But to the traveler's extreme displeasure the pistol remained unwaveringly trained on his heart, the click of its being changed from half to full cock loud in the night.

"Binding my hands, however?" the traveler continued, eyeing the pistol and pretending to an ease he was far from feeling. "You'll find Bacchus recalcitrant if you try to lead him without my hand on the reins. Why don't we agree to a compromise: aye to the blindfold, nay to the bonds."

"Aren't you going to try to get away from us?" Prissy complained. "How utterly depressing. It's never that way in books. You should be riding *ventre-à-terre* across the countryside, with Alfie chasing you on Sukey and firing warning shots over your head. Have you no pluck, sir?"

"None—not while your cohort keeps his cannon trained on me."

"Not loaded anyway," the boy shrugged, still aiming it carefully. *"Bang!"* he said. "That's about the best it'll do. Trigger's rusted solid, don't y'see? Not safe."

Even so, the traveler observed the uncocking of the pistol and its return to the boy's belt with no little satisfaction. "Thank you, Lord," he murmured, having a fair acquaintance with the depredations possible with antique firearms in untutored hands.

"I don't think this one'll be any use to us," Prissy pouted, turning to her male companion. "He hasn't the least spark of imagination or courage, and we need someone with a deal of both. Besides, it's well-known excessively large men are dullards. A dullard'll be no use at all. We need a very clever man. And, he's laughing at us! I don't care to be laughed at." She whirled back to the traveler towering over them, stamped her foot petulantly. "You mustn't laugh at us," she said, then peered more narrowly at him in the bright moonlight. "Why, I don't believe he's even titled, Pru. He has the air of a prize fighter, and look at his clothes! That greatcoat is threadbare."

"I've been traveling, with no opportunity to regularize myself," the traveler explained, bending so the younger girl—Pru, apparently—could tie the scarf over his eyes. "My apologies if I don't suit your notion of what a kidnap victim should be."

"I don't believe he's even a gentleman," the older girl grumbled in disgust. "He sounds precisely like a superior sort of servant. What I wanted was a titled gentleman—a true hero who'd be able to unearth some wonderfully unpleasant fact about Cousin Philip among his London acquaintance, and have him banished to the Americas. Everyone knows they're quite uncivilized, and so the first time Cousin Philip played his tricks he'd be dead. And do something about Mr. Hatch as well, so Phoebe won't have to wed anyone unless she wishes. This lummox will be useless. Why, I doubt he can even read or write. Who and what are you, sirrah?"

"I? A solitary traveler, as you've already observed," he smiled.

"I mean your name," Prissy demanded with no little impatience.

"Since you're not planning to hold me for ransom, d'you really need it?"

"Well," the schoolmistressy one said as she tightened the scarf over his eyes, "we must call you something, mustn't we? There—you may mount, and I'll lead your horse. Tell him to permit me, please. Otherwise you'll have to walk, and I doubt you'd like that. The snow is rather deep in spots.

"As to your name, it's impolite to be forever addressing someone as 'you' and referring to him as 'he.' Phoebe's always been clear on that point, and Mama concurs."

"Goodness, I didn't realize. But kidnapping is totally polite according to Phoebe?"

"He's laughing at us again," Prissy muttered.

"No, he's merely having a bit of fun at our expense," Pru disagreed, "and I can't say I blame him. On the surface this is all quite nonsensical, as we've explained none of it to him yet. Please sir, what may we call you?"

The oversized kidnap victim did his best to moderate his tone, continuing more seriously, "Put that way, and in deference to Phoebe and your mama and their notions of propriety, you may call me Peter."

"Peter what? I presume you have a family name, and as you're considerably older than we are, it wouldn't do for us to call you by your given name."

"Such punctilious kidnappers! Well then, my full name is, ah, Peter Oakwood." Or, close enough, he added wryly to himself.

"Thank you," the serious little voice said. "Now, if you'll be so good as to mount, Mr. Oakwood, and tell us what business you have in the neighborhood? You're not a guest of Lord Soames's after all, are you."

"No," Oakwood returned, swinging back into the saddle. It wasn't a lie. Soames wasn't expecting him, and so he wasn't properly his guest as yet. "Sorry to disappoint you, but I'm not."

"Then why are you here? You don't appear to have funds to be gadding about for amusement. Besides, this isn't the time of year for pleasure trips."

"I'm seeking employment," Oakwood invented on a stroke of genius. No matter what he decided about this ridiculous situation, that would serve. "As you can tell from my appearance, my pockets're rather to let at the moment, and I've heard the local lord is a liberal employer, and a fair one," he expounded, positive this last, at least, was true.

"What sort of employment?"

"Oh, I'm willing to turn my hand to most anything."

"I haven't heard Lord Soames was seeking anyone, have you?" Pru said doubtfully.

"No," Alfie's voice concurred, "and you may be sure if he was Emma Trask'd be speaking of nothing else, besides recommending Cobber for whatever post his lordship had to offer."

"Perhaps he's not," Oakwood returned equably, "but even so I'm sure of a full belly and a place to sleep. That's a great deal to a man in such straits as I. Can you offer as much?"

"Well, there's bread and cheese," the youngest said, "and a scrap of yesterday's rabbit pie, and I've gathered windfalls from the orchard for you. And there's a fire laid, but we didn't dare light it for fear a spark might set the cottage to burning. Besides, if we'd found no one it would've been a waste of good firewood."

"It would, indeed. How provident of you!"

"Well, it's unpleasant to gather this time of year."

"He's laughing at us again," Prissy sulked. "I say we set him free and try again tomorrow, Pru."

"And I say we daren't risk another attempt," Alfie returned, "so it's him or no one."

"Then let it be me," Oakwood said genially. "You children've tumbled into some sort of bumblebroth, haven't you."

"We're not children," Prissy retorted, cut to the quick. "Alfie'll be eighteen in a few months, and I'm fifteen. I suppose you might call Pru a child for she's only just turned thirteen, but she has more sense than Mama, and Mama's almost three times her age. If you can't tell the difference you won't be the least use, and it isn't a bumblebroth. It's a disaster!"

"All the more reason to retain me in your service. I'm rather good at disasters."

"Besides, we daren't let him go until he agrees to help us," Pru said with unassailable logic. "Otherwise he'll sound the alarm and all will be at an end."

"And we certainly can't have that," Oakwood grinned, "now can we?"

* * *

The cottage wasn't as bad as it might've been, Oakwood decided. At least it offered shelter from the bitter cold.

Old, and clearly abandoned for a multitude of years, but then he'd expected that. The thatched roof appeared solid enough despite its age, which was all that mattered given the short time he expected to reside there. Probably some derelict property of Soames's, unless he'd lost all sense of direction on the short, twisting journey.

"Cozy," he murmured, as he gave the place a cursory inspection while the children watched him anxiously, Prissy's china blue eyes pleading for approval, Pru's light brown ones defying him to find fault.

A battered lantern stood in the center of a deal table so enthusiastically scrubbed it was almost white. Smoke might curl from the poorly trimmed wick, but that was easily remedied and its light—assisted by a pair of stubby work candles skewered on iron spikes protruding from the fieldstone chimney—was adequate. He wasn't, after all, expecting anything so luxurious as White's or Brooks's, or any of his own well-appointed and immaculate establishments.

These imps of Satan had planned carefully for their victim's sojourn.

The main room was commodious enough, if inconveniently low-beamed for one of his height—Oakwood topped six feet by a generous measure—and showed evidence of the housewifely attentions of at least one pair of youthful hands. He picked up a battered pewter tankard from the table in the center of the room, smiling at the chipped crockery and unmatched utensils.

A bed of rough wood posts had been dragged in from the windowless bedchamber-storeroom backing on the fireplace, its rope lattice repaired, a thin straw tick rolled at its foot, the stuffing protruding through the loose weave.

His eyes narrowed as he spotted an old harness hanging by the door. The implication that his captors planned to bind him before leaving didn't please him in the least. He might've per-

mitted them to abduct him, but he had no intention of their holding him prisoner. As for how they intended he should see to
nature's needs so confined, he had no notion. Then his eyes
danced, and his estimation of their providence rose another notch.

Beneath the crude bed was a chamber pot. Even more surprising, a basin and ewer sat at the bed's foot, what had to be a coarse
towel draped over them. His respect for the intelligence of at
least one of those with whom he had to deal rose several more
notches. Whatever their problem, these scamps clearly were desperate for some adult assistance, and doing their best to ensure
adult approval in order to gain that assistance.

The dirt floor had been swept clean. The fire Alfie was attempting to light was well-laid, though Oakwood suspected the
deadfall the children'd gathered was damp. Certainly it was assiduously resisting the gangly boy's efforts.

He lifted the much-mended napkin covering a basket on the
bench by the door, grimaced at the unappetizing slab of grayish
meat pie and the oily yellow cheese wrapped in greasy paper.
The withered windfalls were no less repugnant. The crock of
pickled something-or-other oozing brown goo wasn't much better.

"This is all fresh despite its appearance, I presume," he said,
unaware his voice had taken on a schoolmasterish tone.

"Of course," Prissy said, jumping down from the stool onto
which she'd clambered to light the candles in their crude sconces,
her golden curls dancing. She sank to her knees beside Alfie.
"Can't you get it lit?" she asked. "We haven't much time, and
there's so much to tell him."

"We brought fresh food each night, and then Alfie ate it on
the way home," Pru informed Oakwood from the storeroom door,
her arms full of blankets which she proceeded to set on the rough
bed. "He's always hungry."

"Understandable," Oakwood murmured. The sandy-haired
lad was at just that age when starvation was a perpetual condition.

"These've been hung out to air and thoroughly beaten, so you
needn't fear they're inhabited, even if they're musty. You're much
too important to us for you to fall ill," the diminutive girl ex-

plained, turning back to Oakwood. "There're two onions in the storeroom, and a cabbage, and a pot for cooking, and a kettle of fresh snow to melt by the fire as the creek is frozen over."

"How superlatively organized you are."

"We've done our best. I hope you don't crave tea, even if you do sound like a superior footman. There wasn't a way to bring fresh without the loss being discovered, and then we'd've been for it. I'll begin saving used leaves for you tomorrow. As Phoebe insists we use them over and over ourselves they won't be very nice, but they'll be better than nothing. Oh, and there's the makings for porridge in that tin box so the rats won't get to it."

"Rats? You expect me to share my lodgings with rats?" Oakwood demanded in an offended tone, eyes twinkling.

"The roofs thatched," Pru returned with the practicality of a country-bred girl, "and rats and mice will've set up housekeeping as no one's been living here regularly. We got rid of most of the droppings, but you'll have company on occasion."

"I'm only surprised you haven't provided me with a cat, as well."

"Pru suggested it, but I didn't know if you'd like it," Alfie said, puffing on the feeble smolder he'd managed to encourage. "Some men don't care for cats."

"If it's a choice between cats and rats, I'll take the cats and welcome."

Oakwood glanced about him more carefully, childhood memories surfacing.

He knew this place. He should've realized that the moment he labeled the cavern behind the chimney a bedchamber-*cum*-storeroom. Better yet, he knew precisely the direction in which Soames's bachelor establishment lay. They'd snuck here to play at rebels and redcoats often enough when he visited as a boy. True, that had been summer and now the paths were snow-covered, but he should be able to find his way easily enough once he'd disembarrassed himself of his youthful abductors.

Just as he was about to offer his services as fire-starter, a curl of flame licked the heavy log. Alfie sat back on his heels, a look of triumph suffusing his narrow features.

"Aren't you afraid someone will notice the smoke?" Oakwood asked. "Derelict though this place is, I doubt whoever owns it would take kindly to my presence."

"Lord Soames won't mind," Pru said dismissively, shifting the basket to the table and struggling to pull the bench over. "It's been occupied from time to time—returned troopers mostly, seeking assistance at the castle. Lord Soames doesn't hold with hanging those who're destitute, and he approves even less of workhouses. That's why the roof's in such excellent repair. Why, he doesn't even have a gamekeeper these days, feeling those who poach won't abuse the privilege. All in the neighborhood know they're welcome to any rabbits or hares."

"A kind man, and a wise one," Oakwood returned, taking the heavy bench from the girl and setting it across from the settle by the chimney. "I'm surprised you haven't sought his assistance rather than throwing yourselves on the mercy of a stranger."

"I told 'em to, but Prissy wouldn't listen," Alfie explained in a tone so filled with masculine disgust it was all Oakwood could do not to burst out laughing. "Insists it's got to be someone who doesn't know the district, and so will be totally impartial. Me, I think she's got fluff where her brains're supposed to be. Knowing everyone'd be a deal more use if one's trying to catch a murderer, wouldn't it?"

"A murderer?"

"Well, a blackmailer at the very least."

"I truly believe you'd best explain the entire matter," Oakwood said, sinking onto the settle, pulling off his sodden boots and stretching out his long legs to toast, then gesturing at the bench across from him. "In detail, if you don't mind."

What he received from Prissy and Alfie was a tangled tale of parental beatings, of food withheld and incarcerations meted out with a liberality he found astonishing, of an accident in Soames's woods which perhaps hadn't been an accident at all, the whole suffused with hints of listening at doors. Finally at his wits' end, he raised a powerful, muscular hand for silence. The pair broke off in mid-argument as to an exact sequence of events. Oakwood turned to Pru.

"Who is Cousin Philip?" he asked.

"Philip Fordyce, Mama's cousin at several removes," she said.

"And who's Phoebe?"

"Our half-sister."

"And who, in the name of heaven, is this Mr. Dorning?" The name had a familiar ring to it.

"Clarence Dorning? In the name of heaven, he's the village vicar," Pru giggled. "He's a connection of Lord Soames's, and holds the Chedleigh Minor living."

Good Lord! Dandy Clare was involved in this, whatever it was? Oakwood scowled, giving himself a moment to remember details. "Describe him, if you would."

"Mr. Dorning's the village idiot, more like," Alfie explained in a tone of disgust, resting knobby elbows on knobbier knees. "Don't dress as a vicar should. Wants t'be a beau, y'see, but as he's Quality and related to Lord Soames no one dares say a word. Plays the gallant whenever the ladies're about—at least those who have sufficient consequence to interest him—reads his sermons from books, rides with the hunt when he can cage a mount, and wears his collars past his ears. Cousin Phoebe's barely exchanged two words with him, but he's safe, being unlike Uncle Parmenter."

"That's clear enough."

Same man, no question, and a more obnoxious, toadying, tale-bearing runt never existed when they were boys. He'd only encountered this particular wart on the aristocratic Soames rump once, but that once had been enough.

Oakwood turned back to Pru. "Now, in the simplest terms and without the least conjecture on any of your parts, what's to do?"

The girl frowned, chewing the tails of her mouse-brown plaits as she scowled into the feeble fire.

"A week ago tomorrow Papa's body was found on Lord Soames's land," she finally said. "That's where we are right now—Lord Soames's land. His death was ruled a riding accident. None of us was sorry Papa'd died, you understand. That's not conjecture," she added with a touch of apology. "That's a fact. Papa was a most unpleasant man. That's a fact as well. Two days later he was buried, and Mr. Hatch came from Market Stoking to read Papa's will. He's Papa's solicitor. Papa left Mama less than a pittance, and Prissy and me nothing at all. Underhill, Papa's money, everything went to Phoebe."

"Who is a purse-pinching witch whom you all detest," Oakwood said ruminatively. "You suspect her of—"

"Detest Phoebe?" the trio chorused, clearly stunned by the concept.

"You've got it all wrong," Prissy protested. "We adore Phoebe."

"It's Papa we detested," Pru explained, "for all we know it's bad manners to admit it, but if you're to help us you must know precisely how everything was. Now Papa's dead, we don't detest anyone."

"Papa was an ogre," Prissy threw in with a shudder, "a variable monster!"

" 'Veritable,' Prissy," Pru corrected absently, "not variable. Indeed, he was *invariably* a monster. He was, too, Mr. Oakwood. That's quite the proper term. Well," she corrected herself with a slight frown, "perhaps we detest Aunt Trask—she's Papa's sister, and wanted Underhill for Cousin Cobber, and made him offer for Phoebe as soon as Papa's will was read—but she's more annoyance than bane. Say rather we dislike her immensely."

"But you adore your half-sister?" Oakwood said with a slight frown. "And she cares for you as well?"

"Oh, yes! And Mama," Prissy declared enthusiastically. "We love her dearly, too. We're not unnatural, any of us, no matter what Aunt Trask claims, nor what she says about Papa's corpse being brought home in a dung cart. Most suitable, if you ask me. Of course I'd never say so to Aunt Trask."

Oakwood collapsed in what he hoped appeared a coughing fit. Certainly Alfie and Prissy pounded his back hard enough to show faith in his supposed incapacity, and Pru was quick to provide him with a mug of icy water. At last he waved them off, convinced their tender ministrations would leave him sore for a week.

"Mama and Phoebe're more like sisters," Prissy continued as

if there'd been no interruption, "being so close in age. They were forever trying to protect each other from Papa. Being so much younger, we were mostly safe so long as we hid from him. Papa found us uninteresting as we weren't boys. Oh, he'd birch us if we annoyed him, and send us to bed without supper, but as supper was rarely very nice that was no great loss. The weals healed quickly enough. Phoebe concocted the most wonderful ointments for us, having great practice at it. Phoebe can cure most anything. Our still room's magnificent, for all the rest of the house isn't much."

"And your Aunt Trask is merely an annoyance." Oakwood turned back to Pru. "Where do I fit into all this? It would seem the sun shines on you at last."

"It's Cousin Philip," Pru said after sending worried glances at her coconspirators and receiving encouraging nods from them. "He's all but accused Mama of murdering Papa. There's no way she could've. Mama's too fluttery and vague, don't you see? She wouldn't've had the strength of mind, let alone the strength of body.

"But Cousin Philip's told Phoebe he'll go to Lord Soames with his tale if she doesn't marry him so that he can acquire Underhill and never lack for money—it's a very prosperous place, though nothing so grand as a true estate—and then things would be as unpleasant as when Papa was alive, and we don't want that. But suppose," she hesitated, "well, it would be smashing if Cousin Philip was the one who'd murdered Papa and then claimed it was Mama who did it, and totally in character—blaming someone else for his own faults, don't you see, and trying to profit from them at the same time. And since Phoebe would never confront Mama, he'd get away with it. Phoebe doesn't ever speak of unpleasant things to Mama."

"This sounds like the merest moonshine."

"Well, it isn't," Prissy protested, incensed. "We heard Cousin Philip through the door after everyone'd gone into the dining room once the will was read and they knew they'd get nothing from Papa's death but a cold lunch, and not a very good one either, as there was nothing but old boiled mutton and cheese."

"And?" Oakwood demanded, hiding his impatience.

"Phoebe must believe there's the possibility of a scrap of truth in Cousin Philip's insinuations," Pru sighed, "which is what concerns us."

"Not a very intelligent woman, then."

"Phoebe's brilliant! It's just she's very protective of Mama. Mama's had a lot to bear, and with the terms of Papa's will being so unexpected I don't believe Phoebe was thinking clearly, only there's nothing she can do about that now.

"Cousin Philip's pockets're always to let, but now he's discovered a way to remedy that, and as Phoebe must marry someone and produce a male heir, he's constituted himself the solution to both his problems and ours. Cousin Philip would be no better than Cousin Cobber, for if Phoebe were to marry him, then Aunt Trask would be forever about the place making our lives miserable. That's the thing she's best at. Besides, Phoebe has a tendre for Mr. Dorning. Her heart's broken—I'm sure of it—though she goes on about Cousin Philip as if she really cared for him, which she couldn't possibly, having detested him since forever."

"Cousin Philip's as evil as Papa, don't you see?" Prissy threw in, unable to contain herself. "No gentleman would blackmail a lady, would he?"

"No," Oakwood agreed, "no gentleman would."

"So we must rescue her, only we don't know how. Cousin Philip would make a perfectly abdominal husband, for all he claims he means none of us any harm."

" 'Abominable,' brat, not 'abdominal,' " Oakwood murmured absently. "What d'you think of all this?" he asked, turning to Alfie as the only other male present, and therefore possibly capable of rational thought despite his youth.

"There's something havey-cavey about Uncle Parmenter's death, no question there," Alfie responded without hesitation. "A riding accident? Why, he was probably the best horseman in these parts. Only half a dozen mounts, but they're all the best money could buy. Even has a pair of Watford hunters, which tells the tale."

"Hunters of Chronicle Watford's breeding?" Oakwood inquired with some surprise. "The Twin Oaks Stud?"

"Two of 'em, both blacks. Devil-May-Care and Devil-a-Bit."

"Mr.—Parmenter, is it?—treated himself well."

"As well as he treated everybody else badly," Alfie agreed. "Cousin Philip's a gamester and worse, by the bye. The girls're right to want Phoebe to have nothing to do with him. It's just I don't think kidnapping a lord and hoping he'll tumble top-over-tail for Phoebe and call Cousin Philip out and marry her's very sensible. Phoebe ain't the sort men tumble for, besides which, dueling's been outlawed dunamany years."

"It has indeed."

"But you ain't a lord, which gives me hope you'll be of some use. No lord'd be willing to dirty his hands helping people like us. Prissy had that wrong, for all her idea was sound enough once we got rid of that part.

"Oh, we're gentry of a sort, I suppose, or at least Phoebe and the girls are, but Aunt Mabel's nothing but a tradesman's daughter even if she did marry Uncle Parmenter, who was landed even if he was an ogre. She and my father are brother and sister. My father inherited the mill on t'other side of Market Stoking from his father, who had it of his. It's not a manufactory, y'understand. We just grind corn for the farmers hereabout," the boy concluded with a touch of apology. "That's trade, pure and simple, for all we're prosperous enough."

"Nothing to be ashamed of," Oakwood responded absently, conscious of three pairs of eyes trained on him. "Most of the aristocracy're nothing but leeches. Absentee landlords milking the land dry so they can play the swell in London, unlike your Lord Soames. So, what is it you want me to do?"

"Prove Mama didn't murder Papa," Prissy said with a simplicity of expression that startled Oakwood, given what he'd observed of her so far. "Then Phoebe won't have to marry Cousin Philip, and can have Mr. Dorning if she can bring him up to scratch—not that he's such a great bargain, being a prosy bore and two-faced as he can stare, but at least he doesn't hit people, and I suspect that's all Phoebe can see. Phoebe's wonderful! She deserves a reward for protecting us from Papa all these years, and she's done her best to see we didn't lack for education into the bargain. She made sure Papa hardly remembered we existed most of the time, and if you'd known Papa, you'd understand what a blessing that was."

"It would be pleasing if Cousin Philip could be punished for making Phoebe miserable, as well," Pru added. "But, mostly we just want Mama's name cleared, and Cousin Philip chased away so he won't be able to belittle us or plague Phoebe anymore."

"And you're not inventing all this in an attempt to see your sister well-fixed? No dreams of a London Season, or a handle to your names?"

"Cousin Phoebe wouldn't care for it," Alfie responded flatly. "She's above such silliness. So's Pru. Prissy might want it, but she wouldn't like it if she got it."

"Oh, I might," Prissy returned dreamily. "A handsome lord and a coronet would be wonderful."

"Ugly old man and a slip on the shoulder, more like," Alfie returned matter-of-factly. "Besides, you ain't a lord," he said, turning to Oakwood, "just someone like us, so all's right and tight. Now, sir, will you help us?"

"All you need do is ask about the neighborhood, and you'll learn Papa was precisely as we describe him," Pru cajoled. "Cousin Philip as well."

"I see. Perhaps," Oakwood said thoughtfully, "the best plan might be for me to apply to Lord Soames for that position I've heard mention of. Then I'd have a right to be here, and asking questions would be much easier."

"Then you'll help us?"

"I'll consider it, and give you my answer tomorrow. It'll probably be yes, but," he said, gesturing at the peg with its burden of harness by the door, "I absolutely draw the line at bonds. If I must trust you, then you must trust me."

"Don't think I could've managed to tie you up in any case if y'hadn't wanted it," Alfie admitted, flushing furiously. "Glad I don't have to make the attempt, but Prissy would insist we make sure you couldn't go to the authorities. Closest we could come to shackles and chains was old harness. This is a gamekeeper's cottage, after all, not Lord Soames's dungeons."

"Fair enough—no authorities until I've had a chance to unscramble this mess, and discuss what I learn with you. Where can I stable my mount?"

"There's naught but the shed behind the storeroom," Pru apologized as they rose to leave, "but there's a stall of sorts in it. That's where we put your horse. I'm afraid that's one thing we didn't think of—real stabling. I'll return with more food and some tea early as may be, and we'll try to get hay to you somehow."

"I'll see you tomorrow, then," Oakwood smiled. "What hour, if I may be so bold? I wouldn't want you to find me at my toilette," he explained at Pru's rising brows.

"Oh, when I can," she shrugged. "Now all the excitement regarding Papa's death is over, Phoebe's set us to our lessons again. It'll be afternoon. That's when she insists we take walks, even in the coldest weather, and gather deadfall for the fires. Papa's temper was always foul in the afternoons, and Phoebe didn't want us at home for fear we might annoy him and make things worse."

Then the children slipped from the cottage, Alfie to mount his jenny and take off in one direction fortified with the slab of pie and several windfalls, the girls to trudge through the snow in the other as Oakwood stood at the door watching until they disappeared in the night, his lips twisted by a wry, self-deprecating smile.

Dear God, what had he gotten himself into?

Two

Some two hours later—after seeing to Bacchus, banking the fire, extinguishing lantern and candles, and plowing interminably through more snow than he'd've dreamed existed the week before when making the decision to join Hotspur Soames's bachelor house party for the holidays—Oakwood found himself before the forbidding fortress called Penwillow Castle, seat of the Earls of Penwillow.

Of course it wasn't a genuine castle. Its exaggerated crenelations, its dim solars, stationary portcullis, sealed lancets and immovable drawbridge were of fairly recent construction—a Gothic phantasmagoria created by the first earl during the reign of James the Second, and improved upon by each subsequent generation except the most recent. It wasn't that Soames's taste surpassed that of his progenitors. It was simply that Soames, having come into the title only three years previously, hadn't had time to add his touch. Of his father's affixing Italianate balconies and French doors to the formidable brick structure the less said, the better.

Oakwood grimaced, examining the snow-kissed visual feast before him. As a lad he'd thought Penwillow Castle the grandest place in all of England, comparing his own father's residences most unfavorably to it. What boy, given the choice, would opt for cool Palladian elegance when convoluted medieval magnificence was at hand? Now the monstrosity's only attraction lay in the fact that, with all its protuberances, it was a marvelously easy thing to scale. Oakwood knew that from experience.

Of course he could pound on the iron-studded main door, or

hammer the grimacing black gargoyle's head against its iron plate until someone came. He could even tug the heavy rope hanging beside the main entry, setting the great bell in the tower to pealing, and so rouse both the quick and the dead.

The trouble was, so far as Oakwood knew, Raft—Soames's major domo—was still shuffling about the place in his customary miasma of port, snuff, and old age, and Raft would recognize him on the instant unless his eyesight had failed to the point where he recognized no one, not even himself. If there truly was something questionable about Parmenter's death, an innocuous stranger had a far better opportunity to uncover it than a marquess. The chances of the villagers remembering him were poor. The chances of Raft saying, "Why, it's young Master Piers come to visit!" and then spreading the alarm through the servants' quarters, and from there through the neighborhood, were excellent.

Oakwood followed the arrow-straight drive across the wooden drawbridge, strode under the portcullis and into the central courtyard, memory coming into play.

It had been years since he visited the place.

His eyes narrowed as he studied the bastion-like walls lining the courtyard. The preposterous brick pile didn't appear to have changed much.

Dim lights shone through drapery cracks in one of the bedchamber windows on the level above the great hall. The question was who slept—or did not sleep—there these days? Soames, peripatetic and restless, admitted to changing bedchambers as often as most men changed their coats—an exaggeration, but only a slight one. A darkened, and thus possibly empty, chamber would be best. There was no sense attempting any ground floor windows. Most were sealed, always had been. Besides, he required an aperture large enough to accommodate him. No, a midnight climb was needed.

He removed his hat, set it on the verge of the frozen fountain in the center of the courtyard, then unwound the scarf from his neck, folded it and placed it inside the hat. Next came his gloves, which he stuffed in a pocket. He peeled off his battered greatcoat, folded it carefully and laid it on the fountain's verge beside his hat. Then, with a shudder, he resignedly followed it with his old tweed hunting jacket. Penwillow Castle might be scaleable, but not encumbered by bulky clothing—a lesson he and Soames had learned early on. If he caught his death in the service of Miss Phoebe Parmenter, he hoped Alfie and Prissy and Pru would mourn him.

Then, shivering mightily, he trudged through the snow leaving massive depressions in his wake. Oakwood rubbed his hands vigorously against his plain waistcoat, reached high above his head to grasp the first of a series of great knobs protruding from the decorative stonework around the front door.

"For King and Country," he murmured, hoisted himself to the first level, clung desperately to the wall, "and good Saint George! And Miss Parmenter, whose predicament may be the end of me."

Above and around him arched a double bank of high relief sculptures of supposed Soames ancestors, anchored to iron posts in shallow niches and offering easy purchase. Unfortunately the niches were closer together than he remembered. That should've made it easier. Instead it made it infinitely more difficult. And the spaces between the decorative stone knobs sticking out from the brickwork like steps had shrunk until they were in all the wrong places and barely offered toeholds. Of course no longer being sixteen, and several stone heavier into the bargain, might have something to do with that.

He scrabbled for the next handhold, which was inconveniently close if he took the nearest (Sir Terwilliger) and inconveniently far if he went for one more (Lady Esmerelda). Nothing fit.

Penwillow might've been heaven for boys. It was hell for a man of his height and solid girth. Determinedly he moved up another niche (Lord Godwin, battered as ever), then another (Lady Pamela surrounded by her plethora of babes who'd died in infancy).

The things one remembered from one's childhood!

"Dear God, did we really scamper up and down this thing as if it were a ladder?" he panted. "We must've been fools!"

The first balcony was almost within reach. Gingerly Oakwood

moved his left foot up one knob, seized good old Sir Chively around the shoulders, dug his toes in, glanced down and shuddered. The fall to the cobbled courtyard was at least thirty precipitous feet, and there was another ten feet to go before he could grasp the marble baluster and pull himself up. Worse, his fingers were iced to numbness, his toes aching with cold, his eyes bleared by tears from the cold. Worse yet, the healthy sweat he'd worked up clambering over hill and dale had frozen against his skin, making him wonder if he'd survive the night's foolishness.

Well, if he didn't want to make an absolute idiot of himself—which he suspected he'd already done—he'd better move up another niche, and then another. Otherwise he'd come to a distinctly messy end on the cobbles, and he rather suspected neither Soames nor the children would forgive him the solecism.

"Gentleman Jackson's," he gasped, breath clouding before his face and making sight extremely difficult, "definitely does not prepare one for this sort of absurdity."

He grunted, reached above him, knocked the fresh snow from the next niche, seized it firmly where it met the facade, then snaked the tips of his fingers around someone's upper arm. Lord Percival's, perhaps.

Then he pushed and hauled, straining against the icy stones. Slowly, with infinite effort, he gained three full levels. The balcony's floor and the balusters were just within reach. He sighed, reached out, grasped the satyr's nearer horn, prepared to swing himself up—the method he'd employed as a boy. The horn broke loose, whether from age or his adult weight there was no way to tell. Scrabbling for purchase, Oakwood flung the dratted thing away. It struck the fountain, then clattered to the snow-covered cobbles.

"Damn and blast!" Oakwood muttered. "I'm certifiably out of my mind."

There was, quite simply, no way he could climb any higher. He was too cold.

Then, before he could think about it, he lunged for the satyr's body, flinging his arms about it as if it were his mistress rather than frozen marble he embraced. For a miracle, the half-goat, half-man held. With infinite care he settled his left arm about it more tightly. Then, forsaking the scant security the knobs granted his toes, he heaved upwards and grasped the balustrade itself.

In the old days it'd been easy: shift his other hand to the balustrade, twist and push outward in an acrobat's swing, tuck up legs, hook heels over the edge, bend double and slither, and he'd been home free. This time it took a bit more, but finally he dragged himself over the balustrade and collapsed on the balcony.

"For dinner I shall kill them all," he muttered, "very slowly, and with infinite satisfaction. And for desert I shall tweak Pru's plaits until she begs for mercy."

Once his legs and arms stopped trembling and his heart regained its usual, rather lethargic pace, Oakwood stood, tried the opposing French doors. Solidly latched, just as he'd feared. He couldn't remain on the balcony much longer without becoming a block of ice. With a sigh, he pulled off his waistcoat, wrapped it around his fist, sending a quick plea to whatever gods had guarded an oversized man attempting a boy's trick, that the chamber be empty, hauled back and treated the window panels' junction to an example of his famous punishing right. The two halves flew apart, frames shattered.

With a relieved groan and nursing bruised knuckles, Peter Oakwood stumbled through the ornate embrasure, tangled in heavy velvet draperies and crashed to the floor dragging them with him. Something else crashed to the floor. It sounded expensive.

"Damn!" he muttered, snagged in dusty passementerie tassels and satin ropes, mouth filled with cobwebby silk liners. He tore them from his face, sneezed mightily. "Damn, damn, damn! I'm too old for this sort of nonsense."

"I tend to agree," a cultured voice drawled above him, accompanied by the click of a pistol being cocked, "no matter how old you are. Certainly I don't enjoy being broken in upon at this or any hour."

"That's the second time someone's held me at gun point tonight," Oakwood grumbled.

"Really? Fascinating. Make a habit of breaking into the homes of your betters, do you?"

"Not generally. First time was by a band of the infantry, if you please. In the woods. Would you mind stepping back a few paces? I don't want to lurch into you and end up with a bullet in my shoulder or worse."

"You don't sound like the usual housebreaker."

"I'm not," Oakwood sneezed. "Step back, there's a good fellow. Here I come."

Fighting an ocean of velvet that billowed and surged, and was at least as determined to provide humiliating tumbles as any mischievous wave at Brighton, Oakwood rose from the entrapping crests like Aphrodite from her shell, teeth chattering, nose streaming. He sneezed again, a convulsion that bent him double.

"Good God—is that you, Duchesne?"

"At your service, Ware," Peter Oakwood gasped, sneezed again. "Uncock that bloody thing. I've no desire to be blasted to kingdom come for my pains."

"What're you doing here at this time of night half dressed? Accosted by highwaymen?"

"You might say so," Oakwood chuckled, sneezed. "Damnedest thing I've experienced in all my thirty-two years."

Justin Ware uncocked his pistol, set it on the chest by the bed, shrugged into his quilted dressing gown, divested one of the pillows of its case and tossed the delicately embroidered thing to Oakwood.

"Here," he said. "Handkerchief'd be useless, the condition you're in."

Oakwood nodded, sneezed repeatedly, blew his nose.

"Why the devil didn't you knock like a sensible man?"

"Because I'm not sensible."

"Could easily've shot first and asked questions later," Ware insisted, struggling to shift the draperies and close the French doors as Oakwood stumbled further into the room. "Not particularly good for your health."

"I realize that as well. Raft still about?" Oakwood asked, blowing his nose again.

"A bit past it, but yes. You know the tradition here: No servant's ever put to pasture until he requests it. Raft has yet to make the request."

Ware angled the rod against the windows, then bundled the draperies in front of them to more or less shut out the icy drafts.

"There's your answer," Oakwood said, broke into another flurry of sneezes. "A fire-capped mountain's unmistakable, and I don't want it bruited about I was here."

Oakwood wrapped himself in the coverlet Ware tossed him, pulled off his boots and sodden stockings and stumbled barefoot to the fireplace, teeth still chattering.

"Be a good fellow and get me a glass of brandy. I feel like one of Gunter's ice sculptures. And fetch your nephew from whichever bedchamber he's selected as this week's perch. I need to confer with him."

He sneezed again. A welcome glass of brandy was thrust in his hand. He downed it in a single massive gulp, held it out.

"Another," he pleaded, sniffling, "and I'll be fit as a fiddle. Most amusing thing's happened, but before I decide what to do I need Soames's opinion."

"Nothing to do with a ladybird, is it, because he'd not be the least use."

"Good Lord, no! I'm perfectly capable of handling the petticoats unassisted."

Ware emptied half a scuttle of coal on the grate, poked it vigorously. Oakwood sank into a winged chair beside the chimney, placed the tumbler on the flanking table, tucked the coverlet more securely about him, inched his bare toes toward the fender and held his hands to the fire.

"Lord, but that feels good," he said with a grateful smile.

"What the devil're you doing here? Soames said you weren't coming."

"Didn't intend to when I wrote, but that was early November. Lot's happened since then. Figured Soames wouldn't mind."

"Course he won't. Quite the opposite."

"You know the people about these parts?"

"Only their names and reputations. I don't come often. This is the first time in years, actually."

"Doesn't matter. I'll want you both. You've always had a solid head on your shoulders."

Justin Ware gave a puzzled nod, slipped from the room. A few minutes later he reappeared with a disheveled, yawning Hotspur Soames.

"What's to do?" the young earl inquired, running his hand through his sandy hair as he shambled over to the drinks table and helped himself to a tot of brandy, then glanced at the windows. "Good God," he said, turning muzzily to his uncle, "what've you two been about?"

"I'll pay for the damage," Oakwood said.

"Yon idiot's been scampering about the facade, just as you did when you were boys," Ware explained, square-jawed face blank, dark eyes twinkling merrily, "and bursting through windows with the results you see."

"In this weather?" Soames demanded incredulously.

"Almost didn't make it," Oakwood admitted with a sheepish grin. "I owe you a satyr's horn as well."

"Broke one off, did you? Well, you've put on a few stone. How's good old Godwin? And—Esmerelda, is it? One looks like butter wouldn't melt in her mouth."

"Godwin's still missing an ear and half his nose, and Esmerelda's simper's as sickening as ever. I gave them your greetings on the way up."

"My thanks. I'm sure they've missed us."

Soames took the chair on the other side of the fire as Ware pulled over a low chest and joined them. Oakwood flushed under his wiry friend's derisive gaze.

"Never took you for a fool, Piers," the earl finally said. "What're you doing here? More to the point, why'd you choose to arrive in so unconventional a manner?"

"Not much choice, given old Raft."

"Hiding out, are you?"

"Not precisely, though in a manner of speaking."

"I believe," Soames said, "you'd best begin at the beginning.

You weren't planning to join us, according to your scribble. Claimed His Grace and Serena'd miss you during the holiday season."

"Not on their honeymoons they won't. Both newly married," Oakwood explained at Soames's thunderstruck look. "Remember Serena's governess? The one who didn't mind frogs, but insisted they belonged out of doors? Preferably in a pond?"

"Very well," Soames said with a reminiscent chuckle. "Rather a formidable female, for all her diminutive size. Delightful sense of humor, as I remember it, and far better educated than the average governess."

"That's the one. Well, the pater married her. I suppose it'd been coming on for years, though it did seem a bit sudden. Billing and cooing like a pair of turtle doves."

"I'll be damned!"

"And Serena? Leg-shackled as well, and quite the blushing bride, believe it or not. Fellow by the name of John Macy. No title, but he's a sterling fellow and Serena never cared about such things in any case. He's a crony of Rawdon's," mentioning an acquaintance more of Ware's generation than their own. "Now they're all on their wedding journeys, and I was least wanted."

"Poor fellow," Soames chuckled. "So, you decided to join us after all for lack of anything better to do."

"Didn't think you'd mind."

"Mind? Don't be ridiculous—I'm delighted. Should be able to offer you an interesting time. Freddy Derringer's prepared a monograph on the victory at Mylae, and Tim Bladesell's unearthed some new information on Xantippus. Heaven knows what Roger Andersby has for us. He's being mysterious, but I suspect it's something to do with Hannibal and his elephants. I did tell you this year's topic is the Punic Wars?"

"I'm not here to refight old battles," Oakwood protested. "Haven't you all left off that foolishness yet?"

"Doubt we ever will," Soames grinned. "Great fun. Billiard table sees a lot of use, even if it isn't for billiards."

"No ladies about, I suppose?"

"Never! Have to be forever dancing attendance on 'em if there were, and be cursed with Great-aunt Genevieve to act as hostess into the bargain. Dreadful woman, Great-aunt Genevieve. Inveterate matchmaker. Can't think of a worse way to spend the holidays. No, there's just the four of us and Uncle Justin. Five, now you're here."

"I know what you mean about your aunt. Thing was, you see, the pater's been putting a bit of pressure on," Oakwood continued, squirming slightly. "Wants me leg-shackled as well, and the succession seen to. With him flown the coop, I thought I was safe. Then a lady of his acquaintance started parading every passable chit in London beneath my nose. Even some who weren't passable, which surprised me as that's not Lady Cheltenham's style."

"Oh dear," Soames murmured sympathetically.

"Tried to seek shelter with Jeanine—Delisle, you know, my latest," Oakwood rambled on between sneezes and sips of brandy, "and found her unbearably tedious. Been with me six months. That's about par. Paid her off, gave my staff the holidays at double pay so they could make a real celebration of it, and bolted."

"Still doesn't explain why you arrived half naked in the middle of the night, or why you scaled the walls rather than knocking at the door," Ware protested.

"No, it doesn't, does it. Well, you see, I was kidnapped."

"What?"

"Or accosted by highwayboys, er, girls. Well, both, really. Highwaychildren? Yes, I suppose that's what describes them best: highwaychildren."

"There's nothing but brandy in his glass is there, Uncle?" Soames asked.

"Same exact stuff you and I're drinking."

"Duchesne," Soames said, turning threateningly on his friend, "I am not as easily diddled as when we were boys."

"And I gave over diddling years ago. You have, or had until recently, a neighbor by the name of Parmenter, did you not?"

"Yes, Portius Parmenter. Squirish type, well-fixed. Died in a riding accident a week ago."

"If you hadn't," Oakwood growled, "I'd be about to commit

mayhem, after which you could swing me at the crossroads or incarcerate me in Bedlam, whichever seemed more appropriate. What manner of man was he?"

"A bully," Soames returned promptly. "Had a quick temper and a slow mind. Nothing but a churlish, clutch-fisted boor, when all's said and done."

"He abused his wife and children abominably according to local report," Ware elaborated at Oakwood's questioning glance. "All sorts of unpleasantnesses. Given the laws, there wasn't much anyone could do."

"So they were telling the truth."

"Who was telling the truth?"

"My abductors—a troop of infantry named Alfie, Prissy and Pru. *My* name, by the bye, is Peter Oakwood until I decide differently. I'm seeking employment, and sound amazingly like a superior footman. Remember the cottage a mile or so from the creek? Gamekeeper's place in your grandfather's day? That's the current shooting box of Piers Duchesne, Marquess of Stovall— who doesn't currently exist."

Oakwood chuckled at the thunderstruck expression on Soames's open, pleasant face. "I suppose I'd best explain what's to do," he said.

"Yes, I rather think that might be an excellent idea," Ware threw in.

"First tell me two—no, three things. What manner of woman is Mabel Parmenter, your unpleasant neighbor's widow?"

"A gentle soul," Soames responded promptly. "Daughter of Robert Gusset. Dead now, but he owned the mill near Market Stoking. Nick Gusset, his son, has taken it over. Alfie's *his* son. Mabel Gusset married above her, thanks to her face. Pretty in that vapid, milk-and-water way so many fools tumble for. You've seen Prissy? Add a few years and a stone or two, and you have the mother. Parmenter's death can't help but be a welcome release for her."

"Interesting. Phoebe Parmenter?"

"Parmenter's daughter by his first wife. Spinsterish, intelligent, not unattractive, infinitely kind. Takes after the Parmenters

in looks. Brown hair, brown eyes, the usual. Her father chased
off all suitors or she'd be long wed. Excellent housekeeper, you
see, and she didn't cost him a groat. Taught the girls, as well."

"I do see. And Philip Fordyce?"

"My, you have a lot of questions." Soames's brows rose.

"Fordyce, if you please," Oakwood repeated. "Who is he?"

"Mrs. Parmenter's cousin at a few removes," Soames
shrugged. "Pleasant enough chap, resembles the Regent as a
young man. Same golden curls as his cousin, though I doubt
his're natural. Likes to ape the fops. He'll probably run to fat
eventually, just like Prinny. No visible means of support, currently betrothed to Miss Parmenter, if only unofficially. I'm
paying his shot at the George as he's short of funds. Wouldn't
do for him to lodge at Underhill now as Mrs. Parmenter's far
too vacant to act as a duenna, and I certainly don't want him
here. Have one of my men patrolling the place at night—
protection for the ladies."

"It all tallies, thank God. Miss Parmenter seem pleased with
her betrothal?"

"And still more questions? You've become a regular Bow
Street Runner. Pleased enough," Soames continued at Oakwood's scowl. "All simpers and blushes. As I said, Fordyce's a
good-looking fellow, and charming to the ladies. Something of
a toady, something of a mushroom. Tries to weasel his way into
the lower reaches of the ton whenever he's in Town."

"Fordyce is perfectly respectable," Ware protested.

"What if I were to tell you Miss Parmenter detests the man?"
Oakwood settled the coverlet more comfortably around his
shoulders and leaned back in his chair. "That it's all an act? That
Fordyce is blackmailing her into marriage?"

Ware froze, balloon of brandy halfway to his lips.

"I'd laugh in your face," Soames chuckled. "Well, I am, aren't
I?"

"What were the terms of Parmenter's will?"

"Miss Parmenter got everything," Soames sighed impatiently,
"or as near as makes no difference, but to touch it she has to
produce a male heir. Rather an *idée fixe* of old Parmenter's, a

male heir. Couldn't get himself one, you understand. Of course, at that point it'll be Miss Parmenter's husband—Fordyce, in the event—who'll have control so long as Parmenter's solicitor approves the match. For now she's purse-pinched, for until she's wed she has sufficient funds to support only herself, but must see to the four of them. Five, if you count Fordyce."

Oakwood nodded, chewing absently on his lower lip and frowning. "Prissy and Pru overheard the happy pair," he said at last. "Apparently your respectable Mr. Fordyce all but claimed outright Mrs. Parmenter murdered her husband, and threatened to come bearing you tales if Miss Parmenter refused to wed him."

"Fustian," Ware spluttered.

"It seems Miss Parmenter is much taken with the local vicar, you see," Oakwood continued, ignoring the interruption.

"Clare Dorning?" Soames grinned. "If she is, she's better off with Fordyce."

"Clare's really your vicar? The same Dandy Clare as when we were boys? How the mighty've fallen or the weak risen, or some such. Point is, he may not be to our taste, but the children swear Miss Parmenter's heartbroken, and that she detests Fordyce."

"Nothing there to detest," Ware protested. "A genuine nonentity. It's probably that older girl causing problems. Just the age for it."

"They want me to ferret out the truth if I can, for they agree there's no way their mother could've killed their father, pleased as they'd've been if she had."

"Unnatural pygmies," Ware muttered. "They deserve a birching!"

"It seems to me," Oakwood returned acidly, "that they've already had far too many birchings in their short lives."

"True enough," Ware agreed, flushing. "I was only speaking figuratively."

"I doubt they'd understand the distinction. Not certain I do, come to that. All they want is their half-sister free to marry where she will," he continued more equably. "To me that seems a reasonable enough request."

"If there were any truth to it, which there can't possibly be,"

Ware insisted. "Fordyce's a feckless fribble. As for Mrs. Parmenter killing her husband? A physical impossibility. You'll understand when you see her."

"Uncle Justin has the right of it there." Soames reached for the decanter, refilled their glasses. "Parmenter was a bull of a man. Mabel Parmenter? A tiny golden-haired thing without a brain in her head, about as much physical strength, and always sickening for something. Quacks herself constantly. Kill Parmenter? It'd be like pitting a mouse against a boar."

"There's always David and Goliath," Oakwood murmured. "Of course the children hope it was Fordyce did the foul deed—if foul deed there was—and's lying to Miss Parmenter to feather his nest."

"Don't be ridiculous!"

"I take it you don't want me to look into the matter?"

"Didn't say that at all." Soames went to the bare window through which the wind shrilled like a lost soul. Impatiently he readjusted the rod, stuffing draperies in the cracks. "We'll have to shift you to another room until this is repaired, Uncle. We'll say it was housebreakers, and you chased 'em off. No, it's just," he said over his shoulder, "the man's death's been ruled an accident. He's been buried, the will read, and no one regrets his passing. Why muddy the waters?"

"What if Fordyce is genuinely blackmailing Miss Parmenter?"

"Why concern yourself with such people? The Parmenters're barely gentry these days." Soames stuffed a drapery corner in the last gap, turned and shrugged. "Lot more than that in the past, but recent generations've come down in the world. Happens to a lot of families. Not sure what started the slide. Probably backing some pretender who never made it to the Abbey. As for Underhill, it's gone to rack and ruin. House was still a showplace in my grandfather's time. Fine old manor on a hill, lots of antique paneling, marble fireplaces, that sort of thing. Predates the castle by considerable. Famous gardens, too. Nothing left of 'em now. Pity.

"Managed to avoid 'em all until Parmenter met his end in my

woods. Now I haven't much choice. Oh, I like the ladies well enough, and certainly they've all had a great deal to bear, but let them sort out their own problems."

"My brother-in-law's barely gentry," Oakwood spat, incensed. "Same thing's true of my stepmother. Doesn't mean I respect them any less for a lack of blood that's supposedly blue. Perhaps I respect them more, having made something of themselves in a world that did its best to stop them." Then he paused, eyes narrowing. "This doesn't sound in the least like you, Soames. Have an interest in the heiress yourself?"

"Good Lord, no!" Soames spluttered as he regained his seat by the fire.

"The widow, then? She must be fairly young."

"I've no more desire to be leg-shackled than you do," Soames returned firmly. "Eventually I suppose I'll have to, but eventually isn't today, and I certainly wouldn't want Mabel Parmenter. Empty attic, and a vine of the most clinging sort.

"Certainly I intend to assist them when possible," he shrugged. "Planning to speak to Miss Parmenter tomorrow about purchasing two of her father's hunters, as a matter of fact. Valuable bits of bone and blood—Twin Oaks breeding—but food and coal're more to the point at the moment. So's circumventing old Parmenter's will and Hatch's eagle eye."

"Then what's your objection?"

"I've none, really. It just seems a rather odd sort of thing to do—investigating the death of a man no one liked. Heaven knows what you might uncover. Wouldn't want to be forced to take any action I mightn't care for."

"That's why I'm perfect. I learn something better forgotten, I forget it. I'm also unbearably bored. Never thought seeing the pater and Serena wed would do that to me, but most everything seems pointless at the moment."

"I still don't like it," Ware insisted. "Fordyce'll make Miss Parmenter a decent enough husband, and once an heir's produced they'll none of them lack for anything. Underhill's an excellent property."

"I've heard gambling mentioned."

"Really?" Soames frowned. "Now that's something of which I wasn't aware. Only know Fordyce to nod to. He's come visiting at Underhill for years. A paltry sort, but there's a deal of distance between paltry and disreputable. Stoop to blackmail? I doubt it. Neither the intelligence nor the backbone."

"Not if the children're to be believed, and I rather suspect they are. Well, if you won't give me your blessing, that's that," Oakwood sighed. "I'll collect my things in the morning, find some other place for the holidays. Wouldn't want little Pru to know I'd played her false, or Alfie either. Rather prepossessing, that pair. No harm in Prissy, either. Rather dotes on Miss Parmenter, and being fond of my own sister, I empathize."

"Here now, who said anything about your leaving?"

"Prissy has it in her head they require a hero to rescue Miss Parmenter. While I'm not the hero type, I feel for the young woman if she's being forced to wed against her wishes," Oakwood continued, laying it on with a trowel, "especially if she marches to the altar in a spirit of self-sacrifice, believing she's saving her stepmother's life. Kindred spirit, given the pater, though of course he's nothing like Parmenter."

"Put like that," Soames said hesitantly.

"Thought you'd see it my way," Oakwood grinned. "How much chance is there of Clare recognizing me?"

"Idiot never sees beyond his nose. Often not that far."

"He's fulfilled his boyhood promise, then. Should be safe enough. I can stay in your gamekeeper's cottage? And bruit it about you've hired me to do something? Might even have me serve at table, if you've any livery would fit."

"That's no good. Pretend you're a surveyor, or a designer of gardens, or some such. Give you an excuse to roam about with no questions asked."

"You're both mad," Ware said in disgust. "The whole thing's a hum invented by the older girl. Forever with her nose in romances, from what I understand."

"I'll need some decent food delivered," Oakwood continued, ignoring Ware. "Takes considerable to keep this carcass stoked.

And dry wood, and blankets that don't smell of everything from fish to moldy straw. The children'll provide me with a cat."

"A cat? Whatever for?"

"Mice. Probably rats, as well. Thatched roof, remember," he winked. "If one has a thatched roof, according to Pru, one must keep cats or suffer the consequences. She wanted to provide me with one, but Alfie wasn't certain I'd like it. Men often don't like cats, you see."

"What I want to know," Soames said, eyeing his giant friend from his mahogany-colored curls to his bare feet, "is precisely how they managed to capture you. That part, at least, is beyond credibility,"

"Oh, I permitted it. Encouraged it, in fact. It had all the earmarks of an adventure, and after the past month I'm ready for one of my own. Sick unto death of others' adventures. Highly overrated, adventures are, unless one's at the center of 'em."

"Come on now—tell the tale."

"Only if you'll feed me," Oakwood pleaded. "I'm gutfoundered, and this brandy's going to my head. Oh, and I'd appreciate it if you'd have my coats and hat retrieved. They're by the fountain. I'll need fodder for Bacchus, by the bye. In fact, it'd be princely of you to send a groom 'round to see to the old fellow now and then."

"Don't want much, do you," Soames chuckled.

"Wouldn't mind a warm armful, either. Something with curves in all the right places. A dimple or two wouldn't be amiss, come to that. If it can cook and clean and see to my clothes, all to the good."

"Afraid you'll have to provide for yourself. And no poaching in the neighborhood, if you please. Villagers wouldn't like it, and you've no notion what a prosy bore Clare's become when he sets his mind to it."

"Has he, now?"

"Thorn in the side of every red-blooded man in calling distance."

"Jealousy, pure and simple. I'll be circumspect—no worry

there—but there's something I must know or perish from curiosity: Was Parmenter truly brought home in a dung cart?"

"I saw it was well cleaned first, and lined with straw," Soames protested as Oakwood broke into helpless laughter.

Phoebe Parmenter teetered on the stool, arms stretched above her head as she looped another length of fabric over the thick rod. The conglomeration was beginning to look almost elegant. Impatiently she flicked a strand of mouse-brown hair from her eyes, lost her balance, stumbled to the floor, climbed back on the stool.

"I do hope no one thinks we're unnatural, not showing greater distress at your father's death."

"You care?" she shrugged at the sound of her stepmother's plaintive voice as she squinted against the midmorning sun. A twist, a tuck, another few pins and she'd be done with this one. "Even with the dance they led us after Papa's will was read?"

Behind her, Mabel Parmenter glanced uneasily around the tiny bedchamber as she worried a loose thread on the lace-trimmed coverlet Phoebe had unearthed in the attics.

"This isn't right, not any of it, you know," she protested. "Word of my having changed bedchambers is certain to get back to Sister Trask and Nick, and I dread to think what they'll say. As for what you're doing to this room? We'll never hear the end of it!"

"What we do is neither your brother's business, nor my aunt's."

"They'll make it their business and I'll bear the brunt. I always do."

Phoebe sighed, turned to study her stepmother. The little widow was reclining at the head of an old-fashioned bed that hadn't seen use in a generation, her dimpled hands fluttering like trapped birds. The bruises had faded a bit and her right eye was no longer swollen shut. And, for a miracle Mabel seemed a trace less fearful this morning. At least she wasn't flinching at the slightest sound. That was progress of a sort, she supposed.

Ah well, she'd done her best. The fire on the grate had banished the morning chill, rendering the room almost habitable. The dried asters gracing the bedside table, the pannikin of water steaming on the hob, the pot warming before it gave the tiny room an unaccustomed sense of comfort. Two cups and the tea caddy waited on the mantel.

"I won't have you feeling guilty," Phoebe snapped, then sighed at her stepmother's pained expression. "Besides, where you sleep is now your concern, one of the ancillary advantages of widowhood."

The widow's nervous shudder and accompanying wince at the sudden movement of her injured shoulder forced another sigh from the slender young woman.

"I suppose if you really think it necessary, we can give it out this chamber's easier to heat," Phoebe conceded reluctantly. "Everyone knows we must economize given how things were left, and you're known to suffer from chills."

"That would be best. You know how the village is: If the vicar coughs at one end, Granny Mitchell at t'other tells all the world he's sickening for lung fever."

"So long as you don't insist on being moved back into Papa's old bedchamber."

"Never!" Mabel said with another shudder and wince. "Oh, never—please!"

"I thought not," Phoebe said with a grin that faded at the terror in her young stepmother's eyes. "I'm sorry," she sighed. "I'll never suggest such a thing again, even in jest."

"I'd rather die, truly."

"And I'd rather die than cause you pain—you know that."

Phoebe turned back to pinning up the swaths of ancient chintz with a determination bordering on the fanatical.

She wouldn't let Mabel stop her, not ever! They might have to endure Philip Fordyce sporadically now and permanently later, and those of his fiats they couldn't circumvent once the vows spoken. They didn't have to endure constant reminders of Portius Parmenter. Shifting Mabel from the dungeon-like master bedchamber two days before had been one of the wisest things she'd ever done. These days Mabel slept the night through rather than rousing the household with nightmarish screams.

"I do care what the village thinks of us, you know. A man has died," Mabel protested. "Even though he was clutch-fisted and unpleasant—"

"Unpleasant? He was the cruelest, most hard-hearted man I've ever known!"

"And you've known so many? Death is an awesome thing. We should be mourning it, if not him. Everyone will say so, and make our lives most uncomfortable if we don't do as they see fit."

"Mourn Papa?" Phoebe laughed from where she perched before the window. "No one would believe it if we did!"

"Still, it's not right, behaving as if—"

"Forget the village! What d'you think, Mabel?"

She clambered awkwardly from the stool and gestured at the new window hangings—actually nothing more than lengths of flowered chintz she'd just tacked over the rod. Not for nothing had she spent the countless hours, locked away on her father's orders, exploring the dusty upper regions of the old manor house to keep boredom and misery at bay.

She cocked her head, studying the effect, hands on her hips. The poppies glowed like suns, red and yellow and orange against the sparkling white background and bright green leaves. Around her ankles lay yards of tattered, sun-scorched dull bronze velvet trimmed in forest green and gold—the remains of the little chamber's former decoration.

"I think that's much better, don't you, Mabel? And there's enough for bed curtains to add another touch of color. I'll start on those as soon as we've had our tea"

"We shouldn't be enjoying ourselves—"

"When else have we ever known the least enjoyment in this house? I've suffered the place longer than you have. Enjoyment? We've earned it a thousand times over! Christmas will be splendid this year."

"Oh, but I don't think, I mean Sister Trask, and then there's the vicar and my brother, and his lordship is sure to look askance at—"

"We'll manage gifts for the girls somehow," Phoebe interrupted with forced gaiety, pushing more straggling wisps of light brown hair from her eyes. "They've known little enough joy either, poor things. There'll even be more than a lump of coal for you, and we'll have holly and ivy on all the mantels, and a kissing wreath, and a pudding so rich Papa'll spin in his grave. I'm determined that'll be his permanent condition for the rest of my natural life, so don't try to stop me."

"Phoebe, dearest," Mabel protested weakly, the faintest hint of a smile lighting her china blue eyes, "you really must moderate—"

"I shall moderate nothing! Nothing, d'you hear? Not anything! I remember your father well enough, child though I was when he died just after you and Papa were wed. Old Grim-and-Grizzly, that's what the children hereabout used to call him, and rightly so! A more repressive man I never saw, unless it was Papa."

"Phoebe, don't," Mabel protested with a die-away sigh, fumbling among the cordials and vials at her bedside for the vinaigrette. "You're all about in your head. My father was everything that was upright and just."

"And grim. I know there was someone before Papa, a young man visiting in the neighborhood, quite handsome in a quiet sort of way, back when Mama was still alive. Aunt Trask nattered on about how he was bound to give you a slip on the shoulder, and then he disappeared and you married Papa not a year later. Was he a vicar? Certainly Grim-and-Grizzly Gusset would've considered such beneath him, not being well-enough endowed with worldly goods to suit his sense of consequence."

Mabel cast a nervous glance at her stepdaughter, now fussing with the pannikin on the hob. A full day's allotment of coal for Portius Parmenter's office burned on the grate, squandered on this one room so she could be warm for once, rather than shivering as if she'd contracted the ague, and forever coughing at the stench of wood smoke.

"That's not wise to speak of," she said hesitantly. "Those're the leaves from breakfast, I hope? We can't afford to use them just once."

"To blazes with what we can or can't afford. No, I'm using fresh. Pru threw out the old by accident. Besides, we've earned it. As with your fire, economy begins tomorrow or the day after, not today."

"I still find it difficult to believe your father won't descend on us, take one look at all this frivolity and raise his fist," Mabel shuddered.

"Well, he won't—not ever again, and I'm glad, and I don't care who knows it. We've just been released from prison and I bless whatever caused his death, and if God wants to damn me for that, let Him."

Phoebe rinsed the pot, emptied the water in the slops jar, spooned in a generous portion of pungent leaves from the caddy, relocked it, then poured more hot water in the crazed earthenware pot to steep.

"And why isn't it wise to speak of that time, I'd like to know?" she demanded, refusing to be distracted. "You had dreams once, before Papa decided you'd make a suitable brood mare."

"Phoebe—please!"

"I found miles of red ribbon in the attics two winters ago," Phoebe continued as if her stepmother hadn't spoken. "We'll make it into bows and twine it 'round the banisters and festoon the doorways with it. Why, we'll be merry as grigs! Who was he?"

"Who was whom?"

"Your young man—the unsuitable one."

"Leave it be, Phoebe," Mabel sighed. "Sister Trask was correct—he was most unsuitable for me, just as I was for him. Had we wed, he'd've been cast off without a farthing, and so should I."

"Highly born then, I suppose? Titled, even? Someone you met through one of the girls at that seminary you attended in Bath?"

"No, just someone I encountered by accident," Mabel demurred wistfully. "Nothing came of it. Nothing ever could've.

Now that we've disposed of my past, such as it was," she said more firmly, setting the vinaigrette aside as not offering quite the remedy she desired, "I believe it's time we discuss your future and this nonsense regarding your marrying Cousin Philip. That's the shortest road to Weeping Cross I ever heard of! Why, he'd leave you penniless within a year."

"Not surprising you never guessed," Phoebe said, her face hidden as she unrolled more of the chintz preparatory to cutting it in lengths to hang at the head of the bed. "Quite excellent actors we were, don't you think?"

"I think you're lying, though what your purpose is I can't fathom. Philip would make an abominable husband."

"He won't beat us, and he won't starve us or shut us in the attics, and he won't chase you from Underhill."

"And it's on that basis that you've decided to wed him? Did he promise you a goose for Christmas as well, the way Alfie did?"

"Not quite, but he's said since we first pledged our love that we'd be comfortable, and I believe him. There's no sense discussing this yet again"

"Since you first pledged your love, indeed! You've detested him forever, and he's ignored you as beneath notice. Why this sudden change? Besides, I happen to have it on the very best authority you're suffering from a tendre for our vicar."

"Flummery!"

"Not according to Prissy."

"Prissy would see love eternal in a pair of worn boots."

"She'll grow up," Mabel said with a sad smile, leaning back weakly against her pillows, "and soon enough so long as she doesn't witness her elder sister indulging a disastrous lack of foresight. Under those circumstances she'd grow up far too quickly, and wed wherever she could merely to escape Underhill. I shouldn't like to see her repeat her mother's folly."

Phoebe sprang to her feet, crossed to the mantel, uncovered the pot and poured the tea, her movements jerky.

"Have done, I say," she protested softly. "I've loved Philip for years, but had Papa realized it he'd've forbidden him the house.

Neither of us could've borne that, so we kept our secret well and Philip toadied Papa at every opportunity to ensure his welcome."

"I almost believe you. Almost, but not quite—though what you see in Mr. Dorning I'll never understand. Everyone knows his soulful expression has more to do with a longing for his supper than saintliness. Besides, he bears tales at every opportunity."

"You'd best believe me, for Philip and I intend to be wed as soon as possible no matter what Lord Soames says. Delaying the banns until after the first of the year so I may recover my spirits, indeed! You'll notice Mr. Hatch voiced not the least objection to Philip." She set the steaming cup of fragrant tea beside her stepmother, smiled tenderly, for once forgoing the pleasure of leaping to the perpetually abused and misunderstood Clarence Dorning's defense. "Won't you please wish me happy?"

"Not until the New Year," Mabel protested with an abstracted air, retreating to the vagueness that had been her refuge for years. "Grant me that much time to adjust to the notion. Everything can wait 'til then, can't it?"

Phoebe straightened, gazing at her stepmother, the slightest of frowns drawing her brows together. "I don't think so," she said.

"But we've been so busy, you see," Mabel continued plaintively, dimpled hands moving restlessly on the coverlet, "what with your father being brought home in a common cart, and Lord Soames here every day attempting to offer what assistance he can, and his uncle doing what he can as well and proving more nuisance than aide. I'm totally fatigued from all the commotion, especially as I must play the gracious hostess whenever they take it into their minds to appear, and pretend my shoulder doesn't pain me, and that there's nothing in the least wrong with anything.

"A wedding, on top of everything else? Even one of the quietest sort? I haven't the strength to even consider such a thing at the moment, really I haven't," she complained fretfully. "I'm amazed you could be so selfish as to believe I did."

"Well," Phoebe sighed, "I'm afraid you're going to have to consider it, no matter how you feel about the matter."

Three

To characterize the morning as chilly would've been as inappropriate as to label Atilla the Hun a mite testy. The countryside was in the grip of an icy fist as powerful and unrelenting as that of any blacksmith.

Phoebe Parmenter slipped the sledge harness from her shoulders, shivering as she pulled her worn brown cloak more tightly about her.

She'd already gathered enough holly, ivy and pine to make an excellent beginning on the Yuletide decorations. What she lacked was mistletoe, and mistletoe she was determined to have.

But not just any mistletoe.

The easiest would've been to plunder the orchard. Clumps of the parasite clung in the highest branches like disorganized nests no matter how her father had fumed. Even an army of small boys had never been sufficient to knock it all down.

But, fanciful though the notion might be, mistletoe was a pagan thing, its use in kissing wreaths a remnant of traditions unbelievably ancient. Apple tree mistletoe might do for others. At Underhill this first year of Christmas celebration it had to be searched out where the Druids had found it: among oaks deep in a snow-covered wood. Perhaps it would bring them luck. They had need of some, given Papa's will. More importantly, she had need of some.

Phoebe scowled, stifling the unwelcome thought.

At least Philip Fordyce departed each night at a reasonable hour, thanks to Lord Soames's groom. Mick Bodger was invariably respectful, pretending he was only alerting Fordyce to his presence and assuring him the ladies of Underhill would be safe in his care until morning. Actually it was a deal more than that. Bodger was always accompanied by one of his sons. Both were armed, a detail that caused Fordyce to scowl even as he resisted departure. She wasn't certain what he thought to gain by being so disagreeable. He had her and, through her, Underhill. That should've satisfied him, but for some reason it didn't.

No, she had need of Druid mistletoe because, no matter what she pretended to others, Phoebe regarded her impending nuptials with a dread that cut to the bone.

It was the search for mistletoe clinging to ancient oaks rather than sprouting in a mundane orchard that had brought her deep into Lord Soames's woods. And, she'd found it: a grove of trees so tall, so thick-trunked and heavy-branched they might date from the days of the Druids themselves. There was even a flat-topped boulder swept free of snow in the center of the circle, hinting at an ancient altar.

She stood there planning her assault, the crude sledge the girls used for transporting deadfall trailing at the end of its rope harness. She gave no consideration to the fact that she was a spinster, a recently bereaved daughter, a betrothed country heiress unversed in the climbing of trees, and twenty-six years old. Her only thought was for the possibility of a mistletoe miracle.

A fat clump taunted her on a branch just above another offering a secure perch in what had to be the most ancient tree in the grove. The only problem was how to reach it. Nothing offered an easy solution, not even a bit of deadfall she might throw to knock the mistletoe down. Fortuitously, half way between the ground and the lowest branch were a pair of thick knobs with depressed centers offering toe-holds where lower branches had broken off. She gauged the distance, the scattering of higher branches like so many crude steps, nodded, dragged the heavy sledge to the boulder and unloaded it, gave the mass of greenery a reassuring pat, then shoved the sledge to her target and, after a struggle, tilted it against the trunk.

It took a few tries and cost her a pair of sodden boots, a torn hem and snagged mitten, but at last she reached the sturdy branch from which, if she stood on her toes, grasped the branch above and inched out a step or two, she could just reach the clump.

And then she made her mistake: Phoebe looked down, and discovered the first great law of tree climbing: going up was relatively easy if one planned with a modicum of care and were the least agile. Retracing one's path was another matter.

Beneath her, what had been a pristine covering of white when she stumbled upon the grove had been trampled into a confused jumble of footprints and runner tracks. The Druids, she concluded whimsically, would not be best pleased at this sullying of their sacred spot, and were probably exacting revenge. In fact, she admitted, teeth chattering as much from fear as cold, neither was she best pleased.

It was a fool's errand in any case. Nothing would change what her father had forced on her with his unconscionable will. There was a bitter justice to it, she supposed: Papa unwittingly ensuring she only exchanged one form of servitude for another. At least Mabel and the girls might eventually escape the worst of the consequences.

In the meantime, here she was miles above the earth with no visible means of returning short of an ignominious—and dangerous—tumble. It would be criminal not to make the attempt after all that effort.

Eyes clenched, she brought herself to her toes, sliding up the rough bark. Then, clinging desperately to the trunk, she groped for the next branch. Air—nothing but air. Then a twig. She seized it thankfully, slid her fingers up searching for the parent branch. The dratted thing proceeded to snap. Her feet in their old boots began to slip.

"Oh, bother!" She flung herself against the trunk, clinging to it for dear life.

"Miss Parmenter? Is that you? Dear heaven, what're you doing up there?"

The vicar's familiar voice, for once devoid of its pedantic drawl, was the most welcome sound she'd ever heard.

"Escaping a wolf," Phoebe giggled nervously without thinking.

"A wolf? In these civilized environs?" From somewhere beneath her came the creak of a saddle, the jingle of bridle and bit. "Oh come now, that's hardly probable, is it? Are you certain you didn't mistake a fox?"

She risked a peek with its attendant vertigo. The vicar was invisible and, from his tone, shocked by the circumstances in which he'd discovered her, but assistance was at hand. Certainly no gentleman who'd gallantly sheltered her under his umbrella on a particularly inclement day only weeks earlier would abandon her now, no matter what his opinions regarding the impropriety of her current situation, and for all he'd lectured her mercilessly on the use of servants to run such degrading errands as delivering nuts to the George on the previous occasion.

"No, Mr. Dorning, I didn't mistake a fox," she confessed.

This was hardly the image she'd hoped the fastidious cleric might carry in his heart. A vicar's bride? Climbing trees? Especially after being caught traipsing about the countryside in the rain and mud pushing a barrow loaded with nuts, a jar of soup and a loaf of bread for Granny Mitchell hidden beneath the lumpy sacks?

Ah well, there was little chance of that as things stood, no matter what longings she'd cherished since his first appearance in the neighborhood. Whatever else might be said of him, Mr. Dorning would have made a safe and self-effacing mate, and heaven knew she would have made a frugal cleric's wife.

"It was a rabbit," she explained, attempting to interject a bit of humor in the silly predicament. "Such a big rabbit! And, so ferocious. Far worse than any wolf, believe me. Damn me for a coward if you will, but the beast treed me."

"Damn you? Miss Parmenter!" he reproved. Then, quite seriously he added, "You fear rabbits? They're quite harmless, you know, and excellent eating. My housekeeper has an outstanding receipt for rabbit stew."

"But they have such big teeth." It might be heinous of her, but she couldn't resist. "Give one nasty nips if one's not careful," she explained, repressing another nervous giggle. "Can you not imagine being nibbled by rabbits? Just think what they do to carrots and cabbages! And, tender young lettuce. I do believe that's what the brute considered me, now I think on it: a tender young lettuce."

"Miss Parmenter!"

"Why, being nibbled to death would take forever—a dreadful fate, and one I don't deserve in the least."

"I presume," the vicar suggested after a moment's consideration, "you're indulging in humor."

"Yes, Mr. Dorning," she sighed, "I'm indulging in humor."

And so fell one more illusion.

The vicar wasn't merely preachy and vain, his gallantries those of one seeking to ingratiate himself with an eye to future advantage—all of which Mabel had insisted forever, and the children as well. He wasn't merely serious and dedicated to his calling, as *she'd* insisted. He was totally lacking in a sense of the ridiculous.

How lowering—that she could misjudge so! Still, she felt she could be forgiven. She had, after all, passed only the briefest of time in Dorning's company, and that generally under her father's disapproving eye following Sunday services, the vicar's compliments labored, her own incoherent responses stumbling over themselves like clumsy puppies in an effort to gain favor that would never've been forthcoming.

"Well, if that's the case—and entirely inappropriate that is, given the recent death of your male parent," he was forging on repressively, "and you're not escaping a fox, then what in heaven—"

"What does it appear I'm doing, Mr. Dorning?"

"Taking leave of your senses, if you want the truth."

There was a another jingle of bridle and bit, and crunching that told of the vicar's mount coming closer. She risked a second peep.

The sight wasn't entirely unanticipated: the vicar, resplendent in a new many-caped greatcoat and curly-brimmed beaver. With all his worldly goods did he the tailors of London endow, though not the very best tailors. He couldn't afford those, given that Lord Soames didn't supplement the living. It was a generous one, had supported old Mr. Smythe most comfortably. Of course Mr. Smythe's ambitions hadn't run to cutting a dash among the ton, merely to caring for his parish. She'd always realized that, no matter how completely she'd had the rest of it wrong.

But, Mr. Dorning? Astride Devil-a-Bit?

"Thank you for instructing me regarding my faults," Phoebe responded contritely. "That's what I always want—the truth."

To which she was being treated to an inordinately large dose. Clarence Dorning, a knight in shining armor? It seemed Mabel had been right about all of it, even if she didn't generally possess the cleverness for such astute analysis: Phoebe had constructed a non-existent paragon from her dreams and despair. Of course, this time it was only the two of them, and Dorning had no need to pretend to spurious gallantry. Still, that was a poor excuse for her blindness.

"What're you doing with my horse?" she demanded more severely.

"I, ah, passed by Underhill to call on Mrs. Parmenter in her hour of sorrow, say a few prayers, don't you know? Provide consolation for her insupportable loss, and assure her of an eventual joyous reunion. Quite in keeping, y'understand. She, ah, offered me the loan of him as my own mount'd pulled up lame in my effort to be of service to her."

"Had it indeed?"

"Such magnificent steeds shouldn't go unexercised in any case."

"That's all right, Mr. Dorning. I understand the circumstances. Going to the castle, were you," she muttered bitterly, "to impress his lordship with your attention to your parish duties, and his elevated guests with your eye for a fine bit of blood and bone?

"I'm also a trifle inconvenienced, being stuck up here," she called more clearly. "D'you think you could help me down?"

"I? A man of God? Climb a tree? It would be neither right nor fitting."

"I suppose it's right and fitting to abandon one of your parishioners in a most precarious situation?"

" 'As ye sew, so shall ye weep,' " the vicar quoted not quite accurately. "Finally found a good use for that one. Never understood it before, frankly. What Mrs. Trask would say if she could see you—"

"Bother Aunt Trask! She won't learn of it unless you go bearing tales, which I'm assured you won't."

"As your father's sister and the senior female of your family, your comportment is of immense concern to her," he said, apparently struck by a new idea. "Why, only this morning Mrs. Trask was commenting on the fact. Indeed, it's she who should have the governing of you. Much too flighty to see to yourself," he pontificated, "and your stepmother, bowed down by grief as she is, is in no way fit to serve in such a capacity.

"You should invite Mrs. Trask to form part of your household until such time as you're wed, and a sensible man can assume responsibility for regulating you. From all appearances, you've great need of such regulation."

"That's one counsel of yours I feel I must refuse to consider," Phoebe snapped, teetering on the branch. "I suppose you'd wish for my aunt to remain once I wed? Mr. Fordyce and she don't generally see eye to eye. That would make for a most uncomfortable household."

"In such case it would be above all wise to invite her, especially as you shouldn't be considering Mr. Fordyce as master of Underhill. He's only your stepmother's cousin. Cobber Trask, being your father's nephew, has a far greater claim on your affections."

"And on Underhill?"

"Naturally," he insisted, warming to his theme. "It's God's providence your father should have a nephew both unwed and of the proper age to assume his position."

"And the proper intelligence to be master of Underhill?"

"His mother knows what he doesn't, having been born and raised there."

"So that's the way of it," she murmured. "Did Aunt Trask promise you Devil-a-Bit if you brought me to a sense of my family duty?" she demanded more loudly.

"That wouldn't be proper!"

"Did she?"

"Something of the sort may've been mentioned, given such mounts will be superfluous once you wed Cobber. He's not a follower of the hunt."

"But Mr. Fordyce follows the hunt whenever he has the opportunity, and it's to him I'm betrothed."

"I thought we'd already agreed on his unsuitability," Dorning protested. "My cousin did well forbidding the banns when Mr. Fordyce made his untimely announcement following the reading of your father's will."

"His lordship forbade the banns? I don't remember it that way, but my memory must be faulty given the excellence of your education and the paucity of my own."

"Believe me," Dorning preened, "the banns were forbidden. My cousin has a clear sense of the fitness of things and an even clearer understanding of his responsibilities as the representative of the great world in this little corner of England, just as I have a clear sense of the moral imperatives laid down by the God I serve."

"And which god might that be?" she muttered bitterly. "Mammon?"

Clinging to the tree, she studied the elegant pair beneath her, ignoring the dizziness that gripped her. She'd considered young Mr. Dorning everything that was desirable since the first Sunday he mounted the pulpit. His brow was high, his gestures graceful, his manner all that was pleasing. At least so she'd considered them. Fool!

"No," she countered thoughtfully, "you merely stated your and my aunt's opinions—which, I may tell you, have no force with me."

"I see," he said, head tilted back, observing her through cool, silvery gray eyes. "You have so little respect for the spiritual advice of your vicar?"

"When he pretends worldly advice to be spiritual, yes."

"The matter of whom you marry is spiritual."

"And I thought it to be wildly carnal," she muttered, then, at his questioning glance, shook her head. "I was merely talking to myself—a very bad habit, I know."

"You won't reconsider?"

"Jilting Mr. Fordyce? I cannot."

"I see I'll have to take this matter up with my cousin. Perhaps you'll listen to his counsel as your temporal lord where you won't to my canonical one, for I know he'll agree marriage to your cousin rather than your stepmother's is the only moral possibility available to you. Your father's family mustn't be done out of their inheritance."

"My father's family's already been done out of their inheritance," she snapped, tried beyond endurance, "thanks to my father's will. Or, d'you consider his widow and younger daughters to have less claim on him than his sister and her son?"

"Far less, for there're no ties of blood."

"No ties of blood? To Prissy and Pru? You're mad!"

"The ties are much stronger to Mrs. Trask," he insisted, "given she and your father shared the same parents. His daughters carry only his blood, if that."

"What?" Phoebe thoughtlessly started to spring forward, wavered, grasped the tree as if it were a long-lost lover. "Precisely what do you mean by that?"

"I believe you understand the implication, Miss Parmenter."

"And precisely who gave you such a notion? Aunt Trask?"

Mr. Dorning was conspicuous for his silence.

"You realize Underhill's been little better than a prison?" She hurled the words as if they were arrows, delighted to see he flinched as he backed Devil-a-Bit from beneath the tree. "Complete with floggings? D'you realize it'd be no better were Aunt Trask to take up residence? Poor Cobber isn't nearly so clumsy as she'd have the world believe."

"What I believe is that you exaggerate, Miss Parmenter. Mrs. Trask is in every way a fine Christian woman, just as your father was the perfect example of an English gentleman. Flighty girls're highly prone to unfortunate exaggeration, as Mrs. Trask has pointed out," he said piously, "especially those with no sense of family duty or pride."

"Dear God!" she muttered.

"Precisely, Miss Parmenter. Think on it."

"I shall. Oh, I shall! I'll consider many things. Where are you going?" she cried in alarm as he continued to back the black towards the center of the clearing.

"Why, to the castle, of course, as was my original intention," he said, tipping his hat. "I promised my cousin I'd call on him at the earliest opportunity now all his guests've arrived. Wants them to make my acquaintance as an excellent example of sober bachelorhood whom they should at all times emulate."

"I don't believe a word of it! Forcing yourself on their acquaintance is more like it, and his lordship too kind to put you in your place," she muttered.

"Do have a pleasant morning, Miss Parmenter."

"My horse! Devil-a-Bit! I insist you return him to my stables immediately!"

"Your stables, Miss Parmenter? Say rather to your father's stables, and as I have the loan of him from your father's widow there's not much you can do, is there. Forbid your vicar the use of a mount no one rides? Make it impossible for him to attend to his parish duties because of a selfish whim? What would that do to your stock in the neighborhood, I wonder? It's not very high, that I can tell you, and I have your groom's assurance my own poor mount will be in no condition to carry me about for some weeks.

"In the meantime," he said with a cheery smile, "I have the use of this great fellow, and a promise that Devil-May-Care shall be pressed into God's service as well should the need arise. That will raise your stock in Chedleigh Minor as nothing else could, for believe me, the village doesn't look kindly on your choice of intended husband. Indeed, all are quite shocked."

"I don't believe you even spoke to Mabel," she called. "I believe you browbeat poor old Tom into permitting you to make free of my stables!"

"Believe what you will," the vicar returned sunnily. "You'll admit it's a groom's responsibility to see to the welfare of the mounts in his care, and in permitting—nay, encouraging—me to exercise them for you, he's seeing to their welfare."

"I'll admit no such thing!" she called after his retreating figure. "Return Devil-a-Bit immediately!"

"And forego my visit to his lordship and my parish rounds? Or be forced to go afoot—totally out of keeping with my position both as vicar and as his lordship's cousin? I think not. Good day, Miss Parmenter."

She watched him turn Devil-a-Bit, stunned. Fordyce, at least, was totally honest regarding his requirements in return for his silence. This grasping leech was determined to get his good from her father's death no matter how the will read.

"Don't so much as consider selling the Twin Oaks mounts," Dorning called silkily from the center of the clearing. "Mrs. Trask would take it in very poor part."

"The idea hadn't even occurred to me," she shouted, goaded beyond endurance. "Mr. Fordyce is most fond of both. Once we're wed, I've assured him they're to be his."

"I think not, Miss Parmenter. They'll be mine. In point of fact, I'm merely taking advance possession of that which's been promised me, one might say. I'll refuse to read the banns, you know, and I'll have my cousin's blessing in my refusal."

"On what grounds?" she demanded, incredulous.

"I'll find one," he replied. "That's the purpose of canon law: to ensure people behave as they ought and as their families desire they should."

"Could you not send assistance, as you consider it beneath your dignity to come to my aid yourself?" she pleaded as he continued across the clearing. "It's uncomfortable up here, and frightfully cold, and I'm in terror of slipping, and I'm dreadfully dizzy."

"You want others to witness you in this position?" Dorning demanded over his shoulder. "I, at least, am paying no attention to those portions of your, well, that which is exposed that shouldn't be. I can't vouch for such a high degree of moral rectitude in others. Besides, were I to assist you I'd most likely ruin my coat. It's a new one."

"So I see." Dear heaven—what had she ever seen in this venal, pompous nonentity? "You intend to abandon me here to fall? Or freeze to death? Or be nibbled by rabbits?"

"Miss Parmenter, your levity's inappropriate. I believe a bit of solitude during which you may reflect on your duty to your father, to his family, and above all to God, is quite in order. It would seem the Almighty had a purpose in transforming those devil's promptings that led you here on whatever unholy errand you had in mind into your current punishment."

"But if I catch my death—"

"You'll be well served. Mrs. Trask has confirmed with Hezekiah Hatch that, should you die before fulfilling the conditions of your father's will, the entire property reverts to that worthy lady, and through her to her son. It's only in the case of attempted gifts to your stepmother and half-sisters that it goes to the Crown. There's so much of which you're unaware, Miss Parmenter, being untutored in how gentlemen manage their affairs to ensure their projects are carried to a happy conclusion. 'Suffer the meek.' "

Dorning paused by the boulder to help himself to a sprig of holly which he tucked in his buttonhole, then continued on his way.

"Mawworm!" Phoebe shouted after him, tears of fury sparkling in her eyes, then settled herself more securely on her uncomfortable perch and surveyed the now empty clearing, feeling a little sick. "Murderer," she mumbled more softly. "Thief."

She'd only been half joking about catching her death here in Lord Soames's icy woods. How sweetly that would fit Aunt Trask's plans, besides being distinctly unpleasant for herself and a great inconvenience for Mabel and the girls. She didn't dare put it more baldly than that, but beneath the flippant analysis lurked a desperate dread at the thought of never seeing another spring.

"Why can't people behave as one has a right to expect them to," she murmured despairingly, "and why, oh why can't mistletoe grow in more convenient spots?"

From beneath her came the crunch of snow.

"As to the former, because our expectations are generally unreasonable," a deep voice chuckled softly, clearly undesirous of attracting the attention of the departed vicar were he still in earshot, "and as to the latter, because that would take all the sport from gathering it."

Phoebe froze.

"Who's there?" she demanded with more aplomb then she felt.

"A gentleman with less concern for his coat than a lady's predicament," came the deep voice, infinitely reassuring in its touch of humor, from somewhere to the side of her tree. "But then my coat's not in the latest style, so I suppose the comparison's unfair."

"It should be Prissy here," Phoebe muttered, clenching her eyes against the way the trees whirled about. "This has all the earmarks of the tales she and Mabel are forever reading." Then, more loudly, she said, "Where are you? More to the point, who are you? Or don't you believe in answering a lady's questions?"

"Naturally, when they're to the point. What d'you think you're doing up there? Aside from escaping ferocious rabbits?"

"Dear heaven—did you hear it all?"

"Most of it, I imagine. Vicar fancy you for himself, does he?"

"Hardly," she said, again peering uneasily from her high perch and stifling her rising gorge. "Just Papa's hunters, and not all of those. Mr. Dorning might not be able to tell the difference at a horse fair, but Chronicle Watford's stud is so well-known even he's heard of it. Papa acquired a pair of Twin Oaks hunters a year ago, and Mr. Dorning fancies them for himself. Beautifully schooled, great goers, and highly unsuited to a cow-handed vicar. Did you observe how uneasily he sat in the saddle?"

"I did indeed. A paltry fellow."

"Where are you, or am I now consorting with disembodied spirits?"

"I'm the godlet of the grove," the stranger said with a hint of ghostly menace, "come to spy on mortals and punish them for desecrating my holy place."

"Dear me!" Phoebe giggled involuntarily. "How shocked you must be by our modem garb."

"Not very fetching," he agreed. "Much preferred those flimsy things my priestesses used to wear. You need a bit of jewelry about you as well, if I remember correctly. Possibly a breastplate such as Boadicea might've worn, or a necklace of some sort. Be a trifle chilly in nothing but those though. Need a warm cloak as well, speaking of which, wouldn't you rather be on *terra firma* than cavorting up there?"

"I'm not cavorting. I'm stuck."

"Are you? And here I believed you were maintaining your perch out of choice."

"Of course I'd rather be below," she laughed uneasily. "Better yet, beside a toasty fire with a cup of hot cider warming my hands and my feet in a mustard bath and a quilt about my shoulders. Well, almost."

"Only almost? Sounds far preferable to where you're currently housed."

"I did so want that clump of mistletoe," she said, releasing the trunk long enough to point at the dark globular shape above.

"First let's get you down. Then we'll see about your holiday decorations."

"Who are you?" she demanded again. "Not that I'm generally of a suspicious nature, but I've never heard your voice. I'm very good at recognizing voices."

"As you surmised, a stranger in these parts."

"What are you doing in Lord Soames's woods?"

"I might ask the same of you."

"You can see what I'm doing, for pity's sake—robbing his lordship of a bit of mistletoe. At least that was my intention. What's your excuse?"

"I, ah, I'm surveying the game population for his lordship."

"At this time of year?"

"One can tell a great deal from tracks."

"Really? I never thought of that."

"There's obviously a great deal you've never considered," he chuckled, "starting with the fact that that which goes up must eventually come down. The only question is, how? There's no way I can come up after you. Totally impossible, I'm afraid."

"Whyever not?"

"Take a look," the stranger said, appearing from behind the opposite side of Phoebe's tree.

"Dear heaven," she murmured, blanching.

"Too great a chance the branches wouldn't hold me. Then where'd you be, with me in the snow and most likely unconscious, and you up there? That would really set their jaws to wagging once they found us!"

"It would indeed."

Her rescuer was a giant, bigger even than Papa. His clothes were coarse: merely a cap he'd just doffed, an old gray greatcoat with a scrap of heavy brown tweed showing between missing buttons, a tawny scarf wound high about his neck, boots that'd seen better days, a pair of stained wool gloves faced in leather. Hair that shone like mahogany, even in the thin winter light. And a stubble of beard on his chin. Altogether a rough, disreputable character. She shrank against the trunk, discounting the twinkling hazel eyes and ready, good-natured grin.

"I believe I prefer to remain where I am," she said warily, "and take my chances on Mr. Dorning suffering a flurry of compunction. I'm safe enough up here."

"Until your arms grow numb. Then you'll come tumbling down with no one to break your fall. I don't intend to freeze in this clearing for your sake. Neither do I intend abandoning you to your fate."

The voice held precisely that tone of impatient male authority she most hated. Phoebe shook her head, clinging determinedly to her perch.

"Come now," the ruffian ordered, all pretense at good humor fled, "don't be a little wet-goose"

"I believe I prefer that possibility to the others. Besides, what assurance do I have that you're who you claim to be? There've been discharged troopers creating all sorts of havoc in the neighborhood recently."

"No assurance at all, but I am," he said, striding to the boulder and placing a well-oiled gun on its smooth surface beside her greenery. "The name's Peter Oakwood, which is rather propitious given the spot you're in, don't you think?" he added with another infectious grin as he returned to the tree's base and peered at her through the branches. "I don't covet your hunters, and I promise not to encourage you to marry Cousin Cobber or attempt to foist Aunt Trask on your household."

"For which I'm infinitely grateful, but not grateful enough to trust myself to your kind ministrations," she snapped nervously. "D'you think you could go to the castle if you're truly an employee of Lord Soames's, and fetch some assistance?"

"And risk word getting back to Aunt Trask, as it's certain to do? You know all great houses are hotbeds of gossip."

"I hadn't thought of that."

"Do," Oakwood said with a touch of mock severity. "Or, are you lily-livered?"

"Oh, most definitely lily-livered—on both counts."

"Your aunt I understand, given what I overheard—and no, I don't make a habit of listening at doors, even out-of-doors. What's the other?"

She clung to her perch, eyes narrowed.

"Dear God—you fear me more than you fear an inflammation of the lungs?" Oakwood demanded, clearly stunned. "I assure you, I'm most respectable, highly trustworthy, and not given to playing fast and loose with maidens in distress."

"Let's say there're some risks I'm prepared to take, and some I'm not."

Oakwood stood beneath the tree, scowling up at her. "Are you missish?" he finally inquired. "I didn't expect that."

"As we've barely encountered one another, I don't see how you could expect anything of me. Who are you?" she said, returning to the main point. "How can I believe you when you say you're an employee of Lord Soames's?"

"You can't," he shrugged, "as I'm certain even the most excellent belowstairs news service hasn't had time to spread word of my presence yet. I'm afraid you'll just have to trust me."

"I daren't," she said, her pallor underscoring her words.

Oakwood shifted, trying to get a better look through the branches. "My poor girl—what've they done to you?" he asked almost involuntarily at the brief glimpse of a skinny scrap of terrified femininity clinging to the tree, white-lipped and huge-eyed.

"Nothing that need concern you, sir."

"But I believe it must. Dragons to be slain? Wicked witches to be dunked in a pond? Villainous vicars to be vanquished? Pots to be mended?" he teased, deliberately lightening the mood, whether for her sake or his own even he wasn't certain. "Behold Peter Oakwood at your service! I'm especially good at witches, having not the slightest aversion to water. Less proficient at pots, unfortunately, but I'm willing to give 'em a try if you've any in need of bottoming."

The faint giggle was welcome to Oakwood's ears. He wished he could see the object of his concern more clearly. Naught showed but a bit of face pinched from the cold and a smudge of dark clothing. The voice was well enough: light and musical, and ringing with humor when it wasn't trembling with anxiety. The rest was left to imagination. Given Soames's description, his had run to severe expressions, watery myopic eyes, spinsterish diction, and chilblains—apparently an error.

"Seriously," he said, "we must get you down. I'll go to Soames's stables if that's what you wish, but even old Bodger likes a touch of gossip along with his pint. As things stand, any tales your Mr. Dorning—"

"He's not my Mr. Dorning," Phoebe snapped.

"Ah well, misimpressions are so embarrassing, don't you agree? And here I was thinking he'd disappointed you in some manner."

"He did, not that I have any true claim on his consideration."

"Other than he's the local vicar, and riding your horse without your permission?"

"There's that, of course."

"Indeed there is. In the circles to which that idiot aspires such matters aren't taken lightly, believe me."

"You know so much of the ton?"

"Enough to know that," Oakwood said firmly. "If you've no intention of gifting the vicar with a pair of handsome hunters, you should make the matter clear to your stepmother before gadding about again in search of mistletoe. As Ciber said, 'Possession is eleven points in the law.' "

"Poor Mabel," Phoebe sighed. "It wouldn't matter what anyone said. If Mr. Dorning so much as frowned at her she'd grant him anything he wished. Mabel abhors unpleasantness, and she's had far too much of it in her life."

"So that's the direction of the wind?"

"Hardly. My goodness, but this conversation is improper!"

"And most enlightening. Given the task I have to perform for Lord Soames, it's best I understand the personalities of the neighborhood."

"What have they to do with game preserves?"

"One never knows when a scrap of information'll come in handy. See here, we're wasting time. You're frozen to the bone from the sound of those chattering teeth. Yes, I can hear 'em all the way down here. Now, are you going to descend of your own free will, or do I start firing gobbets of snow to knock you off your perch?"

"Just go for help, please."

"No—too much risk of too many tales being born about the village. Your Mr. Dorning doesn't strike me as the close-mouthed sort, not if he was—what word shall we use? Conferring? Yes, that'll do—conferring with your aunt earlier."

Phoebe watched as the hulk who claimed to be a man scooped up a handful of snow and began shaping it into a firm ball.

"You wouldn't!" she protested.

"Indeed I would, if that's what it takes."

"You, sir, are no gentleman."

"Not currently claiming to be one. Merely in his lordship's service, and increasingly grateful for the post. I'm finding Penwillow and its environs more and more to my liking." Oakwood stepped back a few paces to where he could see the dark, huddled figure silhouetted against branches and bright blue sky. "My aim's quite good. Bowler for my school's eleven. Strong arm, keen eye. Watch."

Oakwood shied the sparkling ball at the next tree, striking a clump of mistletoe dead on. Snow fluttered to the ground along with a few glossy green leaves.

"Demonstration enough for you, milady?" Swiftly he bent, assembled another ball, sent it flying after the first. Four balls later a battered clump of mistletoe lay at the foot of the tree. "Now," he said, cocking his head and peering at Phoebe, hands on his hips, "let's see what we can do about getting you down from there."

"Not by the same method, I hope?"

"If that's what's required."

Oakwood's tone was so menacing as he assembled another ball that she knew he was teasing. It was a comforting thought—that this great bear of a man could tease even when he was most serious. And serious she realized he was. Mr. Oakwood, bless him, had no intention of abandoning her as Clarence Dorning had.

"How would you prefer to do this: carefully under my direction, or precipitously under a barrage of snow?" He watched the quivering figure for a moment, unwilling sympathy for the young woman swelling. "Trust me, Miss Parmenter," he said more gently. "Providence guided my steps to you. Now you must place your confidence in me. If you do, I promise all shall come right."

"Tell me what to do," a contrite voice floated to him. "I'm not customarily such a ninny."

"No, given what I've heard of you I'm certain you're not, but even the best of us have our less temeritous moments."

"And what've you heard of me?"

Oakwood flinched at the wary tone.

"Nothing more than what your Mr. Dorning had to say," he soothed. "You've been rather put upon of late, what with one thing and another, haven't you. So, let's go about solving the most immediate of your problems."

"If you please," Phoebe quavered, "I'm ready now."

It took a bit of doing. Her hands were blocks of ice in their much-mended mittens, her feet their equal in sodden boots. Worse yet, female clothing didn't fare well among tree limbs and twigs. In the end, she hung topsy-turvy from the lowest branch, cloak snagged. Then came the sound of rending fabric, and she tumbled into Oakwood's waiting arms. The soft whimper of gratitude, the desperately clutching hands twisted his heart as no faint, no attack of the vapors could have.

With an uneasy clearing of his throat, Oakwood gently set the young woman on her feet, smoothed the straggling light brown hair from her face as he kept a supporting arm about her shoulders. She wavered, emitted a shuddering sigh, then moved slightly away from him and attempted to put herself to rights.

"There now, that wasn't so dreadful, was it?" he said.

"N-no, at least not when one considers the alternative."

Concerned hazel eyes met grateful deep brown. The earth paused briefly in its career, or so it seemed to the pair in that clearing. Then Phoebe Parmenter gave herself a shake and Peter Oakwood scuffed the toe of his boot in the snow, not quite certain what to do with himself.

"I'm perfectly recovered," she said with more assurance than she felt.

"My dear girl, you're frozen to the bone."

"A brisk walk home shall set me to rights." She attempted to pull her cloak around her, found she was dealing with a pair of wings. "Oh, dear," she murmured, examining the jagged rent. "Oh dear me!"

"Not to worry. That thing can hardly be your best," Oakwood consoled with a forced chuckle.

"No, it's not. It's my only one," she admitted with a resigned shrug. "Ah well, a few stitches'll set it to rights. Mabel's most proficient at such repairs, thank goodness, as I'm hopeless with a needle." The young woman stumbled to the base of the tree from which Oakwood had battered the mistletoe, retrieved the scattered bits. "This wasn't what I had in mind. Still, I'm most grateful."

Silently Peter Oakwood helped her reload the cumbersome sledge. When they were done she turned, held out her hand.

"Thank you, Mr. Oakwood," she said, attempting to ignore the intimidating bulk of the man before her and concentrating instead on the dancing hazel eyes. "I'll examine the pots when I reach home, see if any are in need of mending."

"What? Oh yes, of course." He seized her hand, retaining it a trifle longer than was totally proper. "It'll all come right in the end," he said for the second time. "That much I can promise you. I do mean it, you know."

"Yes, well, it has, hasn't it? I'm out of that silly oak thanks to you, and the girls'll have a kissing wreath, though not such a splendid one as I'd planned. Still, it'll be more than they've ever had before."

"Are you sure that thing isn't too heavy for you?" he asked, casting a dubious eye at the laden sledge.

"Heavens, no! Once one gets it going it's easy, and there's a brake of sorts for going down inclines."

She retrieved her hand with a tremulous laugh, settled the sledge's harness over her shoulders and forged across the clearing. At the verge she turned and waved.

"Good-bye, god of the oaks," she called.

"Until we meet again, little Druidess," Oakwood murmured, watching the slight figure trudge away pulling its burden of Christmas greenery.

There were certain questions he had for Pru and Prissy now he'd encountered Phoebe Parmenter, but he had two even more pressing bits of business. One was a trip to nearby Market Stoking, or possibly Pilchester. Surely he could find a lady's ready-made cloak in one of those places. It would have to be plain wool, he supposed. If he had his choice, it would've been velvet with sable trim. Little pagan priestesses whose heads barely reached his shoulder deserved only the best.

The other, he scowled, was more immediate: a conference with Soames. Something had to be done about Dandy Clare and Phoebe Parmenter's Twin Oaks hunters.

Four

"What the devil? Ware, come see this," the earl called, pulling back the breakfast parlor draperies for a better look as he cleared a circular spot in the frost with the flat of his fist. "Damme, but it's cold!" he muttered.

One of Parmenter's magnificent black hunters stood in the courtyard, Clare Dorning swinging from the saddle, many-caped greatcoat tangled about his legs.

"I mean, what the devil d'you make of it?" Soames demanded as a groom dashed through the archway leading to the stable block.

"Clumsy as ever," Justin Ware murmured, observing the transfer from steed to cobbled yard with no little amusement. "It would seem our esteemed cousin's decided to grace us with his presence. Why don't you put the poor sod out of his misery, and invite him to stop with you through the holidays? He calls given the slightest excuse, generally at the hours when meals're taken."

"The damned horse, Ware—not the man. That's one of the Parmenter hunters. What in the name of heaven is Clare doing with the beast?"

"Attempting to dismount without killing himself. With only minimal success, I might add. As to what he means making free of the Parmenter stables? I haven't the foggiest notion, but details of ownership've never meant much to that nodcock when he spotted something he coveted. Ask him yourself."

"I will. Believe me, I will! This's gone beyond the point of farce. In here, d'you think, or should it be some venue more formal and, ah, intimidating?"

Ware cast a glance over the littered breakfast table just vacated by Soames's lie-a-bed young guests in favor of a comfortable afternoon in the billiard room. "Certainly this won't cow the clown," he yawned. "Wouldn't cow anyone. Do as you wish. I'm of a mind to take myself to Underhill, see how the ladies fare."

"Not at the moment you're not." Soames laid a determined hand on his uncle's arm. "You'll bear me company until we get to the bottom of this, and then rid ourselves of dear Clare. Why I offered him the Chedleigh Minor living I'll never know."

"Great-aunt Genevieve importuned you, and it was easier to say yes than no." Ware disengaged his arm, fastidiously smoothed the forest green sleeve of Bath superfine with a wry, almost apologetic smile. "Rather intimidating, Great-aunt Genevieve. You always have taken the path of least resistance."

"For my sins. Well, that's about to change. I believe the bleater's attempting to cheat Miss Parmenter of her patrimony."

"Wouldn't dare. After all, he must know you'd come after him with whip cracking were he to attempt it. This isn't the same as when you were boys."

"Leopards don't change their spots. He wants something."

"Naturally. Clare always wants something. Easiest course's always been to give it to him."

"Not this time—not if it's what I believe it is." Soames reviewed the untidy room with disgust, considered ringing to have it straightened. There simply wasn't time, though the notion of the two of them still supposedly at breakfast and not offering a morsel to his insinuating relative held distinct appeal. "The library, d'you think?" he suggested.

"You want impressive? Use the hall itself, complete with armor, torches, banners hanging from the beams, and an echo that puts Saint Paul's to shame. And you'll leave him to cool his heels—and the rest of his anatomy—for at least ten minutes."

"No, I want to know what's to do. I mislike my suspicions." Soames combed anxious fingers through his sparse sandy hair, straightened his rumpled neckcloth, cast a rueful glance at his shapeless coat and stained leathers. "I'm presentable, aren't I?"

"You'll never be touted as Brummell's successor, if that's what you mean. Yes, I suppose you'll do," the older man grinned good humoredly. "You'd more than do if you'd ever consider replacing old Chalfont with someone not quite so doddering."

"Replace my father's man? Before he requests me to? Wouldn't hear of it!"

"And your grandfather's."

"Oh, come now—he's not so ancient as that."

"Ask him, if you don't believe me. It's not the quality of your clothes that's lacking, my boy. It's the care of 'em."

" 'My boy?' " Soames paused at the breakfast parlor door, hand on the dragon's head handle. "Don't press me, Justin. There's but eight years between us."

"A veritable lifetime," his uncle grinned. "All depends on what one puts into eight years, don't you see? I've managed considerable, what with one thing and another. Well, since you insist, let's see what your ferretish cousin wants."

"You always did have a flair for the *bon mot.*" Soames placed a finger to his lips, cracked the heavy door and peeked through the slit.

Clare Dorning was being divested of his greatcoat, old Raft teetering on unsteady legs as he battled miles of heavy fabric and numerous capes. It was suddenly a question as to whether the coat would drag Raft to the flagged floor, or Raft would drag Clare. The battle was unequal. With a despairing cry, the antiquated butler surrendered to engulfing billows of wool. Clare gazed in horror at the heap.

"My coat, you doddering old fool!" he yelped. "My beautiful new coat! It only arrived yesterday, blast it. If you've spoiled it, I, I'll—"

"You'll what, Clare?" Shoulders squared, Soames strode into the great hall, caught between disgust and laughter. "Well, aren't you going to give the poor man a hand, Vicar? 'Vanity, vanity,' dear cuz. My, that the righteous should sink so low."

"See here," Dorning blustered, lips whitening, "y'ought to have servants who're up to the mark, Soames. I mean, isn't fitting. An earl has a certain position to maintain."

"Do I, now? Thank you for reminding me."

"And his guests have a right to certain expectations," the vicar came close to whimpering, gazing in dismay at his new coat. "That cost me—"

"Is that what my guests've got? Expectations? Interesting. Completely forgot about that little detail in the heat of the moment." Soames knelt on the dull flags, gently began to disembarrass Raft of his dark shroud. "You in there somewhere, old friend?" he called. "We'll have you out in a trice, don't worry."

"Shocking," the vicar muttered. "Positively shocking!"

"Y'don't have to come calling if y'don't like the way I run my establishment, Clare," the earl snapped. "Get off your blasted coat, will you? You've got the poor man trapped."

Lower lip outthrust, Dorning stepped back, careful not to tangle himself in the mess as he glanced at Ware, who'd just entered the hall still nibbling on a cold muffin.

"I say, it really isn't fitting. You know it isn't," Dorning insisted.

"Leave it, Clare," Ware said around the muffin. "There're topics on which the head of the family isn't to be importuned, one of 'em being the staffing of his homes."

"Well, he ought to listen. Great-aunt Genevieve says—"

"Forget Great-aunt Genevieve. Conduct yourself as she dictates, and you'll be transported for debt before you're much older." Ware surveyed the clutter with a resigned smile. "Here—let me give you a hand, Soames. Place resembles a blasted draper's."

With both gentlemen making an effort Raft's wrinkled features emerged, his thin hair—customarily brushed to cover his liver-spotted pate in a futile attempt at the illusion of vigorous middle age—projecting skyward in a curved comb, his watery eyes peering in confusion from one to the other.

"Nasty things, greatcoats," he mumbled. "Sorry, m'lord, but the demmed thing attacked me."

"There, there, we'll soon have you put to rights," Soames consoled, eyes twinkling as he gently shoved the hair shelf down. "Just a bit more, and you'll be disembarrassed and on your feet."

"Appreciate it, m'lord. Most tolerant of you."

"Not in the least. Always glad to be of service, old fellow. Nasty tumble you had there."

It took a few tugs and some clever disentangling—rather like the assembling of a superior puzzle, though in reverse—but at last Raft was waveringly erect and being assisted to an enormous carved chair to one side of the fireplace. The butler sank onto the thin red velvet pad covering its hard seat, and shook his head.

"Thought I was a goner for sure that time," he sighed.

"How about a tot of brandy to set you to rights?" Soames suggested with a nod to his uncle. "Frightening things, great-coats."

"Terrifying," Raft agreed. "Seemed to have a life of its own, it did."

"See here," Dorning protested, "I'm your guest, and your vicar into the bargain. You should be seeing to me, and so should Raft, instead of which you all—"

"Oh, you want me to see to you? Well, and so I shall," Soames snapped, turning as Ware fetched the old man a tumbler of brandy from the drinks table beside the chimney. "Precisely what d'you think you're about, helping yourself to the best of Miss Parmenter's stables?"

"Don't know what you mean," Dorning blustered.

"Saw you arrive from the breakfast parlor windows, Clare. That was Devil-a-Bit you were riding, unless it was Devil-May-Care."

"Oh, that. Didn't help myself at all. Mrs. Parmenter offered."

"She did? Amazing! Why?"

"My own mount fetched up lame when I called on her just a bit ago. Went to offer spiritual counsel in her hour of need."

"Fetched up lame? How convenient!"

"Truly, I swear it! In the spinny behind their orchard, if you must know."

"What'd you do? Force the beast through a rabbit warren until it injured itself?"

"Now see here, Cousin Soames, just because—"

"And what business had Mrs. Parmenter giving you leave to appropriate the best of their stables? Or did she merely offer you a mount when you importuned her, and you gave her permission your own interpretation? And where was Miss Parmenter during all this? Wasn't it more properly she of whom you should've made the request?"

"Wasn't there. Besides, why should a vicar have to ask—"

"You have a strange notion of a vicar's position *vis à vis* his flock if you believe it runs to helping himself to whatever he fancies of their belongings," the young earl snapped. "Where was Miss Parmenter?"

"Not there, I tell you! Besides, it wasn't that way at all. Their groom was only too glad to have me exercise the brute."

"Indeed? And was Miss Parmenter equally delighted?"

"I keep telling you she wasn't there, for pity's sake," the vicar came close to shouting as his retrieved his greatcoat, anxiously smoothing its fabric. The purloined sprig of holly he'd tucked in his buttonhole tumbled to the floor.

"What's this?" Soames demanded, picking it up. "Where'd you get it?"

"In the wood."

"Whose wood?

"Yours. I didn't think you'd mind. It's only holly, after all."

"It's been cut, not broken. Who gave it to you?"

"No one. I got it for myself."

"You did? Then show me your knife."

"I found it in the path. Someone must've dropped it."

"Miss Parmenter, perhaps?" Ware came towards the younger men, eyes narrowed. "I happen to know she intended to forage for Christmas greenery. Mentioned it yesterday when I stopped by to see how they did," he explained at Soames's raised brows. "Accompanied old Bodger while the rest of you were refighting some campaign of Scipio's on the billiard table. Petticoat boredom seemed preferable to lance and spear. Besides, I wanted to assure myself Fordyce returned to the George without a fuss."

"And why did Miss Parmenter find it necessary to inform you of her plans? No, don't bother to answer," Soames chuckled. "I can imagine a thousand reasons."

"None of which would be correct," Ware protested, flushing.

"Offered to take her into Market Stoking, see about some Christmas gifts for the girls. Get a token for Mrs. Parmenter as well. Decided to put it off until tomorrow."

"So?" Soames said, tone insinuating, as he shifted his attention to the vicar. "Miss Parmenter was gathering greens and you helped yourself? Where was she?"

"I didn't see her," Dorning insisted. "Honestly, I didn't! The stuff was just lying there. Why shouldn't I take a scrap? She'll never miss it. I left her where she was."

"Ah—now we're getting somewhere. And precisely where did you leave her?"

"In the wood. See here, Miss Parmenter's been behaving most improperly since her father died. As her vicar it's my responsibility to see she has time t'reflect on—"

"Where did you leave her?" the two men chorused.

"It isn't my responsibility if the silly woman wants to climb trees and can't get down again," Dorning protested.

"You irresponsible whelp!" Ware exploded. "I don't give a tinker's dam if y'are Great-aunt Genevieve's favorite. This time you've gone too far! Why, she could catch her death out there."

"It's God's judgment if she does," Dorning insisted piously, holding up his hands. "Mr. Parmenter left things most uncomfortably."

"Dear God," Ware murmured, "and I thought him merely a posturing fool!"

"Too far by more than half," Soames agreed, giving the bell pull beside the fireplace an angry tug. The embroidered strap dating from the first earl's days parted company with its anchor, tumbling to the floor. "Blast and damn!" he snapped, flinging it away. "Quicker if we see to ourselves in any case.

"Raft, we'll be gone for a bit. Help yourself to more brandy if you wish. You've had a bad morning. If any of the fellows come seeking me, tell 'em I've—tell 'em—oh, tell 'em anything you wish, blast it. Y'usually do. Come on, Dorning—here's your coat. You'll have to show us where she is."

"See here, I'm not going out again so soon. I'm frozen to the bone as it is. D'you want me to catch *my* death?"

"Wouldn't mind in the least. Easier than being forced to chase you from the neighborhood. I wonder how one goes about re-scinding a living?"

"One doesn't, not if one doesn't want Great-aunt Genevieve descending on one," Ware said wryly. "Instead, one oversees one's dependent's actions with an eagle eye."

"What a bother!"

"Still better than contending with Great-aunt Genevieve."

"There's that. C'mon, Dorning. It's show us the way, or have your face washed with snow."

"I'm a vicar. You can't do that!"

"Don't try me. Oh, blast—who can that be?"

Soames seized the massive handle of the great oak door, pulled it open, shivering in the blast of cold air. Peter Oakwood loomed beneath the portico, twisting his cap in his hands and casting a wary eye at Dorning. Behind him Joe Bodger was leading a lathered Bacchus through the arched gateway to the stables.

"Sorry t'trouble yer, m'lord," Oakwood grunted with a school-boy's wink, ducking his head as he shoved his cap low on his forehead, "but happen I come on a neighbor o'yours in t'wood, yer lordship. Female a'huntin' fer misslow stuck'n a tree. Got her down, seeing's I knew y'wouldn't be a'wantin'—"

"S–stubble it, Oakwood," Soames choked. "Get your carcass inside. It's bloody cold out there."

"Who's that?" Dorning asked suspiciously as Oakwood stepped into the great hall and Soames shut the door behind him.

"New employee, arrived two nights ago," Ware managed, striding over to Oakwood. "Should've used the servants' en-trance, you fool," he hissed.

"And stop pretending to sound like an uneducated lout," Soames murmured. "Y'won't be able t'keep it up, and then where'll you be? What's to do?"

"Miss Parmenter's safe and sound for the moment," Oakwood mouthed with a hard glance at Dorning, "but we've some matters to discuss. Quite a few of 'em. The brew's fermenting. And I always thought the country a dull place!"

"What new employee?" Dorning demanded, drawing himself

up. "I don't recognize that fellow. It's your duty to employ locals, Cousin Soames. I happen to know Cobber Trask's seeking—"

"And can spend the rest of his life seeking," Soames retorted. "Who I do or do not employ is no business of yours, Clare!"

"My parishioners' welfare is my business," the vicar insisted, then cringed at the menacing look Soames threw him. "See here, it is my business. Mrs. Trask was saying only this morning how—"

"Emma Trask can natter from now 'til doomsday, for all of me."

"She's a fine upstanding woman, just as—"

"Just as her brother was a fine upstanding man? Even you can't be that much of a fool, Clare."

"You shouldn't call me a fool. Not fitting—to call a vicar a fool."

"Odd shoes fit odd feet," Soames snapped, "and your feet are among the oddest I've ever seen. Can't help but wonder if they're cloven."

Spluttering, clearly anxious to gain some sort of upper hand, Dorning stalked over to Oakwood and wrenched cap and scarf from his face. "Look here, my man—Dear heaven," he gasped, staring at the mahogany locks trimmed in a modified Windswept style, the clear hazel eyes, the bulk of the man, as he retreated a few steps, "that looks like—"

"Peter Oakwood, at your service, sir," Oakwood said with a deferential tug of his forelock and a twinkle in his eye.

"Impossible! You're Piers Duchesne. You're the Marquess of Stovall, by damn! I'd know you anywhere. Not likely to forget, not after the tricks you pulled when we were boys. What're you doing here?"

"That's torn it," Ware murmured to Soames.

"Not yet. Piers's up to something, and enjoying himself hugely."

"What sort of rig're you running this time?" Dorning demanded in a nervous squeak. "Stay away from me, Duchesne, I'm warning you. I'm a man of the cloth, now. Y'must treat me with respect."

Oakwood shook his head. "Peter Oakwood, sir," he insisted deferentially. "No notion who this Chesney fellow you're speaking of may be."

"Duchesne, damn you! *Duchesne,* not Chesney. Duke of Hampton's heir, as you know perfectly well. You're not going to flummox me this time."

Oakwood shrugged, managing to convey an air of extreme embarrassment.

"Oh, dear God in heaven," Dorning breathed, eyes like scummed milk at the bottom of a pail. "You're Hampton's by-blow, that's who you are! That should be worth something given the position he holds in the government. He's sure to want t'keep it quiet. Where's he been hiding you? How much does he pay you to stay out of the way?"

"I don't believe that's any business of yours," Oakwood growled, eyes turning to flint. "If necessary, I'll convince you mightily of the fact, vicar or no vicar."

"Who's your mother?" Dorning demanded, unable to restrain himself. "That little governess he's wed? Oh, yes—I keep abreast of London news. It's invaluable if one aspires to a bishopric. Your mother Miss Chumme that was? Is the duke going to acknowledge you now they're wed? For a consideration, I'll make it my business to bring him to a consciousness of his duty. I'm a man in orders, you understand. Much more convincing than just anyone."

"My name," Oakwood repeated, making the words as distinct as one would when addressing an idiot, "is and always has been Peter Oakwood."

"No it isn't," Dorning giggled with nervous glee. "At least, it may be—Oakwood and Duchesne? Clever! I know my French that well, at least—but you're Hampton's by-blow. You're Hampton's by-blow, by damn! Marquess of Stovall aware of your existence? What does the grand and mighty Piers Duchesne think of you? I wonder what he'd pay to keep news of you from the ton!"

"This clod's an idiot," Oakwood snapped, turning to the earl. "Is there any reason we have to endure his presence, my lord?

I've come about that matter we were discussing yesterday, and would appreciate being able to conclude our business."

"Of course," Soames agreed easily. "No, Mr. Dorning was just about to depart. Afoot," he added, turning a steely glance on his cousin.

"See here, Cousin Soames, you can't expect me to walk all the way to the village in this weather!"

"Do your soul good."

"But I've delicate lungs, and my boots—"

"Then favor those lungs by not prattling on forever about matters you know nothing about." Soames handed the vicar his great-coat. "Put this on, and make yourself scarce before I lose all patience with you."

"I have the loan of Devil-a-Bit from Mrs. Parmenter," Dorning whined, "and I'm riding him back to the village, and I'm going to be riding him from now on, and there's not a thing you can do to stop me!"

Soames's smile should've been warning enough. When it appeared it wasn't, Oakwood cocked an eyebrow.

"Would you like me to escort your vicar to his home?" he asked, flicking his crop against his boot. "Glad to do it, my lord. The other matter can wait if it must."

"No, that's all right, I believe," Soames chuckled as Dorning, with a terrified glance at Oakwood, stuffed himself into his great-coat and pelted from the great hall, cramming his hat on his head and slamming the door behind him with a resounding thud.

"That was not well done of you, Master Piers," old Raft cackled, raising his tumbler of brandy in salute as the echoes died away.

The three gentlemen whirled on him, words of protest dying at the stern glint behind the twinkle.

"I drink to you nevertheless. Not well done at all, but 'twas done infinitely well, you young scapegrace!"

"My name," Oakwood insisted, "is Peter Oakwood."

"Course it is, Master Piers! I may not be a rooster on the strut, but I'm not ready for the stew pot, either. What his lordship'd say to all this," the old man continued, gesturing at the portrait of Soames's many times great-grandfather above the fireplace, "only heaven knows."

"Probably cheer us on, the old reprobate," Soames grinned. "You'll keep your peace about this?"

"Now when did I ever nark on you lads?" Raft chuckled. "Too much amusement to be had t'other road."

"Shameful waste," Emma Trask scolded a short time later as she removed her heavy cloak and coal scuttle bonnet, depositing them on a bench by the door and gazing in disgust at the lavish fire burning on Underhill's parlor grate. "You don't learn to be more provident, Phoebe, you'll come home by Weeping Cross."

Phoebe clenched her lips and hands, and held her peace. It wasn't that her aunt's visit was unanticipated any more than her waspish words were. It was just that, after over a week of enduring both on an almost daily basis, she was close to the end of her patience. At least this time the woman hadn't caught her doing something she'd consider improper. With her stock of greenery well-hidden, this afternoon she'd merely been reading in the parlor and keeping Mabel, who wasn't feeling well, company.

"And what's all this?" her father's sister demanded, turning to survey the striped green and white damask curtains, dark eyes glinting angrily.

"We're cheering the place up a bit for the girls in anticipation of the holidays. They've never known a Christmas celebration, and we felt—"

"Christmas celebration? Porty didn't hold with 'em. Nothing but an excuse to chouse honest men of their hard-earned brass, he said. He was right, too. Y'shouldn't be doing what your father didn't hold with, girl, and him barely in his grave. Can't you govern your stepdaughter any better than this?" she snapped, turning on Mabel. "Course, y'always were flighty. Tales about you all over the village when you were a girl. Tales everywhere now. Gussets never change."

"I, well, I didn't see any harm in it," Mabel sighed, nervously twisting the scrap of lawn that had once been her favorite hand-kerchief between her fingers.

"Did Hezekiah Hatch approve all this waste?" Emma Trask whirled back on Phoebe. "For I'm certain he didn't. Not your father's intention for you to flit about playing the great lady. You're squandering his brass, just as I knew y'would given the chance. Oh, I warned Porty how it would be, but did he listen? Not he! Should've married you off to Cobber twenty years ago, just like I said at the time."

"When he was barely eight," Phoebe protested, "and I but six?"

"Yes, well, be that as it may, it's been done before. By royalty! What's good enough for royalty should be good enough for you."

"How are you doing this afternoon, Sister Trask," Mabel murmured in an attempt to return the call to what a call should be. "Please forgive me if I don't rise to greet you, but I'm not quite myself. Would you care for some tea?"

"Tea? Outlandish brew. Tankard of mulled cider'll do, and another for Cobber. He's seeing to the gig. Be with us in a moment. Eager to see you," Emma Trask continued, leering at Phoebe. "Right fond of you, my Cobber, and anxious as to how you're going on. Won't approve this nonsense in the least," she concluded, gesturing at the partially redecorated room. "Entirely out of keeping. Where're the old hangings?"

"Upstairs. I thought to employ them as dust covers once they're mended," Phoebe replied patiently. "Not good for much else, the condition they're in."

"More waste! Those're perfectly good hangings—far better than anything I have at home. I'll take them, and thank you. Fetch 'em down. Well, get along with you."

Then, with narrowed eyes, she strode to the windows, fingered the striped material Phoebe had tacked up in much the same style she'd achieved a few days earlier in Mabel's new bedchamber.

"Good fabric," the woman muttered. "Far too good for these trollops." Then she turned, brows rising when she discovered Phoebe still sitting by the fire. "Well, aren't you going to fetch my hangings?"

"No, Aunt Trask, as they're mine, not yours, and I have a use for them."

Emma Trask shrugged, pointed at the new draperies. "Shoddy goods," she said. "How much did they charge you? I'll warrant you were robbed. Give you half what you paid, relieve you of 'em. Doing you a favor, my girl, so you'd best do as I say."

"But we like these," Mabel protested, desperately mangling her handkerchief. "So much more cheerful than the burgundy velvet that was in here before."

"Much too bright. Damage the eyes. You always had weak eyes, Mabel. Wouldn't like to see you blind before your time, all for the sake of some cheap cloth. I'll give you five shillings for the lot."

"No, thank you," Phoebe said. "We like them."

"Don't be foolish, girl! You've squandered your money, haven't you. How'll you eat unless you sell 'em to me?"

"We'll manage."

"You'll starve, more like, or find yourself in the workhouse. Never been a Parmenter in the workhouse, never! Until now, that is," the older woman prophesied darkly. "Oh, I warned Porty how it would be, but I'm only a woman and he wouldn't listen. Always had more brains than Porty, always! Told him not to marry your mother, and I told him not to marry *her.*" She pointed in disgust at Mabel. "And, I was right! Stop torturing that rag, Mabel. One'd think you were an idiot.

"And where, may I ask," she shrieked in sudden horror, "did you get that," pointing at an exquisite enameled clock on the bookcase. "Never seen it before, and I grew up here, girl and woman. Don't believe I've seen that chessy-loungey thing you're lazing on either, Mabel. Well, out with it: Where'd all these fripperies come from?"

"The same emporium where I acquired our new curtains," Phoebe returned mischievously, ignoring Mabel's imploring whimper. "Indeed, I'm intending to replace the curtains throughout the house. The bed hangings, too. Atticus's stock is positively amazing, and well within reach of my purse."

"Atticus's, you say? Never heard of the place."

"Dustibus Atticus's, to be precise."

"Queer name. And just where's this emporium? Pilchester? I ain't heard of you shopping in the village, nor yet going to Market Stoking, and if you had I'd've heard. Besides, there's no such place in town or village. If there was, I'd know about it, that you may be sure," Emma Trask concluded on a note of triumph, "so you stop trying to diddle me, my girl. I cut my wisdoms before you were born."

"Naturally you did. No one's disputing that."

Emma Trask regarded her niece through narrowed eyes, but try though she did, she could find no cause for insult in the fact that the hussy had agreed with her.

"Well, when're you going to get my cider?" she demanded for lack of anything better with which to take issue, settling on the settee in front of the fire. "Terrible cold, driving out here in the gig. Like to catch my death, and Cobber sneezed the whole way, but nothing would do but we come calling. It'll serve you right if he catches his death and leaves you a penniless spinster to the end of your days."

"Poor Cobber. Are you sure it wasn't you insisted on calling?"

"In this weather? Don't be more foolish than you can help, girl." Emma Trask's eyes narrowed as she turned to her sister-in-law. "Where's that foppish cousin of yours, Mabel? Didn't see him about the place when we arrived, nor he ain't at the George. We stopped to ask on the way."

"Cousin Philip? I'm not certain. He said at breakfast he had errands to run."

"Gobbling up your shillings, no doubt. The sooner that bold-faced coxcomb takes himself off permanently, the better for everyone."

"Phoebe dear, Sister Trask's mulled cider?" Mabel pleaded in despairing accents, cramming her handkerchief in a cranny of the chaise lounge. "And, Cobber's? We wouldn't want the poor man to catch a chill."

"Philip taking himself off permanently would be quite impractical, don't you think, Aunt Trask?" Phoebe said, head high, ignoring both her stepmother's fluttering signals for restraint and her aunt's glare. "We're to be wed, after all."

"Ain't wed yet," Emma Trask returned with an attempt at good humor, and failing miserably at it, "nor yet've I heard of the banns being called. Spoke with the vicar this morning, and he's in complete agreement. A Parmenter, wed *another* Gusset? For that's all the tailor-worshipping fool is when all's said and done, a Gusset. Isn't to be thought of! Gussets're a feckless lot, as I've told you time out of mind."

"You'd best accustom yourself," Phoebe snapped, "for that's how it's going to be."

"No, it's not. Ain't going to be that way at all, you'll see. And why ain't you in mourning, I'd like to know? Had time and enough to arrange it," she grumbled, once more turning on Mabel. "Heathenish, that's the way you're comporting yourselves, and Porty not a week in his grave! Positive heathenish. Whole village's full of it."

"With you fanning the flames, I'm sure. There aren't funds for proper mourning," Phoebe interrupted before Mabel could respond. "Papa ensured that, and I won't countenance dyeing what few clothes we have as we won't be able to replace them for far longer than the time we'd have to wear blacks."

"Clever excuse, but it won't wash given you can stand new hangings. Fordyce egging you on? Living on credit and counting on the day when you've a son to frank you? Well, you needn't think I'll go running to old Hatch demanding he give you funds for mourning, nor yet that you're going to shame me into buying 'em for you. You're not as clever as you think, my girl. Worst possible way to honor Porty's memory."

"I couldn't agree with you more," Phoebe smiled. "Isn't it pleasant to find ourselves in accord for once?"

A commotion beyond the parlor door brought the woman to her feet, sour expression lightening. "That'll be my Cobber," she said. "Now we'll see how you brazen out your latest follies, for I can tell you now he won't approve."

"Why should Cobber's approval be of the slightest importance to me? No, Mabel, I will not hush! I'm through hushing. I may

never hush again! If that's not polite of me, then so be it. However
much you may think——"

"My nerves!" Mabel Parmenter raised a trembling hand to
her forehead as she fumbled for her vinaigrette among the shawls
draped over her legs with the other. "My nerves, dearest Phoebe,"
she pleaded, at last finding the desired vial, unstopping it and
inhaling deeply. "They're shattered, positively shattered. Have
some consideration."

"You don't need your nerves now Papa's dead," Phoebe
snapped, "so play me no Cheltenham tragedies! I'm not about
to take a cudgel to you, and Aunt Trask can't do much more than
be unpleasant, which she always was in any case."

"Well!" that lady exclaimed, drawing herself up, sharp nose
quivering. "If this is all the respect I'm to be accorded in my
own brother's household——"

"Oh, do be still! It's my household now, Aunt Trask, and it's
Cobber I pity, for he'll have to bear your ill-temper all the way
back to the village," Phoebe rushed on, determined to have her
say before the parlor door opened. "As for Philip, we're to be
wed as soon as may be. Mabel, put that silly stuff away. It smells
positively foul."

"And this," Emma Trask declared dramatically, descending
on her sister-in-law, "is what comes of giving headstrong, in-
temperate, ungovernable girls their heads! If Porty weren't already dead, I'd murder him for the insults he's making me endure
in what by rights should be my house!"

She tugged Mabel's arm. Mabel whimpered, shrinking against
her pillows. The parlor door flew open. Emma Trask whirled,
blanching as Phoebe was overtaken by a choking fit that sounded
very much like hysterical giggles. The earl, his uncle, and the
stranger she'd encountered in the earl's woods crowded in, Cobber hard on their heels.

"Mabel's unwell, your lordship," Emma Trask babbled, bob-
bing a curtsy and simpering at the earl. "Just attempting to assist
her."

"Hallo, Cousin Phoebe." Cobber nodded to Mabel and his
mother, lumbered across the worn carpet to seize Phoebe's hand

and pump it vigorously. "Looking in prime twig, just like a fat chicken with its feathers all fluffed." He glanced at his mother for approval. She scowled, brought her bony hand to her mouth as if stifling a yawn. "Oh—sorry, I forgot." The man seized Phoebe's fingers and planted a loud smack on them. "That's how it's done, ain't it?"

"Hallo, Cousin Cobber. Yes, I understand that's how it's done, more or less," she returned weakly, ignoring Oakwood's murmured, *"Rather less than more,"* and avoiding the eyes of all those present. "You're, ah, looking in prime twig yourself."

"Dandified myself afore coming," Cobber grinned. "Even washed m'hands and combed m'hair. The mother said as how you'd like it."

"I do indeed," Phoebe choked. Cobber's hair spiked about his head in its usual brush. As for his hands—well, perhaps they'd been washed. It was possible the dirt was so ground in he couldn't get it off, poor fellow.

"Important t'please you afore we're wed," he explained. "Won't matter a'tall after, the mother says. Please m'self then. And her, o'course. Y've changed the place a bit." He glanced about him as Mabel murmured greetings to the earl and his uncle, and accepted an introduction to Oakwood. "Not sure how. Brighter, more cheerful-like."

Emma Trask scowled, doing her best to indicate the new curtains at the windows. Cobber followed her eyes.

"Oh—that's it," he grinned. "Should've realized it afore. Y'got new hangings. Very pretty, Cousin Phoebe. Like 'em no end."

"Cobber, you do not like 'em," his mother hissed. "You don't like 'em at all."

"I don't?"

"No, you don't! Waste of good money."

"Oh, I see. Waste of good money," he repeated, attempting a stern tone as he turned back to Phoebe, "even if they are pretty. Shouldn't be wasting m'blunt like that afore we're married."

"We aren't going to be married, Cobber," Phoebe returned patiently. "I'm betrothed to Mr. Fordyce, remember?"

"The mother says we're to be wed, and as she says so, then we're to be wed and that's that. Fordyce don't come into it. Was talking with the vicar just this morning about calling the banns. Once that's done you'll stop your foolishness, she says."

"I do believe," the earl tossed into the stunned silence, "that you're a bit previous, Cobber. Miss Parmenter hasn't agreed to your offer, and so the calling of banns would be totally inappropriate."

"Don't see how," Cobber protested, full lips working. "M'mother's always right about everything, so she's right about Phoebe marrying me. Phoebe's got to. No other choice."

"Not quite, lad." Soames cast a sympathetic smile at his beleaguered hostess. "It's not good form, you see—to insist a lady's going to marry one if she hasn't agreed."

"But the vicar agreed," Cobber complained in some confusion.

"I believe you'll find he's changed his mind if you approach him again. Besides, it's not his agreement you require. It's Miss Parmenter's."

"Is it always like this?" Oakwood murmured to Ware as Cobber stomped across the room to stare sulkily at the fire, muddy brown eyes vacant.

"Since Parmenter's death? More or less."

"Dear Lord!"

"Told you she's quite the country heiress. They've been coming from as far as Market Stoking and Pilchester. If you've any influence with Soames, forget those silly girls' tales and get him to agree to her marrying Fordyce as soon as possible. Calling the banns is the only thing'll put a stop to the poor woman being importuned at every turn."

"But if the girls're right—"

"Doesn't matter. Fordyce, whatever his faults, is infinitely preferable to that pair, don't you think?"

Oakwood's eyes flew from waspish mother to bumbling son, back to Ware, expression unreadable.

With a resigned sigh, Phoebe slipped from the room as the ill-assorted gathering sorted itself out, and darted down the dark passage to the kitchen to order refreshments, shrugging at Mrs. Short's news that they'd almost no tea and no coffee or chocolate. Soames was waiting for her by the windows when she returned, an easy smile on his lips.

"Devil-a-Bit's back in your stable, Miss Parmenter," he said softly as she joined him. "You won't be troubled so again, that I promise."

"Thank you, my lord, you're most kind," she murmured.

"Wanted to apologize for my cousin's behavior. Clare's understanding's never been the best. Not bright enough for the army and he failed miserably as a schoolmaster, which is why I got him."

"Think nothing of it. We're none of us responsible for the actions of our relatives."

"His, however, were particularly despicable. At the least, he should've sent someone to your aid."

"Oh, my," she said with a blush, "I see word of my attempt at poaching some mistletoe's reached you. I know it was hoydenish, but I did so want to surprise the girls."

The earl nodded, grinned. "I'd very much've liked to've seen how P-Peter Oakwood got you down from that tree."

"Rather efficiently, in the end. A forceful man, your new employee. What is it precisely he's to be doing for you?"

"Greek folly, complete with landscaping. Time I put my mark on the place."

Phoebe's eyes flew to the mahogany-haired man seated beside her aunt, the slightest of frowns puckering her brows. Oakwood glanced up and winked as Emma Trask droned on about the historic importance of the Parmenter family in the district, and the distinctly inferior position of the parvenu Gussets.

"Clever fellow, Oakwood," the earl continued, warming to his theme. "Excellent reputation. Devoted disciple of Capability Brown's. He's the one designed the vistas about the place for my grandfather, y'know, and I want something in the same style."

"But I thought Mr. Oakwood mentioned a game survey?"

"Game survey?" The earl glanced at Oakwood. "Well, that has to be done first, don't you see? Wouldn't want to kill off the stock putting the folly in the wrong place. If we did, there'd be a lot of families going hungry, speaking of which, we brought a brace of ducks and some fruit from the succession houses. Grapes, strawberries, that sort of thing. Gave 'em to the woman answered the door—Mrs. Short, isn't it?"

"Yes, Mrs. Short," Phoebe said absently, eyes still on Oakwood. "Thank you so much, my lord. They'll be most appreciated."

"Thought they might. If you've need of assistance at any time, be certain to inform me."

"We're managing rather well, actually," she said, turning back to him with a determined smile. "So long as Aunt Trask doesn't take it into her head to convince Mr. Hatch to be late with my allowance there should be no problem. Of course, it would help if you'd approve calling the banns between Mr. Fordyce and myself"

"Plenty of time for that after the New Year."

"Given Papa's will, we really shan't be comfortable until I have a son kicking in his cradle. That won't happen immediately."

"Even so, I think it best to wait. Instead, I was wondering if you'd sell me those Twin Oaks hunters of your father's? That would relieve the pressure considerably."

"That's something I never considered until today. No," she sighed, "it wouldn't work. Mr. Hatch'd take the money as forming part of Papa's assets, and so something to which I've no personal right. Besides, Philip's quite fond of them."

"Food for the table and coal for the grates are of slightly more importance than Mr. Fordyce's desires, don't you think? Hatch needn't know. I'd thought to leave the pair with you until after you're wed to avoid just the difficulties you mention."

"But what good would that do you?"

"I'd have the satisfaction of knowing you're not having to pinch every penny," he smiled, lilting her hand to kiss it.

"Well! So that's how it is!" Emma Trask shrilled, leaping to her feet.

Earl and heiress whirled to face the irate termagant, Phoebe blushing furiously, Soames paling.

"Oh, heavens," Mabel moaned. "Mr. Ware, do something."

"No wonder his lordship won't countenance banns being called, nor yet agree as my Cobber's the best one for you," Emma Trask stormed on. "Wants Underhill for himself, clear as the nose on your face! Not surprising. Marches with his lands, after all. I warn you, my girl: All you'll get from the likes of him's a slip on the shoulder. Ask your stepmother, if you don't believe me. No male heir then—at least not one's born on the right side of the blanket, and Underhill'll come to me just as it should've in the beginning. Good thing, too."

"You quite mistake the matter," Soames threw in with a nervous smile. "I was merely being polite."

"Biting a woman's hand ain't polite. It's an invitation."

"Oh, I see," Soames returned, goaded beyond courtesy. "It's proper for your son to salute Miss Parmenter's hand, but not for me."

"Besides, I watched you both. *You,*" she declared magnificently, complete with pointing finger, "were *flirting* with my niece."

"Indeed? Is that what I was doing? Thank you for informing me. I wasn't just sure, you see, not having much practice in the art."

"And you," she snarled at Phoebe, "were encouraging him, and your father not a week dead."

"Aunt Trask, please!" Phoebe implored. "It was no such thing. His lordship'd just informed me he brought us a brace of duck is all."

"Ducks? What've you to do with ducks? Meat's too rich. Better give 'em to me. You don't want to be afflicted with gout, and duck's a prime culprit. Cobber and I're accustomed. You ain't, and you got to keep your health until you've produced a son. Duck's the quickest way to ruin it. Make you run to fat. But," Emma Trask concluded on a note of triumph, "y' can see how it is plain as day. He's trying to bribe you."

"I said we should've brought Cousin Phoebe something," Cobber complained from the fireplace. "Supposed to bring something when you come courting. Then you're owed, and they feel obliged to say yes. All your fault, Mother. Now she'll marry the earl, and where'll I be?"

"I do believe it's time we were leaving," Ware said, rising from where he'd been doing his best to shield Mabel from the contretemps. "Your guests'll be missing you, Soames."

"Indeed they will," Soames agreed.

"But I've ordered tea," Phoebe protested, glancing at the door.

"Which I know you can ill afford. I'm sorry," the earl smiled. "I'll send some with Bodger to replace it this evening. Yes, Mrs. Trask," he said over his shoulder, "another sinful gift. Another bribe. Another step down the slippery road to hell."

Then, very deliberately, he raised Phoebe's hand to his lips once more, retaining it far longer than was proper or necessary as she again blushed furiously.

"And there," he murmured, "is another. How you bear that woman I'll never understand, Miss Parmenter."

"Mother, what's this?"

Cobber was staring at a scrap of marble that'd come loose from the mantel. The door to the hall opened and Prissy and Pru came in, cheeks reddened by their walk in the cold. They froze at the sight of Peter Oakwood standing beside their aunt, eyes flying guiltily from him to their sister and the earl, then—in horror—back to their aunt.

From the open door came the sound of an amused cough.

"My goodness," Philip Fordyce said, raising his quizzing glass to examine the assembled company as he leaned on an elegant walking stick, "what have we here?"

Five

The accusations and counter-accusations caused by Cobber's discovery of the broken mantel were instant and acrimonious, the unexpected arrivals of Fordyce, Prissy, and Pru adding to the pandemonium. At last, with a determination at great variance with her customary manner and visibly trembling, Mabel shouted the combatants down. The company turned to her with stunned looks, Emma Trask barely containing herself, Cobber still protesting his innocence of any wrong-doing under his breath.

The mantel had long been in that condition, Mabel said in the sudden silence, throwing quelling glances at her daughters when they made to protest yet again.

Then, clinging to Ware's arm, the little widow sank back onto her chaise, fingers scrabbling in the crannies.

Mr. Parmenter had done it in a fit of pique, she explained hesitantly, upon hearing the vicar—not Mr. Dorning, but dear Mr. Smythe, his predecessor—had been invited to dine of a Sunday, necessitating a table more lavish than customary. Mr. Parmenter had refused to have the damage properly repaired, insisting on a dab of glue instead as the corner break was on the slant and only needed to be encouraged not to slip off.

"You remember the incident, do you not, Phoebe?" she concluded, throwing an imploring glance at her stepdaughter.

"Indeed I do," Phoebe nodded, smiling from the hard circle of Fordyce's arm as her gaze flitted from one interested auditor to the next. "The girls'd severely annoyed him, and he wasn't in the best of humors. As I recall, they'd already been sent to their rooms—a common enough occurrence."

"If they were sent to their rooms," Emma Trask snapped, "you may be sure they deserved it! Pair of insufferable hoydens, both of 'em."

"Naturally. In your eyes we deserved any punishment Papa saw fit to impose. In fact, you often discovered occasions for punishment that didn't occur even to him," Phoebe responded, throwing her aunt a withering glance, then turned back to the others. "It's not of the slightest importance now, but in an effort to placate my father Mabel and I scurried about doing what we could, for of course we were blamed. Our invitation had caused Papa's anger and its righteous expression, you see."

"Perfectly right, too," Emma Trask muttered, ignoring the disgusted glance thrown her by his lordship. "Inviting Mr. Smythe, indeed! Nothing but a prattling old fool, that one. No sense of who mattered in the village and who didn't."

"Our best wasn't very good," Phoebe continued, smiling up at Fordyce. "As you can see, we keep mending it, and still it comes loose at the slightest touch."

Oakwood eased the offending chip from Cobber's grip, ran his finger lightly along its shattered edge, then the mantel, eyes narrowing.

"Simple enough to set to rights properly," he said. "Glad to see to it for you, Mrs. Parmenter, if you'll permit me?"

"I don't know," Mabel dithered. "We're so accustomed to it like this—"

"Come now, Cousin Mabel," Fordyce broke in, voice dripping condescension. "Don't be ridiculous! Of course we'll be glad to have it repaired. Leaving such damage unattended to simply isn't done. Tomorrow or next week matters not, so long as it's taken care of. I'll have that fragment for safekeeping, if I may," he continued, joining Oakwood before the fire. "You know how the ladies always misplace things. Minds like sieves. I don't believe I have the pleasure of your acquaintance, do I?"

"No, sir, you don't. Name's Peter Oakwood," Oakwood replied good-humoredly, extending one hand while retaining the bit of broken marble in the other as Pru and Prissy watched wide-eyed from their post by the door. "His lordship's employed me for some work about the place."

"Oh, I see." Fordyce glanced from the man's proffered hand to his rough clothing—country tweeds that were clean enough, but hardly new or in the latest style—his nose pinching in distaste as he turned to the earl. "Not sure I approve your introducing a common laborer to my fiancée's notice," he protested. "I thought he was just one of your usual covey of eccentrics. Obviously I was—"

"But then Oakwood's no common laborer," the earl smiled easily. "Highly respected in his profession. I consider him a friend, always have. Certainly you can't resent a man who makes his own way rather than living on the charity of others?"

"Indeed? My mistake." Fordyce turned back with a shrug, hand reluctantly extended, only to discover Oakwood had both his crammed in his pockets. "No offense, I hope," he said with a patronizing smile. "Well, give me the marble, my good man."

"Need it for measurements," Oakwood demurred. "Don't worry, I shan't lose it."

Flinty hazel eyes clashed with hard blue. At last Fordyce shrugged again. "Peasant!" he murmured too low for the others to hear. "I'll deal with you later."

Oakwood merely nodded, fingers still exploring the fragment in his pocket.

"Where've you been, girls?" Mabel broke the uneasy silence.

"Where they shouldn't, I'll warrant," Emma Trask snapped. "Well, answer your mother, you little heathens! Where've you been?"

"We partook of a preamblupation," Prissy said.

The corners of Oakwood's mouth quivered, as his eyes sought Phoebe's. She flushed, whether from mortification at the girl's error or his own amused glance he had no way to know.

"We met Mr. Dorning returning to the village," Pru added. "He was sitting on a stile complaining of his boots, and using words I thought vicars didn't know."

Phoebe choked, terrified of meeting Oakwood's eyes.

"Go to your room, girls," Mabel managed weakly.

"Again?" they chorused.

"Again and immediately." Emma Trask stormed across the parlor. "If the vicar used words he shouldn't know, you shouldn't know 'em either. Besides, it ain't for you to be criticizing a man of God," she declared, raising her hand to box Pru's ears. Phoebe was at the girls' side on the instant, drawing them away. "If Mr. Dorning said 'em," Emma Trask concluded on a triumphant note, "you may be sure the terms were perfectly proper, though not necessarily suitable for your tongues. Vicar'd never speak improper."

"I shan't survive my stay in the country with my ribs intact," Oakwood murmured, joining Ware as Mabel implored her daughters to absent themselves before Emma Trask created yet more difficulties. His brows rose as Fordyce bent down by his cousin's chair and picked up what appeared to be a scrap of cloth. "How d'you bear it?"

"First time I've been at the castle since I was at Oxford," Ware returned as the girls held their ground. "Normally keep to London and Bath, with the occasional foray to Brighton when the Regent's in residence. Delightful chap, no matter what anyone says. Paris, of course, with the late unpleasantnesses over. Behave yourself, dammit!"

"Not likely. This is too amusing."

"Amusing?"

"One might believe one were assisting at a splendid farce after enduring some Gluckian excess," Oakwood returned with a chuckle. "Town's a dead bore by comparison. All else aside, those minxes provide constant diversion. Clare, employing vocabulary a vicar shouldn't? I could barely contain myself."

Ware seized his arm, pulling him well apart from the others.

"I'll have you know these're real people," the earl's uncle said furiously in a low voice, "with genuine tragedies and pains, not a burlesque intended for your diversion! The blows they've suffered were real, blast you."

"Where's the harm in seeing humor where it exists?" Oakwood returned with an offended frown. "Miss Parmenter saw the humor of it, and you're not complaining at her laughing eyes. What's your interest here, that you should defend them so vigorously?"

"I've none at all, unless it's that of concerned temporary neighbor."

"That's not the attitude you're taking."

"My attitude? Look to your own!"

And then Soames was at their side. "I suspect we'd best take ourselves off," he said in an undertone. "Fordyce is in one of his moods, Mrs. Parmenter has the look of a highly put-upon lady, and Miss Parmenter's in not much better state. If we can manage to ease that Trask woman and poor Cobber from the place as well, all to the good."

"There you'll never succeed," Ware forecast. *"She* has the look of a female ready to indulge in lectures, and not about to be robbed of her enjoyment."

But, somehow Soames managed it, though even he wasn't quite certain how.

In the flurry of departure, Pru managed to waylay Oakwood, whispering to him that she and Prissy had great need to confer with him. After all, he'd been in the neighborhood two days, or almost. Hadn't he discovered anything to the point?

The girl's gaze flew to where Fordyce, possessive arm once more circling Phoebe's waist, was playing lord of the manor as he ushered guests from the house, thanked his lordship profusely for the brace of duck, and deviled Emma Trask in any way he could devise. That he in turn was being deviled by Soames, who made a show of kissing Phoebe's hand again and complimenting her on her efforts at redecoration, didn't miss anyone's sharp eyes, least of all Oakwood's.

"There's one solution, by damn," he murmured, watching with raised brows, "if it can be managed."

"What solution?" Pru demanded.

"Never you mind, young lady. Just got an idea is all, but I'm making progress—of that you may rest assured."

"We'll see you tonight," she hissed. "You've a lot to explain."

* * *

Dinner at Underhill that evening was superficially no more strained or unpleasant than customary.

Fordyce took the head of the table as usual. He carved Soames's ducks. He helped himself to the best of everything. He sent Flossie, the maid-of-all-work, for another bottle of claret. He spent what little time he wasn't eating and drinking teasing the girls, quizzing his betrothed, and playing the charmer with his cousin.

It was, in sum, a polite hell in which nothing was as it seemed.

Had a stranger been dining with them, the undercurrents, the subtle barbs would've gone unnoticed, Phoebe decided. Half the time she herself couldn't believe them to be what they were. Reluctant peeps at Fordyce's hard blue eyes gave confirmation, however. He might not rule with cudgel and fist as her father had, but rule he did, and with a far cleverer, far more unopposable hand. The pattern of their days was being set.

Her eyes sought her stepmother's bruised face as Fordyce turned his unwelcome attentions back to Mabel, again twitting the poor woman about the mantel. Mabel raised a trembling hand to her forehead, claimed a migraine and begged to be excused.

"Oh, but my dearest cousin," Fordyce smiled, holding her in her seat, "we haven't had the sweet yet, and I know how particularly fond of sweets you are. What is it to be tonight? Those excellent grapes I see on the serving table? Or has Mrs. Short concocted a trifle? I do love a trifle oozing raspberries and cream."

"It's not the season for raspberries, and our table doesn't run to sweets, dearest Philip," Phoebe interposed in an attempt to draw his fire. "We won't have the funds for such extravagances until, well—" she broke off in embarrassment. Then, taking a deep breath, she plunged on, frowning as he helped himself to yet more wine. "My father's cellars're limited, Philip. When what's there is gone, we won't be able to replace it."

"Oh, come," he taunted, splashing more wine in his glass, "not even for me? Not even for dearest Cousin Mabel's sake?

Wine's the staff of life, you know—not bread. She's appeared particularly peaked these last days. The shock of old Porty's death, no doubt. I'm most concerned for her health. Wine is a priority—for her, and for me."

"Mabel doesn't take wine, as you know."

"Nevertheless, I'm sure you'll manage." He gave her one of his most engaging smiles, an angelic thing that never quite reached his eyes, as he raised his glass in her honor. "You're such an excellent contriver, my dear. Why, I do believe you could manage most anything you set your mind to. Certainly I've seen wonderful examples of your inventiveness these last days."

"How kind of you to say so," she sighed.

It was an encomium she only wished were true. If it were, Cobber would never have leaned against the mantel, loosening the obviously hastily repaired corner.

She hoped they'd all believed Mabel's and her inventions, but she doubted it. Certainly Fordyce, with his constant references to the incident, didn't. Of course he was merely cautioning her, as he did a thousand times a day, that he held Mabel's life in his hands. A spider catching flies in its net, that was Fordyce: quite dreadful for the individual fly, but not of much importance to other flies. A nonentity, and yet for them a most maleficent one.

Oakwood was another matter. There were, she shuddered, no terms strong enough to describe that dangerously sharp-eyed, lazy-seeming, rough-garbed giant.

"Isn't that right, my dear?"

Phoebe's head snapped up, gaze flying from her stepmother to her sisters, then to Fordyce, who had just spoken.

"I'm sorry—I wasn't attending," she apologized. "You were saying?"

"The girls just pointed out the mantel wasn't broken before today. A fiancée who lies? I'm not sure I approve," he said, purest acid underlying his mock quizzing.

"You weren't there, and neither were they," Phoebe returned easily. "Naturally we lied. Poor Cobber stumbled and brought his fist down on it, but if you think I'd've said what really happened in that company, you're way off the mark. Aunt Trask would've killed him with reproaches for breaking *her* mantel, and probably taken a switch to him when they returned home as well. We said the first thing that came to our minds, one building on the other's story. Given Papa, the tale was believable enough."

"And that's the truth of it?" Fordyce demanded, narrowed eyes spearing her over the rim of his glass.

"With no varnish on it." Dear Lord—would she never have done with lies? First it had been Papa, in an attempt to shield Mabel and the girls. Now it was Fordyce. She must've become skilled over the years. He seemed to believe her now, even if he hadn't at first. "It's never been repaired," she concluded, "because it only just happened."

"I'd wondered. The break appeared new."

"It is. I'll thank you to keep the secret for Cobber's sake. He has enough to bear. You as well," she said sternly, turning to the girls. "Least said, soonest mended—especially as Lord Soames's new employee seems to have knowledge of how to repair it. There must've been a flaw in the marble for it to shatter so easily, for all poor Cobber's more ballast than sail. Girls, if you'll remove the covers and ask Flossie to clear the rest of the table? I believe we're done, aren't we, except for Lord Soames's grapes?"

The rest of the meal passed without serious incident.

Punctually at nine Mick Bodger arrived. This time he was accompanied by Oakwood, who smiled easily at Mabel and Phoebe, and explained that he'd come to accompany Fordyce to the George as he'd a longing to quaff a pint and enjoy some company. The gamekeeper's cottage was lonely, no matter how snug it might be. Short of creating a scene, there wasn't much Fordyce could do about his unwelcome escort. And, for some unaccountable reason, Fordyce's departure was more expeditious than customary, his salute to his beloved's cheek far less lingering and offensive with Oakwood towering in the entry, expression neutral, eyes watchful.

At last the front door was closed and locked, the key hung on its hook. Bodger, as always, tested from without and declared all right and tight. Footsteps crunched in the snow, faded, along with the murmur of voices.

Phoebe gestured for Mabel to wait, then leaned against the door, listening. This time, for a blessing, there was no hint of Fordyce returning in an attempt to convince them there was no reason why they shouldn't permit him to stay the night at Underhill now the formalities had been seen to. Of course he might make the attempt later, but with Bodger and his son making rounds, and the impressive Oakwood escorting him to the George, the chances were slim they'd be disturbed this time.

The slightest of frowns puckered Phoebe's forehead as she turned to face her stepmother in the gloom.

"What really happened to the mantel, Mabel?" she said. "I need to know."

"Must we speak of it?" Mabel's hands fluttered among her shawls, her eyes darting longingly to the staircase. "I don't want to remember."

"Papa?"

"Not the way you think, but yes, and almost as you said. It wasn't really a lie, you know."

"I suppose the only difference is it happened days ago, rather than well in the past," Phoebe sighed, putting her arms around her pretty, gentle stepmother, "and Mr. Smythe was in no way involved. Oh, Mabel! My poor, poor dear."

On these tender words, Mabel Parmenter dissolved in tears. They lingered in the icy entry, the widow stifling her sobs against Phoebe's shoulder and close to hysteria, her stepdaughter as comforting as she knew how to be. At last Phoebe lit one of the candles and helped Mabel up the stairs and into her bed in her new and cheerfully redecorated room, soothing her with kind words and loving assurances, bathing her aching temples with lavender water, and fetching one of her favorite cordials.

She was exhausted by the day's troubles, but only when her stepmother's eyes finally closed was Phoebe able to return to the parlor, bank the fire and snuff the candles. She lit the old pottery veilleuse in its pan of water on the entry table, blew out the unprotected candle that had burned there all evening and pinched its wick. Then, ever mindful of their safety even with Mick and Joe Bodger patrolling until dawn, she lit her own candle from the veilleuse's tiny flame and went into the kitchen to check the back door.

Standing in the center of the table in a pool of moonlight was a crude basket, a dark bow on its handle. Another gift of food from Lord Soames, brought over by Mick Bodger? His lordship's persistent thoughtfulness was close to embarrassing.

Once she'd checked the door she went to the table, holding her candle high.

There, nestled in sparkling silver tissue, lay an enormous ball of mistletoe. Someone had decorated it with holly sprigs: two for eyes, and a series of smaller ones in the shape of a smiling mouth.

"Oh, dear heaven," she murmured, "Mr. Oakwood! This will never do."

Piers Duchesne, Marquess of Stovall, popular London *bon vivant* and man about town, better known to the residents of Underhill as Mr. Peter Oakwood, leaned back in his chair in the George's taproom, fingers curled around the tankard of ale he'd been nursing for the past two hours, studying the tawdrily elegant opportunist across from him.

The place boasted the usual company found in such gathering spots: tenants from Penwillow, a handful of village tradesmen, a traveler caught far from his destination at nightfall thanks to a carriage mishap, a squirish type or two, a pack of schoolboys intent on making the most of their short reprieve from Aristotle and Pythagoras in the manner of any spirited young animals.

The smoky, uncomfortably low-beamed room was much the same as he remembered it from his youth: laughter, conversation, the rattle of dice, the occasional scrap of song. Except? Except in the nook he'd selected for its deep shadows.

If country folk could be said to indulge in the cut direct, they'd been indulging since the moment he ducked beneath the low lintel with Philip Fordyce on his heels. Even getting service'd been a struggle. He'd finally instructed the barmaid to leave the bottle for Fordyce, given the man's thirst and his own desire to encourage deep drinking.

As for a welcoming word or pleasant glance? Those didn't exist.

And it wasn't the traditional taciturnity that greeted a stranger, for the voluble burgher with the smashed carriage was being accorded treatment worthy of a prodigal son. No, the ostracism was direct, intensely personal, and couldn't be laid at his own door. After all, no one knew him here. At least they thought they didn't. Yet the barmaid constantly and stubbornly refused them service whenever possible by the expedient of becoming deaf and blind when they hailed her. As for the service itself?

Oakwood'd been assiduously avoiding a puddle of ale for the past hour—the dregs of some other guest's drink the girl'd ignored when they took the table. And when she brought Fordyce's first glass of brandy and his own ale, she'd managed to spill those in addition.

Odd, indeed. None of it made sense. Fordyce was Soames's guest at the George and Phoebe Parmenter's intended husband into the bargain, if only unofficially. Either of those factors should've assured him a warm welcome.

Certainly the man was proving an unobjectionable, if somewhat condescending companion despite his acid tongue, now his ire at being wrenched from Underhill was dulled by several glasses of brandy. Indeed, he seemed increasingly grateful for Oakwood's company, was treating him almost as one would an intimate. Quite the raconteur until he'd fallen into morose silence only moments before, perhaps quelled by being sent to Coventry by all but the stranger who'd escorted him to Chedleigh Minor.

"Strange will," Oakwood now threw into the silence, anxious to encourage the man's tongue. "Mr. Parmenter must've been quite the humorist, albeit an unpleasant one. A superannuated daughter forced to wed or starve when there's no need? Demeaning to say the least for Miss Parmenter and everyone around her."

"Funny thing about that," Fordyce chuckled, eyes lighting at his own cleverness. "Opposites, Phoebe and I, when it comes to old Porty's will. I don't have an heir so I don't need lands, and I haven't any lands so I've no need of an heir. Yet here I am in hot pursuit of both, and a wife into the bargain. Don't have one of those either, at the moment. It's the lands that count, of course, and the guineas—old Parmenter saw to that. Wife an' heir're merely necessary nuisances. Whereas Phoebe has 'em all, excepting the heir and the husband, and so she's in hot pursuit of both. Perfect match, Phoebe and I."

"Won't do her much good to marry, from what I've heard. Doesn't that crony of Parmenter's—Hedges? Hicks?—in Market Stoking control the purse strings?"

"Hatch. Hezekiah Hatch, God damn his pusillanimous soul to everlasting hell."

"Rather an impediment to wedded bliss," Oakwood prodded, curious to see what Fordyce would make of the sly innuendo.

Fordyce took a gulp of brandy, drained the bottle in his glass, set both aside, straightened his satin cuffs, adjusted his florid waistcoat—had the man never heard of Brummell's edict that one should dress to perfection in the morning, then take no further notice of one's appearance?—leaned forward after a hasty glance around the taproom.

"There's that, of course," he said conspiratorially.

Blast, but the man was a parody of every ivory-turner and Captain Sharp in London: charming when it served his purpose, but as weaseling and devious, and as predictable. What did Miss Parmenter see in the conniver? She appeared to have at least a modicum of intelligence, even if she did get herself stuck in oak trees.

"What're you doing in Chedleigh Minor?" Fordyce asked after a moment, voice dropping still further. "Not the tale you've been putting about. The real reason."

"Trying to better myself."

"Down on your luck, are you? Know the feeling. We might do each other some good, if you're interested. What's Soames paying you?"

Oakwood's brows rose as he mimicked the affronted silence of an honest man who considered his hire no one's business but his own and his employer's.

"All right, we'll leave that aside. How busy's he keeping you?"

"I'm my own master in that respect. These things take time."

The vague response had the desired effect, for Fordyce nodded, eyes narrowing.

"Like to earn a few extra pounds? Without much effort?"

"I might be interested."

"You've the right of it: old Hatch controls the purse strings, but he's as crabbed as they come. The least thing could summon him to his reward. I'd be infinitely grateful to any who might render Phoebe's life a bit easier by encouraging him on his way."

"Understandable. Generous of you."

"Thing of it is, I daren't muddy the waters. Must be above reproach. A whited sepulcher. Don't want any questions, and there're questions enough already."

"No, one must take infinite care in these situations," Oakwood agreed, rather proud of himself.

"A hundred pounds grateful," Fordyce said with a wink, "once my own pockets're properly lined. Interested? All for Phoebe's sake, y'understand. And m'Cousin Mabel's, o'course. Must see to Mabel, or Phoebe'll call the whole thing off no matter where her best interests lie."

"Not wise," Oakwood murmured. "Too many're likely to suspect a precipitous depature from this vale of tears, especially given the circumstances of Parmenter's death, no matter who encourages your nemesis on his way. Besides, isn't there some other pettifogger waiting to take his place?"

"Too right," Fordyce grimaced. "Just a notion. Probably a bad one."

"I rather suspect it is. What did happen the day Parmenter died?"

"The grand and elevated Lord Soames says it was an accident. Who'm I to cavil at nobility's conclusions?"

"But you do?"

"Let's just say I saw things no one knows I saw, drew the obvious conclusions, and'm turning 'em to my advantage. My father never sired fools, for all he was a fool himself, nor did m'mother give birth to any."

"Given that, there must be some way for you to make old Hatch see reason."

"Always the possibility of making it worth his while t'loosen the purse strings and look the other way," Fordyce agreed with a nod. "Cleverly, of course. Direct approach won't work. I've been making inroads, but it'll take time, and time's a commodity of which I've precious little. Rusticating at Parmenter's expense when all this came about."

Oakwood nodded once more, sighing gustily in an effort to simulate empathy. Fordyce nodded, chin dropping to neckcloth, then jerking up.

"Heard today Matthew King of Pilchester and Squire Darner's youngest've both tried it—approaching Hatch," he said, words slurring. "Clumsily, though, very clumsily. They didn't succeed. No finesse, y'understand. I, on t'other hand, am possessed of infinite finesse—a quality neither of those idiots've ever cultivated. Might've succeeded had they th'least knowledge of human nature, but they don't."

"Whereas you, by contrast, possess such knowledge in depth."

"Have to," Fordyce shrugged. "I'd starve otherwise, not being the sort to earn my keep by th'sweat of m'back."

Oakwood kept his expression neutral as he swept the room with his eyes. Every back contrived to be turned in their direction. So, he was certain, did every ear, physical impossibility or not. Fortunately, the general clamor was great enough that none could've caught more than one word in ten.

"I'm amazed you trust me this deep on such short acquaintance," he murmured.

"You look an honest sort, if not overclever. Got t'trust someone. Can't pull it off solo. Too complicated. Been keeping m'eyes peeled for one who might assist me."

"I see. Sound anxious to bring things to a conclusion. Why? Been anticipating your vows?"

"With Phoebe Parmenter? Not likely! Thought of bedding her's chilling."

The man's rueful smile didn't quite erase the insult. Oakwood chose to ignore both in the interests of furthering his education regarding one Philip Fordyce and the death of Portius Parmenter. "There're other beds," he suggested, "if you find your own too cold and have no taste for hers."

"Indeed there are." Fordyce leaned back, eyes roving the crowd. "Even here in th'neighborhood. Fine merchandise! Some as fine as any London has t'offer."

"Indeed? I hadn't noticed."

"Glad t'point you in the right direction, if y'wish. Favor to a fellow sufferer with shallow pockets. No? Have it your own way, but there're plenty about: widows, serving wenches, younger sisters doomed t'spinsterhood and anxious t'try a man's wares.

"Plan to take full advantage of 'em, once I have the wherewithal to indulge—not that I've ever required pounds to pay for my pleasures, but the choices've been damned limited up t'now. That's about t'change. Won't be a curious virgin in the area when I'm done. Promised m'self that as a reward." Fordyce's eyes narrowed at Oakwood's frown. "Not the thing, to importune a wife once she's done her duty," he said self-righteously. "Ladies don't like that sort of thing. Phoebe and I understand each other."

"You mistake me. I only meant there're other plums ripe for the picking if this one's too far past its prime for your taste."

"Ah, but none so ready t'fall in m'waiting hands. Tree's been shaken. Plum's falling. Just have t'catch it, is all." Fordyce took the final swallow of his brandy, fastidiously wiped the back of his mouth with a lace-edged handkerchief he then tucked in his cuff. "That's th'thing about overripe plums: they fall readily from the branch. Y'saw how she treated me, all dimples and simpers. I'll play the besotted beau until the vows're said, an' maybe a bit longer if it amuses me. After that, it's every man for himself. As for m'better half, she'd best keep her place and remember what she owes me. I won't countenance a wandering wife."

"Thought her not a bad sort, myself. A few decent gowns, a new style of dressing her hair, and she wouldn't be unprepossessing."

"That dried-out spinster? Nothing'll warm her up, believe me. Damnable thing for a man to survive, but 'needs must when the devil drives.' "

Then he seemed to shake himself, raising bleared eyes from his glass.

"Dashed fond of Phoebe, of course," he insisted unsteadily. "Keep forgetting it's safe t'admit it now. Deal of play-acting the two of us indulged in so her father wouldn't tumble to our 'tachment an' chase me off like he did all the others. Make her the best sort of husband. Told her that. She agrees."

"Indeed? I must compliment you both on sterling performances then, if your words of a moment ago were a sample," Oakwood said dryly. "I'd've thought you despised Miss Parmenter, and were merely after her inheritance."

"Not a bit of it." Fordyce shook his head sadly. "There'll always be those who subscribe to the theory, though. In their interests, starting with that pernicious aunt o' hers. Wants Phoebe t'marry her son, y'see. Cobber Trask, bah! Mutton-headed gelding, thanks to his mother. Barely knows his name, let alone how t' find his mouth with a spoon. Phoebe's had a deal t'put up with from that quarter, believe me. For years. First tried t'splice 'em when she was barely fifteen. She refused, was shut in the attics on bread an' water for a month. Only reason Porty let her out was his comfort. House'd become a shambles while she was up there. Almost left m'self, conditions were so bad."

"Ah, yes. I witnessed an example of those importunings this afternoon, you'll remember."

The whole thing remained puzzling, indeed grew more so, from Fordyce's discrepant tales to his sporadic bouts of empathy for Miss Parmenter's plight to their cool reception at the George.

There was no reason Oakwood could discern for the villagers' obvious contempt. An acid tongue filmed with honey and a self-serving bent weren't that unusual in one who depended on others for the very air he breathed. Neither was inconsistency in service of survival. Certainly Miss Parmenter hadn't appeared to resent the would-be fop's attentions. Quite the contrary. She'd dimpled and cooed, a bit treacly, but quite the pattern card as besotted females went if one cared for that sort of thing.

That Oakwood didn't, and so had avoided the marriage mart with all the tenacity of a terrier burrowing for rats, was neither here nor there. At least the woman didn't affect lisps and pouts as the London belles did, or pretend to twist her ankle or be overcome by fainting fits when he was in her vicinity. She was as limpid as a country stream. Of course, she hadn't the slightest notion who he was, so the comparison wasn't a fair one. Phoebe Parmenter might prove every bit as conniving and venal as the rest, given the opportunity. Yet that notion didn't fit the young woman perched on a branch in a winter-bright wood, trapped by her desire to scramble after mistletoe.

Oakwood shied from the thought as dangerous, not certain how, but with a suspicion it might be. He pulled himself together with a shake, took a sip of his warmish ale, and glanced at his suddenly taciturn companion. Ware might be right: a tempest in a teapot, with a pair of pubescent girls resentful of their father's will inventing Gothic melodramas by moonlight in an effort to render life a bit more interesting for themselves and a bit less comfortable for those around them.

The possibility displeased him, just why he couldn't say.

But Fordyce, Parmenter's murderer? The girls had that wrong, for all it would've made solving Miss Parmenter's problems easier. Yes, the man knew more regarding what'd occurred than he was willing to say, but had he been behind it he'd've hired it done, just as he'd attempted to hire out Hatch's demise moments ago. Definitely not a man of direct action, and there was little on earth more direct than murder.

No, Fordyce was no shining example of British manhood. Neither was he the oily reprobate the girls described. If having one's pockets to let, if merely considering insalubrious methods to line those pockets, if disliking employment as a cure for those same shallow pockets and seeking remedy in a profitable marriage were crimes, at least half the great families in England'd had criminals in their past. Probably more.

Of course the evening was proving a bit of a sparring match as well.

Now, with his neckcloth loosened and waistcoat unbuttoned, Fordyce lolled in his chair, eyes bleared by drink, expression a mite fuddled.

"Miss Parmenter does appear a pleasant sort, and greatly put upon by her father, from what I gather," Oakwood probed once more, in his turn treating the room to the sight of his broad back. "I can see why you're taken with her."

"More'n taken. Besotted with Phoebe," Fordyce agreed with a foolish grin, draining his glass and wiping his lips with the back of his hand. "Spirited, for all her governessy ways, and I do like 'em with spirit. Have a dull time of it otherwise. Always treated me like an insect before. Pretended to, I mean."

And now they were getting somewhere at last. Treated like an insect? By one's beloved? Before the knot was even tied?

Face it: heiress that she was, Phoebe Parmenter could've had her choice of any unattached man within leagues of Underhill. He was back to it again: why the penniless Fordyce unless blackmail of some sort was indeed involved? That raised ugly possibilities unless Phoebe Parmenter was as enamored of Fordyce as the man claimed, and after an evening in his company Oakwood was developing grave doubts about that.

Of course the ways of the heart were mysteries into which he'd never delved, though the evidence given his eldest sister and their father was clear enough: When Eros loosed his stinging darts, logic flew out the window.

"Then your understanding is of recent date?" Oakwood inquired at his friendliest, now determined to acquire enough ammunition to spike Prissy and Pru's guns no matter how he felt personally about the matter. "Quite a romance, given the tales I've heard of how they've all lived up to now."

"Not so recent as all that. Already told you." Fordyce sat straighter, shoved his empty glass to the edge of the table, turned the empty bottle on its side and waved his handkerchief in an effort to attract the barmaid's attention. "Here, you, Tess!" he shouted. "Some service here, blast it! No way to treat a guest in an honest house!"

Heads turned. Frowns lowered. Oakwood squirmed as pair after pair of eyes skewered him contemptuously.

"Known each other for years, y'understand," Fordyce continued, ignoring the purdah to which they'd been consigned. "Ever since Cousin Mabel married Parmenter. Came to visit 'em within a month of the marriage. 'Course, Phoebe wasn't but a schoolgirl then. Nasty things, schoolgirls, but she's come around. Most do, eventually."

"Must've been uncomfortable, being a guest in that household," Oakwood suggested, in his turn signaling the barmaid with equal lack of success. "Don't see how you bore it, myself."

"One can endure most anything if there's a roof over one's head and a meal on the table, and one ain't being charged for either. Never've been particularly before-hand with the world. Not consistently, at any rate. Cards aren't always cooperative."

"But the way Parmenter treated his wife and children? Mrs. Parmenter is your cousin, I believe?"

"Only a distant one," Fordyce shrugged. "Barely close enough for me to beg the privileges of a guest. What passed between her and old Porty had nothing to do with me. Didn't want t'forfeit my welcome, y'understand. Couldn't afford to, and it wouldn't've made a particle of difference anyway—not that I'll treat her and Phoebe the same, mind you. Not my style. Genuinely peaceable, an' that's the truth, unless I'm pressed beyond what a man can bear. Anything else's too much effort."

"You're practical."

"Have t'be, in my position."

Fordyce leaned back once more, surveying the taproom with loathing.

"Damnable place—Chedleigh Minor," he muttered. "Damnable people. Damnable position t'be in. Damned if I'll stand it any longer. Better man than any of 'em."

"I can't say I blame you," Oakwood returned with spurious sympathy, "but you haven't much choice, have you? Not if you want to wed Miss Parmenter. You'll be enduring it the rest of your life."

"Only when I'm at Underhill, and a month should see to the getting of an heir unless m'sensibilities revolt too drastically. Once that's taken care of I'll treat 'em to the sight of my heels, and good riddance!"

"I see. Still doesn't explain how you'll frank yourself if the terms are as I was informed."

"Oh, they're precisely as you were informed. Pre-cisely. Canny bastard, old Porty. Thought he'd chouse me, but I have my ways. How practical're you?"

"Infinitely practical."

"Interested in joining with me, then? I could do with a bit of assistance given m'nose must be cleaner than the average to achieve what I must without suspicion falling on me. Caesar's wife an' all that, y'know. There's nothing these rag-tags'd rather than t'see me chased from the neighborhood if they could manage it."

"Not at the moment, I think." Oakwood sighed gustily, doing his best to look genuinely regretful. "Too risky. I daren't incur Lord Soames's wrath, you understand. His pockets're deeper than Miss Parmenter's ever will be. A shame, as I could do with the blunt."

"You'll keep mum? Wouldn't want all this bruited about. Isn't a soul who'd comprehend m'motives."

"Of course not."

"Other ways to handle Hatch, if I must. Know a few things about him, too. All for darling Phoebe's sake, y'understand. Want to see her comfortably fixed. Don't want old Hatch ruling at Underhill. He'd make her life miserable."

"Naturally, fond of her as you are."

"Fond? Yes, I am. Damned fond, no matter what anyone says. Good word, fond. I'll have to remember it. Better'n besotted. More accurate, too."

Oakwood smiled at the barmaid as she stalked to their table at last. She tucked a wisp of hair in her cap and swiped at the puddles with her cloth, propelling half the spilled ale into Fordyce's lap, the rest into Oakwood's, then stretched her lips in a thing that could in no way be called a smile, her eyes as cold as Scotland in January.

"You're wantin' something?" she snapped.

"Another bottle of your best brandy for Mr. Fordyce," Oakwood murmured, slipping her a coin. He was damned if he was going to spend the rest of his time in Chedleigh Minor being distrusted and despised, and having things spilled on him in an attempt to encourage him on his way. If he did, he'd learn nothing. He'd also have nothing to wear. "No, nothing more for me. I've still a long ride back to Lord Soames's estate, and I must be out early on his business." That ought to do it.

The barmaid bit the coin, slipped it into her cleavage, eyes assessing.

"You're that stranger the vicar was prattling about earlier, then?" she said, high-pitched voice warming slightly. "One as is here about a folly or some such?"

"I might be. What did the vicar say?"

"It true you're some famous duke's by-blow?"

Fordyce's head snapped up, his eyes narrowing.

"No," Oakwood chuckled, "nothing half so interesting, I'm afraid."

"Y'are monstrous big, though," she commented, running a practiced eye over him. "Vicar got that right. Ain't usually right about anything, so I wondered."

"Name's Oakwood," Oakwood said, rising. "Peter Oakwood, at your service. I accompanied Mr. Fordyce from Underhill when Lord Soames's men arrived to stand guard for the night."

"So that's how it be," she shrilled, voice rising in the manner of the London Watch calling the hour. "Come from Underhill. Went there on his lordship's asking, I'll warrant? Wise on him. His worshipfulness here don't like the George, nor yet think his bed's soft enough or his room clean enough, or the food more'n passable which, given t'mistress is a fine cook, is nothing more'n a nasty-minded sot tryin' t'make trouble.

"Brandy for Mr. Fordyce," she said still more loudly, giving Oakwood the first smile he'd received in that place the entire evening. "I'll get it right away."

"Y'see how it is?" Fordyce grimaced as the wench made for the bar. "Think the worst of me, every last one of 'em, when all I'm trying to do is see to their precious Miss Parmenter's future. M'own too, of course. Naturally."

"Naturally," Oakwood agreed.

On her way the girl paused at one of the trestle tables, murmuring to first one, then another. Heads swiveled. Eyes widened. Tentative nods were sent in Oakwood's direction. He nodded ruefully in response, shrugged, well pleased with himself.

Then he regained his seat, long legs stretching across the floorboards. The room had warmed in the last few moments, even if no one had built up the fire. If he could outlast Fordyce and the hour didn't become too late, he might yet learn something of genuine use.

Six

The moon was high when Oakwood finally quit the George after assisting a sodden Philip Fordyce to his room. He retrieved Bacchus from the sleepy stableboy, paused in the inn yard studying the small village.

The night was peaceful unless one counted the gaggle of schoolboys stumbling home, in their cups and warbling a ditty that would've horrified their mothers. Oakwood watched their uneven progress with amusement, remembering his own salad days. One lad staggered into a drift. His companions pulled him out, dusted him off amidst much laughter, and they continued on their way.

"Silly gudgeons," Oakwood murmured, breath clouding in the frigid air. "They'll pay the piper for their overindulgence tomorrow, won't they, old boy?"

The big gelding snorted his agreement, jingling bridle and bit.

Oakwood mounted with a sigh, turned Bacchus's head toward Soames's woods, which began a mile beyond the village.

On the surface of it he'd learned nothing of use that evening, except that Fordyce was no worse than many and a bit better than some. The man was either innocent of the girls' accusations, or infinitely more clever than Oakwood believed.

He needed time to sort this out, and time was precisely the commodity with which he wasn't to be gifted. Weeks had shrunk to days. Fordyce was bringing the nuptials forward, intending to surprise his betrothed.

No sense in delay, he'd claimed during his unsteady progress up the back stairs, and to blazes with Soames and his insistence

Phoebe be permitted time to recover her equanimity while a period of mourning was observed. It wasn't his lordship's pockets that were to let, Fordyce'd grunted, nor was he being inconvenienced by the delay. Hezekiah Hatch would give his official blessing once certain things were pointed out to him. Given his tacit one already. The ladies needed a protector—the sooner the better.

Oakwood and Bacchus clopped along the lane, saddle creaking in the cold, tree branches arching over them like the spines of a cathedral vault. Only color was lacking, the world washed in liquid moonlight, the shadows as stark as if it were high noon. An animal screamed in the woods. There was a howl, long and plaintive. Then, silence.

If the girls were right, was that how Phoebe Parmenter felt? Like a small animal, struggling instinctively, but resigned to her fate for all of that? Somehow the image didn't tally with the young woman he'd first met that morning.

Nothing quite fit.

So Fordyce had provided himself with a special license, heaven knew from which bishop or how he'd raised the funds—special licenses didn't come cheap—though he'd hinted that had been the reason for his absence from Underhill that day. He'd pulled the blasted thing from his pocket, waved it under Oakwood's nose.

There was no question it was precisely what he'd claimed.

That Fordyce intended a hole-in-the-wall affair little better than a bolt to Gretna Green and vows sworn over the anvil appeared to trouble him not in the least. Expeditious, he'd said with a wink, was desirable, and expeditious he'd have. The neighborhood would accustom itself once a new master reigned at Underhill.

Oakwood scowled as Bacchus daintily picked his way down the snow-covered lane, lifting his hooves high, tossing his head and snorting in the cold. As on the night of their arrival, the world was a glittering place touched with magic. All it lacked was fat flakes descending from a vagrant cloud.

But it was entirely different as well.

When he'd been traveling this bit of road then, he'd yet to encounter his youthful abductors. He'd never heard of Portius

Parmenter. Certainly he'd never heard of Philip Fordyce, and he'd never seen the fading bruises poorly hidden by rice powder on Mabel Parmenter's face, or the way she favored arm and shoulder. He'd never encountered Phoebe Parmenter seeking mistletoe in a winter wood. He'd never pocketed a scrap of chipped marble.

A fresh scrap of chipped marble with touches of glue clinging to its slanted break and tiny black grains imbedded in the upper edge.

Mabel Parmenter and her stepdaughter had been lying that afternoon. Lying determinedly, and almost successfully. He'd been trying not to think about that, but there it was: he couldn't help himself.

Again, something didn't ring true.

The implications didn't please him. They didn't please him in the least.

Of course he wasn't satisfied Fordyce's motives were as altruistic as the man claimed. Hardly. Not when, well above par, he'd more than hinted at disposing of Hatch before discarding the idea as impractical. But then, were any man's motives entirely altruistic when it came to marriage?

Still, that wasn't the main problem.

Oakwood slipped his hand inside his greatcoat, fumbled for his shooting jacket pocket, once more fingering the heavy scrap of marble. He could feel its slanted, raw edge even through his gloves, cutting along a vein, the glue slickening it.

The only possible conclusion was the thing hadn't been broken when and how Miss Parmenter claimed, but if within the last few days, under what conditions?

Had she discovered her father beating her stepmother—a usual enough occurrence given all Ware and Soames had said. Had that beating been dangerously worse than customary? Had she intervened, with permanent results?

And had Fordyce witnessed the entire thing? He'd hinted at something of the sort. Even helped them stage the accident in Soames's game preserve? And then, certain of his ground, offered for Miss Parmenter as soon as the will was read, knowing there was no way she could refuse him? If that was the case, he'd probably originally intended to offer for his widowed cousin. Clever of him, to wait until he was certain how things stood. Clever and devious, and infinitely calculating.

Oakwood shrank from the thought, but it would certainly explain Fordyce's hold over the two women. Very easy for such innocents as Prissy and Pru, crammed to the gills with Gothic romances, to later overhear a conversation replete with innuendoes and misinterpret everything in such a manner.

No, the murderess—if murderess there were—had to be Phoebe Parmenter herself, not the lovely, vapid widow. She'd never've had the pluck to defend herself, Ware'd been right about that, while Miss Parmenter'd certainly proved that morning she had the requisite qualities. Indeed, she'd proved she had the bottom for most anything, in his humble opinion. It'd been a good question as to whether she'd come out of that particular scrape uninjured, and all for the sake of a bit of mistletoe with which to surprise her half-sisters.

Foolish girl!

The ghost of a smile quirked Oakwood's lips. The definitely feminine bundle that'd tumbled out of the oak had been too slender for conventional beauty, but it had nevertheless been gently rounded in all the right places. Fordyce was either unobservant or blind, or unnaturally prejudiced. As for the furious blushes, the trace of a dimple in the cheek, they'd been more than arresting. She'd been more than arresting. She'd been everything he'd never believed—

Oakwood shook himself, disliking the path his thoughts were traveling.

Better to remember the look of terror when he'd retained that scrap of marble. Better to remember the way her eyes had sought his with a look of wariness when Soames explained he was a landscape designer along the lines of Capability Brown while he'd laid claim to being a specialist in game management.

Far better.

Far safer—for her, and for his own peace of mind. After all, he'd come haring it to Penwillow to escape entanglements, not indulge in 'em, blast it.

No, the nub of the matter was should Miss Phoebe Parmenter be forced to pay for her defense of her abused stepmother with her life? Because marriage to Fordyce—he was becoming increasingly convinced of it—would be no better than swinging at the crossroads. He might as well admit it instead of thrashing about like a trout on the hook in an effort to avoid admitting the truth: The more sodden the man'd become, the more casually he'd revealed his less admirable qualities. No better than many? True, but far worse than most.

That didn't seem just, somehow. As for the thought of Fordyce's pale scented hands on her, probing and stroking and digging, mind and soul revolted.

He'd had the right of it earlier, Oakwood decided. Soames would have to be brought to a sense of his responsibilities in the matter. The clunch had to marry one day. Underhill marched with his lands. Miss Parmenter might not be a beauty, but she was far from plain and she possessed a freshness of wit and a touch of the unconventional that would keep any husband intrigued for a lifetime. It wouldn't be a bad match, even if a slightly unorthodox one.

No, there was no impediment to Soames rescuing little Miss Parmenter. After all, he rarely frequented Town. It wasn't as if his consequence required a bride of distinguished lineage or tonnish elegance, and Underhill would serve his pockets well.

Besides, Oakwood scowled, he'd been blatantly flirting with the young woman that afternoon, and she hadn't seemed in the least averse. That, if nothing else, had committed him. Soames would thank him eventually. Prissy and Pru would have their noble hero, Miss Parmenter an enviable match, he'd scurry back to London, and that would be an end to it. Deliberately he shied from consideration of the intimacies that would follow the ceremony. Soames was a good sort and his friend, the antithesis of the affected Fordyce. There couldn't be the least objection to him.

Oakwood was becoming, he decided, something rather along the lines of one of Perrault's fairy godmothers. Well, a fairy godfather. He'd make all right and tight, just as they did, and then vanish with the sunrise. He rather fancied that role, he insisted to himself. Why then did the notion of Phoebe Parmenter and Soames exchanging vows ring so hollow?

He reached the little glen where he first encountered Prissy and Pru and Alfie, turned Bacchus's head into the woods, carefully picking his way toward the gamekeeper's cottage. A bray shattered the stillness.

"What now?" Oakwood murmured, certain who lurked just out of sight.

Nor was he in error. Alfie jolted out of a thicket on Sukey's raw-boned back, cap pulled low, scarf wound high about his ears.

"T-taken you long enough," the boy complained, teeth chattering. "Thought I'd d-die of the cold waiting. Where've you been all this time?"

"And a good evening to you as well, my lad," Oakwood grinned. "Why didn't you wait at the cottage? Door isn't locked."

"Girls're there. Didn't w-want 'em to know what I've d-discovered."

Oakwood pulled Bacchus to a halt, turned in the saddle to face his companion. "What might that be?" he asked, unpleasant premonitions banishing his uneasy thoughts of moments before.

"Was in M-market Stoking today, delivering flour to a b-baker's for m'father. Mrs. Pruitt's mince pies're the best for miles about. Melt in the mouth, they do. Not like m'mother's, which're as like to ship's ballast as one can c-come."

"And?"

"I saw Cousin Fordyce clear as d-day, going into Hezekiah Hatch's house."

"Nothing out of the way in that, I should think."

"Don't agree with you there. Don't agree at all. What b-business could he have with Hatch? Honest business, that is. Good thing I don't think like you, too. Delivered the flour qu-quick as I might, and then s-snuck under old Hatch's windows to see if I c-could hear anything. Couldn't, but I took a peep. Had their heads together, drawing up some sort of document. P-papers all over the place."

"Could you see what it was?" Oakwood frowned.

"N-no, but it was big and official l-looking, if you understand what I mean? Lots of seals and things. They were copying it from something else."

"I do, indeed."

"Think it's important?"

"I think tonight's wait has been well worth your while, if that's your concern. Or well worth Miss Parmenter's, if you're as fond of her as you claim."

"Cousin Phoebe? K-keep telling you she's a g-great gun!" Alfie insisted. "Deserves far better'n C-cousin Fordyce, even if there's nothing havey-cavey about the b-business. Deserves better'n Cobber or m-me, for that matter."

"Well, we'll see how things sort themselves out," Oakwood reassured him. "I don't think you'll be displeased in the end."

"Th-that mean you believe the g-girls?"

"I begin to think so, at least in part. It's possible they're in error on some of the details, but in the main they have it right, I believe."

"What about Cousin Philip? Did he kill Uncle Parmenter?"

"No, nothing so straightforward as that, but I believe he knows who did."

"So you'll d-do something?"

"I've already begun, though I've nothing to show for it as yet. Come on, now. We'd best get you warmed up before you attempt the ride back to the mill. But, you're right: not a word of this to Prissy or Pru."

They smelled the cottage—or, more accurately, the tang of smoke trickling from its crooked chimney—long before they glimpsed it through the trees: a squat thing, ancient and dark, only a faint glimmer of light seeping through shutter chinks. Two sets of footprints leading toward Underhill dimpled last night's fresh snow.

"We'll have you feeling yourself in no time," Oakwood murmured to the shivering boy. Then, not wanting to frighten the girls, he continued more loudly, "Let's go in by the back way,

Alfie, and see to your mule and Bacchus. Then some tea to warm us, and a bite for you."

The door sprang open. Prissy and Pru tumbled out, rubbing their eyes and yawning.

"Where've you been?" Prissy asked as she blinked in the moonlight. "Pru told you we were coming. I should think you'd've had the courtesy not to keep us waiting."

"Seeing to the commission you gave me, sleepyhead," Oakwood smiled easily.

"What've you learned?" Pru seized Bacchus's bridle, almost dancing in her cracked boots. "Do you believe us now? I know you said you did, but—"

"Let's say I disbelieve you less and less," Oakwood responded, swinging easily from the saddle and dropping to the trampled area before the door.

He took the bridle from the young girl, threw an arm casually around her shoulders and hurried both Bacchus and her to the rear of the cottage. It was damnably cold out, even colder than the previous night when he'd made a furtive trip to the castle to borrow some books and partake of a decent meal.

"Only that?" she demanded, scrambling to keep up with his long strides. "You're not very trusting, are you."

"Only that," he confirmed, "but I do have some questions for you. Let's see to Bacchus and Sukey, and then—"

"Why won't you trust us?" Pru wailed "We've told you everything, and you've met Phoebe and seen what a dear she is, and if you couldn't tell Cousin Philip is a slimy toad on first acquaintance then you have less intelligence than I thought."

"I did stop by to accompany your mother's cousin to the George," Oakwood protested mildly.

"And kept us waiting forever," Prissy grumbled, dogging their steps as Alfie and his mule trailed behind. "That's the mark neither of a gentleman nor a hero."

"But then I've never claimed to be either." The shed door screeched across the stone sill as Oakwood dragged it open. "That's merely something you claimed for me."

"Soph- Soph— That's sophisticatry!"

"Sophistry," Pru and Oakwood chorused, briefly in accord.

"She's correct, you know," Pru reproved, throwing him a stern glance. "You were the one who rescued Phoebe today, weren't you? When she went climbing trees? Mr. Dorning told us all about it when we came upon him by the side of the road."

"He did, did he?" Oakwood took the lantern from its peg, lit it and adjusted the wick, then hung it back up. "Now, there's one who's no gentleman!"

"No, he's not. He's a snake, and a worm, and a piscopantlian," Prissy declared.

"D'you mean an Anglican dominie with aspirations to a bishopric, or a sycophantic nonentity?" Oakwood chuckled.

"Both!"

"Far be it from me to disagree with a lady," Oakwood said, removing Bacchus's saddle and bridle. "Interesting word you've come up with there. I'll have to remember it. Actually, you're right on both counts, as it happens."

They gave Sukey and Bacchus a good rubdown and covered them with blankets, then went from the shed into the storeroom, taking the lantern and closing the door firmly behind them, and from there into the cottage's main room.

Oakwood glanced around him appreciatively. "You've been busy," he said as he set the lantern on the table and lowered the wick.

No, it wasn't White's or Brooks's, or even his restrained bachelor quarters at the Albany, but the floor had been swept, the food in tin keeping boxes carted over from the castle set on the mantel. A kettle of what he presumed was water steamed on the hob. The fresh straw tick and clean blankets he'd dumped on the settle by the chimney were on the bed complete with pillow, their unappetizing predecessors disposed of. The bed, Oakwood noted with amusement, showed evidence of recent use.

Even a fat orange tabby with a ragged ear curled in front of the fire, paws tucked over its nose. Only the flicking tip of its crooked tail proved the creature lived. It slitted a rheumy yellow eye, gave the assembled company a glare, and returned to its slumbers.

"A superior mouser, I presume," he said with a grin that broadened at their vigorous nods. "Which of you young ladies do I have to thank for the improved appearance of my domicile?"

"Oh, Pru did it all," Prissy yawned as Alfie stumbled over to the fire, dispossessed the cat with a gentle prod of his boot, then sank before the grate and held his hands to the warmth. "I was too sleepy. It's not a short walk from Underhill, especially at night in the snow, and we've had a multitude of busy days and busier nights since Papa died." She tripped to the table, sat, crossed her arms on its scratched surface and laid her head down as her lids drifted closed. "It's dreadful, trying to pretend one is one's customary exorbitant self when one's asleep on one's feet. Wake me when you're ready to leave, Pru," she murmured, voice trailing off. "You can tell me what was decided tomorrow."

The most delicate of snores fluttered her lips.

With a good-humored smile, Oakwood carried her to the bed and covered her with one of the blankets. Prissy's exuberance was most definitely in abeyance at the moment. One down, two to go.

He was, if truth were told, damnably tired himself. Of course, two nights ago he'd been so bored he'd been prepared for most anything. That this particular "most anything" was proving considerably more demanding than he'd bargained for wasn't the girls' fault.

"How'd you manage to sneak past Mr. Bodger and his son?" he said, turning to Pru, who'd sought Prissy's stool at the table once she'd taken some used tea leaves from a small tin on the mantel and set them to steeping, then placed three earthenware mugs on the table along with a small bowl of sugar and, Oakwood was amused to note, the flask of superior French brandy he'd caged from Soames.

"Goodness, that was easy!" she chuckled. "After all, Prissy and I know Underhill far better than Mr. Bodger. Once Mama and Phoebe were asleep, we climbed from our window to the kitchen roof, and from there into a tree and waited until he and Joe had gone behind the barn, and then we slipped into the spinny. We'll return the same way.

"Now, what's this about your actually seeking employment with Lord Soames? I thought you were going to help us."

"I, ah, thought it wise to have a genuine excuse for being in the neighborhood. Yesterday was a dead loss, except for examining the path where your father was found," Oakwood prevaricated. "To learn anything, I must be trusted. No quicker road to that than being known to be connected in some way with his lordship."

"Well, you and he'd best get your tales straight. Phoebe mentioned at dinner you have differing notions of what it is you've been hired to do," Pru cautioned. "You're not as clever as you believe you are. Which is the truth?"

"Both, actually."

"That you're a superior specialist in game management *and* a designer of landscapes? I cut my wisdoms before you were—well, I know better than that, even if I didn't cut them before you were born."

"And I know a bit about estate management as well," he grinned. "Quite a bit, as it happens. They go together, and then I've always been something of a dabbler.

"Why is it you've risked coming to see me?" he attacked, seeking safety in an autocratic tone. "I thought we agreed it would be best if you confined your visits to daylight hours and made them as infrequent as possible, preferably during your afternoon walks. Don't try to claim it was because I needed food. Even if Lord Soames hadn't taken me on, I could've gone to the George, *faute de mieux.*"

"That's French, isn't it? How d'you come to know French? That isn't customary for gamekeepers, or landscape gardeners either."

"Oh, one picks these things up," Oakwood explained airily, turning to hide the flush suffusing his features and shrugging off his old greatcoat, "especially if one's around those of the great world often. Enamored of foreign phrases, gentlemen of the ton are. Even Latin or Greek on occasion, though most times they haven't the least notion what they're saying. I haven't either, come to that."

"Don't you? If I remember correctly, you employed that one to perfection."

"Miracles never cease, do they."

"Apparently not. Who are you? Really?"

"I'm really a jack of all trades, and a master of none," he sighed, turning back to Pru, expression now composed. "A sometime jobber, if you will, turning my hand to anything that's available. Now, are you going to pour that tea, or are you going to permit it to become something suitable for tanning leather?"

Pru gave him a hard look, then reluctantly retrieved the pot from the hob and poured out, in the process depositing a fair number of leaves in his mug. He smiled, shrugged as the orange cat twined itself around his ankles.

"Now," he continued easily, sitting at the table and adding several spoonfuls of sugar to the noxious black brew, "why are you here?"

"There's trouble, perhaps."

"When isn't there? Out with it, minx."

The cat jumped onto his lap, began kneading his thigh with strong, clawed paws. Oakwood dumped it on the floor. It leapt back and settled itself in a loose arc, pink tongue tip protruding slightly between yellowed fangs.

"Well?" Oakwood attempted a sip, almost spat it out. "What's the problem?"

"We overheard Mama and Phoebe. Mama was crying."

"Could you understand what was said?" he asked, leaving aside for the moment the impropriety of listening at doors.

"Not enough for it to make sense. Something about the mantel and Papa."

"Only that?"

"Phoebe did speak of Papa never being able to hurt Mama again, but there's nothing new in that. We've all been saying it since the day Papa died. I know it makes us sound unnatural, but—"

"Doesn't make you sound in the least unnatural," Alfie said from by the fire. "It's the truth, and that's all there is to it."

"I see." Oakwood gestured for Alfie to join them, poured a

dollop of brandy in the boy's tea and a more liberal portion in his own. "Now, I've some questions of my own. First," he said, turning to Alfie, "why is Fordyce so intensely disliked here-abouts? The man may not be particularly prepossessing, but he seems harmless enough."

"Try telling that to Betty Klegg's father," Alfie mumbled, col-oring. "He's the one owns the George. Ran off to London with Cousin Fordyce a year ago, Betty did, and never came back. Broke Willie and Martha Klegg's hearts. Before that she was meeting him in haymows. Just before that she was supposed t'marry m'brother, but he wouldn't stand for spoiled goods so it was called off. Now he's betrothed to the squire's youngest, which is a step up and pleased m'father at the time as she's decently dowered.

"Problem is, m'brother wasn't able to ask Cousin Phoebe for her hand when Uncle Parmenter's will was read, which is why m'father put a gun to my head after Cobber'd said his piece. Didn't accept me of course. Nine years her junior—no hard feelings there. Not ready to be leg-shackled, and being married to Phoebe'd be more like marrying one's sister, but if she'd said yes I'd've gone ahead and done it. That fond of Phoebe, and I wouldn't've lead her a dog's life the way Cousin Fordyce is sure to."

Oakwood attempted to scowl the boy down, indicating Pru—who was placidly sipping her tea—with his eyes.

"Oh, Pru knows about Cousin Fordyce and Betty Klegg. Eve-rybody in these parts does who has ears and eyes," Alfie shrugged. "Y'may be able t'hide such things from city misses, but in the country it's different. We're pretty much in each others' pockets, and there's not much of interest happens except for things like that. 'Sides, Prissy and Pru've grown up on a farm. Tell you pretty well anything, were you to ask 'em."

"We just don't talk about it in front of our elders is all," Pru explained, meeting Oakwood's embarrassed glance with straightforward candor. "You aren't to worry about my delicate ears. They're not that delicate, for all we pretend otherwise for the sake of Mama and Phoebe. They'd be shocked, you see, as they've forgotten how it was when they were girls.

"Besides," she shrugged with an air of resignation, "with Papa making so many jaunts to Market Stoking whenever Mama was increasing—she lost five after me, all of them girls; the last was only this fall—and then jumping on Mama whenever she wasn't, and our room being next to theirs, there's not much Prissy and I don't know of what goes on between men and women, either."

She shuddered, lowering her eyes to her mug.

"Why d'you think we're so concerned for Phoebe?" she mumbled. "Prissy may sound like a fool, with all the big words she gleans from Mama's romances, but she's not. Neither'm I."

Oakwood cursed slowly and inventively without any thought to his company.

At least the tale of Betty Klegg fit Fordyce's casual mention of available beauties and his prowess at the art of patty-cake. A man boasting of his seductions in a taproom was one thing—ungentlemanly, but not all that unusual and easily overlooked as more sound than substance. The reality was another.

Where was Betty Klegg now, he wondered.

"Don't look so angry," Pru scolded gently, covering his hand with hers. "It's over. Papa's dead and Mama's safe. It's just Phoebe who's in worse case than ever."

In response Oakwood set the cat on the floor and rose, striding around the small room like a caged animal, finally stopping by the grate to kick the burning logs, then add another. The cat, with a look of reproof, joined Prissy on the bed.

"I see," he said at last, opening one of the small food safes and retrieving a slab of pork pie and two apples. "Fordyce and Betty Klegg are merely one among many local scandals. Still, I'm surprised no one took a horsewhip to him."

"With Uncle Parmenter tolerating him," Alfie snorted, "and indulging in the same activities? Not likely! And Betty ain't the first—just the most recent. Most've them've been ripe for it, but Betty was a good girl until Cousin Fordyce got her to lift her skirts."

"I see." Oakwood frowned, set the apple and pie in front of Alfie, who gave him a grateful grin, and handed the other apple to Pru. Then, still frowning, he resumed his place at the table.

The orange tabby was back on the instant. "Does Miss Parmenter know of her fiancé's adventures?"

"Everybody knows," Alfie said flatly around a bite of pie. "Told you: There isn't any way t'hide what one does in the country, no matter how it is in London."

"But they're not really betrothed yet. No banns," Pru insisted. "All's rumor so far, and no one'd wonder at it's not being true, and most everyone'd be glad."

"And yet your half-sister's accepted the offer of a penniless coxcomb and gazetted philanderer, even if only unofficially? Well, that answers that one—not that I like it," Oakwood continued blandly with the sensation he was pounding nails in Phoebe Parmenter's coffin.

His effort to control his disgust at what these girls, their sister and mother had suffered showed only in a clenched fist and a certain tightness around his lips. He turned to Pru, fixing her with stern hazel eyes until her own gaze dropped uncertainly.

"Now," he said, "where were you and Prissy and Miss Parmenter the afternoon your father met his end?"

Pru's expression changed from troubled and perhaps a trifle embarrassed to puzzled. "What does that have to do with anything?" she said.

"Everything, perhaps. Come now: Where were you? What were you doing?"

"Prissy and I were out walking as Phoebe insists we do each afternoon," she shrugged. "Nothing unusual about that. We take the sledge and gather deadfall. It's heavy, but we manage. We've never been permitted the use of a horse: one of Papa's rules. The tenants aren't allowed to help, either. They'd be turned off if they did."

"Do you have a customary route?"

"The woods, well away from any paths. We follow the game trails mostly, though now Papa's dead we sometimes take the lane coming home, which is how we happened on Mr. Dorning this afternoon."

"Did anyone see you that day?"

"And give some gabble-monger a chance to go bearing tales

to Papa? Even if we were being useful by gathering deadfall? Certainly not!"

"And, Miss Parmenter? Was she at home when you returned?"

"I'm not sure. I suppose so. She usually is. We unloaded the wood behind the kitchen and sneaked in the back way. Papa'd been in a terrible temper all day, and Phoebe'd cautioned us to play least in sight for fear he'd take a strap to us if no one else was handy. He wanted desperately to hit something. Well, hit someone."

"I see," he said. "D'you know what caused your father to be out of sorts that particular day?"

Pru nodded, blushing.

"Well, out with it!"

"He'd paid for a physician to come down from Pilchester to examine Mama," she said, throwing an uneasy glance first at the bed where her sister slept, then at Alfie.

"Might as well tell him," Alfie shrugged. "You don't, I or someone else will."

"You mean *you* know?" she demanded, incredulous.

"Of course. Whole village knows. We both keep telling Mr. Oakwood what it's like here, but even you don't believe it.

"The physician said Aunt Mabel hadn't the strength to bear Uncle Parmenter another child yet," Alfie continued, turning to Oakwood when Pru hesitated. "Too soon, he said. Then he said, as Phoebe's mother'd born only girls, and Aunt Mabel the same, the fault probably rested with Uncle Parmenter. Said he was some kind of factor. Content? Contact? I don't know. Tale was garbled by the time I heard it. Anyway, he said not having sons could probably be laid at his door."

"Constant factor?"

"Could be. Thing is, Uncle Parmenter was ready to tear that fancy physician limb from limb. Refused to pay him. Terrible row, from what I heard. Called him a quack. Doctor was lucky to get away with only darkened daylights. Saw those myself when he stopped at the George and I was making deliveries for my father."

"Was there such a fracas that morning?" Oakwood asked, turning to Pru.

She nodded miserably. "Papa was beside himself. He broke things. But Phoebe was there when Mr. Bodger brought news of finding Papa. Why?"

"Oh, just a notion I had," he said, absently massaging the area behind cat's ears, and calling forth a contented rumble. "Could your half-sister have been paying a call perhaps, or running an errand?"

"Phoebe? Flee the house given what'd happened that morning? She'd never've abandoned Mama—never! Who would she call on, in any case? We've no friends. Papa didn't permit visiting. He said most of our neighbors were interfering busy-bodies, and would give us notions above our station. Gussets gallivant, he said. Parmenters stick to their perches."

"An errand, then?"

"We weren't permitted. Papa said going in shops would encourage extravagance, and Aunt Trask seconded him. We walked to services on Sundays if he was in a benevolent mood, and Aunt Trask stopped by most every day to natter at Mama and Phoebe. Beyond that? No one dared call. Papa didn't keep a carriage, you see, only his hunters and the farm horses. He rode everywhere, and we went nowhere."

"Got to talk to you in private," Alfie hissed behind his hand. "There's more. Saw Phoebe coming out of Emma Trask's."

Oakwood shrugged, nodded. It seemed there was always more.

"Well, you children had best be going or you'll be missed. It's well into the small hours. I'll take you girls home on Bacchus," he said, giving Pru's plaits a brotherly tug as she tucked her apple in a pocket. Then he retrieved the lantern from the table. "Trust me: we'll sort all this out somehow. Wake your sister. We'll meet you out front."

He threw his arm across Alfie's shoulders, led him back through the storeroom to the shed where he quickly resaddled Bacchus as the boy saw to his rawboned mule.

"You said Parmenter played the philanderer," Oakwood murmured, not wanting his voice to reach the girls, no matter what they claimed about lack of innocence.

"Every chance he got, which was often. Wasn't nothing m'father'd do or say. Claimed it wasn't his concern, and him Aunt Mabel's own brother!"

"Getting angry about it won't help things now. Besides, your father was right: What occurs between a man and his wife is nobody's business but their own." Oakwood colored at Alfie's look of contempt, cleared his throat. "Yes, well, d'you know whose company Mr. Parmenter sought when he went to Market Stoking?"

" 'Course. Everybody knew, even Aunt Mabel: Lizzie Blunt. She's a widow, accommodates most as aren't satisfied with their wives in these parts. Left with eight to feed, don't you see," Alfie explained, squinting over the mule's back, "when a runaway hay wagon squashed her husband flat. She tried taking in laundry, but no one brought her any and so she turned her hand to what most women do when they've no other way to support themselves. Those as frequent her pay in food, or something else she can use."

"Dear God," Oakwood murmured, "Country's as bad as London. Worse perhaps, given it has such an innocent air. And Lord Soames's done nothing—"

"Not much he can do. There're too many need help, don't you see? He can't hire everyone who's down on their luck. Beggar him, that would, and then he couldn't help anyone, not even himself. I always imagined places're much the same," Alfie grunted, tightening Sukey's girth. "People are, whether they've got fancy handles to their names or not. Can't write more'n one thing at a time in the snow."

"Out of the mouths of babes. And who was the physician from Pilchester?"

Alfie grinned. "That was Jonas Whale. And before you accuse me of bamming you, that's his name: Jonas Whale. His house and surgery're in the center of town. You can't miss 'em, and if you do, anyone can give you directions. About Cousin Phoebe—"

"You said in there that you saw her at her aunt's?"

The boy nodded. "Coming out the door looking as if she carried the weight of the world on her shoulders, though what she could've been doing there I haven't any idea. Despises the besom as much as the rest of us do. More perhaps, and with even better reason."

Seven

"Dear lord in heaven, what now?"

Phoebe whirled at the pounding on the front door, jabbing herself on the holly sprig she'd been attempting to tuck in the garland bound to the oak banister with red ribbon. Fortunately her hands were so cold she felt almost nothing.

Perhaps decorating for the season was an art one needed to learn at one's mother's knee? Certainly twenty-six didn't seem the age to begin.

She gave her assaulted thumb a quick pinch and wiped the bead of bright blood on her apron leaving a scarlet smear, descended the worn steps and opened the door.

A burly stranger stood planted on the stoop, cap in hand, breath clouding the early morning air. Behind him on the track were four wagons pulled by mules, their long shadows like patchwork against the snow.

"Yes?" she said, shivering at the blast of frigid air. "Are you lost?"

"This be Underhill Farm?"

She nodded. "Yes, but—"

"And you be Miss Phoebe Parmenter, what owns the place?"

Again she nodded. Behind her the parlor door opened and closed. Rapid footsteps tapped across the bare floor. Mabel's muffled squeal of delight, the sound of more steps on the stairs, told their own tale. The entire family was gathering.

"Good enough, then." The carter turned, signaling the others with a wave. "This be it," he shouted, turned back to Phoebe.

"They said as how you'd look more like a servant than a lady, so I guess all's right and tight. Where d'you want us to put it?"

"Put it? Put what?"

"Coal. Sea coal," he chuckled at her puzzled look. "Best quality. Enough to heat Prinny's Carlton House, with more'n a bit left over for his Brighton digs."

"But I haven't ordered any coal." She shook off Mabel's clutching hands. "This must be intended for Penwillow."

"No, it's for us," Mabel caroled joyfully, dancing on the tips of her toes to peek over Phoebe's shoulder. "Look at it all! Oh, God bless his lordship!"

"Who ordered this?" Phoebe asked, frowning.

"Like the little lady says, the earl sent a messenger yesterday with payment in full. A winter's supply, he said, for a place old as the hills and twice as hard to heat."

"I'd hoped and prayed, but I never really believed—take it around back and knock on the door," Mabel gushed, thrusting herself in front of Phoebe, eyes sparkling. "Cook'll show you where the chute is. Around that way. What bliss! We'll be warm all winter, Phoebe! Can you believe it? Warm! Not a chilblain or ague among us, and no need to go foraging in the woods for branches and twigs ever again."

"Mabel, hush." Phoebe turned back to the carter, paling. "Sir, please wait, if you would. No, don't take the wagons around back. You may see Mrs. Short about some cider, but that's all. Our larder doesn't run to entertaining guests."

Phoebe shut the door in the man's face. Then she took a deep breath, whirled on her stepmother, grasped the pretty little blond woman's arm and hustled her into the parlor, ignoring Pru and Prissy at the bottom of the stairs. She wanted to scream. Instead, her throat was so tightly constricted she couldn't even swallow.

Mabel's mutinous eyes met hers glare for glare.

"Precisely what is all this about?" Phoebe demanded in a low, shaking tone.

Behind them the parlor door opened and the girls slipped in.

"Being comfortable for once in our lives," Mabel snapped. "I don't see how you can have the least objection to that!"

"And just what gave you the idea we aren't comfortable?"

"It's freezing in here. It's always freezing everywhere in this dreadful house. I'm sick unto death of being forever imprisoned in my bedchamber because it's one of the few rooms small enough to heat properly with a wood fire."

"I've made it as pleasant for you as I can."

"With lengths of fabric no one else wants? You expect me to grovel in gratitude for that? And I'm sick unto death of being forever overburdened with shawls, and forced to wear heavy, ugly gowns, and mitts to keep my hands warm. I want to wear what I will whenever I wish."

"But we haven't the funds for that. You know we haven't."

"And why don't we, I'd like to know? Look at me! No, don't turn away—look at me! For pity's sake, look at yourself." Mabel gestured at Phoebe's old brown stuff gown, her gray apron—more suited to the doyenne of a charitable institution than a wealthy heiress. "Have you no pride?" she implored. "No pride at all?"

"This gown is warm, and it's comfortable, and it's perfectly suited to chores about the house," Phoebe protested. "Surely you don't expect me to squander what few shillings we have on silks and muslins? Why, we'd catch our deaths!"

"Don't I just! Silks and muslins wouldn't be amiss, you know. I'm not doing chores, and look at me! I want to catch myself a wealthy, biddable husband while I'm still young enough and pretty enough to turn the trick. I'll never manage it garbed like this."

Phoebe sighed. Mabel's deep blue wool dated from her marriage sixteen years before. She'd grown a bit plumper, but raising the waist and adding an insert to expand the bodice and a flounce to lengthen the skirt had brought the thing more or less into style two winters ago. And, yellowed though it was, there was a froth of lace at the neck and another at the cuffs. At a distance, and festooned with shawls, it was presentable enough.

"You've always loved that gown," Phoebe protested mildly.

"And that's precisely my point: I've *always* loved it. Forever! Well, I don't love it anymore. I despise it! I want to be stylish again. Heaven knows I've earned the right, given what I endured at your father's hands. And now?" Mabel thrust out her quivering lower lip. "Now you're behaving just as he did!"

Behind them, the girls gasped.

Phoebe watched as facile tears welled in her young stepmother's eyes, trembled on the brink of fluttering lids, then spilled over.

"I believe you put your father up to writing that will," Mabel quavered. "No gentleman would ever be so lost to honor as to leave his wife and daughters destitute!"

"If you truly believe that," Phoebe countered hollowly after shushing the girls' protests, "then there's nothing I can say or do to persuade you otherwise."

"And look at this room! Cousin Philip's right: It's tawdry, positively tawdry. Shabby-genteel of the worst sort. Stained walls. Buckled floor. Dingy everything. Why, the entire house is a tomb! And it smells of mold and must. I hate it!"

Phoebe's eyes skimmed the threadbare fabrics on chairs and settees, the worn carpet with its backing exposed in so many places there was no way to hide them all, the tables with their scars and nicks, the patches around the windows where rain had seeped through the glazing. Perhaps it had been bright and attractive once. Now? It was like her cracked boots, marginally serviceable and infinitely commonplace, the scene of so many moments of terror and anguish and pain that, if truth were told, she hated it as well.

"It's not very pretty," she admitted grudgingly.

"Pretty? It's despicable to be forced to exist in such squalor! There's nothing one can do that could set this place to rights short of total redecorating, complete with a master hand from London—or Pilchester at the very least—to ensure it's not botched."

"That's out of the question, now or ever," Phoebe sighed. "You keep forgetting it's Mr. Hatch controls the purse strings until I have a son who reaches his majority, and then it'll be that son who controls everything, not you or I."

"Well, even so, making the pathetic attempt you have is worse than leaving things as they were," Mabel carped, "for it emphasizes every fault; besides which, it's obviously the stop-gap of someone desperate enough to try anything, but unwilling to expend so much as a farthing to achieve a pleasing effect. You may not know how a gentleman's house should be, but I do. When I was at school, I visited in some of the most elegant—"

"Yes, Mama," Pru snapped, "we know all about the visits you made when you were in school, much good they ever did you."

"Hush, Pru."

Phoebe's eyes sought the lengths of striped green damask she'd tacked around the windows only two days before. Dispassionately she noted every flaw and discoloration in the old fabric. Then Mabel had been full of enthusiasm, directing the operation from her place by the fire. When, as the final easily achieved touch, they'd taken Portius Parmenter's portrait down from above the mantel yesterday after their guests departed, they'd let out a very small cheer, not caring in the least that after twenty years the walls had darkened around the painting, leaving an accusing lighter patch the color of a toadstool. The crude watercolor Phoebe had tacked in its place only emphasized the parlor's dilapidated condition the more.

Then, guiltily, her gaze shifted to the girls, clinging together by the door. Their clothes were a hodgepodge of her own mother's, cut down and pieced without regard to anything but serviceability. No right-minded person would even've tossed them in a charity box.

"There's nothing I can do, Mabel," she protested mildly. "You know that. The way Papa left things, I've barely the wherewithal to feed and keep us. Some essentials must be purchased, no matter how frugally we live. You need only be patient. Things will be better eventually."

"You can accept his lordship's gift of coal," Mabel harped, turning her back on them. "Do that, and I'll consider forgiving you the rest."

"But Mama, there's nothing to forgive Phoebe for," Pru pleaded.

"Oh, yes there is," her mother returned darkly. "She's responsible for all of it. If she'd been a boy, none of this would've happened."

"Might as well blame us too, then. We're not boys either, and we could've been."

"Don't contradict your mother," Phoebe murmured distractedly.

"Why not?" Prissy flared. "She's being as silly as she can stare, and just about as unfair and selfish!"

Mabel whirled on them, dry-eyed. "I insist you accept that coal, Phoebe," she snapped. "Do it!"

"Don't you see I can't? To do so would make us his lordship's pensioners."

"You were quick enough to accept those ducks."

"There's a world of difference between a brace of ducks and enough coal to heat this house for an entire winter," Phoebe sighed. "The one merely required a moment's kindness. The other involves considerable expenditure."

"Lord Soames will never miss it. He's rich as Golden Ball."

Phoebe's eyes narrowed in suspicion. "You didn't ask his lordship to—"

"Of course not!" Mabel turned to the fire, shivering expressively as she held her hands to the feeble flame. "I merely hinted to Mr. Ware how uncomfortable we all are, and mentioned how you and the girls must forage for firewood. He was shocked. Prissy and Pru'll ruin their hands doing such rough work, and never find husbands. For you that matters not in the least, but for them it does."

"Then perhaps you should take their place!" Phoebe snapped, driven beyond patience. "Have you not the least pride?"

"You're a fine one to speak of pride!" Mabel screeched, whirling to face Phoebe. "Marrying Cousin Philip? I'd no idea you had so little discrimination. Any port in a storm—is that how it is? Or are you curious as to how things go on between men and women? Well, they go painfully and disgustingly, let me tell you! One has no right to refuse, so one simply endures and prays there won't be a repetition for a few hours. Philip will be no better," she prophesied bitterly on a half sob. "They're all the same."

For the first time when that particular subject was raised, Phoebe refrained from placing a comforting arm around her stepmother's shoulders. Instead she stayed where she was and waited, all expression wiped from her face. Mabel made a great show of sobbing into her shawl, of finding a handkerchief, of wiping her streaming eyes. Prissy and Pru slipped icy hands into Phoebe's equally cold ones, gripping tightly.

At last, when no one came to her rescue, Mabel gave a final sniff and turned.

"Then naturally Mr. Ware mentioned the problem to his lordship," she said, her head high, "and his lordship saw to it. Now, either you will go tell the carters to unload that coal, or I shall."

"No, Mabel, I shan't and neither shall you. I positively forbid it."

"But, it's *my* coal!"

"No, it's his lordship's coal, and always shall be."

For a miracle the girls held their peace, contenting themselves with signaling their displeasure with their mother and their support of Phoebe merely by staying close to the one and avoiding the other as Mabel stormed on.

In the end Phoebe sent the carters on their way, instructed Mabel to make do with staying in her bedchamber if she must, and sent the girls to forage for deadfall in Lord Soames's woods. Lessons, she told them, could wait. No, they couldn't have the use of one of the farm horses. Papa's edicts remained in effect. They didn't want Mr. Hatch to turn off old Tom, did they?

Then, with a sad smile for Mabel, who merely tossed her curls and turned her back, Phoebe returned to her efforts at decorating for Christmas.

The unpleasant little incident, while not precisely a quarrel, had come perilously close to one—the first she could remember between herself and her gentle stepmother. Given how her father had left things, the strain of managing to find food to put on the table and the wherewithal to run the house was telling on all of them.

Poor Mabel! She really couldn't be held to blame.

That they should tumble into disagreement barely over a week following Papa's death wasn't entirely surprising, Phoebe con-

ceded as she stuck yet another holly sprig in the banister garland.
The force that'd bound them in a seemingly indissoluble alliance
had vanished. Now the alliance itself appeared in jeopardy. She
could foresee a time when—wed to Philip Fordyce and with not
even her soul to call her own—their situation might become even
more intolerable than it had been when Papa lived, only it would
be she who assumed the role of heavy-handed villain.

The notion was too depressing to consider.

Happy Christmas, she thought bitterly. It seemed they'd never
know a joyous Yuletide season in this house, no matter how she
tried. Portius Parmenter poisoned everything, present or absent.
It was a lowering thought. Still, she had to try.

Peter Oakwood paused at the head of the little glen where
Alfie and the girls had hidden in wait only three nights before.

A smile quirked his lips as he continued to observe the slight,
dark-cloaked figure trudging along the lane below—Miss
Phoebe Parmenter, apparently heading for the village. Even at
this distance she was recognizable: a certain tilt to her head, an
unconscious grace to her carriage, an elegance despite her impossible clothing. She might stumble beneath the scrutiny of
censorious eyes. He'd seen that yesterday, what with first Mrs.
Trask and then Fordyce taking part in that awkward, tension-
filled gathering. But viewed like this, she was uncommon—
quite uncommon.

The low winter light slanted through the trees, causing her to
pass through bands of brilliant sunshine and deep shadow even
at the noon hour. The year would turn in a few days. Strange, to
realize the winter solstice was upon them. A witching time, his
old nurse had claimed. Odd things happened at the winter solstice. Uncanny things. Things that could happen at no other time
of the year. It had nothing to do with the new religion, and everything with the old.

He'd never quite stopped believing in her tales of frost fairies
and snow demons, and little people who lived beneath the hills.
Certainly there'd been moments these past days when he felt

trapped in some other-when and other-where having nothing to do with the customary existence of a staid English gentleman.

With a shiver that had less to do with the adequacy of his old greatcoat and shapeless heavy tweeds than his thoughts, Oakwood turned his attention back to Miss Parmenter, still trudging through the glen.

He'd been following her for some time, unwilling to startle the young woman and so put her on her guard. Oakwood had questions he wanted to ask the intriguing Miss Parmenter given the morning he'd just passed in Market Stoking and Pilchester. The trouble was, he wanted her totally disarmed when he posed those questions, not a rabbit warily eyeing the fox. The isolation of Soames's woods simply wouldn't do—not this close to the place where her father's body'd been found. The overtones of terror would be inescapable, no matter how carefully he phrased his questions.

Why? Because, however little he wanted to believe it, every indication now pointed to her as Portius Parmenter's killer. Lord knew she'd had motive. Opportunity? That, too. And from what he'd seen she would, in proper circumstances, have been strong enough to pull the thing off. And determined enough. A gallant little woman, Phoebe Parmenter. If only she'd trust him, once she confessed they'd claim accident and have done with the matter. Soames would agree nothing was to be gained by reopening the case as justice had been served, if in a round-about manner. Fordyce would be sent on his blackmailing way, Phoebe Parmenter set free to marry where she willed.

And then?

Oakwood ignored the uncomfortable question, watching as she dodged another drift stretching across her path, its shadow almost purple in the clear light. Even at this distance her careless misstep was obvious, her bending over—apparently to dig yet another clump of snow from inside her boot—a bit pathetic, not a word he would have generally associated with that courageous young woman, even given their extremely limited acquaintance. If she continued in this manner, her feet would be solid blocks of ice by the time she reached the village.

Boots slipping and sliding in ruts worn in the packed snow,

arms windmilling, now she was skidding across a patch so compacted it gleamed like ice, lurching into a tree and tumbling into another drift. Had he been thinking she possessed a certain untutored grace barely moments earlier? He must've been spinning air dreams. The poor creature was as clumsy as a walrus.

Oakwood frowned as she picked herself up once more, brushed the clinging snow from her cloak and tramped on, her steps dimpling the snow at the side of the narrow lane as she attempted to avoid the worst of the ruts. Was that a trace of a limp?

She stumbled again, this time apparently into a hidden pothole, and slammed to the ground, loose snow rising around her in a little cloud. Oakwood gave it a moment, then tore down the steep incline, gray coattails flapping about his legs, his heart pounding out of all proportion to the exercise involved as he twisted through the trees.

"Miss Parmenter!" he shouted hoarsely in the crystaline air. "Miss Parmenter, are you all right?"

But of course she wasn't! Had there ever been such a clodpole as he? Ladies didn't lie immobile in the snow for no reason at all. At least, Miss Parmenter wouldn't. She wasn't the sort.

He lurched across the lane, skidded to an awkward halt, and dropped to his knees on the crusted verge.

"Miss Parmenter?" he said, laying a concerned hand on her shoulder.

A rasping wheeze was her only response.

With infinite care, he lifted her foot from the pothole and gently probed her ankle through the cracked boot. She gave a protesting whimper, her eyes opening to peer muzzily at him over her shoulder.

"I've gone and done it now, haven't I?" she said.

"I'm afraid so."

"Yesterday wasn't enough for me. Oh, drat! You seem to be making quite a career of rescuing me from the consequences of my own folly, Mr. Oakwood."

"How's your vision, Miss Parmenter?" He held three fingers before her eyes.

"One, plus one, plus one equals three, but your head is haloed and there're fireflies dancing about, for all it isn't the season for them."

She laid her head down on the soft bank, her lids drifting closed.

"Here now, none of that!" Oakwood gently eased her over. Face pale. Lips barely parted, the faintest of fogs clouding the air between them. "How d'you feel—beyond your ankle, that is?"

"You're not supposed to notice I have any," she protested, eyes still closed. "The closest a gentleman should come to mentioning such inconveniences is 'appendage.' "

"Rather impractical, don't you think? Even a nose could be considered an appendage under certain conditions, and specificity is highly to be desired when one's speaking of injuries. Surely an ear could be, and there's nothing the least improper about an ear, now is there? Even to your puritanical mind?"

"I am not puritanical!"

"No? Mrs. Grundy appears to have you in her thrall at the moment, nevertheless," he grunted. "Here, let's have you up, and see how it goes."

Strong arm cradling her shoulders, he cautiously levered Phoebe Parmenter until she was sitting, head drooping against his chest. A strange sensation impeded his breathing—an unaccustomed, clutching sort of thing, though not the least unpleasant—as he smoothed a wandering tendril of hair from her eyes, then peered anxiously into their rich brown depths.

"Better?" Dear God—what was the matter with him? His voice had just cracked like that of an adolescent boy.

"A bit," she conceded "Rather half above par, if you want to know, for all I haven't taken a drop of ale, nor ever do."

"Champagne should be your tipple," he commented absently, still puzzled by his reaction to those amazing brown eyes and their long, feathered lashes.

"Instead of which, it's generally cider pressed from the worst of the windfalls in the orchard," she chuckled dismissively. "Champagne? Well, at least they begin with the same letter."

"You've never tasted it?"

"At Underhill?" Her laugh was unforced. "Surely you jest, sir! That, or you've learned less of my father in the time you've been here than I'd expect, given your apparent acumen. Watered claret on those occasions he considered worthy of riotous celebration. Those were few and far between, believe me, and generally had to do with cheating some poor soul of what was rightly owed him. Beyond that? Cider on the good days, water on the bad. Most days were bad. Much healthier all told, I suppose."

"I see. Let's get you on your feet. I'm permitted to acknowledge you have feet?"

"If you must."

With the emotional conviction he was dealing with rarest French porcelain and the logical certainty he was dealing with sturdiest English pottery, Oakwood slipped his other arm beneath her knees and stood, then carefully set her on her feet.

"How's that?"

She shook her head to clear it, blinked, stared about her. "How long was I down?" she asked.

"Barely half a minute, if that."

"You were amazingly quick to come to my rescue."

He let the accusing words hang in the air like so many demons come to plague him. There truly was no credible response. After all his care, she'd caught him out as easily as she breathed.

"Indeed," she continued, "you seem to spend considerable time lurking about. What are you, Mr. Oakwood? And why are you here? Chedleigh Minor's not your customary sort of haunt— on that I'd wager my last shilling, and as I've very few at my disposal, and multiple uses for each, you may be sure I'm convinced I'd win the wager."

"The country, you mean?" He tried a chuckle, found it damnably difficult to meet those assessing, candid brown eyes with equal candor. "It's not been my favorite place in the past, I'll admit."

"Then what are you doing here?"

"Down on my luck," he said simply.

For once his voice had the ring of conviction, perhaps because it was the absolute truth as far as it went. He *was* down on his luck, what with his father remarrying and toddling off to God only knew where on his wedding journey, and Serena doing the same with Macy, and nobody much wanting him about during the holidays with the exception of good old Soames. He'd been, if truth were told, feeling abysmally sorry for himself just prior to haring off to the castle. That he'd given Jeanine Delisle her *congé* the day before his departure had only compounded matters.

Perhaps that was all that'd been the matter with him moments ago.

"Told you that before, I believe," he said with a genuine twinkle.

"There's down on one's luck, and then there's down on one's luck," Miss Parmenter returned tartly.

Dear lord, but she sounded just like Pommie Chumme, Serena's old governess, in one of her moods!

"Come now, let's try that ankle, see how it does," he said. Anything for a distraction. "Lean on my arm and take a step or two."

The results were mixed—once Phoebe Parmenter favored him with a hard look.

She could hobble, but barely, lower lip clenched between firm white teeth, her grip almost painful even through three layers of heavy fabric. Finally, with a grunt of disgust, Oakwood swung her up in his arms.

"Here now—what d'you think you're doing?" she gasped as he plunged between the trees.

"Taking you to Soames's cottage so I can see to you properly."

"But you can't do that! We'd both be compromised!"

Oakwood's delighted guffaw rang through the woods. The unlikelihood of some tonnish miss protesting at being found in a compromising situation with the elevated and wealthy Marquess of Stovall, heir to the Duke of Hampton, was so great as to be nonexistent. Rather, he'd had to watch his every step in Town to avoid entrapment. The change was delightfully refreshing, her concern for him even more so.

"My dear girl, put your arms around my neck so you won't jounce," he grinned. "We'll have you put to rights in no time."

Doing something without fearing the consequences was a rare and exhilarating experience. He was determined to enjoy the situation to the hilt. "Must be damnably uncomfortable for your, er, appendage."

Soames's gamekeeper's cottage was becoming as busy as the Woolwich docks, Oakwood decided as he kicked the door open and strode across the hard dirt floor—not that he had much personal acquaintance with the docks, but one heard tales.

He deposited Miss Parmenter on the settle by the chimney, glanced about.

The Woolwich docks?

The cottage was becoming a regular Hyde Park. People forever coming and going, and not too careful how they left things—especially he, who was the prime culprit.

Harsh winter light streamed through the windows, tangling in the clutter: dirty dishes on the table, a schoolboy copy of Cicero's letters on the unmade bed, shirts and neckcloths to be carted to the castle for laundering—something he'd intended to see to later that day. And dust everywhere, and orange cat hairs despite Pru's efforts the night before. He'd intended to see to those too, later. He'd intended to see to everything later, come to that, if he felt up to it after his morning's excursion. Thank heavens the green wool cloak he'd acquired in Pilchester was wrapped in brown paper and securely tied with string—an anonymous parcel masked by the rest of the jumble.

"Later" had an uncomfortable habit of catching one unprepared, he decided ruefully, arriving either too soon or too tardily no matter what the occasion. It was a damnable nuisance—being forced to see to himself. He needed a valet. More specifically, he needed Burke. Unfortunately, a superior London valet was a luxury to which the shallow pockets of an itinerant landscaper and expert in game management would never extend. Otherwise he'd've summoned the man from his holiday, given him another twice as long and well-paid later.

"Sorry about the cold, Miss Parmenter—I've been gone most

of the morning. About the mess, too." He pulled over a rickety stool, gave it a cursory swipe with his glove, and propped the young woman's abused foot on it. "I'm not much of a housekeeper, I'm afraid."

"Then you should hire one of the women from the village." Phoebe Parmenter glanced about her, nose wrinkling. "Times are hard, and it can't be pleasant living in these conditions."

"Ah, but I haven't the funds for such a luxury, you see. How's the head?" He strode over to the door, pulled it shut and hammered the latch in place. "Still dizzy?"

"Much better, thank you. My understanding is that Lord Soames is a distinctly liberal employer."

"Oh, he's generous enough."

"Then you should be able to afford help of some sort, even if not daily."

"Want the post? A shilling a week and all you can eat. Or one of your sisters, perhaps? The little one with her plaits forever in a tangle. She seems an energetic sort, and wants feeding up."

"Goodness, no! That would be totally improper, but you should do something. This has the air of a gentleman's bedchamber before his valet sets it to rights."

Oakwood turned, brows rising in amusement. Pretty little Miss Parmenter was blushing again, by damn! And he'd thought that a lost art beyond his eldest sister. "And how would you know about such things?" he inquired, hazel eyes dancing.

"Those of us who have to see to ourselves are a bit more careful than you appear to be." Phoebe Parmenter's mild protest was accompanied by the slightest answering twinkle at the back of her deep brown eyes. "Only someone accustomed to having servants about would permit things to get in such turmoil. Who are you, really?"

"Peter Oakwood. Really. I've told you that before. Not very organized, that's all. Never have been. Bane of my mother's existence, if you must know, and the despair of my father's. Besides, it's not very kind of you to comment on my slovenliness."

Surprised to find himself flushing in turn at her skeptical expression, Oakwood glanced about him. He'd never considered how the place might look to a lady when he'd decided to carry Miss Parmenter there rather than the slightly longer distance to the village. For that matter, he'd never considered, when he hared off to Market Stoking and then Pilchester once the sun was up, that he might be returning with a guest. At the time, getting an early start on his inquiries had seemed far more important than attending to dirty crockery and soiled linen.

And most rewarding those inquiries had proved. Parmenter had indeed kept a love nest of sorts in Market Stoking, though sty might be the more appropriate term.

Lizzie Blunt had been delighted to reveal every insalubrious scrap she knew about the wealthy farmer, and there'd been more than a few scraps. Some hadn't been scraps at all. His association with Hezekiah Hatch, for instance, was reputed to've led to the beggaring of more than one honest landowner. Legal documents disappeared and reappeared with distressing regularity when the good solicitor was involved. Upon their reappearance details had invariably changed in favor of Underhill's master, though nothing could be proved. Signatures, seals, attestations—all were as before.

There'd been more. Considerably more. As in Chedleigh Minor, no one in Market Stoking had mourned Parmenter's passing with the possible exception of Hatch, and even he'd been heard to express total lack of surprise.

And Jonas Whale in Pilchester? Now *that* had been an interesting half hour. Fordyce'd come asking questions right after Parmenter's death. Whale admitted to telling the man he'd spied Phoebe Parmenter tearing through Soames's woods not ten minutes after his departure from Underhill.

That information stuck in Oakwood's craw. Why couldn't Miss Parmenter've remained at home? Why, heaven help her, couldn't she've used the road? Or, been deeper in the woods where no one would've spotted her? He was going to have to ask her about it, and he didn't look forward to the exercise.

As for his boon companion of the night before, Fordyce's reputation in the neighborhood equaled Parmenter's in type if not in detail. Parmenter had at least paid his bills, if ill-naturedly and long past their time. The rumors of Fordyce's betrothal to the

Underhill heiress had tongues flapping and brows soaring all over the countryside. Betty Klegg wasn't the only bucolic beauty who'd met her downfall at his hands.

Oakwood hung his cap and scarf on the peg by the door, cleared his throat with an unaccustomed touch of abashment, turned to face the open gaze meeting his.

"I, ah, would you care for tea? There's some about the place somewhere."

"Up there, I believe." Phoebe Parmenter pointed to the mantel. "In that canister to the right of what appears to be a bird's nest just beyond the candle in front of the pot. I seem to recognize the dents. How did you come by it? The canister, not the nest."

"It was here," he shrugged dismissively, dismayed by her sharp perception.

Was she about to identify every bent spoon and scrap of chipped crockery as more properly belonging at Underhill? He wouldn't put it past her. What he'd do then he hadn't the slightest notion. Playing Bow Street Runner was definitely not an art at which he was excelling, for all his earlier successes.

"Here, let me make up the fire," he said, desperate for any activity that might distract her and obviate the need to meet those deep brown pools. "You're shivering. Then we'll see to your, ah, injury."

"Any number of women in the village would be glad of work," she insisted, returning to the original subject much to his relief. "I know gentlemen don't like to be nattered at, but I do think—"

He interrupted her by stirring the fire, clattering things about as he added some wood, then lifted the lid from the kettle of water he'd left in the ashes against his return. Still steaming slightly in the chill room, thank heavens. He moved it closer to the fire, hands lingering by the cheering warmth.

"You're quite the managing female, apparently," he commented when satisfied he'd interrupted her juggernaut, sending a quick glance over his shoulder.

"Not generally speaking, but certainly you require some assistance if you're not to attract every mouse and rat within miles."

"Have done." He dumped a handful of leaves in the pot.

"Regulating my household, paltry and disorganized though it may be, isn't your responsibility. Besides, there's a cat about the place somewhere."

"Yes, there is. Under your bed, in fact." She leaned forward, squinting. "Good heavens—is that Tabitha?"

"Tabitha?" Oakwood set the pot on the table, took a single step and swept the Cicero under the tumbled covers before she could spot that as well, then tugged them over his parcel. "I've no idea. Who's Tabitha?"

"One of our more approachable stable cats." The young woman extended her hand. "Puss-puss," she cajoled, wiggling her fingers. "Tabitha, come here."

The cat eased from beneath the bed with a flick of its tail, minced across the filthy floor and leaped into Phoebe's lap, purr loud in the sudden silence.

"It *is* Tabitha," she said, absently stroking the cat as she stared reprovingly at her disorganized host. "How does she come to be here?"

"Simply turned up. Cats wander, from what I've heard."

"They do indeed, but they rarely set up housekeeping so far from home when close to their time. In case you haven't noticed, Tabitha's expecting a litter."

Oakwood turned on his guest with a broad grin. Phoebe Parmenter's lack of coy euphemisms concerning earthier topics was as refreshing as her sisters'. "So that's why that pernicious feline's so fat," he chuckled, "and eating me out of house and home."

"Well, she is rather cumbersome for hunting at the moment, though she's generally our most skilled mouser. How did you come by her?"

"One might almost think," he continued absently, pouring some water from the ewer by the chimney into a basin, and ignoring Phoebe's uncomfortable question as he seized a rag from the table, "that she'd been foisted on me so others might not have to see to her care and feeding."

"But who would've done such a thing?"

"Who, indeed! Here, let's have a look at that ankle." Oakwood lifted her booted foot, and seating himself on the stool before her, gently laid the foot on his knees. "I can't promise you this won't hurt," he cautioned, "but you do understand it must be seen to? I'm not taking liberties—truly!"

"Heavens, there's no need to treat me as if I were some tonnish London miss with more sensibility than sense. Of course it must be seen to, and I'm perfectly aware doing so will hurt. Such examinations generally do, if past experience is anything to judge by."

"You've twisted it before?"

"So many times," she grinned weakly, "that Prissy claims that foot's already in the grave. Actually, I've become expert at binding it myself. Beyond the first time, Papa didn't hold with wasting money on the apothecary. Indeed, our still room puts his shop to shame. There's nothing we can't cure at Underhill if it's to be cured at all."

"I see. And how did you come to twist it so often?"

"Papa insisted I was clumsy, just like my mother. I suppose I am."

"How kind of him."

Oakwood thought of Phoebe's alternating turns of grace and awkwardness—stemming as much from fits of absent-mindedness as any other cause, he was certain—as he studied the young woman in front of him. He remembered the results of his eldest sister being constantly informed she was hopelessly awkward by their mother, that she was naught but a trial and an inconvenience. Youth and young womanhood hadn't been a happy time for Serena. Clearly it hadn't been any better for Phoebe Parmenter. Worse, probably. At least Serena had never been beaten, whatever else she'd had to suffer.

"I'll be as gentle as I can," he said, empathy glowing in his eyes, and perhaps a touch of something more.

"I'm certain you will." Phoebe dropped her gaze, flushing furiously once again.

For some reason, Oakwood's complexion took on a similarly ruddy hue.

Hands the slightest bit unsteady, he undid the fastenings, careful not to jerk the abused appendage, and doing his best to ignore the oft-mended coarse stocking as he slipped it from the elegantly-shaped, slender foot. Then he probed the slightly swollen ankle, frowning in concentration as he noted a darkening patch just below the bone.

"Does it hurt here? Or here?" A sharp flinch gave him his answer. "Try pointing your toes. All right, now turn your foot side to side. Now up and down. Good—nothing seems to be broken."

"I could've told you that," Phoebe snapped in obvious embarrassment.

"Then why didn't you?"

"You seemed intent on playing knight-errant. Besides, you weren't paying the least mind to anything I said. I've found that's often the way once a gentleman seizes on a notion—especially a harebrained one."

"But then I'm no gentleman. You'd've been safe insisting," Oakwood said with a naughty-boy grin. "Are you sure you didn't secretly enjoy being carried off like some fine lady in one of those romances your stepmother and Prissy devour so avidly?"

"How d'you know about that?"

"One has only to listen to their diction," he grinned, thinking quickly. "Now, let's see about binding this, and then I'll make us some tea. Water should be hot enough."

Skillfully he tore the rag into narrow strips, moistened them, began wrapping the bandages securely around her foot and ankle.

"The water will keep it cool for a bit, help prevent more swelling," he said. "I'll change the bandages for dry ones just before we put the boot back on and leave. Must get you warm first. You're still shivering like a doe in a gunsight. What was your purpose in going to the village?"

"I'd intended to purchase some trinkets for Mabel and the girls. They've never had a real Christmas."

"Well, you'll have to give that over." He secured the end of the last strip beneath a thick spot. "No way you can go to the village now."

"Oh, but I must!"

Eyes that hadn't wavered during his ministrations were suffused with pain. The gently curved lower lip trembled. Damn, but women were impossible!

"My dear girl, think! You've injured your ankle, and will only make things worse if you persist—"

"It's fine, I know it is! See?"

Phoebe set the cat on the floor, rose, took first one hesitant step, then another, as Oakwood watched her through narrowed eyes. She wavered, blanching, gripped her lip between even white teeth and hobbled on determinedly.

"Not doing very well, are you?"

"I stepped on an uneven spot."

"And I suppose there're no uneven spots in the lane?"

"I'll do," she insisted. "I must. It lacks but three days 'til Christmas, and what with one thing and another I've nothing for Mabel or the girls."

"No, you won't do in the least. Even if you would, I won't permit it."

Oakwood scooped her up, staring into those eyes he'd been so reluctant to meet only moments before. They were the slightest bit questioning, a sudden shyness clouding them. Well, he didn't feel precisely himself at the moment either. This slip of a woman had a way of destroying his equanimity that was disturbing in the extreme.

With the slightest of shudders, he shoved the settle closer to the fire with his knee and reluctantly plunked her down.

"Stay there," he ordered brusquely. "You're frozen to the bone. I'll prepare our tea. Then, when you've warmed up a bit, I'll saddle Bacchus and take you to the village. How many places do you need to go?"

"There's no need for you to—"

"Hush! You'll do as I say. Sorry I can't offer you a curricle and pair, but there it is—I've only the one horse, and not a carriage to my name at the moment. We'll simply have to make do."

Eight

Make do they did, to Phoebe's consternation and Oakwood's increasing enjoyment. If the sight of Soames's newest hireling trotting into the village with the recently bereaved heiress perched snugly before him raised brows, so be it. High time someone took a hand in her life. Martyrdom was damnably uncomfortable for everyone involved, not just the martyr.

And it was just as he'd hoped and Miss Parmenter'd feared. Biddies stopped in their tracks, eyes darting in their direction. Curtains trembled at cottage windows. And, well down the way, wasn't that Ware, in Chedleigh Minor on heaven knew what errand? That, if nothing else, would put the cat among the pigeons. The more chaos he engendered, the more likely this impossible situation would be resolved in a manner to his liking. Precisely what that manner might be, however, he took no time to consider.

Oakwood lifted Phoebe Parmenter from the saddle and carried her into the first of the shops to the sharp clang of its brass bell, guarding her ankle and overriding her protests with first a frown and then a good-natured chuckle.

Her delight at how far her few shillings stretched, purchasing three times what she'd expected, pleased him even more. Mitty Potts, one of a pair of antiquated sisters who kept The Ladies' Emporium and Furnishings Bazaar—certainly far too fine a name for the front room they'd turned into a warren offering sundries and lady's trimmings—scurried at his bidding, pocketing the pound he slipped her and nodding her understanding that it was to extend Phoebe's mite.

Hair ribbons and a volume of essays for Pru, a small looking glass and some silk flowers for Prissy, a flask of inexpensive scent and lace mitts for Mabel took an eternity and much consultation to select. More time was expended wrapping them in brown paper and tying the parcels together with string. Oakwood shook his head when Miss Potts offered him change.

"Keep it on account for her," he murmured, "against the next time she comes shopping for herself or her family."

"You're a saint, no matter how it is you earn your keep, soiled hands or no, and no matter what the vicar hints about your parentage," Mitty Potts returned in a pleased whisper as Phoebe limped from bin to table to rack, exclaiming over the oddments they contained. "High born is as high born does. Aren't many like Lord Soames. Now, if you could just be doing something to solve poor Miss Parmenter's more serious problems, we'd be that delighted here in the village."

"I'm trying. On my honor, I'm trying my very best."

"Try a little harder, then. We're that fond of her in Chedleigh Minor. Always managed to send a basket to them as was ailing or in trouble, even if she couldn't take it herself what with that horrible man watching her like a hawk to make sure nothing left his larder but it went in his own belly, and keeping her to the place as if it were a jail and he the chief turnkey."

It was just as Mitty Potts was passing Phoebe's parcels to Oakwood and an oblivious Phoebe was fingering a figured woolen shawl of rich royal blue that the shop door crashed open, its unlovely bell clanging like a blacksmith's hammer. Clarence Dorning stalked through, a dandified avenging prophet with fire in his eye, brimstone in his voice, and snow crusting his boots. Miss Potts drew against the shelved wall as Oakwood sent her a wink and a signal to remain silent. Phoebe whirled, coloring furiously.

"What," Dorning bristled, stumbling into a bin of bolt ends and lace scraps in his haste, and grabbing the table that served as counter to keep his balance, "d'you think you're doing, Oakwood, compromising a young woman who already has a deal to answer for? Before the entire village, no less!"

"That what I'm doing? Goodness! How shocking!"

Oakwood frowned Phoebe down as Sarah Potts came bustling through the curtains dividing the little shop from the rest of the cottage, attracted by the commotion. The future duke turned, massive body following massive head, as if he were leading the figure in an elegant dance, Phoebe's parcels dangling from his hand.

"And here I thought I was merely assisting a young lady with her Christmas purchases," he said with a air of genuine puzzlement.

"A likely tale!"

"Precisely what Mr. Oakwood's been doing, as you can see from that bundle he's carrying," Mitty said. Then she leaned closer to Sarah and continued in a whisper, "And that liberal with it as well. On account." She showed her sister the remaining crowns and shillings in her pocket, nodded in satisfaction at Oakwood. "Fine man, this one is," she said more loudly, turning to the vicar, "not like that horror Miss Parmenter's about to tie herself to, so you'd best contain yourself, Mr. Dorning."

"And how many shillings did he slip you to say those kind words?" Dorning sneered.

"Found Miss Parmenter injured in the lane," Oakwood explained at the vicar's furious look. "Twisted her ankle in a hole, and was more there than here from knocking her head against a stump when she fell. Played the good Samaritan. Surely you approve, knowing your Bible as you do?"

"Bible's for church, not for providing excuses for riotous living."

"Riotous living? *Here?* You're all about in your head. Miss Parmenter could've caught her death lying in the snow. Shocking, the state of the lanes hereabout. I merely brought her into the village to complete her errands, as she insisted she'd continue no matter what her condition."

"Don't believe a word of it! Trying to get on her soft side, are you?" Dorning drew himself up to his full height, which was minimal, and thrust out his chest, also minimal. "Like the idea of all those acres, and Parmenter's fat coffers? Won't work. She's already betrothed."

"My, how anxious you are to defend Fordyce's preserve."

"Please, Mr. Oakwood," Phoebe broke in, tugging on his sleeve while Mitty and Sarah Potts eased forward, eyes flashing. "I'll not be having you make a scandal of me in the village. You may leave whenever you wish. I can't! Given I must remain here—"

"Hush! No one's making a scandal of anyone, unless it's your precious vicar making a scandal of himself."

"Too right, too right," Mitty Potts threw in, incensed.

" *'Honi soit qui mal y pense,'* " Sarah added indignantly, dredging up the famous motto of the Order of the Garter from heaven knew what source, but pronouncing it so poorly, and on a questioning note—"Honey swats key mole! Why pence?"— that it took Oakwood a moment to recognize the thing and Dorning comprehended the reference not at all, which was perhaps as well.

"Besides which," Oakwood continued, stifling a chuckle and turning on the vicar with a vague air of menace, "I have it on the best authority nothing's official between Miss Parmenter and Mr. Fordyce."

"Please, Mr. Oakwood! Have done!" Phoebe hissed. "And you two, as well," she implored, turning to the sisters. "I'm already in the suds to my neck as it is. I'll thank you not to thrust me deeper."

"Stumbling out of 'em, more like," Mitty said with a wise look at Oakwood, "for all you've no notion of it as yet."

"And whose authority might that be?" Dorning jeered, ignoring both the young woman whose cause he was supposedly championing and the little shopkeepers.

"Why, Miss Parmenter's," Oakwood said, in his turn disregarding Phoebe's increasingly desperate tugs on his sleeve and *sotto voce* pleas. "And Lord Soames's, of course. Banns haven't been read yet—not that I've heard."

"Oh, dear heaven help me!" Phoebe murmured, casting her eyes to the ceiling.

"Poaching, that's what you are!" Dorning ranted on. "Probably what you intended to begin with, coming here at such a

time. Marquess of Stovall let you know of the opportunity? Or
even the old duke? Send you here to line your pockets? Relieve
themselves of the charge of you? Wouldn't put it past them!
Thorough blackguard, Stovall. Always was. Entire family's off-
center, starting with the duke. I'll wager anything you wish his
current wife was his convenient for years! I'd win, too. And poor
Mr. Parmenter barely cold in his grave."

"In this weather? Your poor Mr. Parmenter's probably hard as
iron by now," Oakwood snapped, "and not likely to thaw 'til
spring—if then, given the tales I've heard about him. Don't be
more of an idiot than you can possibly help, Dorning."

Phoebe's eyes flew desperately from Soames's increasingly
arrogant and incensed hireling to the fulminating vicar as the
shopkeepers leaned over the table, the better to hear every detail.

"Serve you right if Fordyce gives you a whipping," Dorning
railed.

"What? Not call me out in defense of his lady-love? Or is the
man a lily-livered poltroon in addition to all else?"

"Mr. Fordyce? A gentleman of the highest order? Call out a
baseborn servant?" Dorning snorted. "You've delusions of gran-
deur!

"This fellow's not the thing, you know," he continued, turning
on Phoebe with the self-importance of one about to impart delightfully disastrous news, "whatever you may think. Not at all
the thing! His, ah, well, his father and his mother, well—"

"They anticipated their vows?"

"Never even made 'em," Dorning proclaimed, glaring at Oakwood as if to dare him to offer contradiction. "I have *that* on the
very highest authority—Lord Soames himself, whom this fellow
is so quick to quote—so you can see you've no business with
him when you're already betrothed to Mr. Fordyce, who's a gentleman of the ton and far more than you deserve. Should've
thought you'd hold yourself in higher respect."

Dorning had the grace to color at Oakwood's derisive snort.

"Sometimes," Phoebe muttered, "I have high doubts about
your antecedents!"

"Hush!" Oakwood murmured too low for any but Phoebe to hear.

"As for any injury to Miss Parmenter, I should've been summoned," Dorning pressed on. "I'm the vicar, after all. Better yet, being you weren't that far from the village, you should've sent for Mrs. Trask. Most fitting one to see to her—her own aunt. Interference on the part of a menial is what I neither can nor will accept. Remember the place God assigned you, and keep to it."

Hard on these words the door crashed open once more. Emma Trask stormed the threshold, slamming the door so forcefully the bell continued its jangling for some moments.

"Couldn't believe it when Granny Mitchell came bearing me tales of what she'd seen," she panted as she leaned against the table-*cum*-counter to catch her breath, then whirled on Phoebe. "Told her it couldn't be. Told her it was her eyes going from bad to worse. Told her you couldn't be so lost to all propriety.

"Well, I was wrong, and I admit it! Just what d'you think you're doing, missy, gallivanting about the village with one who's no better than he should be? The very least you could've done was ask Cobber's escort, given he's already made it known he—"

"I believe I shall faint," Phoebe murmured too low for any but Oakwood to hear as her aunt spewed fury, indignation and reproach. "Oh, what a muddle!"

"Might be the best notion," Oakwood agreed, turning his back on the others. "Don't worry—I'll catch you."

"Don't be more of a nodcock than you can help!" Phoebe snapped at full voice.

"Nodcock?" Emma Trask's face, beet-hued from ire and cold, turned a brilliant purple. "Just who d'you think you're calling 'nodcock', missy, I'd like to know?"

Phoebe cast Oakwood a despairing glance. Then, as Nick Gusset barreled through the door roaring recriminations at Phoebe's ignoring Alfie's prior claims on her company, the beleaguered young woman gave a soft mewling cry, took a single step forward, hand rising to forehead in the traditional manner of young ladies too put upon to tarry among the sentient, and threw herself into Oakwood's waiting arms.

"Didn't have to do it so vigorously," he murmured, scooping her up. "And stop giggling or I'll laugh, and then we'll truly be in the briars.

"Now see what you've gone and done!" he continued so all could hear, voice dripping disgust. "I'm taking Miss Parmenter to the George, where I hope she may recover her spirits and her strength following the unwarranted importunings of those who should have her best interests at heart—which not a one of you have with the exception of these kind ladies, having more concern for your hides than hers."

"For God and Saint George," Mitty Potts caroled in delight.

"And the good old king into the bargain, God keep him," Sarah chimed in.

The soft-spoken hireling they'd all regarded as a nonentity in their small world met the furious glares of vicar, aunt and step-uncle with one equally furious.

"I shouldn't, if I were you," he growled as Dorning, Emma Trask and Nick Gusset made to bar his way, protesting the impropriety of his plans. "I really shouldn't, an' you value your health. And if you make to follow us? Well, I shan't be responsible for my actions, which is another matter you might consider. I've seen entirely too much of the lot of you, and so has Miss Parmenter.

"Good day, ladies," he said, turning to the Potts sisters. "My thanks for your assistance, and keep you well. I'll be returning later." He gave a quick nod at the soft, deep-fringed woolen shawl of royal blue draped on one of the display tables.

On those words Oakwood was through the door and striding down the village high street, the snow squeaking under his boots, Phoebe's parcels dangling from his hand, the ghost of a saucy schoolboy's whistle streaming from his pursed lips on clouds of warm breath.

"Put me down!" Phoebe hissed, peeping at him from beneath lowered lids.

"And spoil the greatest sport this place's seen in many a year?

Not likely. Besides, if I put you down they'd know that faint was a sham, and then you'd truly be for it. Now hush, my dear. We're almost there. Keep still until we're in a private parlor, assuming the place boasts one."

"Yes, of course it does. And I'm not—"

"Hush, I tell you! Leave all to me."

And then they were at the George's door, and Oakwood was kicking it without regard to who might be within or what they might think of his assault or the damage it might do.

"The house!" Oakwood bellowed at full throat. "Eh, Klegg! I've Miss Phoebe Parmenter with me! She's been taken ill!"

The door sprang open. Martha Klegg hovered behind her husband, drying her hands on her apron. With a quick glance at the young woman in Oakwood's arms, Klegg stepped back. Oakwood stamped his feet to knock off the worst of the snow, ducked his head and passed under the lintel.

"I'll have your private parlor. Make up the fire, and hurry about it. Mulled ale for me and your best claret for the lady. She's frozen to the bone," he shot at Klegg, who gave another nod and strode toward the taproom. "My mount's down the way," Oakwood called after the innkeeper. "Big bay gelding, answers to the name of Bacchus. Be grateful if you'd retrieve him for me."

"What happened to the poor dear?" Martha Klegg fussed, ushering Oakwood and his insensate burden to the back of the inn and up a twisting flight of stairs so narrow he had trouble navigating them. "As if she didn't have troubles enough!"

"Twisted her ankle, among other things. We'll want whatever you have available in the way of a meal," he said, as he followed her down a short hall, and into the only private parlor the George boasted. "I'm sharp set."

"I'll see you settled and the fire lit first. There's mutton stew or roast chicken, mushroom fritters, pigeon pie, and apples laced with cinnamon and honey."

"Excellent. And anything else you have to hand, while you're about it."

Oakwood glanced about the unheated parlor, and laid Phoebe

on a settee well away from the drafty door, tucking a pillow beneath her head.

As with the taproom the night before, it was precisely what one could expect of such a place: low-ceilinged, chintz everywhere, with bright sunlight streaming through minuscule windows, plenty of sturdy furnishings, and an excess of country fairings to lend it elegance, complete with a cheap engraving of the king in his better days over the mantel. The place smelled of beeswax and dried lavender.

"Bring triple portions of everything," he instructed, bending his gaze on Martha Klegg with a good-humored smile.

"The stew *and* the chicken?"

"There's a deal of me to keep up and I've had a busy time of it, what with one thing and another, and no time to fuel the engine."

"The stew, triple portions of that, and a chicken, and an extra on the spit just in case. And everything else, you say? Won't take but a moment, all being ready.

"What really overset her? Miss Parmenter's not the sort to faint at such a trifle as a twisted ankle," Martha Klegg prattled as she set kindling and logs on the grate. "Not but what she's born enough to cause a hundred indispositions, poor dear, and her stepmother no more use than a rabbit. Less! One can at least skin a rabbit and put it in a pot, and get some good of it that way. Can't say the same for Mabel Parmenter. A waste, for all there's not a mean bone in her body—nor any other kind, if you ask me!"

Phoebe moaned and turned her face to the wall.

"And her father what *he* was, which is no better'n a broadbellied, heavy-fisted monster," the innkeeper's wife scolded, "and that aunt of hers a harpy if ever there was one. Emma Trask was his fit sister, bone and blood and temper, that's for certain.

"And then there's the high and mighty Gusset-that-isn't. How such a sweet lady, who's a favorite in all the neighborhood, let me tell you, managed to get herself betrothed to Philip Fordyce I'll never understand, for even she knows what he is, and never had the least use for him 'til now, and that do bear looking into, if I say so myself."

Martha Klegg rose stiffly from her knees, folded her arms beneath her generous bosom. "The sooner an end's put to that mismatch, the better," she proclaimed sternly, giving Oakwood a look that would've sent him running for his life only days before.

As it was, it merely caused him to flush and nod. "You'll get no argument from me on that head," he said.

"Sod—forgiving the language, but that's all he is—'ll lead her a life'll make the one Porty Parmenter led her mother and stepmother seem a bed of roses," Martha Klegg insisted, "and beggar the poor dear into the bargain—you mark my words! And leave her to fend for herself and the rest of them, and likely a babe as well. End in the poorhouse, they will. Isn't a soul hereabout wants to see her come to that, not even her aunt, for all *her* idea isn't one I hold with, nor anyone else, either. Cobber Trask, who's got mashed turnips for brains, and always will? Wed to Miss Parmenter? It don't bear thinking on!"

"I doubt there's the least chance of that," Oakwood protested, eyes flying to where Phoebe lay on the settee, back rigid with insult.

"You don't think so? That's where you're wrong. Nothing Emma Trask'd do would surprise me. Nothing! Well, I'll be getting your meal. Himself'll be here with your wine and ale in a trice. Surprised he isn't already," she said, giving the mantel a swipe with her apron, "but could be there's some come importuning him as needs putting in their places. Wouldn't surprise me none. Saw you ride into the village with Miss Parmenter. *And* saw that Trask woman come gleaning nightshade like the witch she is, and Nick Gusset lumbering after her like his breeches was on fire. Like as not they'll all come chasing you here. Thought you should know."

The door closed with a sharp crack. Phoebe sat, glowering.

"Let's get you settled by the fire," Oakwood said. "You're frozen to the bone. Here, lean on my arm."

"I'm perfectly capable of seeing to myself," she snapped, "no matter what you, and apparently the entire neighborhood, think. Dear heaven—to be the subject of such gossip! I'd no idea."

She jumped to her feet, took two steps, winced, took another unsteady step.

"Don't be a ninny. You're ankle's hurting you worse than ever."

"The condition of my ankle's none of your business."

"I've made it my business, begging your pardon, and all the rest of it as well. It's that or abandon you to drown in a sea of disaster, and that's something I find I don't care to do. Your Mrs. Klegg and the Misses Potts have the right of it."

Oakwood removed her old cloak and tossed it on the settee. Then he scooped her up once more, ignoring her protests and delighting in the excuse for further propinquity. Phoebe Parmenter did indeed make a delightful armful, one he was increasingly loath to relinquish once he had her where he wanted her. Reluctantly he deposited the young woman in a wing chair by the fire, and propped her aching foot on a tabouret.

"Now, we'll have no more protests out of you," he grinned. "Just sit there and get warm, and remember to look vaguely ill when Mrs. Klegg returns." Then, on a considering frown, he added, "How *did* you come to accept Philip Fordyce? The man's a thorough reprobate, from what I've learned."

"I find him everything that's charming," Phoebe protested, holding her hands to the fire.

"Oh? Really?"

"I detest such supercilious drawls!"

"Taking exception to the way I speak?"

"Indeed I am."

"Let's have at least a modicum of honesty between us," he sighed. "Otherwise there'll be little I can do to assist you."

"And just why should you wish to assist me—not that I've the least need of assistance! Charging about with more the air of a bull in a china shop than a knight in shining armor. Crushing all before you. Overriding everything and everyone. Certainly you've the size for it!"

"Damned if I know. You've a waspish tongue when displeased. Honey catches more flies than vinegar, in case you hadn't heard."

"Interfering blockhead!" she muttered.

"Termagant!" he riposted, then chuckled. "You'd think we were a pair of scrubby schoolboys having at it in the schoolyard. I wonder why?"

"I haven't the slightest notion."

"You don't? Truly? Amazing! I, by contrast, am beginning to discern several possible reasons, little as I expected it, heaven help me. What an education this foray into the hinterlands is proving," he chuckled, "for I'm generally the laziest of fellows. To bestir myself on anyone's account? Unheard of! The pater'd be pleased were he to learn of it—which he shall in time, no doubt. As for my sister, whether she'll laugh harder than she'll cheer is the only question. She's no sylph and rather unconventional, so there'll be a deal of one or t'other."

The notion of his playing matchmaker would indeed tickle Serena's risibilities, and those of the beau monde into the bargain.

"You have family?" She looked up at him, flushing. "No one's ever mentioned any, with the exception of Mr. Dorning."

"Did you think I sprang full-armored from the brow of Zeus?"

"Not appropriate. That was a lady."

"Athena, to be precise. No, I suppose it wasn't. Yes, I have a family."

"I don't think the worse of you for being, well, because your parents—"

"Because Dorning told you I was base-born? Glad to hear it. I suspected you were more independent-minded than to subscribe to his constipated views. One of the things I like best about you: that you're independent-minded."

Oakwood removed his cap, unwound his scarf, divested himself of his greatcoat, and settled his old tweed hunting jacket more comfortably across his broad shoulders. Then, with a considering look from beneath lowered brows, he sank into the matching wing chair opposite Phoebe and leaned forward, forearms resting on powerful thighs, hands clasped between his knees.

"Well, let's have it," he said.

"I'm sorry; I don't catch your meaning." Phoebe shivered, shrinking as if to elude both him and his uncomfortable questions and even more uncomfortable compliments, watching him warily. "Have what?"

"The truth, Miss Parmenter. Or, may I call you Phoebe? I think I shall, no matter what you say, viewing you rather in the nature of a younger sister as I do. Never had one of those before. I find I rather like it. What sort of hold does Fordyce have over you, Phoebe?"

"Hold?" she said, ignoring his highly improper use of her given name. "Over me? Whatever can you mean?"

The door opened. Klegg hurried in carrying a bottle of claret, a glass, and a tankard of ale. The serving wench from the night before followed close on his heels, toting a well-provisioned tray.

"Have your gelding bedded down in the stables," Klegg said. "Stableboy's giving him a rub-down and a measure of oats."

"My thanks. He's a reliable mount. I shouldn't care to slight him."

Oakwood's brows rose. The acrid tones of Emma Trask shrilling an ill-humored duet with Dorning's grating tenor flowed up the stairs and down the short hall, Gusset providing a *basso continuo* counterpoint. The innkeeper kicked the door to and shrugged.

"They won't come bothering you, that I promise," he said, "or my name's not Willie Klegg which, being it is, means you've no cause for worry." He set tankard, wine and glass on the mantel, pulled a gate-legged table so ancient it gleamed like ebony between Oakwood and Phoebe, lifted the leaves, swung out the gates, rested the leaves on their posts, and nodded to the girl. "Set that down and hop to it, Tess. Miss Parmenter's shivering like a stoat with a knife to its throat."

"Hope you're feeling more yourself, miss," the serving girl said, casting Phoebe the sympathetic glance of one who'd known her all her life as she set the tray on the table. "You do be that pale, and flushed with it, too. Sure you're not sickening for something? And just before Christmas, of all the bad luck, and you

able to enjoy the season for the first time in dunamany years!
First time ever, more'n like."

"I'll do, Tess, thank you for asking. More wearied than ill, I
believe."

"And so you might be, traipsing into the village all the way
from Underhill in this cold, and his prissified dandiness leaving
you to it with nary an offer of assistance. Fine gentleman he is!
Off at the crack of dawn, Lord knows where, and with no thought
to anyone but hisself and his head. Regular tosspot last night,
and paying for it dear this morning. A pickable worm, just like
he was when he first come here, and a pickable worm he'll always
be, just like you said at the time.

"Glad you didn't suffer, sir," the girl said to Oakwood, busying
herself with setting the covers as Klegg retrieved wine and ale
and placed them in easy reach of his guests. "Made considerable
indentures yourself afore y'left, an' that's the truth."

"Ah, yes, well, hard head," Oakwood mumbled uncomfortably
at the reference to his previous evening's dissipations and the
company in which the girl implied he'd enjoyed them.

Phoebe shot him a look of combined reproof and censure laced
with not a little humor. Then she frowned, eyes narrowing.

"Mistress says t'ring if you want more, sir, but this should get
you started," Tess prattled on. "I'll be bringing a pot o' tea and
the tart herself's set t'warm on the hearth later, an' some fruit
and cheese. Nuts too, if you want. Walnut crop's that good this
year—sweet as sugarplums, and that's the truth. You want me to
carve, or'll you be doing it, sir?"

"I'll manage," Oakwood smiled.

"Here now, Tess—let's leave them to it," Klegg interposed,
placing a hand in the small of the voluble serving girl's back and
propelling her toward the door. "Mr. Oakwood has the air of a
starving man for all his courtesy, and an impatient one."

"That fine a gentleman, he is," Tess agreed with a wistful
glance over her shoulder. "You mark my words, Mr. Klegg: He
ain't no gamekeeper," she babbled more softly, for all her pierc-
ing voice carried to the pair by the fireplace, "nor yet a fancy
gardener t'the nobs, no matter what he or Mr. Dorning says. Has

an air, he does, just like Quality. A real air, not like Mr. Fordyce, what hasn't no business marrying Miss Parmenter, no business at all."

"Might be as well to lock up behind us," Klegg called as he closed the door. "I can't be everywhere at once and the devil knows what them three below intends."

Phoebe shivered uncontrollably as Oakwood followed the inn-keeper's suggestion.

" 'Tis I will have to pay the piper for all this, you know," she said on a quavering note. "For months, if not years!"

"Not unless you truly desire it. Fordyce's long outstayed his welcome, don't you think, playing sour notes all the while? I'd say it was time you seized him by the neck and wrung it 'til his eyes popped. I can think of a few other necks you ought to wring as well, while you're indulging in the exercise. Glad to shoulder the task for you, if you've little taste for it. Throttling's more the province of gentlemen than ladies. Certainly I've the hands for the job!"

She shook her head at his fierce words and stern look, lips compressing.

Oakwood rattled the door against its lock, returned to the fire-side, picked up the carving knife, tested its blade against his thumb nail, then set to carving elegant slices of juicy breast meat complete with caps of golden skin, disjointing thighs and drum-sticks and wings with the skill of one well accustomed to the exercise, aligning them neatly around the plundered carcass. Then, with a quick look at the frozen girl, paler than ever in the ruddy firelight, he filled a plate with the choicest morsels, added some peas mashed in cream, a slice of pigeon pie, a pair of mushroom fritters and a hearty portion of stewed apples, and set the plate before her along with the boat of bread sauce.

"Eat," he said, as he poured her a glass of wine, ignoring her mutinous look. "You've the air of a starving orphan. I'll feed you myself if I have to, so don't try me further than I can bear. I expect to see your plate emptied in reasonable short order." He cast a considering glance at the tureen of stew, a brow cocked. "You want some of this?"

She shook her head, eyes widening at the thought.

"I'll have at it as is then, begging your pardon. Ladling it on a plate'd only make it cold, and there's nothing more foul than congealed mutton stew—or congealed anything, for that matter. What's intended to be hot should be hot."

He set the tureen at his place, balanced the platter of chicken on the fireguard, tore a hunk from a loaf of bread still warm from the oven, seized a serving spoon and set to with a good will while Phoebe watched in amazement.

"Told you it takes considerable to fill my stokehole," he chuckled between bites. "This concoction's not bad. Your Mrs. Klegg has as excellent a way with a stew as she does with words to dissect a character, and the sense not to claim it's a ragout into the bargain, for a ragout it's not. No wine, you see. A true ragout must have wine, and a splash of cognac as well if the chef knows his craft.

"As for the spoon, look at that puny thing." He pointed to the conventional one by his place. "Why, it'd be lost in my paw! Much better to admit I'm what I am, and select my utensils accordingly. Now, eat! I'll not have you wandering the countryside with the air of a starved chicken when there's a remedy at hand."

Phoebe eyed first her host and then her plate with reluctance.

"Are you certain you can afford all this?" she said.

"Won't beggar me, if that's what you mean."

"Because I've only sixpence remaining."

"Don't worry yourself about my pockets, my dear. I'll meet our shot with crowns to spare. Now, for once in your life, eat 'til you're bursting at the seams, and never mind if the rest of the world's starving, because it isn't."

"How indelicate," she murmured.

"Indelicate or not, I want to see some roses on those pretty cheeks of yours, and a bit of plumpness to 'em as well, and cherries on your lips. No more ghosts flitting about, understand? Eat, blast it! Soames gave me an advance," he added more equably, seeing she was serious about his ability to stand the nonsense of a rather mundane nuncheon at an out-of-the-way country inn.

It was an unaccustomed experience—having a young lady

concerned as to whether he could frank any nonsense he wished, and dubious concerning her right to be a charge on him. He rather enjoyed it. Certainly it raised the country girl another notch in his estimation, if that were possible.

"You spent the evening with Philip?" she inquired, hands still resting in her lap.

"I did indeed, for my sins. Eat!"

"Why?"

"It didn't seem the thing to abandon him when we arrived. Not the warmest of receptions. Don't care for him here any more than they do elsewhere. Now, eat. Meals're serious business for a man of my size. We'll talk later."

"I can't see what you'd be wanting with Philip," she complained, picking up fork and knife and sending him a narrowed glance. "I'll wager he's a deal beneath your customary companions, no matter who you are."

"What? Aren't you going to regale me with a recital of his charms?" Oakwood sighed, pausing in his steady consumption of warm bread and hearty stew to throw the girl a parody of a shocked look. "Certainly I'd've thought that was the duty of a betrothed—to bore on forever concerning the glories of her intended."

"I never bore on about anything," Phoebe protested, caught between blush and insult.

"True enough, you never do," he grinned good-humoredly.

And indeed she didn't. He was becoming more convinced by the minute that dullness never dwelt in Miss Phoebe Parmenter's vicinity. Certainly it hadn't that day. A life lacking dullness was not a thing to despise. Soames was sure to agree.

Besides, dammit, he felt protective towards her. Ready to take on the world in her defense if need be. Before he quitted the region, he had every intention of seeing her life regularized, her future one of sunshine and happiness. Indeed, if she'd permit it, he had every intention of giving the bride away. Hezekiah Hatch, from what he'd learned of the man, didn't deserve the honor.

"Now eat, blast it, or at least keep still until I'm done. I've told you we'll talk later."

As for that way she had of looking at a fellow with those immense brown eyes, slightly shy, slightly dubious, slightly hopeful and yet not daring to hope, it was enough to wrench a man's vitals, and that was the simple truth.

"And if I want to talk now?"

"Have at it, if you enjoy the sound of your own voice. You shan't be hearing mine."

He glanced at her again, softening his admonition with a warm smile that made the girl flush as rosily as he might wish. Then, with a determined blanking of his mind, he turned his attention back to the steaming tureen.

After that there was silence in the sunny private parlor as Oakwood made his way through the stew, sopping up the last bits of gravy with the last of the bread, essaying mashed peas, pigeon pie (which he found to be well above average), fritters and stewed apples, and occasionally spearing a slice of chicken with the tip of the carving knife to replenish Phoebe's plate.

At last she shook her head. "I can't," she said as he bent to select yet another morsel for her. "Not another bite, or I'll expire."

He glanced from the depleted platter and serving dishes to her plate, nodded, refilled her glass with claret, then drained the bottle into his empty tankard.

"All right," he said, "now we've satisfied the inner woman, let's move to the outer. What's Fordyce's game, other than feathering his nest at your expense? And why the devil're you letting him do it? Because that's what he's doing, plain as the nose on your face. What sort of hold does the bounder have over you?"

Phoebe sighed, a look of beleaguered patience too obvious to be anything but spurious replacing her fleeting look of terror.

"Dearest Philip has no hold over me," she said, "unless it's the hold of long attachment. I can't think what leads you to believe he might."

"Very neatly done, but not quite neatly enough. If not you, then whom? One of your half-sisters? Your stepmother?"

"I can't imagine what you mean—truly I can't."

Oakwood leaned back, studying her through narrowed eyes

as he swirled the wine in his tankard. "Why're you marrying him, then?" he said at last.

"I've known Philip for years," Phoebe prevaricated.

"And despised the wastrel as long as you've known him. I have that on good authority."

"Whose!"

"Beyond the Misses Potts and Mrs. Klegg, who're bound to have the truth of it, being acquainted with both of you since time immemorial? Why, even Tess hinted at your aversion. A 'pickable worm', indeed. Conjures up visions of pitchforks and pig wallows, that does. Fitting place for him to end, when all's said and done—a pig wallow. Never you mind. Let's just say my source is unimpeachable."

"Lord Soames, that's who it must be. He seems a dithery sort, but he's not. Have you been listening at doors? For he'd never discuss such a matter with you—never! It's not just the village that's talking then," she sighed. "It's his lordship, and Mr. Ware, and probably every soul within twenty miles as well."

"So why marry him?"

"I haven't married Philip yet," she mumbled, staring blindly into the fire.

"But you're going to unless something changes, aren't you. What's that something?"

"I haven't much choice, given the terms of Papa's will. Mr. Hatch seems to accept Philip as suitable, and I'm delighted by the prospect of becoming his wife. Delighted, I tell you! Besides, we'll starve if I don't marry someone and produce an heir. Mrs. Klegg has the right of that, if nothing else."

"But why Fordyce?"

"Why not? He's ready to hand, and most anxious to fill the post. Besides, we've been attached for years. Hiding it desperately, you see, for fear of Papa."

"And daffodils bloom in hell, tended most tenderly by his Satanic majesty! He's convenient, I'll grant you that, and he's not totally repulsive to look at if you care for the type that rolls its hair in papers every night. I don't. I rather doubt you do, either. Too pretty by half and forever concerned with his prettiness."

Her telling shudder gave Oakwood pause. He was pressing her unmercifully when, between the pain from her injury and concern over her family and the brouhaha in the shop, let alone the two glasses of claret she'd consumed and the third he'd just poured her, her defenses were at low ebb. He'd gotten nothing out of her at the cottage, less than nothing on the ride into Chedleigh Minor, and he needed something, if only to show him how best to proceed in foiling Fordyce's schemes and assuring the poor girl could achieve a life that included at least contentment and security. So far, Soames remained the best notion he'd had.

"What really happened the day your father died?" he said after a moment, determined to press his advantage while he still had it, and gentlemanly conduct go hang.

"Papa went riding and came a cropper." She laid her head wearily against the chair back, sighing. "I've told you that before. Countless times, it seems."

"So you claim. Did he, really?"

"I resent your implication," she snapped, closing her eyes as if to blot out the world and her future, and him along with both. "If you won't leave the subject be, I shall depart immediately. On foot and alone, d'you understand?"

"My dear girl, I'm only trying to help you in my own poor way."

"And a very poor way it is, too!"

"What really happened to the parlor mantel? That corner's fresh broken."

"I've already told you that as well."

"You're being most uncooperative. Why?"

"Because I see no advantage to cooperation. Papa's dead. He's buried. His death was ruled an accident. Leave it be."

"I'm afraid I can't."

"What are you, a Bow Street Runner?"

"I? A Runner? With this bulk? My dear girl, you're bamming me!"

"I've wondered, given you appeared so suddenly in the neighborhood with no better excuse than seeking employment at Penwillow—which Lord Soames most conveniently provided you. Does he doubt the manner of Papa's death? Has he opened a private inquiry? Did he send for you?"

"So many questions! No, his lordship didn't send for me. I arrived in precisely the manner it appears: unheralded, and of my own will. Why not consider someone else if Fordyce has no hold over you?" he persisted, returning to the main point. "Surely the neighborhood has something better to offer than that mushroom?"

"No, there's no one, or at least no one who's preferable," she said, fingers twisting. "Mr. Dorning is all, and I've come to detest him as much as I—"

"Aha! And so you admit the truth at last?"

"It's the wine speaking," she murmured distractedly. "Not a parcel of truth to anything I say. Even you should be able to see that. All about in my head."

"No, I don't see it at all. It would seem to me almost anyone would be preferable to Philip Fordyce—Dorning excepted, naturally. Oh, and Cobber Trask and Alfie Gusset. They're among your suitors as well, I'm told."

He paused, studying the slight, bedraggled figure before him, replete now with the first decent meal she'd probably had in her life.

Paler than winter sun dictated.

Thinner than she ought to be.

Hands roughened by hard work, the knuckles cracked.

Gowned abominably in brown stuff, and with hair so plainly dressed it was a parody of every serving maid's.

And, gallant. Determined to see to her little half-sisters and stepmother, come what might. So much for her catalogue of faults. A gentler life would see to them, and her virtues would never fail her or anyone else, Soames included.

As for his earlier conviction that she must have had something to do with her father's death, impossible! No, whatever had happened to Portius Parmenter, she bore none of the responsibility. Only a short time in her company had taught him that much. If she were the culprit, she'd've admitted it instantly. Anything less would've been out of character. She was clearly protecting some-one, but whom? Certainly not her stepmother. That left only Soames or Ware. Soames? Again, impossible. No motive.

But, Ware? Now there was an intriguing notion. He'd consider it later. The question was, why would Phoebe Parmenter feel called upon to protect Ware, of all people?

Whoever it was she shielded, one thing was certain: she was being forced to pay the price for another's misdeed. And that price? Marriage to Philip Fordyce. Prissy and Pru had that right, at least. Nothing else explained the match.

And so, having constituted himself her champion, what was he to do? Well, in for a penny, in for a pound. It would come to the same in the end, no matter when he spoke, and speak he knew he would, over and over, until he convinced both Phoebe Par-menter and Soames his was the proper solution to all their prob-lems. That the prospect of Phoebe Parmenter bearing Soames's son and heir didn't particularly appeal was neither here nor there.

"Lord Soames, for instance," he said on a low, diffident rumble.

"You're offering up your employer in Philip's place?"

"Why not? He knows something about running an estate, and I promise you the most beautiful garden in England as your wed-ding gift. And, some decent clothes into the bargain, both for you and the girls. I can convince him to provide those, at least."

"It's very kind of you, but Lord Soames is so far above my touch it's laughable."

"I believe he'll agree with me that you're wrong."

"A menial? Convince his employer where and when and how and whom he should wed? Oh, come now! Besides, we're barely acquainted. I've seen more of his lordship since Papa's death than I did the entire rest of my life. Those from the great houses don't consort with those who dwell in places like Underhill ex-cept on the most formal occasions, and I've attended precious few such fêtes give Papa."

"You know he's honest, steady, gentle, generous and kind—qualities you share, by the bye. And intelligent—another quality

you share. That, I believe, is something better than what you
know of Fordyce."

"You do have a way of wearing one down. All right, I'll admit
it: I'd like to find someone else," she said, "but I can't."

"Yes, you can," Oakwood returned with a cajoling smile. "Just
think: all the food you'd ever care to eat, and your stepmother
with a place of her own, and the girls properly seen to. Soames
could do it all, including sending Fordyce packing so effectively
you'd never have anything to fear again. Most any honest man
could, and would be delighted to as a favor to you into the bargain.
You're quite a fetching little thing, you know, with a sparkle that'd
attach any man."

"My thanks for the compliment, but no. As for Lord Soames,
it simply wouldn't do. It's Philip or no one, and as it must be
someone, it's Philip."

"My dear girl—no, I suppose you won't listen, and even if
you'd listen, you wouldn't believe me. All right then, if you're
going to be difficult, why were you at your Aunt Trask's the day
your father died?"

Her eyes flew to his with a combination of disbelief and anger.

"You've been asking about my activities around the village?"
she fumed.

"You were seen leaving her cottage, and later crashing through
the woods. What business had you there? I'd've thought you'd
avoid that virago whenever possible."

"Not that it's any business of yours, but Papa'd ordered Mabel
examined by a physician from Pilchester. I knew what was coming, begged Aunt Trask to lend Mabel the protection of her presence. Aunt Trask refused. She said Mabel was playacting to avoid
her duty in Papa's bed. Some truth to that, perhaps, but she was
nevertheless in a weakened condition from the last miscarriage.
It hadn't been that long. When I got home it was over. Papa'd
beaten her within an inch of her life after the physician left, and
then gone off riding his acres. Mabel had retired to their room.
An hour later Mick Bodger arrived to inform me of Papa's accident, and then we brought him home in Lord Soames's dung
cart."

"And that's the truth of it?"

"That's the truth, however unlikely it may seem."

"Who found your father?" he asked on a sudden frown. That was one issue he'd never considered.

"Philip," Phoebe said with a sigh. "It was he alerted Lord Soames, as it'd happened on his land and Penwillow Castle was closer than Underhill. Lord Soames had me fetched while he organized himself. Now, have done. My head's swimming. There must've been something wrong with the chicken."

From below rose renewed shrieks mingled with the sound of smashing crockery and Jehovah-like exhortations. Then an enraged bellow topped them all, and the sound of boots taking stairs in a furious tattoo.

"Oh, dear," Phoebe murmured. "That must be Philip come to horsewhip you, for I believe you've compromised me most vilely now I consider the matter. Riding into the village with you is nothing compared to being closeted here."

"At Mr. Klegg's suggestion," Oakwood grinned. "A clever man, Mr. Klegg. I'll have to remember to reward him well. As for you, my dear, I believe you'll have to reconsider my proposal of Soames as a substitute, for more likely than not Fordyce'll rescind his offer when he finds us alone, being the sort to believe the worst of everyone as he's his own measuring stick. Soames, on the other hand, will never believe a word of harm against you."

"Philip? Give up Underhill? Not likely! He could find us in the most fervent of embraces and overlook it beyond a word or two of public chastisement, believe me. As there's nothing to be done, unlock the door quickly and no one'll be the wiser. We can say Tess only just left to fetch us a tart."

"I think not." Oakwood stretched out comfortably as fists pounded on the door, determined Fordyce wouldn't prove quite so forgiving as Phoebe anticipated, no matter what ruse he had to employ. "You might try fainting again," he suggested companionably, "if this commotion isn't to your taste."

"Faint? Why, then they'd think they *knew* you'd compromised me, and witnessed the seduction with their own eyes! As it stands, we may come through if only we keep our wits about us."

"I've not the slightest desire to keep my wits about me. Indeed, there're those who'd say I've already lost 'em, and am likely to lose 'em further before the year gets much older."

The door to the little parlor burst open, jamb splintering. Fordyce loomed in the ragged aperture gripping a crop, golden curls mussed, many-caped greatcoat unbuttoned, boots dripping melting snow on the carpet.

"Aha!" he proclaimed in fine theatrical style. "They were right!"

Nine

Oakwood yawned and waved Phoebe, who'd sprung to her feet and was blinking wildly, back into her chair.

"I wonder when that self-important cipher'll learn some couth," he murmured loudly enough to reach the irate Fordyce's ears. "Probably never, given the evidence."

"Couth? I'll give you couth!" Fordyce ranted. "Phoebe, get yourself home. I've not given you permission to gad about the countryside."

"Do I require your permission to go anywhere? Dear me, I can't think when that happened," she protested with no thought to safety as Dorning, Emma Trask, Nick Gusset, the inn's entire staff, and what seemed like half the village crowded through the open doorway, Klegg with blood streaming from his nose and both daylights darkening at an alarming rate, Martha Klegg with a livid weal across her cheek.

The cheery parlor, hardly generous to begin with, shrank to minuscule proportions.

"See here, I'll not be submitting to your sauce, no matter what you think," Fordyce blustered at the head of the crowd. "I may be a peaceable man, but enough is enough. Now, get back to Underhill where you belong, Phoebe, or do I give you a taste of my crop?"

"Only thing the chit understands," Emma Trask crowed in triumph. "Told every soul in the village so, but oh no, not a one of you'd listen, knowing so much more than a mere woman. Porty had it right, and so you can see! Doesn't know her place, needs to be taught it every minute of the day. Same was true of her mother. Same's true of that fool Porty married the second time, and both her brats into the bargain."

Phoebe, taking heart from the steadying glance Oakwood threw her, defiantly took a sip of her claret.

"Merciful heaven above! Scoundrel's been plying her with spirits!" Dorning gasped. "And you," he squeaked, rounding on Klegg, "have been aiding and abetting him! On your knees for your sins, and implore the Lord's forgiveness, and perhaps one day He'll hear you."

"Was Him turned water to wine," Klegg said, incensed, "and I never heard as where He passed the women by when He was pouring it. You tend to your sermons, and I'll tend to who I'm to be serving and who I'm not."

"And quite excellent spirits yours are, Mr. Klegg," Phoebe trilled, ignoring Dorning's horrified natterings and Fordyce's temper-purpled face, "enlivening my own most delightfully. Why, I haven't felt so carefree in years! You may remove the covers, Tess. I believe Mr. Oakwood is ready for one of your excellent tarts, Mrs. Klegg, once you've cleared the room of these intruders."

Then, as if noticing the woman's abused cheek for the first time, she leapt to her feet, took a hobbling step toward the inn-keeper's wife. "Merciful heaven above," she gasped, impishly aping the incensed cleric, "whatever have you done to your face, Mrs. Klegg? Is that a burn? Oh dear, it looks dreadfully painful! Do someone get Mrs. Klegg some snow to put on it. Best thing for burns there is—snow. Bruises, too. You might get some for Mr. Klegg's eyes and nose as well."

Phoebe retreated to her place by the fire, sinking gratefully into the chair. Goodness, but the floor was unsteady. It must be the fault of her ankle. And she was feeling a bit more than dis-tinctly odd.

"It ain't a burn, and well you know it." Fordyce had apparently recollected himself. The affected drawl was once more in place. "Fishwife struck me across the shoulders with a poker when I demanded to see you," he snapped, "and so I gave her a taste of her own."

"You struck a defenseless woman? In the face?"

"She isn't defenseless—not by a long sight!"

"I didn't come after you until you'd knocked my good man down when he blocked your way," Mrs. Klegg protested over the excited murmurings of the crowd, clearly anxious her part in the fracas be accurately detailed. "Twice! I do have some control over *my* temper."

"Dear me, whatever is the world coming to?" Oakwood rose, bulking over the assembled company like a man o' war circled by skiffs. "You assaulted our good host? And his lady? Why, Mr. Fordyce, I'm amazed! And you such a peaceable man by nature, as you keep informing everyone," he reproved mildly.

"Lady? That female isn't a lady by any stretch. See here, what're you doing with *my* fiancée shut up in here all by your-selves?"

"My dear Mrs. Klegg, Mr. Klegg," Oakwood continued, ig-noring the interruption, "are you thinking of bringing charges against this fellow? Because that might be best for all concerned. Assault's a criminal offense, I believe. His lordship handles such matters in these parts, doesn't he? Perhaps someone might fetch him."

"Charges? I'll charge you!" Fordyce roared, raising his crop and shaking it but warily keeping his distance. "What the devil've you been doing with my fiancée?"

"Consuming an excellent meal, until you so rudely interrupted it. You can see the remains on the table. Wonderful mutton stew, by the bye, Mrs. Klegg. I recommend it to anyone with an empty belly and a desire to fill it while enjoying the process. Superior cook, Mrs. Klegg is," he informed the company at large. "I speak on the best of authority, having eaten my way across the length and breadth of England several times."

"No one cares in the least about your eating habits," Dorning snapped.

"See here, Oakwood, you've no business with Phoebe—not without my permission," Fordyce insisted, clearly attempting to calm himself.

"And here we're back to it again," Oakwood said with a long-suffering sigh. "Permission, which it is your prerogative to grant or withhold. On what authority, if I may be so bold?"

"You may not!"

"Because if it has anything to do with your betrothal, nothing's formalized to my knowledge. Given Miss Parmenter's of age and her own mistress, I fail to see what business it is of yours what she does or doesn't do."

"Hush, Mr. Oakwood," Phoebe begged. "Please! You're thrusting us both ever deeper in the briars, just as I knew you would."

"I'm not thrusting anyone anywhere, my dear," Oakwood smiled. "I'm extricating 'em. Or you, to be precise."

"Business? *Business?*" Clearly against his better judgment, but propelled by some inner demon, Fordyce stalked forward until he was just beyond Oakwood's long reach, snapping his crop against his boot. "And what business have you calling Miss Parmenter 'my dear'? What business have you with her at all, come to that!"

"Ah—and here we return to it once more. I thought we might. Some things are too much to hope for, such as sense in one who lacks it!"

Oakwood's pained expression caused not a few titters among the crowd. Even Phoebe, beset though she was, gave a wan half smile.

"Well?" Fordyce demanded, drawing himself up, but taking a precautionary half step back in case Oakwood decided to move.

"You can see perfectly well what business I had with the lady. It was my pleasure to see her not quit a table half-starved. Beyond that, we were discussing the position of bailiff at Underhill once she'd seen to some purchases."

"The devil you were!"

"The devil we were, indeed. We'd just concluded the bargain when you burst in like a bull in a china shop."

The sly glance Oakwood sent Phoebe, the wink, the reminder of their earlier conversation, gave her pause. Well, and why not? She did require a bailiff; she was unable to see to everything herself. Even in the best of times she'd never been involved with farming matters. Papa'd forbidden it, not wanting her to know more of his affairs than was absolutely essential for the smooth running of his household. That her head was spinning didn't mean she couldn't think rationally, or see to both her best interests and those of Underhill.

"We had, Philip dear," she said in support of Oakwood's fabrication, the "dear" ringing false even in her ears. "Just concluded our bargain, that is."

"Isn't any way you could've," Fordyce declared on a triumphant note. "Hezekiah has to approve anyone who's hired, and he won't approve of Oakwood in a month of Sundays—that I can promise you."

"Hezekiah?" Oakwood's brows rose. "Not Mr. Hatch?"

"We're by way of becoming well acquainted," Fordyce blustered.

"Yes, so I understand, but to the extent of employing given names? I'd no idea!"

"See here, Phoebe," Fordyce continued, flushing as he turned to his love, "you get yourself home on the instant and forget all this nonsense, and I'll overlook finding you secreted with that rotter."

"You will? How kind of you, Philip." She managed the words, but only barely, each consonant ringing a trifle too clear and clipped even in her own ears.

"*I* certainly think so, and I'm sure everyone here will agree with me. Had designs on your virtue, I'll warrant, and your pockets as well."

"And you don't?" she spluttered, forgetting wisdom as Oakwood chuckled broadly. She took another sip of her wine, glaring first at her would-be husband, then Dorning over the glass's rim. "I must be all about in my head, for those are precisely the things I thought you had designs on!"

Neither the crowd's appreciative murmur nor Fordyce's glare, not even Oakwood's cautionary frown affected her. Claret was wonderful stuff—red as blood, and making one's own flow twice as fast, giving one a courage one never knew one had. That must be why the room was spinning just the tiniest bit, and not tainted food at all—all that unexpected courage when the entire world was crashing about her ears.

"Sooner the wedding's brought forward the better," Fordyce blustered, maintaining his distance. "I keep telling you that, Phoebe, but you're as deaf as any woman when a man speaks sense. This travesty just proves my point. A lady, hiring her own bailiff? And a perfect stranger into the bargain? And dining with him? Behind a locked door at a common inn? It's clear you've no more sense than a peahen, and need me to see to you."

"I'll have Cobber take her home in the gig," Emma Trask threw in, tugging on Fordyce's sleeve, clearly anxious to have a more important role in the drama than she'd managed until then. "Been hobbling about. Saw her at the Emporium, tottering like a crone. Why, Oakwood had to carry her. Taking unwarranted liberties, of course, but there was nothing I could do but stand by and watch given I'm naught but a frail female. Injured her ankle again no doubt, the clumsy cow."

"Now that," Oakwood growled on a note of such menace that even Phoebe shivered, "is a description of my new employer which I will not permit of anyone."

"Oh, do be still," Phoebe murmured. "Things're bad enough as it is. You'll only make them worse if you keep on like this."

"If," he said clearly, frowning her down, "by making things worse you mean teaching this harridan you call 'aunt' some manners, then I have every intention of seeing them worse. To make an omelet one must first break eggs. Or, heads."

"Country sayings, now? Dear Lord, preserve me!"

"He just might, if you leave things to me. Or, a lord."

"And just what arrangements've you made with this lummox?" Fordyce sneered, inserting himself into the sudden silence Oakwood's cryptic words caused.

"Month's trial, no pay, which should please Mr. Hatch," Oakwood said before Phoebe could more than open her mouth. "At the end of the month we'll see if we suit. We do, I'll receive back wages. We don't, I'll leave neither richer nor poorer than I arrived. Meantime, I'll be taking up residence at Underhill. Bound to be a sight more comfortable than Lord Soames's old gamekeeper's cottage."

"I won't have it!" Fordyce exploded. "I simply will *not* have it!"

"Not much choice that I can see," Oakwood shrugged, placing a calming hand on Phoebe's shoulder as her eyes flew from one man to the other. "You have no authority at Underhill. As far as that goes, I'm not aware you have any authority anywhere."

"Tell him, Phoebe," Fordyce snarled. "Tell him, or by heaven, I'll—"

"You'll what? Take that crop to her? Not wise. Given I'm now in Miss Parmenter's employ I'd feel it my duty to come to her rescue, and I rather suspect you'd come out the worse for the experience. I'm known to have a rather heavy hand when I wish, and in your case I wouldn't feel called upon to restrain myself."

"And just how're you going to fulfill your obligation to his lordship? Or is that all a sham to insinuate yourself into the neighborhood, just as Dorning claims?"

"Oakwood? Oakwood, you in there?"

The crowd parted in a sudden hush, a latter-day Red Sea obeying God's command as if it were Moses himself at their back, and not merely the Earl of Penwillow. Justin Ware followed in his nephew's wake, eyes darting about the room, coming to rest on Oakwood, cold accusation in their depths.

"And that," Phoebe whispered in despair, rising to make an unsteady curtsy, "has fine and truly torn it. My felicitations, Mr. Oakwood. I'll be a scandal for the rest of my days, thanks to you."

"Not a bit of it. All's well. My lord," he continued, bowing, "you couldn't've arrived at a more opportune moment. There's been a bit of a problem," Oakwood's gesture indicated Klegg's eyes and nose, Martha Klegg's cheek, and Fordyce's crop, "which I believe you stand in the best position of solving."

The instant din, each putting forth his or her view of the precise problem and the exact nature of the solution the earl should employ, built on itself, reverberating from the plaster walls until Phoebe thought she'd go mad.

Soames sent Oakwood a humorous, despairing glance and shrugged.

"Here now!" Oakwood bellowed. "One at a time, if you please. His lordship can't understand a word of your racket. Such behavior in greatness's presence," he reproved in a more normal tone as the babel subsided. "I'm shocked, truly I am."

He swung his wing chair from behind the table, setting it in the center of the room much in the manner of a throne or a judge's bench.

"If you'd honor us by taking a seat, my lord," he said with a bow and a flourish, "we may proceed with the, ah, proceedings, as it were. In the ancient and accepted manner naturally, as practiced in these environs, and entirely according to local custom and tradition."

"Don't press your luck, jackanapes," Soames murmured as he passed his boyhood friend and accepted the proffered chair. "Ware tells me—"

"Ware knows precisely nothing. Just keep your wits about you, and we've naught but clear sailing ahead. Bit of justice to see to first, of course, and a lady's future after."

In the event it was Fordyce who was seen to, and in a manner most inimical to both that gentleman's sensibilities and his *amour-propre*.

Klegg insisted he'd no longer have the high-flying mendicant on the premises, citing his eyes and nose and Mrs. Klegg's assaulted cheek as reasons for his disfavor, and hinting darkly at the insult of being forced to toady to his daughter's seducer. There weren't enough pounds in all England, the innkeeper declared, to render Fordyce's presence palatable an instant longer—not that it'd ever been palatable to begin with.

Not a one of the many words Fordyce said in his own defense, including several hints regarding his future position at Underhill and his control over its heavy coffers, and the power both would give him in the neighborhood, served to sway the indignant innkeeper or his equally indignant wife.

No, they'd no desire to press charges—at the moment, that was. However, if that bottom-of-the-barrel dregs remained in the area, Klegg glowered, even he couldn't swear to what measures he might resort to rid them all of one who was, when all was said and done, nothing but a burden to them all, and dear little Miss Parmenter the most burdened of all. Everyone knew what one did with dregs. Pigs never minded what they ate.

The chorus of approval his words called forth caused Phoebe to flush painfully as Soames glanced first at her and then at Oakwood, who was hovering protectively behind her chair. Oakwood shrugged.

"I won't have you at Penwillow," the earl said, squaring his shoulders and turning back to Fordyce, "so there's no sense asking."

"I'm not leaving," Fordyce protested. "My interests're here. This is a common inn. They've got to house me."

"Not if you haven't the wherewithal to meet your bills. Certainly I'm not going to frank you after today's display."

"Then I'll repair to Underhill, where I should've been to begin with except for your interference."

"That you will not," Oakwood rumbled. "Try it, and your legs'll never carry you again. Hands and knees perhaps, but not your legs."

"You then, vicar." Fordyce's smile was all that was ingratiating, desperation lurking in his eyes.

"Can't. If my cousin doesn't want you, it'd be worth my living to house you. It's not that grand a living, but it's all I have at the moment and I'm that grateful for it, and say daily prayers for the soul of him who gifted me with it, calling God's blessing down on his head."

"God's curse, more like," Oakwood murmured.

"Mrs. Trask," Fordyce snapped, now with the air of a cornered badger, whirling on Phoebe's aunt, "surely you have room and to spare for your future nephew?"

"With you gone, it's Cobber or no one for that flighty niece of mine. Why'd I want to stand your friend when doing so'd take

the food from my own nursling's mouth, and pounds from his
pockets as well? You can sleep in a hedgerow, for all of me!"

"Mr. Gusset? No, I suppose not. You've a son to establish,
too."

"Two of 'em, and one you choused of his rightful bride, not
that he hasn't done considerably better by himself since," Gusset
growled. "I've as much reason to send you from the village riding
a rail as Willie Klegg, and twice the stomach for it!"

Fordyce's eyes roamed the crowd, obviously searching for an
ally, lighting on Phoebe, his own narrowing.

"My dear, I believe it's time for you to speak in my behalf,"
he said. "That, or hold the nuptials here and now, so I'll not find
myself in that hedgerow your aunt so kindly offered me. Certainly we've enough witnesses to do the deed, and the vicar into
the bargain."

"Perhaps," she quavered, ignoring Oakwood's warning frown,
"you might seek lodgings with Mr. Hatch in Market Stoking?
It's not all that far from Underhill if one has a horse, and you
do."

"Damnably inconvenient. Much easier to be wed and be done
with it."

"There's nothing I can say, dearest Philip, truly there isn't.
None of this is as it seems. You've been most remiss in wildly
leaping to unwarranted conclusions. Perhaps if you were to
apologize for your actions? No, I can see that wouldn't do, for
by your lights you've done nothing in the least out of the way."

"Indeed I haven't," he agreed, scowling at first Oakwood and
then Soames. "Where there's smoke, there's fire."

"Please, Philip, don't make bad worse," she sighed. "I was
walking to the village and twisted my ankle. Mr. Oakwood
brought me the rest of the way and assisted me in making some
purchases—there's the bundle right over there. If you don't believe that's how it was, you can ask Mitty and Sarah Potts. Then
Aunt Trask and Mr. Dorning and Mr. Gusset came crashing into
the shop, making all sorts of dreadful accusations. Apparently I
fainted, and that's the last I know 'til I woke here."

"You've never fainted in your life. Never! Not even the time

old Parmenter took after you with a horsewhip and laid your
back open."

"Well, this time I did, Philip. Now, if you don't mind, I believe
I should like to return home since Mr. Oakwood and I have concluded our business."

"Cobber and I'll take her in the gig," Emma Trask said, bustling forward with the self-importance of one who knows herself
to be indispensable. "Just need a moment to fetch him is all. In
fact," she said on a spiteful note, pulling Phoebe to her feet and
dragging her toward the door, "you'll walk, missy! No need for
us to fetch you here, then go back in quite the opposite direction."

"Miss Parmenter? Walk a half mile without even her cloak,
and on an injured ankle? I think not." Soames was instantly at
Phoebe's side, disengaging Emma Trask's clutching fingers as
Phoebe winced. "Uncle," he said, turning to Ware, "as we came
in your curricle, perhaps you could—"

"I'll not hear of your going out of your way for the sake of a
silly chit gadding about where she'd no business to be, nor yet
Mr. Ware either." Emma Trask seized hold of Phoebe once more,
tugging so hard the young woman was afraid her arm would leap
from its socket. "Totally out of keeping with your position, your
lordship, and his into the bargain."

Not to be outdone, Soames firmly retained his grip on
Phoebe's other arm, in his turn bracing his legs and giving a firm
tug.

"Oh, but I insist," he grunted. "You do too, don't you, Ware?"

"Naturally. Could even bundle her between us. Slip of a
thing."

"I've business with Oakwood," Soames said between
clenched teeth, exchanging Phoebe's arm for her shoulder as
offering better purchase, "given he's signing on as Miss Parmenter's bailiff and intends to move to Underhill. Plan to accompany
him. Borrow a mount from Mr. Klegg, with his permission."

"No need," Emma Trask grunted in her turn. "No need at all."

Phoebe glanced desperately to Oakwood, still lingering by the
fireplace and watching the proceedings with a humorous glint
in his eye as she was pulled first one direction, then the other.

"Here, both of you, we're not at a country fair and Miss Parmenter's not a rope and there's no prize I know of waiting for the one who takes her back to Underhill," he said, striding over to the trio and disengaging Phoebe's arm and shoulder from her would-be escorts.

"Thank you," she murmured. "That was becoming a trifle painful and more than a trifle embarrassing."

"Well," he murmured in return, swinging her up in his arms and carrying her to the settee where her cloak still lay, "that's what happens when you go gadding about with irresponsible strangers, and then depend on wild lords and wilder aunts to rescue you from the results of your impetuosity."

"I suppose I should've depended on the irresponsible stranger instead?"

"Indeed you should. He, at least, knows how to rescue damsels in distress." Oakwood stood her on her feet, picked up the old brown cloak and settled it on her shoulders, tying it firmly at the neck. "I see you mended this thing. Hardly worth it, d'you think, especially as you claim to be no needlewoman? Actually, the stitches are quite fine. Equal to anything I've seen."

"Mabel did it. As to its being not worth the effort, given it's truly the only one I possess the effort was well worth it."

"Ah, yes, your only cloak. I wonder what Christmas will bring you?"

"Not a cloak," she chuckled, diverted, "of that you may be sure!"

"And if it did?"

"Then," she said quite seriously, meeting his warm hazel eyes and blushing furiously, "I'll know we're still in the age of miracles, even in the nineteenth century."

"They still occur, you know, miracles do. I've found living proof of it in this very village: A young woman who, no matter how desperately beset, still retains both her grace and her humor."

"Here now—what're you two talking about?"

Both turned at the sound of Philip Fordyce's irritated voice.

"Settling when I shall see Miss Parmenter again," Oakwood

said, and, "Merely retrieving my cloak and parcels," Phoebe insisted.

"Well, which is it?"

"Both," Phoebe snapped, picking up the parcels. "Thank you so much, Mr. Oakwood. If you'll report to the house at the dinner hour, I'll tell Pru to set a place for you as well as the rest of us."

"I'll not be having you—"

"Philip," Phoebe broke in with all the firmness she could muster, ignoring the crowded room, "I believe you'd best see to the packing of your traps and transporting them to Market Stoking as Mr. and Mrs. Klegg no longer want you at the George. Perhaps you'd be well-advised to send word ahead to Mr. Hatch? I'm not certain he has much of a household, and may be put to some effort to accommodate you."

"See here, Phoebe, there's no need for that," Fordyce wheedled. "I can doss down with Oakwood at Underhill without putting anyone to the least inconvenience, keep an eye on him for you at the same time. Keep an eye on each other, come to that. He's every bit as unmarried as I am, or at least I suppose he is, and it's not in the least suitable that you—"

"Fine idea," Oakwood said quickly. "Glad of the company, Fordyce. Are you in need of a cart? I'll send one, just as soon as I'm at Underhill and settled in."

"Whatever are you about?" Phoebe hissed in Oakwood's neck, face turned from the room. "I don't want Philip staying at Underhill! Or you either, come to that."

"You'll see, my dear," Oakwood murmured. "And I'll be wanting a key to the house. Fine solution to all our problems," he said loudly, overriding the instant chaos this new arrangement called forth from villagers and nobility alike. "No assurance Mr. Hatch would've felt it incumbent on him to house a relative stranger, after all. Even one with whom he's well-enough acquainted to employ given names.

"Now, Mr. Ware, if you're ready to see this young lady home, I'll carry her to your curricle."

"Put her down," Fordyce snapped. "I'll see to carrying her if she's really injured herself, which I take leave to doubt."

"Oh dear, are you sure you can, Philip?" Phoebe quavered. "I'm not a feather, you know. Appearances can be deceiving."

"Don't be silly. Of course I can carry you."

"He'll drop you," Oakwood cautioned softly.

"I know, but what can I do?"

"Refuse him the privilege of so much as touching you."

"I don't believe that would be politic."

Phoebe slipped reluctantly from Oakwood's grasp, handed him her parcels. One contained the bottle of scent for Mabel. No reason to risk having it broken just because circumstance forced her to risk her neck.

"Let's give it a try, then," she said, turning to Fordyce and repressing a shudder as she held out her arms.

He did give it his best, Phoebe had to grant him that, chivalrously restraining grunts and muttering merely the mildest of oaths at the weight beneath which he labored rather than giving them full voice. Of course, by the time they were halfway down the short hall he might've had breath for little more.

In fact, he stubbornly persisted, staggering behind the Kleggs and Oakwood with the rest trailing behind, and actually made it not only to the head of the stairs, but down two steps before he gave out, taxed beyond what he could bear. There was a moment's confusion, complete with flying arms and thrashing legs. Then Phoebe and Fordyce were sitting tangled on the stairs, both disheveled but in no wise injured in anything but their pride thanks to Oakwood's broad back blocking the way.

"Thank you, Mr. Oakwood," Phoebe murmured.

"Thank him!" Fordyce snapped, incensed. "What're you thanking him for? I'm the one carried you."

"And dropped me. He stopped us from plunging down the stairs."

"Tripped me," he muttered. "What're you made of, blast it, lead?"

She felt him squirming beneath her. Dear heaven, but the man made an uncomfortable pillow—lumps and protrusions and hard things everywhere.

"Mr. Oakwood, I believe I could do with your assistance," she faltered.

"No objections this time, Fordyce?" he said, turning carefully on the narrow stairs as the Kleggs scurried down to be out of the way.

"None at all, thank you! Just rid me of her."

"You're certain? I wouldn't want to encroach."

"Blast it, man, get her off me! She's heavy as a mule."

"I think it had best be a ride pick-a-back," Oakwood apologized after eyeing first Phoebe and then the narrowness of the stairs, "as they do when they transport a curricle to a race aboard a wagon."

"And what would you know about racing curricles?" Fordyce snorted.

"Seen it done. Even helped a time or two. What you must do Miss Parmenter," Oakwood instructed, "is to place your, ah, perambulatory appendages to either side of my midsection, while I, ah, grasp them beneath their flexion points and—"

"Oh, have done!" she snapped. "Your arms'll form stirrups, and I'll put my legs through and bend 'em at the knee, and my arms around your neck, and we'll manage in that manner as there's no room to pick me up properly."

"Miss Parmenter!" Dorning gasped.

"Stubble it, Clare!" Ware and Soames chorused.

The thing was, Phoebe wondered, had Oakwood muttered precisely the same words at precisely the same instant, or had it merely been her imagination?

"Just don't choke me," Oakwood cautioned, "or we'll both come to grief, and that I don't want."

The technique may've been undignified, especially when employed by a landscape gardener in assistance of a renowned local heiress, and an unofficially betrothed one at that, but there were no more untoward incidents. Fordyce limped painfully after them, favoring first one leg and then the other as he rubbed his abused gluteus maximus and muttered about his beloved's lack of sylph-like qualities loudly enough that she heard him, and far from blushing, was actually forced to choke her laughter against

Oakwood's broad back. The answering suppressed rumble came close to being her undoing.

Then they were out the door and in the inn yard where the stableboy was proudly walking Ware's matched grays. Oakwood strode to the curricle, deposited Phoebe on the seat, and handed her her parcels.

"And that, my dear, will teach you to trust a caper-merchant to do a man's work," he scolded, breath clouding in the frigid afternoon air.

"Yes, sir, I'll keep that in mind if there's a next time," she managed.

"There'll be next times until you learn sense, the need for which I'll keep reminding you until you've mastered the lesson. I'll be requiring my mount," he said, taking the stableboy's place at the horses' heads as Ware swung himself onto the curricle's bench and retrieved reins and whip. "His lordship'll require a mount as well."

"Ain't nothing but Mr. Fordyce's nag," the stableboy returned.

"Then that'll have to serve. You don't mind, do you, Fordyce?"

"Don't know as how I could sit a horse at the moment anyway," Fordyce admitted. "Maybe you could take me up with you and Phoebe, Ware, since it'll save you a trip."

"No room," Ware said, and quickly gave his grays the office.

"Told you we'd send a cart for you, Fordyce," Phoebe heard Lord Soames say as the curricle lurched across the snow-rutted inn yard.

"So long as it's not the one you sent for Parmenter."

"What do you care? It's been given other use several times since."

And then voices were lost, and they were beyond the village with the lane leading to Underhill and Penwillow stretching before them, snowy branches arching above and the little glen where she'd had her mishap what seemed a lifetime ago not far ahead.

Ten

Phoebe was hit by a blast of warm air the instant she opened the front door. Underlying unfamiliar odors was the stench of old boiled cabbage, magnified by the heat. It was enough to make her gorge rise and her head throb, both of which did so instantly and unmercifully.

She leaned against the jamb to catch her breath, then closed the door, still clutching her Christmas parcels.

Dear God, while she was gone Mabel must've used up their entire supply of coal in a fit of self-indulgence! Well, for once the ungrateful wretch could go foraging for deadfall just as she had and the girls did, and to blazes with her dainty hands and the ease with which she caught cold, and learn just what it cost in effort and sore backs to take the worst of the chill off even one room.

And if Mabel so much as dared to mention the nasty smell of wood smoke and the nastier smell of ashes, Phoebe would, she'd, well, she'd say something unpardonable, and she wouldn't beg pardon later, either! Of all the irresponsible acts her stepmother could've performed, this was absolutely the worst.

Phoebe hobbled to the little cloakroom under the stairs, hid her bundle in a cranny, deposited her cloak on its usual hook and her boots in front of it, settled her old gray shawl around her shoulders from habit and slipped into worn house shoes.

Then, knowing there was no way to avoid the confrontation no matter how ill she felt, or how disillusioned, or how much she wanted her bed and a bit of a rest before she had to face Philip

Fordyce and Mr. Oakwood again, let alone the nobility from the castle, she limped across the entry and opened the parlor door.

Mabel lolled on the chaise lounge beside the chimney in the thinnest of her summer muslins from before she was wed, the fabric straining across her bosom. That she'd crammed herself into the thing at all was amazing. And not a single shawl—not one. None of Papa's journals protecting her feet from the cold. No coverlets. Indeed, she sported her one pair of delicate summer sandals, and was waving a fan she'd unearthed from heaven alone knew where, her eyes closed. Dear God, the woman's forehead was actually glowing with moisture, it was so hot close to the fire!

And on the table beside her? A pitcher of what could only be lemonade, for pity's sake. The two lemons Phoebe'd been hoarding for their Christmas punch—gone and irreplaceable, along with the wasted sugar.

Phoebe sank into a chair by the door, tears filming her eyes.

"Why did you do it, Mabel?" she whispered, despising the catch in her voice.

"Is that you, Phoebe?" Across the room her stepmother opened her eyes, smiling sleepily. "Isn't it wonderful in here? Absolute perfection, for once!"

"Why did you do it?" Phoebe repeated.

"Do what?"

"Waste the lemons on a silly drink we never have even in summer."

"Much more fun in winter," Mabel smiled good-humoredly, sitting up. "Makes me feel positively sybaritic, just like when I was a girl and would go visiting my friends from the seminary in Bath. Would you care for some? It's absolutely delicious, and so refreshing. I'll have Mrs. Short bring another glass for you."

"No, I would not care for any lemonade, and Mrs. Short has far better things to do than come running in here. You knew I was saving those lemons. Now there's nothing for the punch."

"Lord Soames'll give us more if only you ask."

"Well, I'm not going to ask. It was excessively kind of him to give us those."

"Then I will, silly girl. What's the use of having grand neigh-bors if one doesn't take advantage of the fact? I'm sure Lord Soames has dozens of lemons."

"I'm sure he does. That has nothing to do with it."

"It has everything to do with it," Mabel yawned. "Don't be tiresome, there's a dear. Would you put some more coal on the grate? I think the fire's dying."

"I will not! How could you be so thoughtless as to burn every scrap we have in a single day? Why, the way the entry felt there must be fires in every room."

"There are, or most of them," Mabel returned smugly. "And it's not every piece, believe me. There's enough for fires all this winter, and probably the next as well."

"Dear heaven, what've you done?"

"Exactly what you'd've done had you one ounce of sense: accepted Lord Soames's gift, and sent him an appropriate note of thanks."

Phoebe shivered, chilled to her very soul.

"I believe I'm the mistress in this house," she said, reining in her fury as best she could and keeping to a reasonable tone. "I refused that coal."

"Out of silly, misplaced pride! Pride goeth before a fall, you know. Besides, to've refused it would've been to offer his lord-ship the most dreadful of insults. Why, he might never've called again, or Mr. Ware either, so I saw to the matter. It only required sending Flossie down the lane, and telling them to wait 'round the curve until you were gone. Took you long enough! I had to have Mrs. Short give them the last of your father's ale for their trouble as I'd no money."

"I hardly think Lord Soames would've taken a refusal in such poor part. Indeed, I believe he'd've understood the reason for it quite well."

Phoebe watched her stepmother, amazed she felt so little sur-prise the matter of the coal hadn't been settled earlier. It had been a miserable scene, the usual feeble fire hissing on the grate, the girls hovering wide-eyed in a corner, hardly able to believe their half-sister and mother were pulling caps for the first time in their lives. And now it was to begin again, apparently.

"You bid fair to become just such another as Emma Trask," Mabel snapped, interrupting Phoebe's brown study. "Well, heaven help us, that's all I can say. At least when it came to your father no one doubted the evil, no matter how little anyone was willing to do about it. With you it's different—the little saint of Underhill!"

"How can you say I'm like Aunt Trask?" Phoebe protested reasonably. "She grabs anything that comes to hand, whether it belongs to her or not." At least she thought she was being reasonable. Certainly she was trying, and it was most miserably difficult when all she wanted was to run weeping from the house and never return. "In what way am I like Aunt Trask?"

"You're a Parmenter," Mabel'd spat bitterly, "always thinking only of yourself and more concerned with appearances and position than the needs and wishes of others. Indeed, you're more like your father with every passing day! We've only exchanged one tyrant for another equally cruel. Besides, I'm forever frozen to the bone, and likely to catch my death if you force me to survive another winter under the conditions your father imposed. Coal only in his office, indeed! Is that what you want—one less mouth to feed? One less body to clothe?"

As Phoebe listened in despair, Mabel moaned for Italy and the Mediterranean—about as attainable as the moon, and probably little warmer at this season—or at least fires in every room. Lord Soames had made that possible. Why should they all suffer from Phoebe's misplaced sense of the fitness of things? Besides, the gift had been for her, not Phoebe. She was delicate, always had been, tending to chills and fevers and heaven knew what other dire maladies the apothecary had never been able to diagnose properly, or that fancy physician from Pilchester either.

And when she'd admitted to Mr. Ware in the most reluctant manner how chilled she was—for he'd been taxing her unmercifully about her constant shivering—Mr. Ware had promised to see to the problem.

"Yes," she confessed as Phoebe sent her a hard look, seeming to think this would rectify matters, "the coal may've been ordered by his lordship, and it was to him I most properly directed my note of thanks, but I'm certain Mr. Ware was the one who handed over the necessary guineas. His is a kind heart, unlike yours. The sin of pride in refusing his charity would be far greater than whichever sin might apply when one accepts it."

"But such a gift from a stranger will create an even worse scandal than if it had indeed come from his lordship," Phoebe protested, head throbbing.

"That's of no importance whatsoever. What matters is creature comfort."

"And moral comfort go hang?"

"If it must. I'm content. In fact, I'm delighted. Why shouldn't you be?"

"Because, however little either of us may like it, this is my house now, and the decision was mine."

"Well, I took it out of your hands, and I'm glad I did!"

"Somewhere I shall have to find the funds to pay the carters to haul it away," Phoebe muttered, pressing her hands against her temples, "and pay Lord Soames or Mr. Ware for what you've squandered into the bargain."

"You do that, and I'll never forgive you. Never!"

"Why, *why* did you do this?"

"Because I wanted to! With all I had to bear from your father—"

"My father go hang! He has nothing to do with Lord Soames's coal."

"He has everything to do with it! Look at my face. Look at it! I'm a hag! These bruises will never fade. I deserve some consideration after what I've suffered."

Mabel flounced on her chaise lounge, lower lip thrust out as she turned her back. Then, negligently, she took a sip of the lemonade, then another.

Phoebe winced.

Certainly the bruises were at their ugliest, she conceded privately—yellowish and green with a touch of lingering purple, even under a heavy layer of rice powder. And they were still painful, that she knew.

Mabel was more skittish than ever since Papa's death, her nerves strung like the tightest wire. Well, and no wonder! She had to be terrified of disclosure, and with Lord Soames and Mr. Ware stopping by almost every day, and Philip Fordyce forever lurking about and saying things that were completely innocent on the surface but had a thousand unpleasant meanings snapping away beneath, things were rapidly going from bad to worse—witness this latest incident.

Lord Soames had to suspect something, for all his air of friendliness and his attempts at flirtation and his constant gifts. Why else would he have summoned what could only be a Bow Street Runner to Penwillow Castle? Papa'd always claimed the earls carried their brains in their purses. She wasn't so certain.

And Mr. Ware? He could only be another of Lord Soames's spies. She'd tried to caution Mabel about him repeatedly, but Mabel had merely laughed and claimed there was that about Mr. Ware which caused her to trust him implicitly. Silly Mabel! If she wasn't careful she'd end up at the crossroads without the least effort on her cousin's part, no matter how many sacrifices Phoebe made to protect her.

"Mr. Ware will be joining us in a moment," she said hesitantly, hoping the battle wouldn't begin again at the mention of the elegant, rather quiet Londoner's name. "He's just stabling his horses."

"Mr. Ware is here? At Underhill? Now? Oh, dear heaven!" Mabel leaped to her feet, quarrel forgotten, tugging at her gown. "And I in this old rag! It was fun to put it on and dream of being a girl again, but I'd never wear it in public. Oh, you must stop him. You mustn't let him in! I must go change. Why didn't you let me know he was here? I swear you're the most malicious girl I ever met!"

"I had other things on my mind," Phoebe sighed, pulling off her shawl and holding it out. "Here, you may hide beneath this."

"It's ugly!"

"It's all I have."

"Well, I won't wear it. Better this gown, dreadful as it is, than that old thing! Oh, dear—am I positively blowzy? I've been resting all day, attempting to recover my strength. Are my curls in order? Are there roses in my cheeks?"

"Mabel, for heaven's sake, it's just Mr. Ware."

"Just Mr. Ware, indeed!"

"Indeed it is," a pleasant masculine voice chuckled behind them. "Just as you say, Mr. Ware. No one else."

Mabel whirled, hands flying to her cheeks. Then she gave herself a little shake. As Phoebe watched, puzzled, her stepmother glided forward to greet their guest, hands extended, eyes glowing, the slightest of smiles parting her lips.

"You've put our coal to good use, I see," Ware said, seizing her hands with a matching smile, then raising them to his lips.

It was quite, Phoebe decided, as if she'd become invisible, or else vanished from the face of the earth.

"Indeed, Mr. Ware, and most grateful for it."

"You're no longer shivering under a mountain of shawls. I'm glad, Mrs. Parmenter."

"So am I, Mr. Ware," Mabel returned softly, "and more thankful for your kindness than you'll ever know."

"I think I can imagine. You've had a miserable time of it. I just wish I could make all the rest of it vanish as easily as I could the cold."

"I think you could do anything you wished, ever."

"There was a time when I thought so, too," he said with a sudden bitter twist to his mouth. "In the event, I was proved wrong."

"But not permanently."

"No, not permanently, thank the Lord for mercies large and small."

Phoebe produced what she hoped was a natural-sounding cough, though to her it was abysmally off.

"Don't you have something to occupy you elsewhere, Phoebe?" Mabel murmured, still smiling at Ware.

"No, nothing of import," Phoebe said, holding her ground.

"Then perhaps you'd be so kind as to fetch a glass for Mr. Ware? I'm sure he'd enjoy some of my lemonade."

"I'm sure, at the least, that you'd both much prefer me at the ends of the earth."

"Whatever can you mean?" Mabel turned then, frowning. "Are you being clever again, Phoebe? Too much cleverness is unattractive in a young woman, you know," she chided gently.

"No, I'm not being clever. At least, I don't think I am. In fact, I think I've been abysmally stupid."

"You have?" Ware said.

"Yes, I believe so. Mabel, why didn't you explain?"

"Explain? Explain what? I do wish you wouldn't speak in riddles, Phoebe."

"Forgive me this one, at least: what, if it exists at all, flourishes without food, keeps faith without hope, and never fails through all time?"

Mabel shook her head, clearly bewildered. "I've no idea," she said.

"And yet you're both the very best example of it."

"We are?"

"You are indeed." Tears dewed Phoebe's lashes. As never before, Philip Fordyce had her bound and chained. "I'm most delighted to meet your unsuitable suitor," she said on a stifled sob, "and I think he's most suitable, and I can think of no one who had a better right to send you that coal, and I earnestly beg your forgiveness for any harsh words I may've spoken, but you should've confided in me, truly you should've."

"Justin thought it unwise."

"Gentlemen don't always know everything."

"Justin does."

"I think," Phoebe said more firmly, "that very soon I shall be able to claim you as a connection, sir. I'm honored."

"So, you've tumbled to us."

"Not difficult. It is you, isn't it?"

"Yes," he said with a sudden, engagingly boyish grin, "I expect it is, if you mean what I think you do."

"Before Papa. Just before Papa. You were the one Aunt Trask railed against."

"Just down from university, liberated at last from the bonds of academe, visiting my eldest sister and old Soames. Best place I could think of to come on holiday. Always happy-go-lucky at Penwillow. Paradoxical, that the most joyous people I've ever known lived in the most forbidding place. Totally besotted, the pair of them.

"I was right," he said wistfully, "it was the best place I could've come. It was also, for a time, the very worst. The major impediment, you understand, wasn't my family. They weren't best pleased with my choice, but I was a very minor, very younger son. It would've blown over quite quickly, given my sister found Mabel everything that was sweet and unaffected. No, it was Mabel's. Mr. Gusset refused to believe I meant honestly by her. Finally there was nothing I could do but leave, and stay away."

"And so he chose Papa instead. That has to be one of the greatest ironies the world's ever seen."

"One of the most unpleasant, certainly. You'll keep our secret?"

"Why? Everyone'll be delighted, starting with Prissy and Pru."

"Soames lives here, and has to hold up his head while he does it. I'd rather the questions regarding Mr. Parmenter's death died down for his sake. For Mabel's as well, so long as you don't mind my assisting you in any way I can. My pockets're rather deep these days, thanks to some welcome bequests."

"Within reason. You've the right if any one does, but you'll have to watch yourselves. Another scene like the one you treated me to, and the entire world'll know."

"You don't mind?" Mabel's voice was hesitant, almost fearful. "It's dreadfully disrespectful to your father's memory—this happening so soon following his death."

"I think it's wonderful!" Phoebe beamed. "Absolutely wonderful! The girls shan't be a charge on you, that I promise," she said, turning back to Ware. "I'll arrange for allowances when the time comes, and dowries, and everything else that's proper."

"My dear Miss Parmenter, there's absolutely no need—"

"There's every need. It's a matter of honor—mine, not my father's. They're my sisters, you see, and I love them dearly and want to assure their futures. And, my name's Phoebe, not Miss Parmenter, at least when there's only the three of us present.

"Now," she said with a wan smile, "if you'll forgive me, I find I'm unutterably wearied. It's been a long day, and my ankle aches—I turned it in the lane, Mabel; nothing to worry about, but it's tender and swollen—and my head aches as well, and I should like a rest before dinner. You will join us, won't you, Mr. Ware? I can't promise you a meal such as you'd be served at the castle, but I can promise you precisely the company you'd most prefer."

"So long you don't mind my appearing as I am, I'd be delighted to join you."

"Excellent. We do *not* dress for dinner at Underhill."

From beyond the windows came the rattle of a cart.

"Oh, dear God," Phoebe whimpered, staring about her wildly. "Philip! And Mr. Oakwood, and likely Lord Soames into the bargain, all wanting to know the way to the old bailiff's cottage! Be careful, both of you. Mabel, your cousin has foisted himself on us after all. There was nothing I could do. Mr. Oakwood pressed the point. You'll have to see them settled. I can't! I simply can't, and retain my sanity! Mr. Ware'll explain when he has a chance. Oh, and I've hired Mr. Oakwood as our bailiff *pro tempore.*"

"Mr. Oakwood? Our bailiff? What will Mr. Hatch say?"

"Nothing. It's at no pay. For a month. His suggestion. Mr. Oakwood's, not Mr. Hatch's." Phoebe slung her shawl about her shoulders as she limped to the door. "Mr. Oakwood said hiring him and having Philip on the premises would solve all our problems, don't ask me how."

"Well," Ware chuckled, his amusement not quite reaching his eyes, "if Oakwood said that, you can believe him. Clever fellow, Oakwood. Best get yourself upstairs if you don't want to be caught. I'll detain the gentlemen while Mabel and the girls see to the cottage."

Phoebe nodded, hobbling into the entry and towards the stairs as fists pounded on the front door.

The evening proved interminable. Mabel, clearly anxious to avoid any semblance of particularity, invited Soames and Fordyce to join Ware and Oakwood at the family table. When it was discovered there wasn't a sufficiency to feed such a gathering, old Tom was sent to the castle for reinforcements in the form of already-prepared viands. Raft toddled back with him to oversee the groaning board and discover what the Parmenter cellars had to offer—a matter concerning which he'd been most curious through two generations.

The gentlemen lingered endlessly, not over their port, but over the ladies, each apparently determined to outstay the others. Oakwood and Fordyce were the worst, never quite coming to cuffs, infinitely adept at that civility which bristles and implies but never quite states. It was, Pru scolded their new bailiff under the guise of serving him yet another cup of tea, like being submitted to the torture of listening to fingernails scraping across slate.

Head still pounding, nerves frayed from the combined assaults of Oakwood and Fordyce, terrified Mabel would betray to Fordyce how infinitely his hold over her had increased, Phoebe finally claimed extreme fatigue—which was no lie—and excused herself, shooing the girls up the stairs ahead of her. As if at a signal Soames, Fordyce and Oakwood rose, eyeing each other warily.

"I have a need to confer with your lordship before we take our leave," Oakwood said casting Fordyce yet another derisive glance. "The matter of the game trails and the placement of your folly, and I believe we're close to outstaying our welcome."

"The hour does grow late," Soames agreed, eyes twinkling. In matter of fact the hour, for any gentleman accustomed to London hours—and Piers Duchesne, or Peter Oakwood as he was currently calling himself—was most certainly a London gentleman—was actually rather early. "You'll be able to handle things here for Miss Parmenter and still see to my commission as well, then? I thought you'd give it up."

"Hardly. Construction can't begin until spring, well after the thaws. There's plenty of time for everything."

"Ah, I see. Hadn't thought of that."

"Unconscionable to remain your pensioner now I've determined a few choices for you, but am unable to do anything about them until after the crocuses bloom."

"Admirable," Soames said as Ware was attacked by a coughing fit.

"Want to discuss a few possibilities before I set to work on the sketches, however. Waste of my time and your blunt otherwise, as you're paying me by the piece at each stage of the project."

"Too true. D'you want to join us, Ware? Might be you'd have an opinion or two."

"Oh, I don't think that's necessary," Oakwood interposed as Ware started to rise. "Once there're sketches to consider, then you'll be wanting your uncle. At the moment, though, we'll only be eliminating that which you wouldn't want at all. Far better for Mr. Ware to keep the charming Mrs. Parmenter company, as they're so comfortably settled by the fire."

Soames raised his brows but made no demur, merely indicating the parlor door with a graceful gesture.

Then, as if in afterthought, he turned to Mabel Parmenter. "Madam, where would it cause the least inconvenience for us to be private?"

"Phoebe's father's old office, I think, just at the end of the hall to the left at the back of the house before the kitchen wing. It's something of a shambles, but I had a fire lit in there as well this afternoon, so the worst of the chill should be off."

"Excellent. You're most gracious, accommodating us in this manner."

"It's my pleasure," she dimpled. "There're pens and paper in the office. You'll find working candles on the stand in the hall beside the veilleuse. There's a lamp on Mr. Parmenter's work table, but it may have no oil. Whatever condition it's in, it's the same as the last night he, well, I don't believe Phoebe has yet—"

"You going to wait for me, Fordyce," Oakwood broke in, "or will you be returning to the cottage on your own?"

Fordyce made a great show of yawning.

"I take it y'don't want my advice, Lord Soames," he said on yet another delicate and clearly bogus yawn, "given y'don't want your uncle's? Thought y'didn't."

He paused, as if considering a matter of dire importance, a slight frown furrowing his brow. Then, drawing himself up, he said, "I must thank you for remedying the improvidence of my cousin when she invited so many to dine, my lord, without the least thought as to how she'd feed them."

"I—I didn't think, Cousin Philip," Mabel quavered, blanching.

"I know you didn't. Y'never do. And then my betrothed did naught but throw her hands up in despair when she learned of it. You should've taught her better, Cousin Mabel." He turned back to Soames with an elegant bow. "I was mortified, my lord, that you should receive such shabby treatment in my home. Phoebe will learn to manage better under my direction once we're wed, that I promise you, if you'll be kind enough to overlook it this once. She's inexperienced in the ways of the world, and has no notion what's due your consequence."

"I understand entirely," Soames said, a fleeting look of distaste in his eyes. "Please disregard it, just as I did."

"Too kind," Fordyce murmured. "I'm most grateful for your forbearance, but then it is always so with those of the great world—courtesy compounded by courtesy."

"Encroaching insect," Soames muttered, turning his back on the man as Mabel flushed painfully and Ware clenched his jaws.

"Well, what's it to be, Fordyce," Oakwood demanded in the sudden silence. "Are you waiting for me? I shan't be but a short while."

"No, if it's all the same to you, and with my apologies to the present company, especially you, Cousin Mabel, for deserting you in such a manner, I believe I'll seek the arms of Morpheus.

Totally fagged, given all the excitements to which I've been subjected, followed by such an excellent meal. Far better than the swill Phoebe customarily provides."

"Yes, it's been a rather active time for you," Oakwood agreed sympathetically, "what with this bit of business and that, and making a late night of it yesterday. I'll see you back at the cottage, then."

"Don't trouble yourselves to see me out. I know my way. Your lordship, Ware, Cousin Mabel—a good evening to you. Ah, Oakwood, yes. Later. I shan't wait up for you, though, so don't look to see me until morning, and then not early. Pray keep your activities to a minimum when you do arrive. No crashing about. I'm a light sleeper, and don't care to be awakened."

Fordyce produced another practiced bow and showed himself out of the parlor, still yawning, and not bothering to close the door. From where he stood Oakwood could see the man don his greatcoat in the glow of the single candle lighting the entry, fussily adjust the many capes, then retrieve his hat and gloves and an elegant walking stick that would be all but useless in the rutted snow around the house.

"Won't you be needing a lantern?" he called.

"No, I'll do fine with the moonlight. Almost full, thank you."

Then Fordyce disappeared from view. There was the sound of the front door opening. The accompanying blast of frigid air found its way into the parlor, flickering the candles. Then the door closed, and there was silence.

"And so the party of the first part departeth," Oakwood murmured, "may his soul rot in hell forever and his sleep be most unquiet. Well, your lordship, shall we?"

They abandoned Ware and Mabel to the cozy privacy of the little parlor, Oakwood firmly closing the door behind them and frowning Soames down before he could speak, then lighting a work candle and pointing to the back of the house.

There were two doors on the left at the end of the hall, not one as Mrs. Parmenter had indicated. The first was negligible, merely an under-the-stairs cubby filled with outdoor gear. The second proved the one they wanted, giving on a cheerless room paneled in dark wood. Moonlight streamed through a pair of soaring, undraped windows, striking a littered table set before a fire that had died hours before.

"Perfect," Oakwood murmured, dripping some wax on a battered standish and anchoring the candle in it as the wax congealed in the cold. The lamp, as Mrs. Parmenter had cautioned, held no oil. "I want him to see us conferring, but not clearly. Keep your back to those windows, and yourself between the windows and the light. Hearing's another matter. I don't want him to hear a blessed thing, or be able to guess what we're discussing from the movements of our lips. There're some who can do that, you know—discern what's being said from the movement of the lips—quite accurately."

"What the devil?"

"Fordyce. I'll lay you pounds to shillings he's out there spying on us. And not too distant, either. You'll notice that pane's broken, and stuffed with cloth? And that's a door to the exterior in the corner. Big keyhole, so keep your voice down."

"Listening at doors? Even Fordyce wouldn't stoop so low."

"Perfect phrase," Oakwood grinned, diverted. "And keep your voice down, blast it. Yes, he'd definitely stoop that low, especially if by putting his ear to the keyhole he thought he might learn something of use. The man's a thorough scoundrel. Point is, I've worked it out, all of it. Well, most of it, at least. The most important part."

"What in blazes are you maundering about? Worked what out?"

"The solution to Miss Parmenter's problems, and she does have 'em in plenty, starting with the fact that she doesn't in the least want to marry the widow's cousin. In fact, I think she'd accept most anyone so long as it wasn't Dandy Clare or Alfie Gusset or Cobber Trask, and whoever offered for her was able to keep Fordyce at bay. Has some sort of hold over her, y'see, though she claims he doesn't and I'm not entirely sure what it is, for another thing I'll swear: She didn't murder her father."

"Murder her father? Phoebe Parmenter? Not that he didn't deserve it, but have you taken leave of your senses?"

"It was a possibility I had to eliminate. She had opportunity, you see, and motive. Would've been totally out of character, though. Has to be something else."

"You don't say!"

"I do, but I'd wager my last shilling the man didn't meet with an accident in your woods. Just ended up there. See here, keep your back to the windows and your voice down, I tell you. I want him to see us, nothing more. Men who're unnerved act rashly. I want him rash as they come."

Oakwood rooted about in the clutter until he found a fresh sheet of paper, drew some intersecting lines on it with a pencil stub, added a few circles and triangles for good measure. It could be a diagram, he decided, eyeing it with pride. That no one could be sure exactly what it signified didn't matter in the least. The thing was merely a test.

"Pretend to be considering this," he told Soames, adding another pair of lines. "I'll be pointing to one thing and another. Don't let it distract you."

"You're enjoying yourself immensely, aren't you."

"Never more. This is *my* adventure, not my sister's or my father's. First, a question for you: how often did Ware come visiting at Penwillow in the old days?"

"What has that to do with anything?"

"I'm curious, is all. Seems to've developed quite a proprietary attitude toward the widow of late."

Soames shrugged. "I don't remember," he said. "Not often. I do remember his being here once for most of a long holiday. As for the widow, he's just being his usual chivalrous self. Even treats Great-aunt Genevieve that way. Nothing in it."

"I see. Not the main issue in any case. Thing of it is," Oakwood continued, bending over the table and indicating first one section of the lines and circles, then another, as if he were offering options, "Miss Parmenter needs a husband, given the terms of her father's will. It's that, or they'll starve."

"Doing my poor best to see they don't," Soames murmured, frowning at the meaningless lines, "and Ware's seen to their coal supply."

"Has he? Kind of him. Far more to the point than bushels of roses." Oakwood drew three more lines. "Doesn't obviate the fact that Miss Parmenter must wed, though. We're agreed on that point?"

"I suppose so." Soames's finger traveled the paper, then tapped a circle as if he were reaching a decision, amusement twinkling at the back of his eyes. "Certainly Parmenter did everything he could to force the issue. She has very little choice."

"Well," Oakwood said, straightening up and facing his old friend with a grin, "neither do you. Think on it. You have to, as well."

"What must I do?"

"Marry."

"What the devil're you implying?" Soames roared, whirling on Oakwood so that he stood in profile against the windows, secrecy forgotten in the horror of the moment, ledgers and journals flying to the floor. "If you think for one instant—"

"Hush, blast you!" Oakwood grasped his arm, swung him back to the table, pointing to his diagram insistently. "And consider the matter rationally rather than flying into the boughs like some missish virgin who's just been offered a *carte blanche.*"

"I am not in the market for—"

"I don't give a tinker's dam whether you are or not. Sooner or later you'll have to be, right or wrong?"

"Right, I suppose, but it ain't now!" Soames yelped.

"Why not? There's no one in the world you could find who'd make you a better wife than Phoebe Parmenter. She's intelligent," Oakwood insisted, ticking the points off on his fingers, and in his turn forgetting the need for secrecy in his fervor. "She's pluck to the backbone. She's provident. She's sensible. She's infinitely kind and gentle and loyal. She's a considerable heiress. Her lands march with yours. There's never a dull moment when she's about. She has a delightful sense of the ridiculous. And," he concluded triumphantly, "a decent gown or two and she wouldn't be just fetching. She'd be the sort to plant a man a facer from which he'd never recover, or even want to. Can do it right now, come to that, with just those eyes of hers for the task, and she's a delightful armful into the bargain. Curves in all the right places, for all one can't see 'em given those shapeless gowns and horrible shawl of hers."

"You've fluff in your cockloft!"

"Not a bit of it. Plain common sense. Besides," Oakwood concluded triumphantly, knowing he had reason on his side, "you rescue her from Fordyce and you'll be the hero of the neighborhood. Don't have to set up your nursery immediately if you don't want to. I wager Miss Parmenter'd enjoy an extensive bride trip— Rome, Naples, Paris, even Athens perhaps. Give you a chance to show her off.

"Best of all, if you offer for her Hatch'll never dare say nay, and she won't be cheated of her inheritance. Mrs. Parmenter and the girls'll be seen to, and when they make their come-outs it'll be under the aegis of a countess. They'll be Diamonds, or at least Prissy will, and with a little management Pru'll become a famous Original. And with your assistance Phoebe'll be able to see to Alfie as well. He deserves a wider scope than Chedleigh Minor or Market Stoking. Or Pilchester, for that matter. Too limited."

"Does he? My goodness!"

"He does, indeed. University first. Then we'll see about a profession. I'll be glad to lend a hand, bear-lead him about Town when the occasion offers, see he meets the right people. My father should be of some help as well, and between Serena and Miss Chumme-that-was— No need to look at me like that! I'm not fit for Bedlam. I'm the most rational man you'd ever want to meet."

"Are you indeed?" Soames murmured. "Amazing."

Then, as Oakwood watched his old friend, it was as if a cloth had been wiped across the man's face, leaving it expressionless.

"I see," Soames said. "Interesting solution you've come up with, but you're missing the point. There's a far better candidate than ever I could be, and he has a distinct advantage over me: I suspect he loves Miss Parmenter to distraction, but doesn't realize it. Certainly he speaks of her in the manner of a man smitten beyond reason. And, from what I've observed, she cares for him more than a little in spite of herself."

"Not Dandy Clare!"

"Wind blew in that direction at first, but once she had a chance to see him as he really is? No, it's veered in another entirely, thank heavens. Being lord of all I survey's no sinecure, believe me. Don't know how my father endured it. Just wait 'til it's your turn. You'll see. It's not the land's the problem. It's the people, and one does feel a certain responsibility, dammit, little as one wants to. Deuced uncomfortable."

"He's suitable? Hatch won't be able to come up with something unsatisfactory about him? No skeletons in any cupboards?"

"None beyond a severe case of masculine myopia, perhaps. Oh, he's a bit mercurial at the moment, but once he recognizes his plight that'll pass."

"And he can offer her the same advantages you could? Decent fortune, good name?"

"Absolutely, you gudgeon," Soames grinned. "Better, as it happens."

"Tell me who it is, and I'll put a gun to the fellow's head and march 'em to the altar, complete with special license."

"You will? That would be fascinating to watch."

"Who is it, blast you? This ain't a laughing matter!"

"I didn't say it was, though you're certainly turning it into one. No, don't eat me!" Ware protested as Oakwood rounded on him, fists balling. "I've no desire to have my daylights resemble poor Klegg's. But a special license? Impossible. There isn't time, though it's an excellent notion. Wish I'd thought of it."

"You didn't need to. When I was in Pilchester I hired a courier for a dash to London. I've an acquaintance at the Horse Guards seeing to it for me. Should have a license with Miss Parmenter's name on it by tomorrow evening. Paid the man twenty-five pounds and promised him another twenty-five if he gets it here by then. Figured I'd have you at the altar the moment it arrived."

"Good Lord," Soames murmured. "I can't believe it!"

"Can't believe what? That I can act expeditiously when called upon to do so? The poor woman's in desperate case, I tell you, and there's not much she can do to save herself. Women're still chattels when all's said and done, to be disposed of as their fathers and brothers and husbands wish. When one of 'em tangles with the wrong sort, she might as well stick her spoon in the wall for all the real help she'll receive."

"Done what I could by delaying the banns," Soames protested uneasily.

"Well-meaning, but it isn't enough. Fordyce's been pressuring her to advance the date. Could've been a nasty scene at the George earlier. He's gotten himself a special license as well, for all I believe it's forged.

"Hatch," Oakwood explained at Soames's startled frown. "Alfie tells me he spotted them—well, spied on them—in Market Stoking yesterday morning. Papers everywhere, and they appeared to be copying a document of some sort. Then yesterday evening Fordyce informed me he'd acquired a license. Hasn't the funds for it, that's certain. The inference is obvious. I understand Hatch's indulged in such exercises before, for all it's never been proved."

"True enough. Never sufficient evidence. His forgeries're masterpieces of the art. Either Fordyce can prove something no one else's been able to and is blackmailing the old reprobate, or else he's signed over part interest in Underhill to Hatch once he's wed to Miss Parmenter. Either way, I don't like it."

"Didn't think you would. Apparently Fordyce is afraid someone'll come to her rescue before the knot's tied."

"Is he? Then I suggest you spend every waking moment in Miss Parmenter's company. Nothing he can do if you're at her side to put a stop to his machinations."

"Will you stop grinning like a cat in the cream? Doesn't solve the problem, only delays it, blast you! Can't you understand it's to your advantage to marry the woman?"

"No, quite frankly, I can't. I'm the wrong man."

"She'd accept you, I know she would. Just think: No need to go playing the fool in London, doing the pretty and enduring the boredom of a Season. Terrible waste of time and blunt, especially when she's available, and right beneath your nose."

"And some other noses."

"You haven't listened to a word I said!"

"Yes, I have. I've listened with extreme care. It's you who hasn't heard a word. A special license, by damn! If that doesn't beat all. Indeed, I believe I'll gift you with a hearing trumpet for Christmas. Just stick close as a burr to Miss Parmenter. Only way disaster'll be averted, justice served, and everyone achieve their happily-ever-afters."

"Make it a deal easier if you'd simply tell me who this other fellow is. If she cares for him in the least—"

"I'm beginning to suspect she does."

"Well then, you see? Eminently suitable, and from what you say—"

"Doubt you'd agree he's suitable at the moment," Soames grinned. "No, you'll have to discover him for yourself if you're determined to rush about setting all to rights."

The earl snapped the candle from its wax support, indicated the door.

"Now, if you don't mind, Ware and I have a distance to go before we can seek our beds given it must be by the lanes. He wants his grays back in a decent stable."

"You're riding in Ware's curricle?" Oakwood asked, brows soaring. "At night? I thought you said—"

"Oh, no, I value my head and my teeth as much as ever. I'll beg a mount of Mrs. Parmenter, but there's no way I'll permit poor Ware to travel alone," Soames grinned. "Too great a risk of his being waylaid. This is rather a dangerous neighborhood, don't you know. Besides, Freddy Derringer's reading his paper this evening," he said more seriously. "I'd like to hear it. A bit wild, Freddy, but his theories're always interesting, and the discussions that follow're amusing in the extreme. You're done, I presume?"

"Yes, I'm done as you won't listen to sense. Now I'm going to have to come up with another solution, and I can't think of a one."

"You will, that I promise you. Yes, you'll most definitely come up with another solution, little as you may think it now. A far better one."

Eleven

It was with an air of self-important mystery that Mabel waylaid Phoebe the next morning, taking hold of the young woman's arm through her old gray shawl and refusing to release her.

"I need you abovestairs," she whispered importantly. "Yes, I know Mrs. Short expects you in the kitchen, and I know you've to descend to the cellars and see if you can unearth one last bottle of brandy overlooked by my pernicious cousin, and I know the parlor must be cleaned in case the gentlemen or Sister Trask decide to stop by, but the girls can help you with all that later. Just come with me, and not a word to anyone!"

Phoebe sighed. Heaven alone knew what flight Mabel was indulging this time. Ever since admitting her connection with Ware the poor woman had become increasingly skittish, flinching whenever Fordyce entered a room and blanching at his least word.

Phoebe cast a longing look toward the back of the house. Dealing with Mabel's megrims was not a thing to which she wished to be subjected on this particular morning—not with the way she'd felt since yesterday, eyes burning, tongue furred, and the inside of her skull throbbing as if everything in it had swollen to twice the customary size. Each breath, each step, each word was an effort performed against her will.

"All right, Mabel," she sighed hobbling across the entry and up the stairs, then down the dark, drugget-carpeted hall to Mabel's new bedchamber.

If only she weren't so weary of it all: the fencing with Fordyce and Oakwood, the constant responsibilities, the constant pressures, the fear of saying one word wrong, placing one foot awry, the scratching and scrabbling to put each meal on the table. Even with Lord Soames's considerate gifts, there were problems. One didn't survive on tea or chocolate, or pastries and asparagus and exotic hothouse fruits. One survived on meat and bread, and those remained in short supply at Underhill.

She stood aside as Mabel slipped a key from her pocket and unlocked the narrow door. "What on earth?" Phoebe murmured, eyeing the procedure in surprise.

"Promise me," Mabel whispered, "not a word of what you see passes beyond this room!"

"I promise."

"All right, then." She swept the door open, pushed Phoebe into the little bedchamber, then pulled the door to and locked it from the inside. "I haven't been resting quite as much as you've thought, nor have I been rising quite as late."

The diminutive widow darted across the room, pausing to add some coal to the already generous fire glowing on the grate, then looped the draperies aside and pointed to a jumble of bright emerald fabric lying on her bed. More colorful jumbles lay scattered on chest and chairs.

"There! That's what I've been doing, and *that's* why I haven't gotten any of the new draperies stitched up as yet. I simply couldn't wait another two days. Out of that dreadful brown thing this instant!"

She seized the emerald fabric, held it out. As if at a magician's wave, what appeared to be merely a length of soft wool resolved itself into elegant folds and pleats, high waist accentuated by darker green satin ribbons, the sleeves elegantly puffed at the shoulder, then tightly gathered below the elbow, the cuffs touched with ribbon and old lace mirroring the demure, high lace collar.

Phoebe's mouth dropped open.

"Don't stand there catching spiders with your tongue, for pity's sake! Take off that hideous rag you've been wearing for weeks, and put this on! This instant, Phoebe. I can hardly wait to see it on you. I think the fit'll be perfect. And see? I've made you a shawl of the same material, and trimmed it with braided ribbon fringe."

"So that's where my red ribbon went."

"Only just a little bit. After Christmas I'll change the red for green, but I couldn't resist transforming you into a wandering holly bush at this season."

"Dear Lord in heaven!" Phoebe murmured. "I haven't seen anything so elegant in—well, I've *never* seen anything so elegant."

"Mr. Ware acquired some journals for me just after your father, well, you know. Mr. Ware hoped they'd distract me, and they did. They distracted me most wonderfully, but I was heartbroken for I thought there was nothing I could do about them, for a journal is one thing, but permitting him to purchase fabric?

"Well, I couldn't do that, for I'm not quite the wet goose you think, but I had my heart set on seeing you properly garbed for once, and then you told me about your attic treasures, and so we went up one day, just Mr. Ware and I, when you and the girls were away from the house—and most dreadfully foul it was, all spiders and dirt; I don't know how you stood being shut up in there so often, truly I don't, for I know I should've gone mad— and oh, the things we discovered! Fabrics of all sorts, bolts and bolts, and most in passable condition despite their age. Who purchased them I've no idea, for it certainly wasn't your father, not even when your mother was alive. Some ancestor, I suppose, with an open purse and a flair for such things.

"And you're going to wear it—the dress, I mean, for it's quite the latest style—and look, I found some cambric. Just feast your eyes on this!" What appeared to be a length of white cloth resolved itself into a slim petticoat trimmed with more ribbons and a delicate undergarment resembling a loose corset cover. "Here, let me help you."

Moments later a bemused Phoebe stared at her reflection in her stepmother's dressing table mirror. It was a gown—not a dress. A deceptively simple, supremely elegant gown. And, it suited her to perfection. And it was soft and warm, unlike the rough old thing she'd been wearing for what seemed like forever.

"I had to piece the skirt at the knee for moths had gotten into the fabric, but one would never know for I hid the seams with bands of green ribbon. Now," Mabel fussed, draping the red-fringed shawl over Phoebe's elbows, "if you'd only stop pulling your hair back so you resemble a plucked chicken!"

"No, this is change enough," Phoebe protested weakly. Change enough? Dear heaven! It was as if an entirely different person peered at her from the mirror, and not herself at all.

"Just a few curls? One or two, to soften your face?" Mabel cajoled. "You'd be quite lovely if only you'd give yourself a chance. I've had the tongs heating by the fire."

"Absolutely not."

"Ah well, Rome wasn't built in a day. I know you've always considered me foolish to be so concerned with fashion," Mabel chattered, twitching Phoebe's skirts and adjusting the stand of lace at the neckline, "but there's little else to amuse a woman once she's wed. Of course I never was permitted to put my knowledge to use, for your father didn't care what appearance I presented so long as my belly was fat with yet another babe of his getting. Now? Now," she laughed, surveying the results of her handiwork, "I'm able to do my best, and you'll notice I've learned a thing or two since my girlhood."

"You have, indeed."

Mabel's bride clothes had been fussily girlish parodies of her elevated schoolmates' finery. This creation was the ultimate in restrained elegance.

"This is really for me?" Phoebe said wonderingly.

"Every stitch and tuck of it! It's your Christmas present, but I wanted you to have it ahead of time. And I'm going to make dresses for the girls." Mabel whisked up a deep rose fabric from her chair by the fire. "For Pru. I felt it would lend her color. And this one," she said, seizing a dusky blue, "is for Prissy. Perfect with her eyes, don't you think?"

"I think she'll set every young man's heart within a hundred leagues fluttering!"

"Well, it's a little soon for that," Mabel returned complacently, draping the fabrics over the foot of the bed, "for I won't have her marrying as young as I did for all it's the custom—not unless she's completely sure. My daughters won't follow in my footsteps, or at least not my early ones, not if I can help it."

"But, what of you?"

"There wasn't time to make anything for myself," Mabel said airily, "but that doesn't matter. Perhaps Mr. Ware will have a Christmas surprise waiting for me—I've given him enough hints as to what would suit me best, goodness knows—and even if he doesn't I've still a few things that're passable. You don't mind that I helped myself to some of the fabrics I found in the attic?"

"Not in the least."

"And you're pleased with your gown?"

"Pleased? With this? I'm overwhelmed!"

"Just so long as you're pleased. Mr. Ware thought you would be. It was at his suggestion, to keep my mind occupied so I wouldn't dwell on, well, unpleasant matters. And then you're so hopelessly dowdy. An offense to the eyes, and he didn't believe that to be wise just now, and insisted I see to you first."

Mabel grabbed Phoebe's threadbare brown dress and gray shawl, tossed them on the fire, seized the poker and crammed them deep within the glowing coals. The stench of burning wool filled the room.

"What are you doing?" Phoebe gasped "Those have lots of wear left in them, and are perfect for—"

"They're perfect for nothing, not even rags! If I don't burn them, I know you: you'll continue to wear them, and leave this hanging on a peg. Well, I won't allow it. It's time you had pretty things, and I'm going to see you have 'em. Phah! I never knew burning wool smelled so horrid." Mabel glanced at Phoebe in dismay. "Why, it's rendering the room uninhabitable. Now what am I to do?"

Phoebe chuckled, opened both tall windows, letting in a blast of frigid air. Then she seized the ewer on the washstand and dumped its contents on the fire. Smoke and steam billowed into the room.

"Something may be rescued of them, I believe," she said, pulling the smoldering mass from the grate.

"No, you don't!" Mabel grabbed the charred remains, darted to the window and flung both pieces as far as she could. "There," she said with considerable satisfaction, dusting her hands, "now you'll not be tempted."

"But—"

"Have done, Phoebe. You may command everywhere else at Underhill, but from this day forward I command in your dressing room."

"I suppose all I can say is thank you."

" 'Thank you' will do nicely," Mabel returned with a twinkle, "along with a properly reverential 'Yes, Mama dear,' no matter *what* I instruct you to wear."

They laughed together at the suddenly dowagerish stance Mabel adopted. Then Phoebe sobered.

"And if your cousin doesn't agree?" she said.

"Bother Cousin Philip! I wish you'd chase him from the place, really I do."

"I don't believe that would be wise. Do you?"

"No," Mabel sighed, "I suppose it wouldn't, but I dearly wish it were. There's no word vile enough to describe him. How you can continue to accept his advances I'll never understand. I was all for putting mouse droppings between his sheets, but the girls insisted it wouldn't do. Instead I was forced to content myself with chipping bits from the window surrounds, and providing him with the nastiest blankets I could find."

"Oh, dear."

"And sweeping all the dust in the place under his bed. Philip despises dust, has ever since we were children. He hasn't changed in that respect. In fact, he hasn't changed in any respect: a weasel then, and a weasel now. I didn't think you'd mind, especially as I saw to it Mr. Oakwood had the more comfortable room and was provided with the best Underhill has to offer."

"No, I don't mind."

Mabel nodded wisely, smiling the smallest of secret smiles.

"Rather fetching, your Mr. Oakwood, wouldn't you say?" she teased.

"Fetching?" Phoebe laughed, still examining her reflection in the mirror. "No, I wouldn't call him that. Prepossessing, perhaps, and amusing, and somewhat disturbing, and infinitely dangerous into the bargain—for he's not what he claims to be, though I'm not certain precisely what he is. But, fetching? Never! As soon say a great cloud booming thunder and flashing lightning is fetching, or a flood rolling over the land, sweeping away everything in its path."

"Ah, so there you are, my love. Been hiding from me?"

Phoebe froze at the oily tone of reproof. Then she raised her eyes as Prissy's and Pru's heads snapped up from their efforts at constructing the frame for a kissing wreath.

He was dressed to the nines, as always. A veritable Pink of the ton. The conniving blackmailer looked ready for a saunter in Hyde Park, or a call upon some high-flying courtesan. How he managed it on short funds was the only question. She could swear both Nile green coat and florid wasitcoat were new, and the lace at his wrists was of the finest. Talented and resourceful when something mattered to him—she had to grant the man that.

Of course, it was possible his toggery wasn't the latest stare. No way to know so deep in the country. Certainly he didn't affect a style that in any way resembled that of Lord Soames, which was rather rough and ready. Come to that, it didn't resemble that of the restrained Mr. Ware, who was sitting companionably by the fire with Mabel and, until Fordyce made his entrance, had been reading to them from a volume of Shakespeare's sonnets as they worked on Christmas decorations.

"Of course not. Good afternoon, Philip," she responded, dredging up a smile from heaven knew where. "I hope you passed a pleasant night?"

"Do you, really? Well, I didn't," he said with a yawn reminiscent of the previous evening. "That place wants a new roof and a glazier—drafty as the devil—and there was dust everywhere. I can't think what you were about, not having it seen to."

"The bailiff's cottage hasn't been occupied in years," Phoebe explained, refusing to glance in Mabel's direction. "You'll remember your decision to take up residence there was a last minute thing, for originally you were to seek lodgings with Mr. Hatch. There wasn't time to ready it properly for you. I'm sorry."

"There wasn't time? Certainly there would've been had you applied yourself immediately upon returning to Underhill. Heedless as always, Phoebe. This insouciance when it comes to the comfort of others must cease."

"As I said, I'm sorry. I'll send Flossie and the girls over later."

"See that you do. Better yet, see to it yourself. Then there's a prayer it'll be done properly." He yawned again, a lingering, almost sensuous thing that repulsed far more than it annoyed. Then, with narrowed eyes, he said, "Have I seen that gown before? It's not quite as disgusting as the rest of your wardrobe—if one can dignify the rags in which you customarily show yourself by such an elevated term."

"Mabel contrived it from things she found in the attic—a Christmas surprise she insisted on presenting to me early."

"Thought it had a blowzy, homemade air about it. A shawl should always contrast with a gown, not match it. No sense of style, my cousin, unfortunately."

"I hate him! I hate him—I hate him—I hate him!" Pru muttered under her breath as Prissy slipped from the parlor and Fordyce strolled to the fireplace where a liberal coal fire burned on the grate.

"Hush," Phoebe murmured. "I'm already in his black books. You and Prissy should be put on bread and water for leaving his sleeping chamber as you did. Don't make bad worse."

"I couldn't. Things're already at their worst. If only he'd take himself off, but that's too much to hope for."

"Ware," Fordyce said evenly, either ignoring or not hearing the murmurings behind him as he held his hands to the warmth, "I bid you good day. Damnable place, that bailiff's cottage. Your pigs're better housed, Cousin Mabel."

Mabel shrank toward Ware.

Phoebe frowned, sighed. Blast the woman! She'd give the game away if she wasn't careful, and what Fordyce would do if he detected the attachment between his cousin and the well-to-do

Londoner Phoebe trembled to think. Certainly his price would rise higher than just Underhill and herself. Immeasurably higher.

"I'm sorry you weren't more comfortable, Philip," she said, not in the least sorry, only thankful the shambles to which Fordyce had been treated hadn't been too obviously contrived. "There're no funds for such repairs at the moment."

"As for the bed!" Fordyce grumbled on. "D'you really call it a bed, my dear? I'd've thought you had something better than that lumpy straw tick with which I was provided, and the ropes sagged. As for the blankets! They smelled of horse, or possibly goat. I had to drench my pillow with cologne to counter the stench."

Pru stifled a giggle.

Phoebe's eyes flew reprovingly to her half-sister, then to Mabel.

"I'll see if something better can be found in the attics," she said in an attempt to placate the man.

"Don't bother. I'll be moving in here in the next day or so, and then I expect to have the best bed in the house, and nicely warmed into the bargain. Well, aren't you going to offer me something with which to break my fast? Perhaps a beef steak grilled rare so the blood follows the knife, and some eggs, and a tankard of ale. A pot of chocolate wouldn't be amiss, either, and some muffins."

"You know our larder doesn't run to such luxuries as steak, Philip, and eggs are precious at this season. I'm sure Mrs. Short will provide you with a bowl of porridge if you'll take yourself to the kitchen."

"So unaccommodating! You really must learn better manners, my dear."

"But I'd prefer you saw to yourself," Phoebe continued as if he hadn't spoken. "Flossie and Mrs. Short are elbow-deep in the baking for Christmas dinner."

"Then why don't you see to me?" His smile was all that was cajoling, all that was insinuating. It didn't reach his eyes, which were as blue and hard and cold as ever beneath their elegantly-arched brows. "I've a need to confer with you privately concerning our nuptials in any case, my dear. They're hard upon us, and I'd like to discover your preferences in certain matters."

"Anything you need to ask me, Philip, you can ask in front of my family."

"Oh? Ware's part of the family now?"

The derisive look he sent her had Phoebe blanching. She rose hastily from her seat at the table, scrubbed the sap from her hands with a rag, then removed her apron.

"We can be private in Papa's office, if you wish," she said, knowing it was capitulation, but unable to discern a alternative.

"An excellent proposal. Is there a fire?"

"I doubt we'll freeze in the few moments it will require to conclude whatever business we have. Pru," she said, leaning over her sister's shoulder to examine the frame they'd been constructing, "be sure those twigs are tightly bound with string or the entire thing will fall apart the first time it's touched, and we don't want that. Mistletoe everywhere, and someone knocked on the head into the bargain."

"There's someone I'd dearly love to see knocked on the head," Pru muttered, "and I won't give you even one guess as to his identity!"

"Hush. I'll be back in a few moments. Whatever happened to Prissy?"

"Had to visit the necessary. Guess you didn't notice, enthralled as you were exchanging compliments with Cousin Philip."

Phoebe flushed, then squared her shoulders and led the way into the hall, Fordyce close on her heels.

"Now," she said as soon as the door was closed, "what do you want?"

"My dear, such an uncivil tone!"

"Well, what d'you expect? There's not the least love lost between us. Why pretend otherwise?"

"I expect—nay, demand—courtesy from my betrothed. There's no need for us to be forever at cross purposes. Didn't you learn anything yesterday?"

"What could I possibly've learned, other than you lack a certain couth?"

"Why, that I merely seek my own comfort and ease. And," he continued with a narrow look, "that I'm not best pleased when they're threatened, and won't stand for it. Beyond that? I'm truly a charming, very peaceable man, as you'd quickly understand if you'd only give me half a chance."

"You?" she laughed bitterly. "Charming? Yes, I suppose you may be, given snakes are said to mesmerize their victims. Now, what d'you want?"

"Not here, I think," he said, glancing around the entry. "Much too public. Anyone could interrupt us, including that oversized oaf you've burdened me with as housemate. He snores, you know. Loudly. Didn't like to mention it in there, but you must get rid of him. Immediately. No more of this bailiff nonsense."

"We're not married yet, Philip. You have no say as to who forms part of my household and who doesn't."

"That's where you're in error, my dear, or have you forgotten darling Cousin Mabel? Think of the scandal! Your pretty step-mother's face turning purple, her tongue swelling and thrusting as she twitches on the gibbet, and soils herself into the bargain. How demeaning for her, fastidious as she is! Hanging isn't painless, you know, and it can take considerable time. Hours, I've been told, if the hangman knows his business and someone's slipped him a coin to extend the process. An ugly death, but then why should a murderer be granted a pleasant one? Or should I say 'murderess?' "

"Philip! Please!"

"And then there'll be Ware, distraught and unable to rescue her for all his great name and deep pockets. Oh yes, I've spotted that little *affaire*. And the girls of course, sobbing and blaming you because you were too selfish to avert the tragedy. Poor Prissy. Poor Pru. How long d'you think their love'll last under those conditions? Or their maidenheads?"

"You're despicable!"

"They'll end up as high-priced trollops for a bit—their youth, you understand—and then the price'll sink as their partners wear 'em out with too much vigorous riding. And still you'll have to wed and produce that heir your father so greatly desired, only who'd have a wife whose stepmother swung from a gibbet and whose sisters are no more than common whores? That's a bit much to offset, even for your father's coffers. There'll be none but I willing to take you on then, and so it'll still be me or starve. Resign yourself, my dear. We discussed this the day of your father's funeral, or have you forgotten?"

"No, I haven't forgotten."

"Thought you hadn't, but it was just as well to remind you, I believe," he said, flicking a non-existent speck of lint from his sleeve, then giving her a hard look. "You've been entirely too independent these last days. We shall be wed, Phoebe, unless you want your stepmother in the dock and your half-sisters earning their bread on their backs. The reality of that is something you'd best keep in mind. You balk, and I'll anticipate our vows. Not a gentleman in England'd have you then but me. Spoiled meat belongs to the one who spoiled it. Keep that in mind.

"Now, shall we retire to your father's office? As I said, there're some things we need to discuss."

She followed him down the short hall like a servant. When he made no effort to open the door, she opened it for him and permitted him to pass in before her.

"Come here," he ordered without pretense at courtesy.

He pulled a crumpled sheet of paper from his coattail pocket and smoothed it on her father's work table, first pushing aside some other papers and the stub of a pencil, and scowling at the drips of wax congealed on her father's old standish.

"You really must do something about this room," he complained. "I intend to turn it into a study, and I insist on a modicum of cleanliness and comfort. Now, what's all this?" He pointed to the circles and triangles drawn on the paper, the lines that intersected without apparent pattern.

"I haven't the slightest notion. I've never seen it before."

"I didn't ask if you'd seen it. I asked what it signifies."

"I told you: I don't know."

"You'll have to do better than that, my dear. Lord Soames and that churl of yours are conspiring against me, and this has something to do with it."

"I don't know, Phillip—truly I don't. As to their conspiring against you, you're all about in your head."

"I'd better be. Don't forget Mabel. If Soames were to refuse to act on my information, I'd take it elsewhere. As for Oakwood, I want him dismissed immediately. If you haven't the stomach for it, I'll see to the matter myself."

"Miss Parmenter?"

The pair at the table whirled at the sound of Peter Oakwood's voice. He stood in the doorway, face ruddy from the cold, greatcoat unbuttoned.

"Haven't you heard it's considered the thing for a servant to knock before thrusting his unwanted presence on his betters?" Fordyce snapped.

"And a good morning to you as well, Fordyce. Did you pass a pleasant night?"

Phoebe blanched at the sight of Oakwood's hard, accusing expression.

"Your stepmother said I'd find you in here," Oakwood continued, turning slightly to face her. "Some questions I must ask you about how things're customarily done at Underhill. From what I've been able to determine, the land's in exceedingly poor heart."

"Oh, dear, I'd no idea!"

"Your father was bleeding the place dry, according to your tenants."

"My tenants, not Miss Parmenter's," Fordyce smirked, insinuating himself into the exchange.

"Are they? Not yet, I think, and perhaps not ever. Now, if you'll excuse us, Miss Parmenter and I have serious matters to discuss."

"Oh, I think not. Anything you have to discuss with Miss Parmenter you may discuss in front of me. In fact, you'd do better to discuss it with me instead, and leave my poor darling out of it. Female heads aren't made for business. Wouldn't want to see her tax her intellectual capacity beyond what Nature intended, and succumb to a brain fever." Fordyce placed a proprietorial hand on Phoebe's shoulder, fingers digging until she almost screamed from the pain. "Isn't that right, my dear? Besides, I doubt you'll be here much longer, Oakwood. A matter of days at most, so don't get too comfortable in that sty of a cottage."

Phoebe shivered, desperately trying to read the message in Oakwood's hazel eyes, knowing all too well what she'd find in Fordyce's hard blue ones.

"Come, Phoebe, tell the bumpkin whatever his business is concerning Underhill, it's with me and not you," Fordyce snapped. "Besides, my good man, your arrangement is with my betrothed, not me, and by law I'll be in charge within days. When that happens, you can be sure you'll be chased from the place."

"I shall? Interesting. Well, Miss Parmenter, what's it to be? Does this fellow already rule at Underhill, or have you a scrap of independence left?"

"This once," she quavered apologetically when the silence stretched beyond what she could bear, each man waiting on her decision, and both suddenly seeming her enemy for all she knew Oakwood wasn't, nor ever could be, "I do think it would be best for Mr. Oakwood and me to confer privately, Philip dearest."

"Phoebe, my love, reconsider. Think of your family," Fordyce said, his voice at its most mellifluous. "Cousin Mabel, so utterly dependent on your good sense. And the girls, half-orphaned as it is, and all three destitute and homeless lacking your charity."

Oakwood, the light of triumph in his eyes, strode over to the table.

"Well, Fordyce," he said, "do I show you to the door, or can you find your way?" Then his eyes narrowed as he picked up the piece of paper they'd been examining moments before. "Where did you find this?" he said in surprise. "I thought I'd lost it."

"I was certain you'd be concerned about it," Fordyce jeered.

"Concerned? What a mild word! These're the preliminary suggestions for Lord Soames's folly, and I couldn't remember which ones he'd discarded, and didn't like to ask him again for fear of seeming an irresponsible fool. See here?"

Oakwood pointed to a cluster of lines and circles. "That's the hollow just down from the castle. Lot of fox in there. And up here's a considerable rabbit warren," pointing again as he continued his glib explanation. "Wants the rabbits left in peace, Soames does. Folly wouldn't bother 'em once it was up, but the construction would, what with workmen crashing all over the place. Doesn't care in the least about the foxes, of course. Nasty things, foxes. Cause all sorts of depredations. Then over here—"

"You mean that's all this is?" Fordyce demanded, regarding Oakwood through slitted eyes.

"Why, of course. What else could it be?"

"You tell me. You're the expert."

"I've already told you," Oakwood said in long-suffering tones as he folded the paper and slipped it in a pocket. "Glad you found it. Saves me a deal of trouble. Cold out there, wading through the snow. Didn't want to repeat the process unless I had to."

"Now," he said, all traces of good humor vanishing, "if you'll be so good as to show yourself to the door? And leave it open. Chilly in here. We could do with some warmth from the entry."

Fordyce looked as if he wanted to reopen the argument. Oakwood folded his thick-muscled arms over his chest, cocked a brow, and jerked his head at the open door. With a moue of distaste, Fordyce stalked from the room. Oakwood followed him, watched for a moment, then pulled Phoebe to the windows.

"How did you manage to arrive so opportunely?" she asked.

"Prissy fetched me. She suspected there'd be trouble. Intelligent girl, for all she gives the appearance of total vacuity when she wishes. Probably a defense against your father left from the old days. You'll have to wean her of that. Watch the door," he said in a undertone. "I'll keep an eye peeled in this direction."

"What are you—"

"Fordyce eavesdrops, among other things. Has he been importuning you most dreadfully, my poor girl?"

"Nothing to which I'm not already accustomed."

"Threatening you, then? I'll warrant he has."

"No, merely reminding me of our agreement."

"That all? Then why're you white-faced as yon snow?"

"I wasn't aware that I was."

"You are. I'd give half my fortune—such as it is—to tear that rotter limb from limb."

"What a mess that would make." Phoebe gave him a tremulous smile. "Have at it, if you wish—just not in the house. I shouldn't like to clean up the remains once you're done, and they'd be most dreadfully difficult to explain."

"Believe me, when he does meet his comeuppance there'll be no leavings for you to see to. I'll handle them myself, and gladly."

Oakwood's eyes met hers briefly. Then he returned to his study of the snowy landscape beyond the windows.

"See here," he said, "this morning I was out on the path where your father was found. All over the area, in fact."

"Oh, dear."

"Why 'Oh, dear?' "

"Because that means you *are* in Lord Soames's employ."

"Naturally I am! To build him a folly that'll put all other follies in England to shame. Why I was up there—to review the lay of the land."

"And I'm Queen of the May, with blossoms in my hair!"

"You might be, given the opportunity, and an extremely comely one at that. I like your new gown, by the bye. Something of your stepmother's concocting, I assume? The matching shawl will set a new style, unless I know nothing of such matters."

The derisive look she cast him actually had the man flushing. Well, and so he should, lying to her about his activities the way he was, and emptying the butter boat over her into the bargain. Unconscionable! And well-meaning, that was the worst of it, and likely to cause disaster if he kept on as he'd begun.

"Fordyce was gone half the night," he continued more prosaically after a moment's thoughtful silence.

"I could only wish he'd be gone all night, every night."

"Your dearest betrothed? Whom you're to wed within days, whether the banns've been called or not? I've heard of shy brides, but—"

"Oh, have done!" she snapped.

"It just may be possible to banish him permanently," Oakwood said on a more cheerful note. "D'you have any idea where he went?"

"None in the least, nor do I care."

"I cared. Good thing, too. Took a little jaunt in the moonlight myself, once I'd confirmed his horse wasn't in the stables. Market Stoking first, where he stopped by Hatch's, then a private home near Pilchester. Was at both places a considerable time, or so it seemed hiding out in the cold with my hand clamped over Bacchus's muzzle and snow beginning to fall. Followed your beloved all the way out and all the way back, keeping well out of sight. Wish I knew what he was about."

"Of course his horse was gone. Lord Soames would've taken it. You followed someone else entirely. What a farce!"

"No I didn't. It was Fordyce, all right. Last night your stepmother loaned Soames Devil-a-Bit for the next few days. Didn't think you'd mind. Soames has velvet hands. Nothing like Dandy Clare, who barely knows one end of a horse from the other."

"Dandy Clare?"

"What Lord Soames calls your vicar," Oakwood said, reddening about the ears. "Catchy. I'll have to watch myself."

"I see. Well, that's clear enough, I suppose. I keep asking you who you are," she said, rounding on him, "and you keep refusing to tell me. But, you're no itinerant landscaper, for all you managed the bit about the paper wonderfully just now."

"Didn't I just!" he agreed with a low chuckle.

"Just be careful you don't overdo your cleverness. Philip may be a posturer, but he's no fool. He's lived by his wits forever, and they're rather sharp. What was really on that paper?"

"Nothing."

"Nothing?"

"A few lines and circles scribbled to make him think they were something. As I said, precisely nothing. A ploy. A ruse. Nothing more. I left it here last night to see if he'd filch it and try to determine what it was. Nor did he disappoint me."

"Dear heaven! And he was terrified of it, and questioning me as if I were in the dock!"

"And quite the fetching witness you made, I'm sure."

"Not for him," Phoebe said, sobering. "Philip detests me as royally as I detest him."

"And still you plan to marry him?"

"As I've told you, not much choice. We'll reach an accommodation of sorts given time, I suspect. Many couples go their separate ways after a bit."

"Grim, believe me. My parents followed that time-honored pattern."

"But better than the alternatives. Now, what was it you wanted to see me about?"

"This." He reached in another pocket, pulled out a soiled scrap of fine white lawn bearing the intertwined initials M. G. "Have you seen it before?"

"Dear heaven—that's Mabel's. Her favorite handkerchief from when she was a schoolgirl, in fact. She mislaid it some time ago. Where did you find it?"

"Snow's been melting a bit where the sun strikes it."

"On the path where Papa was found," she said with numbed certainty.

"Yes, on the path where your father was found. And there was some wire tangled in the bushes as well. How Soames came to overlook both I'll never know. Did your father's mount come in lame that day?"

"No, not that I remember. You should ask old Tom."

"I have. There's a wound on his left fore. Tom swears it wasn't there when he came in riderless, nor was he limping. He is now, though."

"But I don't understand. Why—"

"Leave all to me," Oakwood said with a smile so blinding it was as if the sun had peeped from behind a storm cloud. "Fordyce isn't as clever as he thinks—not by a long shot. Neither's Hatch. I know you believe they have you trapped, but they don't. And now, I must insist on your giving me that key to the house I've been requesting. You've avoided it, one way and another, but it's become of importance that I have one. Setting a trap for them, you see."

Twelve

"It's excruciatingly beautiful!"

Prissy pirouetted, gazing in wonder at the family parlor as Ware and her mother watched from by the fire, doing their best to be circumspect.

"Extraordinarily," Pru grunted as she struggled with mistletoe sprigs and string. "At least that's what I believe you mean. Certainly we've none of us been tortured to achieve the effect, even if my fingers do feel like pincushions."

"Yes, that's what I mean," Prissy burbled "Extraordinately beautiful. It is, isn't it, Phoebe?"

"Indeed, dear," Phoebe murmured.

With Christmas Eve on the morrow, the family had gathered in the parlor after an early dinner, the girls intent on putting the finishing touches to the Yuletide decorations, Phoebe determined to keep as many people about her as possible. That Lord Soames had joined them was a bonus, and Oakwood was stubbornly present as well, however little either might be able to do to change her situation.

For she *was* trapped, no matter what Oakwood had claimed the day before. Fordyce knew it, and she knew it. Hezekiah Hatch had to suspect it, for all the mealy platitudes he'd mouthed the previous afternoon when he'd stopped by to poke about the place and see how they were doing.

And it was a trap no one could open.

At least this day had passed pleasantly for a change, given Mabel's cousin had been absent until just before the dinner hour. In midafternoon Oakwood'd taken her out on her father's acres so she could observe their condition for herself, carrying her double on Bacchus as she'd never learned to ride. It was as he'd warned: fields weed-choked and slashed by gullies, hedgerows gone wild, stone fences tumbled down. Neglect everywhere, care nowhere, just as with the house. The land had indeed been bled dry.

Her dismay at the sight of the tenants' dilapidated cottages was even greater than her distress at the ruin Underhill had become. She'd never been permitted to visit them during her father's lifetime, she'd explained miserably, and there hadn't been time as yet to make an inspection.

Things could be put right, Oakwood had told her as they walked back to the house after stabling Bacchus, faces gilded by the setting sun, shadows streaming before them, but it would take time, money and effort in equal proportions, and a deal of all three.

"Then I don't know what I shall do," she'd said as he opened the door for them. "I've no money and no time, and I doubt there's a soul willing to put in the needed effort. Certainly Philip won't care to. Neither will Mr. Hatch."

"Perhaps the responsibility won't be theirs."

"Oh, it will, and the decisions as well. I've never felt so helpless," she'd returned. "Those people depended on Papa. How he could have treated them so I'll never understand."

"And how did he treat you?"

"The same, I suppose."

"And there you have it."

Fordyce'd entered the house hard on their heels, and life had returned to its accustomed uneasy state.

She gave herself a shake, glanced up from the sprays of holly and pine she was arranging in a tall ewer set between the windows, smiling wistfully at her young half-sister's enthusiasm, then found her eyes irresistibly drawn to Oakwood lurking at one end of the mantel. There was a sense of leashed power in the stranger's casual stance, his oversized figure dwarfing the room. His offside lid descended in a slow wink.

There it was again: that finding of humor in a situation where no other would.

And she understood precisely what he meant by that wink, as if they'd shared a thousand secrets and would share a thousand more.

Phoebe shivered and blushed, seeking security in Prissy's familiar, exuberantly whirling figure.

"Positively beautiful, like a fairyland, isn't it, Mama?" the child was gushing breathlessly. "Titania and Oberon's wood, brought within doors!"

"Quite lovely, dear," Mabel agreed, eyes going fearfully to Philip Fordyce, who lounged at the other end of the fireplace from Oakwood, arm flung across the mantel in a gesture of proprietorial elegance, almost as if by grasping first one physical portion of Underhill and then another he could claim right of possession. "Isn't it, Cousin Philip?"

"This mess you've permitted Phoebe and the girls to make? Lovely." Fordyce drawled, draining the last drops of claret from his glass, then glancing about the room with distaste. "I'd've thought you had more sense. If one admires dirt and bugs within doors, I suppose it's attractive enough. For one with the least sense of style, however—"

"Dirt and bugs? There isn't a one," Prissy protested, stumbling to a halt in midpirouette and facing Fordyce with her rounded chin thrust forward. "Don't be so everlastingly tiresome, Cousin Philip! One would think you'd never celebrated the season, and yet I'm certain you have, for as you've never been here at Christmas before, you must've found a more congenital spot to do so somewhere."

"Congenial," Pru hissed from the work table, not bothering to raise her eyes from fashioning red bows and lovers' knots for the kissing wreath.

"Why is it you're so everlastingly unpleasant now Papa's dead," Prissy continued as if no one had corrected her, "whereas you were quite the toadying guest before?"

"That'll be enough out of you, you malicious little hellcat,"

Fordyce snarled, slamming his glass on the mantel and starting for the girl with fist balled.

"May I remind you that you're a guest in this house?" Phoebe murmured as Ware rose from his place by the fire and Oakwood took a step forward.

"Then regulate the chit yourself, Phoebe," Fordyce snapped after an assessing look at the two men and a third at Soames, who was lounging in the chair opposite Mabel and Ware. As if to underscore the boredom he found with the issue, he yawned, then retrieved a snuff box from his coattail pocket, took a pinch, and sneezed violently into a handkerchief stained a yellowish brown. "But, I do insist you regulate her. Preferably with a strong birching and a stint in the attics on bread and water."

"You insist?" Phoebe took a deep breath, turned to face her tormentor. "I don't believe you're in a position to insist on anything, Philip."

"Prissy, apologize to Cousin Philip," Mabel broke in, face paling.

"Claiming Oberon's wood as our current abode's apt enough." Oakwood gave Fordyce a hard look. "I wonder who our jackass might be?"

"See here, if you're referring to me—"

"No, it just seems there must be one, given the events of the last few days. Certainly we all seem at sixes and sevens. Perhaps even eights and nines and tens if one includes *Messieurs* Hatch and Gusset, and *la belle dame* Trask."

"And precisely what d'you mean by that?" Fordyce sneered. "Beldam and beautiful lady? I'm only surprised you didn't manage to fit Bedlam in there somewhere! Cleverness in the presence of your superiors isn't precisely an endearing trait y'know, Oakwood, nor's pretending to knowledge of a civilized language such as French. Purely fortuitous, that pun of yours. In two languages, no less! Keep to your station."

"And here I thought I was," Oakwood murmured, "playing dupe to your jester."

"I must protest, my love," Fordyce said on yet another yawn, turning to Phoebe. "This lout passes all that is civil. If you don't chase him from the place, I won't answer for my actions. A whip-ping's too good for the encroaching lout. Why you permit him in the house is beyond me. Such buffoons belong in the farm-yard."

Soames gave a grin that held nothing but good humor in it.

"There's a fool right enough," he chuckled, "and no, Fordyce, it ain't you despite my landscaper's perhaps infelicitous mode of expression— Y'really must be more circumspect, Oakwood. Puns in two languages, when most of us can barely manage 'em in one?—so don't go soaring into the boughs. Yes, indeed: we've a jester, complete with parti-colored hose and bells on his cap. I doubt I've ever been so well entertained, even at Vauxhall."

Fordyce scowled at the inference, yet clearly couldn't catch the affable young lord's meaning.

Phoebe unconsciously retreated a step as her would-be-husband, lacking a nearer target, sent her a glance that held far more of menace than promise in it.

Her eyes traveled the sprays of pine and yew gracing the man-tel behind him. How incongruous the decorations seemed. Given his attitude of the past days, the reign of Mabel's cousin would be no more benign, no less malignant than her father's. Pretended charm and counterfeit devotion had gone the way of spurious courtesy. "Peaceable," indeed! They'd have this one Christmas if nothing more went awry. Then it would be a return to the old life, with fear dogging their every step.

"Yes, it's perfectly splendid," Pru sighed from her place at the table, then turned to the gentleman who had become her arbiter of taste over the last days. "It is, isn't it, Mr. Ware?"

"You've all achieved miracles, Mr. Fordyce's opinions to the contrary notwithstanding," Ware agreed pleasantly from the chair beside their mother's chaise lounge which had tacitly be-come his. "My felicitations, ladies."

As for Oakwood? Phoebe shivered as his flint-hard eyes seemed to pass over her as if she didn't exist, coming to rest on Justin Ware and Mabel not as if he were their friend, but as if they were his enemies. Whatever could be the matter now, other than the usual? The atmosphere in the tiny room became thicker with every passing moment.

"Thank you," Phoebe murmured, determinedly turning her back on the room and continuing to adjust the sprays of pine and holly set in their pewter container.

"I do think that wants more holly, dear," Mabel caviled. "A few sprigs to the right, and then a longer branch in the center. And perhaps another small sprig on the left? Lowish, but not all the way at the bottom. Middle-lowish, I think, for balance."

"I haven't any more, Mabel," Phoebe said. "This will have to do."

"And do absolutely perfectly it will," Ware smiled.

"Perhaps one or two of Pru's knots, then," Mabel suggested. "It wants more red."

"I think it's perfect just as it is," Prissy protested. "Knots would be too attention-getting, and distract from the whole."

"Detract," Pru said flatly. "Of course you're right this time, Prissy: they'd distract as well. Besides, more holly'd mean Phoebe'd have to gather some tomorrow, and it's colder than ever, Mama."

"Not for a sturdy country woman," Fordyce drawled from where he'd retreated to the fireplace, arm again extended along the mantel bidding fair to undo all their hard work and expose the broken corner. "After all, if Phoebe can create decorations standing on an injured ankle, certainly a short walk in the woods wouldn't prove too taxing?"

"I'm amazed you don't offer to run the errand for Miss Parmenter yourself," Oakwood countered smoothly. "Certainly that would be the mark of a fiancé. Might go far toward convincing his lordship you're worthy of Miss Parmenter's regard—and Underhill, of course—were you to do her the favor."

"If anyone's going out in those blasted woods, it won't be me," Fordyce snapped. "See here, Soames, can't you control this fellow's prattlings any better'n this?"

"Apparently not," Soames replied with a twinkle. "Always been a trifle free with his opinions, Mr. Peter Oakwood has. Be thankful you've yet to truly catch the rough edge of his tongue.

You'll be amazed at his vocabulary and inventiveness if ever that happens, which it just might one of these days."

"Now why is it," Oakwood threw in, "that I was under the distinct impression you enjoyed roaming the woods hereabouts, Fordyce? That's why I suggested it. Especially Lord Soames's woods?"

"Haven't the foggiest notion," Fordyce blustered. "Not that it's any of your concern, but while I may ride out for pleasure on occasion when the weather's fine and the lanes're more or less clear, that's the extent of it. Not a sporting man. Never was. Never will be. And, that's *Mr.* Fordyce to you. See here, Mabel," he said, turning to his cousin and indicating his empty glass, "you sure there isn't any more wine in the cellars?"

"You may go see for yourself, if you wish," Phoebe responded absently, slipping into the chair opposite Pru, and selecting a sprig of mistletoe to insert in the kissing wreath she'd been helping to decorate before Mabel demanded something be placed between the windows to add a touch of color. "There's a lantern hanging at the top of the stairs."

"See here, madam, I won't—"

"Oh, do be still, Philip. I did caution you the cellars weren't inexhaustible. If you don't believe me, go see for yourself. I'm certainly not going to go to the trouble merely to confirm what I already know. That's the last of it."

"You should've sent to the wine merchant for more, then."

"And paid for it with what? D'you think Mr. Hatch would approve such an expenditure for a household of two ladies and two girls? I rather doubt it."

"You might be surprised," Fordyce muttered. "Yes indeed, you just might be surprised what old Hezekiah will and won't approve these days if I request it. Well, fetch me some brandy, then. Rather have that, anyhow."

"There's precisely one bottle remaining." Phoebe stubbornly set her shoulders as Oakwood ambled over to stand behind her chair. "I won't squander it."

Ware made a great show of consulting his pocket watch, of

comparing the time to that of the little clock on the parlor book-case.

"Dear heaven, but it's grown late," he proclaimed in feigned surprise, turning to Fordyce as he rose. "I do believe it's time we were all making our departures. Your guests're sure to be wondering where you are, Soames. Isn't this the evening Derringer's to read his paper about that naval engagement?"

"That was yesterday. Today's Andersby's turn. And it's to be elephants and the Alps—I was right about that."

"Good thing old Ware'd no ambition for the stage," Oakwood murmured in Phoebe's ear as Fordyce watched them, scowling. "He'd've starved."

Phoebe giggled in spite of herself. It was nerves that made almost everything Oakwood said seem amusing, she told herself.

"I agree, sir," Oakwood continued more loudly. "It's time we left these lovely ladies to enjoy the peace and comfort of their home in privacy. Indeed, I rather suspect it'll offer more peace and comfort lacking the presence of at least one of us."

"Then get yourself gone," Fordyce snapped. "Certainly we've no need of you."

"Play along with me," Oakwood murmured, ignoring Fordyce and bending over Phoebe. "I want him enraged."

"Please don't do anything which—"

"Hush. Don't worry. We'll catch him out yet."

Oakwood brushed a heavy hand over the table beside hers, knocking a sprig of mistletoe to the floor as if by accident.

"Oh, pardon me," he said more loudly.

He bent to retrieve the scrap, examining it as if perplexed. Then, with what Phoebe could only characterize as a devilish glint in his customarily soft hazel eyes, Oakwood gave a delighted laugh.

"There's no law says it must be suspended from the ceiling, is there, my lord?" he asked, turning to Soames as he broke off a berry and slipped it in his pocket.

"No," Soames grinned, "not that I've ever heard."

On those words Oakwood swiftly tucked the mistletoe in

Phoebe's hair, pulled her to her feet, gave her a swift bracing look, then lingeringly kissed her cheek.

"See here," Fordyce roared, lurching forward, hand seeking his coattails, "I won't have you sampling goods that ain't intended for your—"

Moving in concert, almost as if they were trained acrobats, Soames and Ware seized Fordyce's arms, effectively anchoring him in place as Phoebe gripped Oakwood, keeping him at her side.

He gave her a tight, rueful smile, covering her hand with his where it trembled on his arm. "Little more than I bargained for," he admitted softly, eyes flying to Fordyce's plunging figure. "Come now, pluck to the backbone'll see us through."

"My, what have we here?"

With a powerful twist belied by his slender frame, Soames forced Fordyce's hand, which was gripping a miniature pearl-handled pistol, toward the ceiling. There was a deafening report. Bits of plaster showered on the three men.

"Good Lord, Fordyce—are you totally foxed?" Ware spat as Mabel screamed and gave every appearance of fainting. "A kiss beneath the mistletoe? Totally traditional, and entirely unexceptionable."

"Wasn't any such thing! Lout's been flirting with her all evening. I won't have it. So's the earl. Been flirting with her. And taking her part. I'm not blind."

"I'll have that," Soames said evenly, prying the pistol from Fordyce's fingers. "Prissy, Pru, see to your mother. I believe there's a vial of *sal volatile* in her work basket. Miss Parmenter, are you quite all right?"

"Like my ceiling, a trifle shattered, but nothing that won't mend in time."

"That's my brave girl," Oakwood murmured.

"As for you, my good man," Soames continued with unaccustomed brusqueness, turning on Fordyce, "I believe it's time you should be making your departure."

Hard on these words the parlor door crashed open, Mrs. Short and Flossie crowding through, eyes wide with terror.

And then, as if miraculously, all were gone from the parlor but Phoebe and Oakwood, Flossie and Mrs. Short and the girls bundling a vaporous Mabel upstairs to her bedchamber, Ware and Soames cramming Fordyce into his coat and hurrying him out into the cold night.

"Dear heaven," Phoebe murmured distractedly, staring at her volunteer bailiff as she pulled her shawl more tightly around her shoulders, "what now?"

"Now," Oakwood said with a tight smile, "I think you should follow your stepmother's example and seek your bed once you've partaken of a restorative. Where's that brandy you're hiding from your fiancé?"

"The kitchen, but I don't want any."

"What you want and what you need are distinctly at variance. I could do with a sip or two myself. Fordyce had every intention of seeing me planted beneath England's pastures as his private form of Yuletide celebration."

"You must leave," Phoebe said, shivering.

"Why naturally, after I've seen to you."

"I mean now. I mean permanently."

"Leave Underhill? I think not. It isn't my custom to be cowed by cowards, or abandon maidens in distress. Ah, Mrs. Short!" He turned to the parlor door as the cook bustled by. "I'll follow you to the kitchen, if I may. Miss Parmenter and I could do with a trace of that brandy you're hoarding. If need be, I'll acquire another bottle for you at the George. And some wine, though Fordyce isn't to know of it. Come to that, I believe I'll have Mr. Klegg decant some vinegar into an empty bottle of his best claret, and leave it where the bounder'll find it but never be able to admit uncorking it."

Mrs. Short's approving laugh boomed from the hall.

"Don't," Phoebe pleaded, chuckling at the thought despite herself, "for if you do it's we who'll pay the price."

"My poor girl, don't you understand? Fordyce's hand must be forced, and forced yet again, until he does something so totally outrageous he'll have no way of escaping the consequences. Almost managed it tonight, though I didn't expect a pistol. His swordstick, more like."

"Swordstick?"

"That elegant walking stick of his is more than it appears."

"But why—"

"Don't ask. And now you, my dear Phoebe, will take your stepmother's customary place by the fire and cease your shivering."

"It's dangerous here."

"By the fire? Come now! We're both quite alive, for all it was a nasty experience."

"Nasty? He intended to kill you. You said so yourself."

"But he didn't manage it, did he?" Oakwood made a great show of examining himself for wounds in the unlikeliest portions of his anatomy. "No, he didn't, that's right," he said, as if in wonder. "I'm very much alive after all. Will miracles never cease?"

"I shouldn't like to see you come to grief over all this," Phoebe responded with a tremulous smile. "The problem's mine, not yours."

"Ah, but I've made it mine. Adopted it, you might say, like a ragged urchin one finds sleeping in a doorway, tear stains on his cheeks and a moldy crust in his fist. I keep telling you it will come right in the end. All I touch turns to gold."

Her appraising glance, her skeptical indication of his baggy, antiquated tweed shooting jacket sent their own message.

"Appearances to the contrary notwithstanding," he insisted, coloring slightly. "This thing's comfortable, perfectly suited to my current employment, and an old friend. Don't disparage it.

"Besides, I was in need of an adventure to set me to rights. Life'd become distinctly dull of late. It's dull no longer, thanks to you. Now go sit by the fire. I'll return with our brandy in a moment."

But instead of doing as Oakwood instructed, Phoebe stood where she was, heart pounding, as he disappeared down the dark-paneled hall. Then she turned to the windows, pulling the bright make-do draperies aside.

The moon shone on last night's sprinkling of fresh snow with the brilliance of a thousand candles in a ballroom. At least, that's what she imagined such a scene would resemble. Even the stunted apple trees seemed enchanted, like crabbed dowagers sharing their secrets as they bent toward each other in the wind.

How wonderful it would be were that what she was viewing—a ballroom, and not the rutted track leading to the village lane, and the old orchard and the nut trees in the spinny beyond it tossing their branches against a sky washed of stars because of the moon's brilliance.

She let the curtain drop with a sigh, then quickly sought her stepmother's place by the fire as firm footsteps came up the hall.

After tossing and turning, and counting the strokes as the clock on the parlor bookcase announced the hours, Phoebe finally rose from her bed some time after midnight, chilled to the bone and wakeful beyond all that was reasonable.

She snugged her new shawl about her shoulders, padded across the icy floor to pull the worn draperies aside and stand barefoot at the window, staring out over the snow-laden fields. The moon had set. Now the stars rivaled its former brilliance, shimmering like chips of ice as they swung across the sky. And the wind had died. It was peaceful, so very peaceful, just as it must have been that first Christmas Eve—and it *was* Christmas Eve morning, no matter how early, with one star shining more brightly than all the others.

How appropriate.

What newborn babe would lie beneath that star come evening, she wondered whimsically. Many, probably. And the sorts of gifts they'd receive? Not gold or frankincense or myrrh, that was certain. A coral for teething, perhaps, and warm shawls and a poppet or two and, if they were fortunate, a silver spoon.

She'd taken out the gifts for Mabel and the girls hours before at Mr. Oakwood's insistence, arranging them on the table where they'd constructed the kissing wreath. The six packages'd been disappointingly drab in their brown paper wrappings. Then Oak-

wood—who'd seemed intent on lingering as long as possible—
had asked if there were any scraps from her gown, and perhaps
some of the green and white fabric she'd pinned around the parlor
windows in lieu of their faded old draperies.

They'd ransacked Mabel's work basket, and purloined ivy
sprigs from the mantle, substituting red ribbon for the string with
which the parcels had originally been secured. How they'd
laughed, like children indulging in a forbidden prank, for Oakwood contended it would be much more exciting for the girls if
they could see the packages without being permitted to so much
as touch them.

"That's the best part of childhood," he'd chuckled in that deep
voice of his, "being able to anticipate a treat for days and days.
We can't give them quite that much, but an entire day and night
of wondering what treasures they'll receive? Believe me, my old
governess used to consider that entirely sufficient."

"Your old governess?"

"Slip of the tongue." He'd flushed on the words, for all his
eyes'd retained their good-humored twinkle. "My mother's employer's children's governess, rather," he'd rushed on by way of
explanation. "Took my lessons with the family, considered Pommie quite personally my own. Of course, she was really for the
girls. I was only under her tutelage briefly, before I was sent away
to school."

"Really?" Phoebe'd murmured, goading him.

And she'd had her reward, for, "I know it sounds strange,"
he'd continued after a moment, shifting the coals, then examining
the poker with apparent fascination, running a finger along its
length, then twisting it this way and that in the candlelight as if
it were a rare sword instead of a battered scrap of iron, "but I
was the only boy in the lot, and my father insisted on it. My being
taught by Pommie only briefly, you understand, and then being
sent off to school. He didn't want me turned into a man-milliner
from overcoddling, and I was the youngest. There was probably
a fair chance of it given my mother, had he not taken an interest."

"Then you *are* a lord's—"

"Oh, I'm my father's son, no doubt there," he'd interrupted, as if not wanting to hear the sentence completed, rattling the poker fiercely among the coals once more. "He even deigns to acknowledge me on occasion, if I'm not being too much of a fool by his lights. What he'd consider me at the moment? A greater fool than ever, according to Soames."

"Lord Soames considers you a fool?"

"So he's told me."

"But why?"

"When I've discovered that, he says, then he won't have reason to consider me a fool any longer."

"And your father?"

"Ar, t'old cove's a right'un, fer ow 'e's gentry-mike," Oakwood said, breaking into broad Cockney as he set the poker in its stand, then turned and chuckled at the startled look on her face. "Oi'm gentry-mike sime's 'im, yer moight sie," he added with a wink, "on'y bit differnt's ow."

Perplexing, perplexing conversation. Perplexing man, come to that—hard-bitten and cynical one moment and a laughing, warm-eyed boy the next, both infinitely appealing. The cynic wore his world-weariness like battered armor shielding a tender core too many times assaulted. And the boy? Always on a spree. He was the one should have Devil-May-Care, not Fordyce or Dorning, or even Lord Soames.

They'd covered the worktable with an old cloth she'd fetched from the dining parlor, pinning ivy and bows over the worst of the darns and arranging the packages for Mabel and the girls so it seemed there were far more than there were.

"Hadn't we best leave space for a gift or two for you?" Oakwood had asked, but she'd gestured at her new dress and shawl, explaining there was no possibility of anything more.

"Your beloved fiancé, then? Surely he'll be put out of countenance if there're offerings for his cousin and her daughters, but nothing for himself?"

"I never thought of Philip," she'd admitted, flushing in her turn.

"How odd. And here I'd always thought the first person a

young woman in love sought to please was the object of her affections!"

"I suppose I consider myself gift enough."

"Far too generous a gift."

"And Underhill, of course."

"It won't come to that, you know. I've told you that until you must be bored with hearing it."

"I'm afraid you're wrong," she'd sighed. "Don't you think I'd avoid it if I could? There simply is no way. I've told you that before, too. Does it bore you? There's even a certain ironic justice to it. Papa must be laughing, wherever he is, which is fair enough given how we all detested him and longed for the time when he'd no longer be with us. Yet he'll always be with us. Life offers no escapes—not for a woman."

"My dear girl—"

"Leave it be," she'd sighed. "I don't want to think or talk about it. The reality'll come soon enough."

Then Oakwood'd climbed on the sturdiest chair in the room and they'd hung the kissing wreath from its bright red ribbons, positioning it just inside the parlor door and joking about how no one would be able to escape it, and even sung snatches of carols, he in a bass rumble, she in her clear soprano. Mrs. Short had peeped in on them coming back down from Mabel's bedchamber, and said the poor dear was over the worst. It had seemed such a commonplace, family-ish sort of scene, with a human warmth missing in that dark house for years, that thinking of it brought tears to Phoebe's eyes.

The coziness, the security were a sham, she sighed, running her finger aimlessly over the icy window pane and shivering. Given Mabel's cousin, they always would be. But, for just that one moment she'd had a vision of how it might be in other families, and she'd found herself bitterly jealous of those not cursed with Portius Parmenter for a father and Philip Fordyce for a husband-to-be.

Mrs. Short had given them both a searching look Phoebe hadn't in the least understood before the sturdy cook headed for her own quarters. Oakwood had made his reluctant departure shortly alter, first putting the kissing wreath to decorous use, then plucking a single waxy white berry from among the glossy leaves and slipping it in his breast pocket with a bemused smile.

That the exercise, for all its adherence to tradition, had left them both a trifle breathless Phoebe'd done her best to ignore at the time and forget ever since. Showing Oakwood to the door, giving him the key he'd again requested and which she'd finally provided, had been a tense and embarrassing scene.

The incident intruded on her thoughts as insistently as a tooth needing the attention of a drawer.

If he was perplexing, she was foolish, Phoebe told herself sternly. Infinitely foolish. How could those brief moments when his finger had lifted her chin while his other hand sought her waist have made her feel she'd come home at last? To lose an entire night's sleep over a kiss was unpardonably missish. But, and she knew this to the bottom of her soul, Philip's attentions would be different, not things she'd welcome, but penances to be endured for her sins. If fate was kind, he'd soon tire of her.

With a shudder Phoebe started to turn from the window, then spun back, pulling the shawl more tightly about her shoulders.

Was that someone watching the house from just beyond the barnyard fence? Too far to tell with the light so poor, and the figure, if it was one, blending with the barn.

And then it moved, separating itself slightly from the dark building behind it. A man, foreshortened given the land sloped down from the house. No features visible, not with the moon set and only the stars for illumination.

Logic said it should be Mick Bodger, pausing on his rounds— for Lord Soames had insisted the man and his son continue to guard Underhill at night even after Oakwood took up residence in the old bailiff's cottage—but somehow she didn't think so. The silhouette was solid enough, but seemed too tall. Philip Fordyce, then, bundled in a surfeit of many-caped greatcoats and shawls because of the cold? Dear Lord, would she never have done with him?

And then she truly realized that no, she never would have done with him, not for the rest of her life. None of them would.

He was moving now, breaking a trail across the crusty snow rather than following the cart track to the house. One arm seemed akimbo, the other flailing to retain balance. What did the parasite want, she wondered.

The answer to that was so simple, so straightforward that she shivered. He'd sworn to have her, informed her damaged goods belonged to the damager to do with as he wished. Was he about to make good on his threat? With only women in the house, his chances for success were excellent.

A whimper of revulsion broke from Phoebe's trembling lips as she shrank from the window. Then something snapped within her.

No way would she submit to such indignity, not ever! Not even for Mabel's sake.

She paused in the center of her bedchamber, head high, shoulders squared, thinking furiously. Fordyce must've stolen the key she'd given Oakwood just hours before, sneaking into his room while the man slept. A thief in addition to all else? That didn't surprise her.

And if that was the case, he might be doing her the only favor he'd ever be capable of doing her.

Phoebe retrieved her new gown from its peg and dashed to the bed, rolling the soft wool into the semblance of a human form. She shoved the bundle between the coarse sheets, gave the coverlet a twitch, then squinted, nodding. The mound wouldn't've passed muster in daylight, but Fordyce would be acting in stealth and not thinking clearly. Probably foxed into the bargain. By the time he realized the difference, it wouldn't matter any more. He'd be dead, or dying. If the beautiful gown was ruined, well, that wouldn't matter, either. Mabel would understand as no other could.

Still barefoot, and silent as the gentlest zephyr twining through a willow, Phoebe eased her door open and sped to the head of the stairs. She paused there, listening. The house was quiet. From the stoop came surreptitious sounds of arrival: the scraping of snow-encrusted boots, a muttered curse, a muffled thump, as if something cumbersome had fallen against the door. Was he so cupshot he couldn't maintain his balance? That would help.

Heart pounding, she tore down the stairs and along the dark hall, making her way in the feeble light of the guttering veilleuse, turned into the kitchen wing, grabbed Mrs. Short's butcher knife from the rack on the wall, pelted back along the hall and reached the top of the stairs just as the key turned in the lock.

She froze deep in the shadows, watching and waiting with the sensation that she wasn't herself at all, but someone else entirely who had the power to command her thoughts and actions with a cold-blooded calm she could never've felt.

The door handle protested as it turned, groaning like a demented ghost.

Dear heaven, would she have the courage? A swift thrust, that's all it would take.

And how would she feel after taking a human life? That was a matter for another day. At least Mabel would be safe, and with Fordyce in her bed with his smalls unbuttoned and himself tumbling out, flaccid and disgusting as a slug, and the gown whisked away before she sounded the alarm, and blood everywhere and herself in hysterics, few would think to ask the right questions, such as when she had taken to sleeping with a knife on her night table.

She gripped the heavy bone handle more tightly as the door eased open and a blast of frigid air surged into the entry. She still couldn't tell who it was, but it had to be Fordyce. She'd never find the bottom for this again.

The heavy silhouette resolved itself into two parts: a man and a bundle. Whatever was Fordyce doing with a bundle? It so closely resembled the form into which she'd forced her new gown that she almost giggled.

You are not, she told herself, *going to lapse into hysterics, my girl!*

Still on the threshold, and with the door open to the arctic night, the man first divested himself of his burden, then his boots. Then he pulled the door to, cursing softly as the hinges squealed and the latch clattered.

Then, as Phoebe watched, he picked up his bundle and turned toward the parlor.

She came down a step, trembling.

He depressed the door handle with the stealth of a house thief.

Phoebe came down another step, eyes widening, then another and another, until she could see into the parlor.

The man was tiptoeing to the table where earlier she and Oakwood had arranged the gifts for Mabel and the girls. He was shifting their packages, making room for his awkward bundle.

Whatever in the world?

And now he was stepping back, surveying the results. Then he was on the move once more, purloining greenery and a bow from the mantel. Then he stopped, as if struck by a sudden thought, turned toward the door, gazing at the ceiling.

There came the sound of a deep rich chuckle. And then he was striding to the door, reaching up, plucking something from above it. A sprig of mistletoe? It had to be. He turned back to the table, began decorating his parcel with the fruits of his foraging.

"It's not considered the thing to watch a Christmas elf at his work," he murmured with his back to the door, "but if you insist on breaking with tradition you may join me and open your gift now, Miss Parmenter."

The knife dropped from her numbed fingers, clattering down the remaining steps to the entry floor.

Peter Oakwood turned at the sound. "That's not how it's done," he reproved in a stern whisper. "When you surprise a Christmas elf, you must go about it very quietly lest you frighten him away."

Then, at Phoebe's continued silence, he came to the bottom of the stairs, picked up the knife.

"What on earth?" he said.

And then he peered narrowly at Phoebe, her hair bundled in a nightcap, her prized new shawl circling her shoulders, her bare toes peeping from beneath her old gray flannel nightdress. She shook her head, unable to speak. Her knees buckled, and suddenly she was sitting on the stairs, face buried in her hands, giggling hysterically.

"What's to do? Phoebe, is that you? And you, Mr. Oakwood?"

Oakwood's head snapped up at the sound of the piping voice. Pru hung over the banister holding a candle above the stairwell, her plaits even more disheveled than usual.

"Your sister believed I was a housebreaker," he whispered. "I fear I've frightened her most terribly."

"Is that all?"

"Yes," he smiled, "that's all."

"But you did break into the house, so you are in a sense a housebreaker," Pru said, coming down a few steps, "for all that we know you."

"Well, I do have a key," Oakwood apologized.

"You do? How did you come by it? Before Papa died there was only one that I know of, and he always kept it with him."

"Apparently there were two. Your sister gave me my choice."

"Prissy did? Why?"

"No," he said with another smile, "Phoebe."

"Why?" Pru insisted.

"Because I requested it. See here, imp, you should be in bed rather than playing Bow Street Runner."

"Is that what I'm doing?" Pru cocked her head, came down a few more steps, ignoring Phoebe, who now was watching the pair of them, her features wan. "It's fun, if that's what it is. I think I should like very much to be a Bow Street Runner when I grow up. What's that in your hand?" She raised her candle higher. "Whatever are you doing with Mrs. Short's best butcher knife?" she scolded.

"Ah—"

"I had it," Phoebe said. "I thought it was—"

"Your sister's overwrought," Oakwood interposed smoothly. "Why don't you get yourself back to bed where you belong, Pru. I'll see to her, and—"

Pru handed Oakwood her candle and sank down on the step beside Phoebe, putting her arm around her half-sister's shoulders.

"You thought it was Cousin Philip, didn't you," she said.

Phoebe nodded.

"And you were going to kill him, weren't you."

"Don't ask that question," Oakwood broke in. "It's not pertinent, for nothing of the sort's occurred."

"You were, weren't you," Pru insisted.

Again Phoebe nodded.

"Well, I call that splendid of you! If only you *had* been Cousin Philip, all our problems would've been over," Pru complained in a governessy tone as she glanced at Oakwood. "That's most unfair."

"There are better solutions to the Philip Fordyces of this world than murder," Oakwood countered repressively.

"Don't be so stuffy! Name one. Well, name one! See? You can't."

"Hush! You'll wake the house, and that we don't want, any of us. Take your sister into the parlor and build up the fire," Oakwood said. "I'll see to putting this away, and then—"

"You don't know where it goes, and you won't want questions about it in the morning. I'll take care of it. You take care of Phoebe."

She rose, held out her hand for the butcher knife. After a moment, Oakwood handed it to her.

"I'll bring back the brandy," she said over her shoulder as she headed down the hall, "what's left of it. I believe you both could do with some. And you'd best be procuring another bottle for us somewhere, just as you promised. Mrs. Short's heart'll be broken if she can't lace the puddings properly. It's the first time she's had the opportunity since she came to Underhill as a girl."

"I truly meant to kill him, you know," Phoebe said dully as Oakwood picked her up and turned toward the parlor.

"I know."

"And I wouldn't've felt the least compunction. At least," she shuddered, for once giving herself up to the feeling of warmth and safety Oakwood's arms offered without demur, "I don't believe I would have, and that gives me the horrors."

"Don't think about it."

"I must."

"No, you absolutely must not. Instead you must learn to trust me. I'll see you out of this, with a little help from his lordship.

That I've promised you, and I've promised some others, and I swear it yet again."

He deposited her on Mabel's chaise lounge beside the fireplace, picked up the coal scuttle. It was empty.

"Prissy and Pru, I suppose," she said.

"That's for me to know and you to guess, but you've quite a few champions."

"What happened to Philip's pistol?" she asked with apparent inconsequence, still shivering with reaction.

"Soames has it, I expect. He or Ware. I'm going to fetch us some coal." Then, as if on impulse, he set the scuttle down and retrieved the bulky parcel from the table of gifts. "My poor girl, you won't have a single surprise waiting for you Christmas morning," he apologized. "Well, not many, but I believe you need this now more than a plethora of surprises then, and this is the main one."

"It's for me?" she said, bewildered. "I assumed it was something Mr. Ware had commissioned you to see to for Mabel."

"Ware can see to his own ladies. Open it. Here, let me light some candles first so you can tell what it is."

The parlor was bathed in a soft glow as Oakwood lit candle after candle, first those on the mantel, then every other he could find.

"All right," he said when he was satisfied, "now you may open it."

Phoebe gripped the cumbersome parcel lying in her lap. She knew it had to be as improper as the suggestive sprig of mistletoe nestled among the ivy and red bows. For a miracle, she didn't care in the least. Blushing at the thought of impropriety didn't mean one cared about such things, after all.

Hesitantly, as if attempting to prolong the moment, she eased the bows and ivy and mistletoe from beneath the plain string lashed around the bundle. Then, very carefully, she untied the string, prudently rolling it into a tight ball so it could be used again, and set the ball on the floor next to Mabel's work basket. At last, so slowly it was almost as if she were fearful of what she might find, she unpleated the end folds, then the center double pleat, and eased the brown paper apart.

"That it matches the trim of the gown your stepmother fashioned for you is the purest accident," Oakwood said diffidently. "It wasn't a conspiracy, I assure you."

Phoebe stared from the parcel to Oakwood, lips trembling. It was too much. Entirely too much. A cloak. A wool cloak the deep rich green of the forest in high summer. Not a rent. Not a tear. Not a darn or a patch. Whole cloth, and so new it smelled of nothing but itself. Then she was clutching it to her, shoulders heaving, as she sobbed helplessly into its warm depths.

"No matter what happens to me next," she managed between gulps, "I am the most fortunate woman in the world. None has ever been so blessed as I."

"It's the veriest nothing, my dear girl. Merely a ready-made cloak, for pity's sake. A paltry thing at best."

"But it's new! No one's ever worn it before."

"I'd've much preferred it to be velvet with a sable hood and lining, and sable at the hem, and a muff to keep your hands warm in the cold."

"What would I do with a velvet cloak?" she laughed through her tears. "Trimmed in sable, for heaven's sake? Can't you just see me, gathering deadwood in Lord Soames's woods in such a tonnish rig-out?"

"Not Soames's woods foraging for firewood, but yes, I can easily imagine you so. In a carriage taking the air in Hyde Park, perhaps. Or a sleigh, traveling to Richmond to view the winter countryside."

"Hyde Park? Richmond? I? Now I know you've gone mad," she grinned, wiping away her tears with the back of her hand. "The closest I'll ever come to them is our spinny. If you think for one moment—"

"I think a lot of things, and I suspect quite a few more. In fact, I almost know 'em." He swung her to her feet, shook the cloak out and settled it over her shoulders, tying the ribbons at her neck in a clumsy bow. "Now you'll be warm until I return with some coal and can build up the fire."

And then he cocked his head, hands lingering on her shoulders, eyes searching hers with a puzzled, slightly bemused expression.

"I believe Soames has the right of it," he said softly. "I've been a complete fool all along. Dear Lord, but my sister'll make fun of me when she learns of this. As for my father and his bride, God bless 'em, it'll be the fatted calf and the finest china and silver, and no wine too rare. Why, nothing'll be good enough for me now I've come to my senses. You said if you received your cloak you'd believe in miracles. Well, start believing in 'em now, for I certainly do. Christmas ones, at least. The solstice, by damn! Nanny was right. Dear Lord, what a joke, and I the butt of it. There must be little people under your hill, busying themselves with us."

"Whatever do you—"

"Come morning, don't let Fordyce get you alone," he cautioned, sobering. "Keep the girls with you. Stay by Mabel. Ware'll be wherever she is. He should offer you some protection from the wretch. If possible, I'll see to it Soames is here as well. His guests've survived without him to date. They can survive without him a bit longer. That would spike the scoundrel's guns as nothing else could. Strangely, your greatest security might be your Aunt Trask."

"You're not suggesting—"

"No, sometimes safety can be purchased at too high a price. I'll burden you with many things to keep you safe, including myself, but Emma Trask isn't one of them."

"Thank heavens! At her I'd be forced to draw the line."

"And I wouldn't blame you."

"I'm generally not a watering pot," she said by way of apology, examining the top button of his greatcoat with apparent fascination. "It's just the cloak was, well—"

"A surprise?"

"An overwhelming one. Thank you from the bottom of my heart, though I'm not sure I should—"

"I promise you," he said, smiling as his arms tightened around her, "the happiest Christmas you've ever had, and perhaps a few more surprises. Remember, I'm the godlet of the oak grove and know more than is permitted mere mortals such as yourself. This is only your first merry Yuletide in a future of unending jollity and merrymaking, my priestesses tell me, so long as you don't lose your head. At least I hope that's how you'll consider it as the years pass, but leave the knives where they belong. You wouldn't like the mess."

Then he pulled her beneath the wreath of mistletoe, tenderly kissed her forehead, then her lips, plucked two more berries and sent them to join the pair already in his pocket.

"You're quite extraordinary, you know," he whispered huskily.

Pru's warning cough from the entry had them springing apart, Oakwood with a rueful grin, Phoebe flushing furiously. A moment later the girl was through the doorway, setting the brandy bottle and two glasses on the gifts table. Dear heaven, how long had she been out there?

"What a beautiful cloak," Pru breathed, turning to admire its soft folds. "And green? That's Phoebe's best color. You got it for her, didn't you, Mr. Oakwood?"

"Indeed I did. In Pilchester. She ruined her old one the day she went searching for mistletoe."

"No, she didn't. It's been ruined forever. That was just its death knell. I believe," Pru said, glancing from one to the other, "that I'll take care of getting us some coal. See to my sister, if you would, Mr. Oakwood? She appears a trifle fuddled."

The girl retrieved the scuttle, flicked her plaits over her shoulders with an impish grin and slipped from the parlor as Phoebe stumbled back to Mabel's seat by the fire.

Fuddled? If that was what it was called, she'd still be fuddled in the next century!

Thirteen

It was a confused and sleepy Nick Gusset who answered the pounding on his door in the middle of the night. Peter Oakwood loomed against the stars, gripping the reins of his mount and stamping his feet in the cold, breath clouding the air.

"What—"

"Ask me in, for pity's sake," Oakwood complained, looping the reins around the post at the door. "It's colder than an ice house out here, and I don't want to leave poor Bacchus standing longer than necessary. Besides, I haven't much time."

Gusset yawned and backed into the narrow hall. Oakwood was across the threshold on the instant, closing the door behind him. More yawning faces appeared at the top of the stairs, among them Alfie's tousled pate.

"What is it, Da?" a voice that wasn't Alfie's called sleepily.

"That's for me to know and you to guess. D'you have any idea what time it is, Mr. Oakwood?" Gusset managed on an even bigger yawn. "Honest folk have to work in the morning."

"Which is precisely why I'm here. Need to run surveys in his lordship's woods. Has t'do with the way the light'll strike the folly various seasons. One man can't do it alone. Thought to hire your younger boy to assist me—Alfie, isn't it?"

"I'll be needing Alfie m'self. Busy season."

"He's a bright one. I'm willing to pay well."

"How well? Alfie makes my deliveries."

"And the wages of someone to take his place while he's gone."

"Mite anxious to have the lad." Gusset cocked his head, eyes narrowing cannily. "Wasn't aware you were even acquainted with our Alfie."

"Seen him about the village a time or two. Trustworthy, according to the Kleggs. Dependable, the Potts sisters tell me. Hard worker. That's the sort I'm looking for."

"Y'don't say."

"Oh, I do. I do, indeed."

From the head of the stairs came the sound of a sharply indrawn breath. Gusset regarded the stranger for several moments.

"For how long?" he said at last.

"Not certain. I'd want him at Underhill, as I'm staying at there myself. That'd make it more convenient."

"I was at the George yesterday, or have you forgotten?"

"No, I haven't forgotten. Shall we say two bob a week for someone to make your deliveries, and a yellow boy for Alfie's services?"

"Two bob's fair enough, but a pound a week? For Alfie?"

"For the entire period, whether a day or a year. I'm no fool," Oakwood continued, stuffing his gloves in his greatcoat pocket and retrieving his purse, "but he's worth that much to me if I'm feeling generous, and I happen to be feeling particularly generous at the moment. Besides, time's money. Alfie'll suit me."

"Don't whip up your horses yet, Mr. Oakwood." Nick Gusset shook his head at the pound and pair of shillings held out to him. "Not sure I'm willing for Alfie t'leave us. Why, it's Christmas Eve, or almost."

"If I have to search out some other lad, heaven knows how long it'll take. I want the preliminaries at Penwillow over so I can concentrate on Underhill. Not the best of landowners, your brother-in-law. I've a deal of mismanagement to undo there."

"You're the first one to notice that," Gusset marveled.

"No, I'm just the first one to state an obvious fact. Tenant cottages're a disgrace, and the land's in such poor heart it'll take years to put right. Showed Miss Parmenter yesterday, thought she'd burst into tears." Peter Oakwood slipped the coins back in his purse. "Parmenter must've gotten his brass from some other source."

"Double-dealings with Hesekiah Hatch. Thick as thieves, for all no one's ever been able to prove anything. Still, any who joined 'em in a venture grew poorer while they grew richer. Always suspected Mabel's wedding old Parmenter was my father's method of paying a debt he couldn't discharge otherwise."

"It wouldn't surprise me in the least. Now, about Alfie?"

To Oakwood his offer sounded perfectly reasonable. Apparently it agreed with Nick Gusset's sense of the fitness of things as well, even if it took that gentleman a few moments to reach his decision, and it was a good question as to whether his recognizing the reality of Underhill's condition or the pound for Alfie's services and pair of shillings to hire a boy carried more weight.

Finally the miller nodded, turned toward the stairs. "Alfie," he called, "pull on your warmest togs and hurry about it. Can't keep Mr. Oakwood waiting all night." Then he threw Oakwood a keen glance. "How're you going to be getting my lad to Underhill? You haven't but the one horse."

"Bacchus is up to carrying us both."

"Is he, now? You're a mountain, Alfie's heavier than you'd think, and once you've got him to Underhill my guess is you've a few more errands. You won't want your mount foundering."

Gusset paused, observing Oakwood with amused tolerance. Finally Oakwood nodded.

"I do have a place or two to go," he said.

"Such as the castle? No—don't tell me. Leave me guessing, but I saw a sight more yesterday than ever that fool of an Emma Trask did. The length of her nose is her limit. Parmenters aren't known for their wits, only their slyness. Phoebe got her wits from her mother, in case you've wondered. Character as well. Nothing of old Porty in her but hair and eyes, for which my silly sister should thank God every day of her life."

"Who, precisely, is Philip Fordyce?" Oakwood asked after a moment's thought, surprised at the miller's volubility.

"You want the truth?"

"If you're willing. No one's mentioned more than some sort of cousinship."

Gusset sighed, set his candle on a stand well away from the door, pulled off his night cap, scratched his bald pate, yawned, shook his head.

"Suppose you need to know?"

"It would help immeasurably."

"Because it's not something we speak of, you understand? Old scandal. Would've left the country because of it, hadn't the living here been so good. But there it is, I've a liking for Phoebe Parmenter. Put up with a lot, and not a word of complaint out of her, and always did the best by Mabel and the girls she could."

Oakwood nodded encouragingly, careful not to seem too anxious. Gusset folded his arms across his burly chest, scowling as if to defy Lord Soames's employee to find anything untoward in his tale.

"My grandfather's sister was by way of being a fool," he admitted at last. "Had her head turned, ended up with Fordyce's father nine months later. No band on her finger, but the fellow saw her well provided for, I give him that."

Gusset's eyes dropped, as if there were something he found fascinating about the floor boards.

"She came home, raised her babe here for a bit," he continued softly, "wandered off again with someone else, ran through the brass was supposed to establish her son. Second fellow abandoned her. Nothing more to be got of her. She died of the typhus a year later. Wrote my grandfather at the end, telling him where she was. My grandfather fetched the lad here, saw to his education, got him a post as a schoolmaster where his history wouldn't be known. Phineas Fordyce, his name was. Still is, so far as I know. Never been a Gusset in the poorhouse, no matter what Emma Trask says. We take care of our own. Phinny married a curate's daughter, and Philip's the result."

"I see. But the name?"

"She took it when she ran off with the second fellow. His was something like to it, and when she died my grandfather felt it best Phinny keep it. Less chance he'd make claims he'd no right to make." Gusset's eyes narrowed accusingly. "Was one of your sort got my grandfather's sister a fat belly. It's always been your sort, causing trouble for our sort without a care as to what happens next so long as you had your amusements."

"My sort?" Oakwood protested. "I'm naught but—"

"And I'm the Regent, complete with creaking corsets and fat old women to keep me warm," Gusset snorted. "See to it you do better than Phinny Fordyce's father did. Phoebe isn't blood, but she isn't water, either."

"If that's true," Oakwood said sharply, "then why did you never lift a finger to help her or your sister?"

"Not my affair, once Mabel married. That's what the law says, and that's what the Bible says, and that's what my father said, and that's good enough for me. All between her and Parmenter, and I didn't want to run afoul of him. Any that did ended up licking wounds that don't heal.

"No offense at the George? I was remembering my grandfather's sister, and not taking kindly to the attentions y'were showing Phoebe. All started at an inn for her, too."

"No, no offense."

Footsteps clattered down the wooden stairs behind them.

"Well, here's our Alfie. Took you long enough, lad."

Gusset turned back to Oakwood. "I'll have the boy take Sukey," he said. "Won't be the first time since Porty died he's ridden off on that old mule in the middle of the night thinking all the world's deaf and blind but him. You can send her back in the morning. I'm sure someone at the castle'll be willing to accommodate you."

Alfie cast his father a nervous glance that had the older man chuckling. Then he was out the door and tearing to the stables as Oakwood extended his hand. Gusset pumped it vigorously and eased the door shut.

"Just see to it that young sprig of mine doesn't come to any harm," he cautioned. "Adventure's fine and well for a lad his age. Had a few in my own time, with my father looking the other way and making sure my mother did the same. But if what I'm thinking's true, this is more adventure than many a man could handle, and Alfie's naught but a boy for all his height and his strong back."

"I'll see to him."

"Don't bother seeing to Fordyce, though. Isn't a one of us'd take a step to pull him from a bog. Stand and watch, more like, and say good riddance when the last bubble broke. Stole every penny he could find from old Phinny when he turned seventeen. Never went back, not even when his mother died. Broke the poor man's heart."

"Then how'd he find such a warm welcome at Underhill?"

"Mayhap he knew something old Porty would've rathered he didn't know. Philip isn't the fribble he seems, nor ever has been. What he wants, he takes."

Gusset cast a glance up the stairs, made a shooing motion with his hand. "Nothing here for you, old woman," he called, "nor yet for you, boy. You've heard it all a thousand times over. Get to your beds afore you catch your deaths. Morning'll come soon enough."

Then he turned back to Oakwood with the slightest of hesitation as footsteps pattered down a short hall above them.

"You've heard how I had our Alfie offer for Phoebe just after old Porty's will was read?" he said finally.

Oakwood nodded.

"You know how Porty left things?"

Again Oakwood nodded.

"Good, that makes it quicker. Emma Trask'd just had Cobber go down on his knees. Poor man didn't know what he was about. Missing a few sheaves to his thatch, and there're times it leaks. Promised Phoebe a chicken on the table every Sunday if she'd marry him. Told her he wouldn't trouble her once there was a boy in the cradle. Lord knows if he has the least idea how to put one there. Probably still thinks fairies leave 'em in crocks by the kitchen door.

"Thing of it is, I wanted to show Emma Trask for the grasping harpy she is—not that Phoebe wouldn't've done a sight better accepting Alfie over that poor fool of a Cobber, even with the difference in their ages. Course I wouldn't've minded Alfie having Underhill, either. He'd've been able to bring it around eventually with a little help, and he's always been fond of Phoebe."

"Why're you telling me this?"

"Better to tell you soon rather than late. Wouldn't want you thinking wrong of me if it comes to matter, and it might. No sense having bad blood when there's no need."

"I see."

"Thought you would. Now," Gusset said, one hand on the door latch and the other held out, "I'll be troubling you for that golden boy and those four shillings—two for the inconvenience, and two for whoever I hire to drive my wagon. Then you can be on your way. Family's family, but brass is brass, and no one's ever said I had thatch missing from my roof. Keep it in excellent repair, as a matter of fact."

Oakwood and Alfie's trip through the night was as swift as poor light, icy lanes, and a mule highly incensed at being taken from her warm stable permitted. Given Oakwood's desperation to have Alfie hidden at Underhill, and himself off to confer with Soames and Ware at the castle, that was surprisingly swift.

On the way he related events since he'd last seen the boy at the gamekeeper's cottage, concluding with the unpleasant incident with the pearl-handled gun.

"Then I should have one too, if that bleater's armed," Alfie protested. "Won't be much use otherwise."

"And make bad worse? I think not. Besides, Soames took possession of it."

"And you think that's the only one Cousin Fordyce has? He's not that green! Might've all been for show, just to make you think he's harmless now."

"Not that clever."

"You think not? I keep telling you he's lived by his wits all the time I've known him. When it comes to things like this, he's clever'n Wellington himself."

"No gun," Oakwood insisted, then grinned behind his woolen scarf. He was *not* looking forward to the time when he'd have a son the age of this stripling. Constant alarums, and that would be on the good days.

"See here, Mr. Oakwood, I do know how to shoot a pistol," Alfie pleaded, "even if that relic I had in the glen hasn't seen use in dunamany years. It was just for show, in case you proved fractious. With something a bit better, I could give a good accounting of myself."

"I'm certain you could—most country boys learn to shoot at an early age—but are you really so anxious to end up swinging from the nubbing cheat for murder? I think not," Oakwood grinned. "A pound wouldn't content your father then."

"Bother my father!"

"The song of all unregenerate young whelps. No, my lad, you'll have to satisfy yourself with your ears and your eyes for weapons. In the most dire of circumstances, your fists."

"And bother the brass," Alfie muttered. "That's all my father ever thinks of—piling up the shillings. I'd've come for nothing, and begged for the chance."

"Of course you would," Oakwood soothed.

"Don't feed me pap!" Alfie snapped. "I've as many teeth in my head as you do in yours. So, what've you discovered? There must be some reason you want me besides Cousin Philip's unpleasantness, for he's always unpleasant if there's no one about he wants to impress. D'you know who killed Uncle Parmenter?"

"Let's say I know who didn't."

"Who's that?"

"Miss Parmenter, for one."

"Cousin Phoebe? You suspected her? You must be mad!"

"I've come to believe I may be," Oakwood agreed with a wry grin. "And you didn't kill him. The girls didn't. And, your Cousin Philip didn't, however much you may wish he had."

"You've already told me all that," Alfie grumbled. "But he *was* murdered?"

"I'm not certain one should call it that."

"Well, he was killed, wasn't he? And not by a fall from his horse, either."

"No, not by a fall from his horse. You had that right."

"How, then? And who did it? Have you—"

"Not related to Torquemada by any chance, are you? Have

done, scamp. There're things you need to know, and those you don't at the moment. Far safer."

Then they fell silent, intent on making the best speed possible without risking injury to Sukey or Bacchus. The shortcut through Soames's woods, so well traveled of late it was like a beaten path, put them at Underhill well before the sun rose. The house was still asleep, looming dark and forbidding on its low rise, the doors locked against intrusion, the curtains drawn. They saw to the stabling of Bacchus and Sukey, waking a sleepy Tom to lend them a hand, explaining Alfie's presence to Mick Bodger and his son, and cautioning the three men to keep a sharp eye out for anything unusual.

Then Oakwood sneaked Alfie into the house, pausing in the entryway to provide himself with a work candle. After lighting it from the little veilleuse and rapidly surveying what was available in the way of hiding places, he decided to have the boy tuck himself in the pantry behind an old hogshead and some sacks that might, in better years, have held flour.

"Keep out of the way," he warned as they artfully arranged the lot in the corner most likely to be overlooked by sleepy eyes during the bustle of beginning another day. "With any luck, each of 'em'll think another rearranged things so the clutter'd be less inconvenient, and consider it too unimportant in the midst of all else to comment on. I don't want anyone to realize you're here for a bit."

"What good will that do? Besides, what of Sukey?"

"Stable's big. She's tucked away where she won't be noticed. As to what good keeping your presence a secret will do, I don't know," Oakwood admitted. "I just know I want you here while I'm gone, and I don't want anyone in the house to know you're here. My ace in the hole, you might say, for I must speak with Soames soonest possible."

"But if no one realizes—"

"Yes, I know," Oakwood overrode the boy, "logically I should be announcing your presence with trumpets and drums. It's the same when you sit at the tables, and a little voice tells you where to place your bet, and how many pounds. Not much of a gamester, but when that little voice speaks, I pay attention. It's not failed me yet, and it's nattering insistently just now."

"But I still say if no one——"

"Enough!" Oakwood snapped irritably, then took a deep breath, struggling for patience. "Pressure's mounting on your cousin," he said more calmly, "which is why I cautioned Mick Bodger and old Tom. Time's passing, and the more time passes the poorer your cousin's chances of becoming master of Underhill, and he knows it. He's acted without thinking once. He may do so again."

"But I keep telling you: Cousin Fordyce don't act without thinking. I wish you'd listen. He's a deep 'un, no matter how silly he looks or how nasty he is."

"Canny? Agreed. Sly? That, too. But a deep 'un? My lad," Oakwood chuckled, "you haven't met a deep 'un in your life!"

"No need to sound so condescending," Alfie muttered. "I know I'm not up to snuff by your standards."

"You're up to snuff by anyone's standards," Oakwood countered flatly, "my own included. Now, get behind that blind, and keep your head down and your legs tucked in. You've visited the necessary, so that should be taken care of for a few hours. Whatever you do, don't sneeze. That'll give the game away."

"Don't you know," a small voice piped from the doorway, "you should never tell someone not to do something, because that's not only precisely what they'll want to do? It's what they'll have to do. Whatever are you playing at back there, Alfie?"

"Blast and double-blast, and a million ring-tailed baboons shitting on the moon," Alfie muttered.

"Quite," Oakwood murmured, choking back a hearty guffaw at the image called up by Alfie's curse, and turning to survey the moppet in nightdress and shawl behind him.

"Well, what're you doing?" Pru demanded, holding her candle high with one hand as she clutched her shawl with the other.

"Hiding, if you must know. And trying not to sneeze."

"Why?"

"Mr. Oakwood doesn't want anyone to know I'm here."

"And so he positions you precisely where I must retrieve

spoons and bowls for breakfast?" She tripped lightly into the pantry, placed her candle on the hogshead, turned to the two lords of creation, hands on her hips, toe tapping. "Brilliant, Mr. Oakwood!"

"Well," Oakwood said with a resigned sigh, "do you have a better suggestion?"

"You must not know much if you think a pantry's the place to hide someone at holiday time—not that I know that much about it myself, but Mrs. Short's been telling us tales about when she was a girl. Why, everyone in the family'll be coming here soon or late to lend a hand for luck!"

"There's that, of course. I should've thought."

"Yes, you should've. Why's Alfie at Underhill?"

"Persistent, aren't you, minx? I'm not that certain myself. I just know I want him about the place as I must be away for a bit." Then, drawing himself to his full height and staring down his nose, he assumed his most schoolmasterish tone and demanded, "And precisely what are you doing up and about at this hour?"

"I heard you. You weren't all the quiet, you know. It's a good thing Mrs. Short's half deaf and Flossie sleeps like the dead with her head under the blankets, or you'd've been discovered long since. Besides, I have every right to be here. You and Alfie don't."

"Ah, I see," Oakwood murmured, "you've changed your mind. You want your sister married to your Cousin Philip."

"Never!"

"Then," he grinned, "I've as much right to be here as you do. Now, where do you suggest we tuck Alfie away?"

"My sleeping chamber? Except Prissy'd have to know. We share a bed. Warmer that way."

Oakwood shook his head.

"The cellars're too far for him to be of use should we need him," Pru frowned. "Does he really need to be in the house? Because there's always the old necessary. No one goes there because—"

"I thank you, no!" Alfie spluttered.

"Then there's only Papa's office or the cubby under the stairs.

That's where Prissy and I hid to listen to Papa's will, and heard Cousin Philip waylay Phoebe."

"Your father's office is a bright room with no hiding places."

"There's that."

"Then it must be the cupboard for you, my lad," Oakwood said. "Not ideal, but better than nothing. Up with you, and let's get these things put back where we found 'em so no one'll be the wiser."

It took only a few moments to settle Alfie, a few more to check on Fordyce, who was snoring in his bed at the cottage precisely where he was supposed to be, and then Oakwood was at the stables saddling Bacchus once more.

"Sorry about this, old fellow," he murmured as he expertly slid the blanket down the big gelding's withers and settled it on his back. "I'd walk to the castle the way I did the first night, but I have this dreadful notion I'm going to require speed. Events, not to put too fine a point on it, are upon us."

Unencumbered by a boy riding a recalcitrant mule, Oakwood made swift work of getting to Penwillow, keeping to the high ground and so shortening the trip by almost two thirds. It was still night when he arrived—not the dead of night, but rather that hour at which a confused bird, its feathers ruffled against the cold, lets forth a single chirp as if to summon the sun.

Oakwood rode into the courtyard, brows rising at the glimmer of light between gaps in the billiard room draperies and the muffled sounds of masculine revelry. Poor Raft, trapped by the exigencies of butlership unless Soames'd sent him toddling off to his bed, or else insisted he doss down in the great hall. Being a servant at Penwillow had never been a sinecure. It appeared to be even less of a one now.

He'd always suspected the scholarly bachelor house parties Soames'd described weren't quite as decorous as advertised. Given Oakwood preferred his jollifications a deal less cupshot, it was as well this strange Yuletide had begun with the "kidnapping" that prevented his joining the castle festivities. Otherwise he'd've been likely to take to his heels after the first brandy-soaked evening, sullen from a splitting head, sick unto death of hearing the Punic Wars fought yet again by drunken would-be warriors, and feeling abandoned by the entire world. Heaven help him under such circumstances, for almost anything could've happened.

Then he considered what would happen within days if he could manage it, and he broke into a bellow of laughter that brought two sleepy stableboys running and caused Bacchus to give a whicker that sounded suspiciously like a chuckle to Oakwood's ears.

"Been riding him hard most of the night," Oakwood said, dismounting and turning the reins over to the first to reach him, then flipping each of the boys a shilling. "He wants a rubdown, a warm blanket, and feeding. An apple wouldn't be amiss, either, if you've one or two about. I'll be wanting him again in an hour or so, so hop to it."

Then, secure in the fact that Bacchus was in good hands—unlike the castle, which limped along any way it could thanks to superannuated retainers like Raft, the Penwillow stables had always boasted the sweetest goers and the most expert grooms—Oakwood strode across the courtyard.

No scaling the walls this time. No indulging in addle-pated schoolboy pranks. Instead, he climbed the broad steps and hammered the black gargoyle's head that served as knocker against its iron plate.

It was a frowzy and sleep-bewildered Raft, shuffling about in ancient slippers and dragging a moth-eaten blanket behind him, who finally answered the future duke's summons. He shivered at the blast of cold air, pulled the blanket around his shoulders, and peered into the darkness.

"Here now, who's that waking an old man from his slumbers?" he yawned, trying to shove his hair shelf in place. "You again, Master Spur, playing pranks with that devil of a schoolmate o' yours? You know the one: big fellow, carrots in his hair."

Not quite so sleepy or vacant after all, for Oakwood could

swear he saw an amused twinkle at the back of the old man's eyes.

"Master Piers is all, Raft," he said, stepping over the threshold, "a few years older than the times of which you speak, and a sight more circumspect and a sight less plaguey and a damn sight bigger, come to confer with his lordship and Mr. Ware."

He gently removed Raft's palsied fingers from the handle and closed the massive door. Then, after observing the butler's struggles, Oakwood raised the blanket high about his wattled neck and snugged it securely, then firmly pressed the stiff comb of hair down until it lay smoothly against the man's liver-spotted skull.

"There," he smiled, "that should do you. Ware and his lordship about?"

"Hiding from those hellions Master Spur's invited for the holidays," Raft said, shuffling towards his chair beside the chimney. "One of 'em got into the pantry, and they've eaten all the mince pies. Played keep-away with what they didn't eat. Pantry's a shambles, and Cook's threatening to leave in the morning. That happens, the George'll be seeing more custom than's usual this season, and some nobs what thought they were rid of their sprigs until after the New Year'll discover 'em descending on the attack."

"The library, Raft?"

"Could be. Or their beds. More sense than t'be playing at Roman generals at this hour, that's certain."

Raft settled himself on his chair after first helping himself to a tot of brandy, then removed his battered house slippers.

"They'll be burning the castle down around our ears one of these days, you mark my words," he grumbled. "Bedlamites, every last one. Do an old man a favor, your lordship, and add a log or two t'the fire? Too heavy for me to lift, and I'm froze to the bone. Don't use coal in here, y'know. It'd be like trying to heat all of England. Sides, wood fire in here's a tradition."

Oakwood added three logs to the fire, pumped the giant bellows until flames were leaping, then strode across the great hall and down a wide corridor toward the rear of the castle. He opened the library door. The remains of a coal fire glowed on the grate. A pair of glasses stood on tables beside mismatched settees to either side of the chimney. Of neither Ware nor Soames was there any sign.

He closed the door, sighed. Even from this distance, he could hear Raft's snores. No sense waking the poor old duffer yet again. With a shrug he started toward the great hall and the massive paired staircases leading to the upper regions of the castle. And then he cocked his head. From behind the doors to the state dining room came a crash. On impulse, he strode across the corridor, opened the doors.

It took him a moment to recognize what he was seeing. Then he entered, closed the doors behind him and collapsed against them, guffawing as he slid his length until he was sitting on the floor.

Fastidious Ware in a cook's apron. Soames, ever a bit rumpled, protected in the same manner. Both on their knees, wielding scrub brushes.

"Dear God, what next?" Oakwood moaned, holding his sides.

"See here, instead of laughing you might give us a hand," Ware snapped. "There's a broom in the corner. My blasted nephew just broke a particularly ugly urn, and it wants sweeping up."

The state dining room, used only on occasions of greatest ceremony when Oakwood and Soames were boys, had clearly been the site of the grandest and most glorious food fight ever to take place in the British realm. No Etonian, no Oxonian revel could possibly've equaled it. Not satisfied with the destruction, some evil genius had apparently flung flour over the whole.

"What's the pantry like?" Oakwood gasped.

"Minor matter compared to this," Soames grinned from his knees. "Just a few crocks overturned. Set the lads to cleaning that up, Cook did, and oversaw 'em. See here, make yourself useful, or get yourself gone."

"Whose fault was the flour?"

"Uncle's. Well, mine really," Soames admitted at Ware's glare. "Came at me with fists flying. Claimed I was a graceless beggar to permit desecration of these hallowed halls. Heavens, m'father and mother would've thought it jolly good sport."

Soames laughed at Ware's derisive snort.

"You know they would've, Justin. Any road, I held up a sack of flour—never you mind how it got up here in the first place—to protect myself, and it burst. That's when things *really* got out of hand. Fellows wouldn't help in here. Said it was our responsibility. Cook agreed. Since Cook holds the keys to the larder, and the fellows like their three squares and copious snacks to fill the random cranny, we more or less do as she says."

"You need a wife to regulate you," Oakwood choked.

"Perish the thought! As well hire an executioner."

"You must all've been foxed past coherent thought."

"If we were, we aren't now. It all started with a bet as to whether Freddy Derringer or Tim Bladesell could eat a pie the fastest. Had a monkey riding on Freddy. Lost the whole five hundred. Story of my life. One of these days I'll learn gaming's not for me. Then Roger Andersby said he could better Tim's time, and things got a trifle out of hand. Well, get that broom and sweep up the detritus. I take it you've a solid reason to be here at this hour, and the sooner this is cleaned up the sooner we can confer. I'd like to see my bed before the sun's too high in the sky."

"Actually," Oakwood said, sobering as he retrieved the broom by the service door, then stared at it as if not quite certain of its purpose, "it's your uncle I'm wanting. Rather have you present, of course, but only in an unofficial capacity."

"More trouble at Underhill?"

"Nothing new since last night. Fordyce is peacefully asleep in his bed, and I presume one of you has his pistol. No, it goes further back." Oakwood set the broom aside, crossed the room to stand over Ware. "You were there when old Parmenter was sent to his just reward, weren't you?" he said.

Ware's shoulders stiffened, then slumped. Wearily he dropped the brush in the bucket, stood and nodded.

"See here, Uncle," Soames said, clambering to his feet and clasping Ware's shoulder, "don't say anything you'd rather not."

Then, at Ware's defeated shrug, he grabbed a decanter of brandy and three glasses from a sideboard massive enough to serve as an elephant's sarcophagus, nodded at the doors leading to the rest of the castle.

"We'd best repair to the library," he said. "We can be a deal more comfortable and considerably more private there. I suspect privacy's something I'll value, and God knows I'm not best pleased to find myself considering serious matters at this hour. It's essential, I suppose?"

"I deem it so. Best divest yourselves of your extra clothing first," Oakwood suggested, "lest you next be accused of playing at ghosts rather than yahoos."

With resigned disinterest, Ware removed the apron, folded it and placed it on the massive table, then straightened his cuffs. More cavalier, Soames merely set decanter and glasses down, tore off his unaccustomed gear and tossed it beside Ware's.

"You'll be even less pleased when I'm done," Oakwood cautioned, retrieving the glasses and leaving the decanter to the young earl. "Several lives quite literally hang in the balance. The last pieces of the puzzle began to fall into place just a bit ago, thanks to Nick Gusset."

They retreated to the library, Soames building up the fire in an obvious effort to delay matters while Oakwood poured liberal portions of brandy in the three glasses.

"It's a council of war, gentlemen," he said when they were seated at one end of a library table massive enough to serve as a small dance floor, their corner lit by a pair of brass triple candlesticks with rectangular bases and dark green shades. Around them ranks of books soared, a full three stories to the frescoed ceiling, with balconies and ladders and circular stairs like so much scaffolding, protruding from the walls. "Let me tell you what I know, and what I've deduced.

"First," he said, ticking the points off on his fingers, "Parmenter didn't meet a natural end, and he didn't go to his just reward on your game trail, Soames. That was merely where he was found. He met his Maker in his own parlor."

Oakwood reached in his pocket, pulled out the scrap of marble from the mantel at Underhill and placed it in the pool of light. Its raw slant glittered like crusted snow filmed yellow in spots, the tiniest of black flecks ground into the upper edge.

"I'll return to that later," he continued, "but my guess is our charming Mr. Fordyce didn't just find him lying there. He watched whoever deposited Parmenter, and's been bleeding the man dry ever since. Or," Oakwood paused, glancing at Ware, "woman.

"Second point: Blackmail's an art at which Fordyce is probably long expert. Think a moment, Soames: What was Parmenter's character? Not precisely the hospitable sort, would you say? Yet Fordyce practically made his home at Underhill for extended periods, a quintessential lily of the field."

"Good God," Soames murmured.

"Precisely. And never seemed to lack the little luxuries of life, such as an excellent London tailor—excellent if one's tastes run to the sort of overblown stuff Nugee concocts, that is. Expensive in any case, for all his plaints of poverty, and always at the height of *à la mode*-ality. I've not the least doubt he had some sort of hold over old Parmenter, a hold so strong the man was forced to let him run tame at Underhill. Probably paid him a generous allowance as well."

"Flummery!" Ware snorted. "Fordyce is Mrs. Parmenter's cousin. What better reason to permit him to visit?"

"Won't wash," Soames countered. "Parmenter despised his wife. Logic says he should've chased Fordyce from the place long ago, but he never did. We were all so accustomed to his being there, we never gave it a thought."

"Well, you should've," Oakwood snapped. "Would've saved a deal of trouble."

"Yes," Soames admitted ruefully, "I suppose we should've."

Oakwood leaned back, face in the shadows, as Ware adjusted his cuffs, then began toying with items on the standish before him.

"So, Fordyce knew something about Parmenter's dealings the man would've preferred he didn't know," he continued softly. "And with whose assistance did Parmenter conduct business?

Hatch's. My guess is, Fordyce has the same hold over Hatch he did over Parmenter. Not quite as good a hold perhaps, but good enough to force Hatch to agree to his wedding Miss Parmenter, and ultimately coming into control of Underhill and old Parmenter's heavy coffers. Fordyce must've become desperate when Parmenter met his end. One of his prime sources of income'd just dried up.

"That's the simplest of it, and the least unpleasant."

Oakwood leaned into the light, picked up the scrap of marble, turning it this way and that in his powerful fingers, then lightly touched the black-flecked edge.

"Let's suppose," he said, looking directly at Ware, "that Emma Trask, for all she's a mightily unpleasant woman, has an ounce or two of sense. Let's suppose there was, many years ago, oh, not a scandal, for that'd be too strong a word. Let's call it a whispering about a miller's daughter, educated above her station and as lovely as a spring day. And let's say there was a stranger in the neighborhood. A highly impressionable young man come to visit his family."

"How did you find out?" Ware said dully. "Did Phoebe tell you? I didn't think that poorly of her."

"No, it only takes eyes to see what's beneath one's nose, not supernatural powers or traitors in one's employ. The rest?

"Well, I've seen Mrs. Parmenter. The poor woman still bears marks of what must have been a horrific beating. According to an unimpeachable source, the lady wasn't yet fit to attempt bearing another child following her latest miscarriage, and her husband wasn't, shall we say, best pleased. He wanted a son, considering girls beneath contempt. If only he'd had the wit to realize it," Oakwood said with a crooked grin, "both his youngest and eldest daughters're probably blessed with greater intelligence and ability than most of the men in England."

"What has that to say to anything?" Ware snapped. "That Mrs. Parmenter and Prissy are merely gentle females doesn't mean they don't deserve a man's protection!"

"And there we come to the nub of it: protection," Oakwood said ruefully. "This is the part I really don't like. Soames, perhaps you'd best leave us to ourselves? I've a matter to discuss privately with Ware. Once we've settled that, we'll call you back and decide what's to be done."

"What sort of idiot d'you take me for?" Soames spluttered. "Ware'd intended to pay a few calls the day Parmenter died. He'd gone off in his curricle." He turned to his uncle. "You went by Underhill, didn't you, hoping to see Mrs. Parmenter. And you did find her, only her husband was beating her, and you tried to stop him. There was a scuffle and you killed him. Probably knocked him into the mantel and he hit his head, and that's how that scrap of marble Duchesne's playing with came to be broken off. Heavens, Uncle, you didn't do just her a favor! You did the entire countryside a favor."

Justin Ware nodded slowly, tiredly.

"And Fordyce's been blackmailing you?"

"Persistently and effectively."

Peter Oakwood set the scrap of marble back in the pool of light, took a sip of his brandy, watching the older man.

"Except that doesn't explain several things," he said as Soames jumped to his feet and began pacing the library, muttering to himself, "does it, Ware? Such as Miss Phoebe Parmenter's grim determination to wed someone she detests.

"Why, I kept asking myself—once I realized you must've accidentally killed the man—was Miss Parmenter protecting you? Because that's Fordyce's hold over her: there's someone she's desperately protecting at an unconscionable cost to herself, isn't there, but you were perfectly capable of protecting yourself. Besides, it made no sense. The only reason a woman'd go to such lengths to protect a gentleman would be if she loved him beyond reason. There wasn't a hint of anything of the sort between you."

"Leave well enough alone," Ware snapped. "She's got to marry someone, for God's sake, or they'll all starve. Why not her stepmother's cousin? They both claim a long attachment. You've no notion what you're saying."

"Oh, but I think I do."

"Uncle, it was self-defense, pure and simple," Soames said, pausing in his pacing. "We'll simply set the story straight, encourage Fordyce on his way, and that'll be an end to it. Oh, there may have to be another inquest, but you'll be exonerated. In fact," he grinned, "you'll probably be proposed for sainthood. Why you fell into such a trap I can't understand."

"Not quite that simple is it, Ware," Oakwood said, "because Parmenter was already dead when you arrived at Underhill."

"Damn you, Duchesne," Ware roared, leaping to his feet, "I've told you to leave well enough alone!"

"And that's the hold Fordyce has not only over you, but over Miss Parmenter. Because, you see," he continued, turning to Soames, "there's no such thing as self-defense when it comes to a wife killing her husband just because he's beating her. If he'd had a knife to her throat perhaps, just perhaps she could justify defending herself. But against a garden-variety beating? That'd be called murder, pure and simple. If it ever came out, she'd swing. It's men're the judges, and men the barristers and the jurors. She wouldn't stand a chance—not with Fordyce ready to swear he saw her do the deed in cold blood, which is what I'm sure he claims he'll do."

"Mabel Parmenter?" Soames snorted as Ware gripped the back of his chair, face drawn. "Kill that brute? She wouldn't've had the strength or the fortitude!"

"My guess is it was a lucky blow to the head. That mantel? It wasn't chipped by a head hitting it. Even Parmenter's couldn't've been that hard. I'd say it was broken by a blow gone awry. Besides, there's a lenticular mark, and something black ground in. The poker, given the evidence. There's a shiny spot on it, scraped clean to bare metal. I checked last night. Tonight? Whatever. Haven't been to bed. Poker'd be a woman's weapon. A man would've used his fists. Even a mouse will roar, on occasion."

"Point is," Oakwood said with a smile, "all's not lost, though every last one of you's been acting the fool. Never was a need to dance to Fordyce's tune, though he's played you most skillfully, one against the other—I'll grant him that.

"Sit down, Soames, for pity's sake, rather than wearing out your carpets! You see," he continued complacently, as first Soames and then Ware returned to their seats, "Fordyce hasn't been quite as clever as he thinks. He's made himself an accessory—if he's going to insist there was a murder, which we could debate at some length, being reasonable men. And that's not the best of it. He's been planting evidence for an entirely different sort of death up on your land, Soames: a wire that could've been stretched across the trail where Parmenter was found, a handkerchief belonging to Mrs. Parmenter, and he's injured the cob Parmenter was supposedly riding. Infinitely foolish.

"You see," he grinned, "Fordyce doesn't believe that sweet, vaporish woman could've killed her husband either, and he has absolutely no notion how the deed was done. It merely suited his purposes to pretend he did."

"What?" the other two men chorused.

"He's been diddling everyone, but he knows only what he saw, which I'd wager was you placing Parmenter's body on the path, Ware. Were you alone?"

"Mabel was in hysterics. All three girls were gone, and Parmenter'd sent Mrs. Short and Flossie packing for the afternoon. Not much I could do," Ware admitted. "I *had* to take her with me."

"Unfortunate, but not irremediable. How much've you paid Fordyce for his silence? And was it in cash, or did you give him a draft on your bank?"

"It was cash. He insisted. Almost all I had with me. Somewhere in the vicinity of eight hundred pounds."

"But that's it? No written communications? No bank drafts? Nothing of that sort?"

"Nothing," Ware frowned, puzzled. "Why?"

"Why? Because it's your word against his, gudgeon. You arrived at Underhill to find Mrs. Parmenter napping in the parlor. The two of you conversed for a proper half hour, or an even more circumspect fifteen minutes. Then you left. End of story."

"But—"

"Who in Chedleigh Minor is going to believe Mabel Parmenter killed her husband? Even accidentally while defending herself? No one! As I said, it's your word against his. We'll send the rotter packing, and that'll be an end to it. There's just one thing I want to know."

Oakwood rose, drawing himself to his full height, a giant of a man, legs slightly apart. Ware shrank toward his nephew, then stood in his turn, jaws clenched, face pale, like a man mounting the scaffold.

"What in the name of God," Oakwood growled, fists balling, "gave you the idea you'd a right to keep silent regarding the truth?"

Ware spread his hands helplessly, eyes wide, shook his head.

"Or the right to sacrifice Phoebe Parmenter, who's worth a hundred of her stepmother, on the altar of your calf-love? Because you'd've kept silent to the end, wouldn't you! And watched an innocent woman sell herself to safeguard Mabel Parmenter's sorry life! And when Fordyce began beating his wife, which he would've as he's just the sort for it, as cowardly as they come and a bully into the bargain, you'd've looked the other way!

"It's a pitiful sort of love, I'd say, that blinds a man to all honor and decency."

"They'd've hung Mabel," Ware protested, backing away from the young giant. "I couldn't let that happen, no matter what the cost."

"What, no backbone? Why didn't you step forward, claim you'd accidentally killed the man while defending Mrs. Parmenter? You'd've been believed."

"I couldn't. Mabel made me promise. She was beyond reason, terrified I'd be transported, or worse. She'd endured enough, damn you!"

"See here, Duchesne," Soames broke in.

"Mabel made you promise? The only possible conclusion," Oakwood bit out, overriding his boyhood friend, "is you're a lily-livered poltroon, and always have been. You lacked sufficient courage to marry the woman years ago. You lack sufficient courage to shield her now, except at everyone's expense but your own.

"Well," he said after a moment's silence, "aren't you going to call me out for those words?"

"How can I?" Ware shrugged. "They're the truth, once one discards the details."

"Just so we understand one another," Oakwood snapped as his hands slowly relaxed. "See you make some changes. Prissy and Pru deserve a better father than you after what they've survived. I'm not sure you comprehend what that means, but you'll learn. Certainly I have these last days.

"Besides, I've no desire to call a coward stepfather-in-law, and I've every intention of marrying Miss Parmenter if she'll have me."

"Mirabile dictu," Soames murmured. "The mighty oak falls."

"So it would appear," Oakwood agreed wryly.

"I didn't mean Miss Parmenter any harm, you know," Ware said. "It's just that Mabel—"

"You may not've meant her harm, but you certainly didn't mean her well. No, don't attempt to exculpate yourself. You do and I'll call you out, which is a thing I've never been tempted to do before to any man, no matter what the nature of our quarrel. There's nothing on God's green earth can justify your actions."

Soames frowned, looking uneasily from his uncle, slumped against the table, to Oakwood, standing with his legs still braced as if ready to attack.

"This goes no further?" he said hesitantly. "I shouldn't like it bruited about Town that my uncle—"

"Oh, it goes no further. Why spread the tale? It's no credit to anyone, and would only make a scandal of innocent victims. I won't see Phoebe so plagued, nor the girls either. Gossip's a vicious thing. Now, leave well enough alone or we both may say things we'll later regret. I do value your friendship, Soames, and I comprehend only too well the quandary your uncle's faced you with."

Fourteen

Phoebe woke to a merciless pounding in her head. As if that weren't enough, it was being echoed by a determined assault on the door at the front of the house. She rolled over groggily.

It was still night, the draperies open at the window just as she'd left them when she finally returned to bed after Oakwood departed the second time. Beyond them a few last stars sparkled. Traces of what might be dawn showed to the east—a graying of the horizon, the trees darker against the sky.

"Dear God," she mumbled, "what now?"

She couldn't've been asleep more than an hour or two.

With weary resignation she crawled from her bed, lit the candle on her night table, went to the washstand and splashed some icy water on her face in hopes that would clear her mind and lessen the pounding. It achieved neither, merely trickling inside the high neck of her gray nightdress, leaving an unpleasantly cold, wet trail down her back and along one arm. Pulling a brush through her tangled hair only made matters worse.

"So far, I do not like this day in the least," she muttered, shoving her feet in a pair of old house slippers, then pulling her new shawl around her shoulders. "That it's Christmas Eve makes not the least difference. Bother Christmas!"

"Phoebe?"

She turned at the sound of the opening door, picked up her candle.

"Yes Pru, I hear them. Who wouldn't? I'm coming."

"Mama's frightened. She's hiding under the covers."

"What a wonderful solution! Why didn't I think of that?"

"I told Prissy to stay with her," Pru explained, trotting along the hall after Phoebe. "That's why there's only me."

"You're never only anything," Phoebe retorted with a wan smile.

They reached the top of the stairs just as Mrs. Short, hair dangling down her back in a wispy plait, was setting her candle on the table, then stomping to the door.

"I'm coming, blast you!" the cook shouted. "No reason to wake the dead! That you, Mick Bodger? Cause if it is, you're about to receive an earful'll make you wonder if you wouldn't've been better born deaf."

She took the key from its hook by the door, slid it in the lock, turned it. The door burst open, sending her reeling against the newel post.

"Good morning, Mrs. Short." Philip Fordyce pushed into the entry, followed closely by a rumpled Hezekiah Hatch, an infinitely sleepy Clarence Dorning, and a stranger of medium size and girth with the look of a country squire.

Fordyce glanced about the entry, then at the head of the stairs.

"Ah, there you are, Phoebe! Good morning, my love," he said with an exaggerated bow that set her teeth to grinding even as she had the sensation of a bucket of icy water being poured over her head.

"Whatever are you doing here at this ungodly hour?" she managed.

"It's our wedding hour, my dear. You may've thought I was jesting when I mentioned advancing the date, but I wasn't. Here's Mr. Hatch to give you away, and Clarence Dorning to marry us, and Joseph Broome, a magistrate from near Pilchester and an old and valued acquaintance, to stand as one of the witnesses. We'll need Cousin Mabel as well, and Mrs. Short. I suggest you join us."

"Like this? You're all about in your head." Phoebe gripped the stair rail until her knuckles showed white, her words masking Pru's sharply indrawn breath. "Besides, the banns haven't been called yet. That's not to happen until after the first of the year.

You do remember what Lord Soames said about a proper period to recoup my equanimity following the shock of Papa's death?"

"Soames? An interfering old woman." He pulled an oblong, official-looking document from his coat pocket, waggled it in the air. "I've a special license, so there's no reason for further delays. You require the protection and guidance of a husband, and we've already determined I'm to be that husband, haven't we? Do tell me you're pleased with my little Christmas surprise."

"Damn him!" Pru muttered. "Well, he shan't get away with it! Don't go downstairs. I'll contrive somehow."

"Infinitely pleased," Phoebe agreed, eyes wide with horror, ignoring Pru' s desperate murmurings. Dear heaven, what could she do now? And a magistrate into the bargain? Clever, clever Philip Fordyce! "Good morning, Mr. Hatch, Mr. Dorning, and— Mr. Broome, is it?"

The stranger sketched an abbreviated bow without bothering to doff his hat.

"Welcome to Underhill, Mr. Broome, and do please forgive my state of undress, but this is an entirely unanticipated pleasure," Phoebe babbled. "Especially at this hour."

Broome shrugged, eyes traveling what he could see of the house as if attempting to determine its value. Dear heaven—she almost expected him to rap his knuckles on the walls, and request an inspection of the foundations.

"Mrs. Short, show the gentlemen to the dining parlor and provide them with tea," Phoebe rattled on, struggling for dignity. She had to think! And couldn't. She needed time. There was none. Where in the name of heaven was Oakwood when she needed him? "I doubt they've had the opportunity to break their fasts as yet, arriving so very early. I'll be down as soon as I've made myself presentable. That will give us time to dispatch Mick Bodger to Penwillow so that—"

"Bodger's already gone," Fordyce grinned up at her. "So's his son. Long time ago. As for fetching Lord Soames, whyever would you want to do that?"

"Common courtesy. Lord Soames is our closest neighbor. I doubt it would suit you to be at odds with him. Mrs. Short, see about some breakfast for these gentlemen. The usual fare at Underhill is bread and cheese or porridge. Which do you believe your friends would prefer, Philip?"

"It matters not in the least, as I certainly won't touch such swill, and don't expect them to either." He turned to Mrs. Short. "A superior ham was delivered by Lord Soames yesterday evening," he said. "We'll have grilled gammon and an omelet, fresh muffins, and a bottle of whatever's left in the cellars. I know there has to be something, given his lordship's care of the ladies. After the ceremony's over. Porridge as usual for the ladies. Wouldn't want them to fall ill from indulging in unaccustomed luxuries."

"There's but three eggs," Mrs. Short protested. "There's four of you."

"Oh, come now," Fordyce smiled, at his most ingratiating. "I'm well aware you've at least a dozen on hand. Such fibs won't do."

"But those're for the Christmas baking."

"They may've been, but they're for my wedding breakfast now, to celebrate my installation as the person to whom you must look for continued employment."

After an exchange of hard glances, Mrs. Short stomped down the hall, back rigid, the flame of her candle a dirty orange stain in the growing daylight.

"Now, downstairs with you, my dear," Fordyce called. "Such reluctance isn't in the least becoming. Prudence, fetch your mother."

"Phoebe may have to obey you in an hour's time," Pru said with a toss of her plaits, coming down the stairs, "but she doesn't yet."

"Ah, but she'd be wise to accommodate me, don't you think?" Fordyce returned suavely. "As a matter of proper female behavior, if nothing else?"

"What I think is that no one's ever taught you manners, any of you," Pru scolded. "Why, you've not so much as removed your hats! Now, into the parlor. You may make up the fire so we won't all freeze to death. There's a full scuttle of coal by the grate. I saw to it myself last night before I went back to bed.

"And I'll take your hats and greatcoats. Gloves and scarves in pockets, please. I don't want to have to sort them out later. Phoebe," she tossed over her shoulder, "hadn't you best make yourself lovely for the ceremony? After all, a lady weds but once if she has the least luck, and in one's nightdress isn't the accepted form."

"I suppose so," Phoebe returned weakly, gripping the banister as she tried to steady her trembling limbs. She didn't believe this. She didn't believe any of it. She couldn't. And yet there was Fordyce smiling up at her, a merciless glint in his hard blue eyes.

"And alert Prissy and Mama," Pru added, giving Phoebe a look the distraught young woman was at a loss to interpret. "I can tell you right now they'll refuse to come down with their hair all on end," the girl said, whirling on Fordyce. "And no, I do *not* think you have the final say in this matter, Cousin Philip. Until the ceremony's concluded, you're only a guest in this house. Isn't that right, Mr. Hatch?"

"By law, yes. However, Miss Parmenter," the elderly solicitor harrumphed, gazing up the stairs at Phoebe and almost licking his lips at the sight greeting his rheumy eyes, "you'd do far better to obey your future husband. No need for any fuss."

"Wisdom is the better part of valor," Dorning agreed. "Pride goeth before a fall, handsome is as handsome does, and sweet submission is the joy and duty of—"

"Oh, do be still!" Pru snapped as Phoebe continued to stare at the gathering in the entry. "Hand me your coats as you pass into the parlor, and I'll see to them. Good heavens! You're tracking snow everywhere, and mud into the bargain. That *is* only mud, I presume, and not something worse? Has no one ever taught you to scrape your boots before entering a house?"

As Phoebe watched in amazement, Pru managed to force all four men through the door, locking it firmly behind them.

"That won't do the least bit of good, Pru," Phoebe gulped.

"They'll come in precisely when I wish them to, and not a moment before," Pru said, glancing from the parlor to the back of the house, then up at her sister. "Don't worry: I know I can't keep them out forever. Now, go inform Mama and Prissy what's happened. I'll be up in a moment. And don't lose heart. All's not at an end yet."

With a resigned sigh Phoebe turned and stumbled down the hall to her stepmother's new bedchamber, her candle now less than useless.

Mabel was precisely as described by Pru: buried beneath the covers, and sniveling softly. Prissy glanced up from where she sat by her mother, rolled her eyes to the ceiling and gave a highly expressive shrug. Phoebe sighed, nodded, went to the windows and looped the curtains aside, letting in the thin gray light of dawn. It promised to be an unusually fair day. What irony!

"It won't do any good for you to hide there, Mabel," Phoebe said, coming over to the bed and jerking the covers back. "It's your cousin, complete with special license, Hezekiah Hatch—yes, at this hour—Mr. Dorning to solemnize the deed, and a magistrate from Pilchester to act as one of the witnesses."

"A magistrate?" Mabel squeaked, sitting up, hands pressed to her chest. "From Pilchester? To act as a witness to what?"

"This is apparently my wedding morn."

Prissy blanched.

"Your cousin insists on your presence," Phoebe continued mechanically, "so if you don't want him to fetch you here, I suggest you rouse yourself."

"I can't!" Mabel whimpered, throwing herself down and groping for the covers. "I'm most dreadfully unwell, Phoebe."

"I don't exactly feel top-of-the-trees myself Mabel. Enough silliness. Standing by my side as I sign my life away for your sake is the least you can do."

"I'll build up the fire," Prissy murmured. "That may help."

"Nothing will help—nothing!" Mabel moaned. "The end of the world's come. Oh, that I should live to see this day! Better your father had killed me."

The door to the little bedchamber opened. Pru slipped inside. A quick glance at Phoebe, another at her cowering mother, and the girl was at the washstand picking up the ewer.

"Mama," she said, turning to face the bed, "look at me."

Mabel cracked an eye.

"D'you see this pitcher, Mama? It contains very cold water. Either you're out of your bed instantly or I'll pour it over you, and *then* you'll be out of your bed instantly."

Mabel's scramble from the bed was precipitous, if awkward.

"Unnatural child!" she whimpered.

"Not in the least. I'm as natural as can be. Now," Pru continued, setting the ewer down and turning to Prissy, "you go help Phoebe dress. And, take your time! There's no hurry, no matter what Cousin Philip says."

"You did unlock the door?" Phoebe asked.

"Of course. They weren't even aware I'd locked it, silly gudgeons."

"This isn't a laughing matter," Phoebe reproved, trying to seize on something to anchor her to reality in the midst of what appeared a desperate nightmare.

"I know that. All of us do, but you'll just have to trust us. I gave Mrs. Short special instructions regarding that breakfast Cousin Philip's ordered. And, they're to have coffee before the ceremony. Cousin Philip knows all about *that* gift of Lord Soames's as well. That should delay matters, if nothing else will."

"What good will delay do us? If Mr. Oakwood were about the place—"

"Well, he's not, which is why we need time. But he'll be back, I'm sure of it. He only left for a little bit, you see. If worse comes to worst, simply refuse to say your vows."

Close to tears, white-faced, Phoebe's eyes sought her stepmother's. Mabel hunched her shoulders, lips quivering.

"I can't," Phoebe said simply.

"Then we'll do it another way."

As she watched, frozen in place, Pru spun to her sister.

"Prissy, you must help Phoebe rig herself out, and dress her hair, and fashion a veil and wreath of some sort, and a posy, and then you must get dressed as well. That should take considerable time, shouldn't it?"

"If I'm particular about it."

"Be as particular as you wish! The more particular, the better. And Mama, I didn't say you were to hurry your toilette. I merely said you must make a beginning."

"You'll be the death of me yet," Mabel wailed. "I shan't survive this day—I know I shan't!"

"Philip was most reluctant to permit us time even to make ourselves decent," Phoebe protested, numbed by the speed with which events were proceeding. "Lollygagging will have him in the boughs, and I must admit I don't enjoy the prospect. Things're bad enough already."

"D'you prefer having Cousin Philip as your husband?" Pru demanded. "Well, do you?"

Phoebe shrugged, sighed, unable to think through her pounding headache.

"Then give them time to have their coffee," Pru insisted.

"What have you done? It's I who'll pay the piper if you've been up to mischief."

"Mischief? I wouldn't call it that. And no, you will *not* go belowstairs and countermand my orders." She caught Phoebe's arm as she headed for the door. "Mrs. Short and I are in complete accord as to their special treat."

"And what might that be?"

"Mama's ipecac. They'll never notice the taste in their coffee, for I've told Mrs. Short to make it very strong, and once they realize what's happened it'll be too late because they'll be much too busy casting up their accounts and dashing to the necessary. Mr. Oakwood would approve, I know," she wheedled as Phoebe hesitated. "We only need a little time, you see. Just a little, Phoebe. Please!"

"What has Mr. Oakwood to do with this?"

"Everything, if you'll only take your time about dressing. He had to go to the castle to clarify some matters with Lord Soames, but he left ages ago. It can't take him much longer."

But they weren't to be given the option, for hard on these words the door to Mabel Parmenter's bedchamber flew open. Mabel dove for her bed with a shriek, pulling the covers to her chin.

Philip Fordyce lolled against the jamb, negligently gripping another elegant little pistol almost, but not quite, as if he were unaware of its presence.

"What slug-a-beds!" he drawled. "Mabel, you'll have to learn to be more punctual. I don't encourage sloth in others, however prone to it I may be myself. As for you," he continued, turning to Phoebe and gesturing with the pistol as if it were his quizzing glass, "I'm shocked, truly I am! Still in your night clothes? Well then, they'll have to suffice. This isn't to be a formal wedding, merely a binding one."

"No!" Pru wailed, darting in front of Phoebe.

"Ah yes, my inventive little Pussykins." Fordyce turned on Pru, uncocking his pistol and shoving it in his waistband, his voice silky. "Imagine who waits you below! Now, I wonder who it could be? Mrs. Short, perhaps? But we know she's there, so that can't be it. Nor Flossie, who's as common as porridge, and twice as lumpy. Who, then? Someone, perhaps, who doesn't generally reside here? Another cousin, related to us both? Now, I wonder what *he* was doing sneaking about, and at whose instigation?"

"What—"

"My dear," Fordyce said smoothly, cutting Phoebe off, "you'll be pleased to learn Alfie—a favorite of yours, I know—is here to watch us recite our vows."

Despairing tears trickled dawn Pru's face.

"Whatever is Alfie doing here?" Phoebe asked, confused.

"Precisely my question."

"I thought he might help," Pru gulped. "I told him to take the best in the stables and fetch Mr. Oakwood. We had him hidden in the cloak cubby under the stairs. Oh, Phoebe, I'm so sorry! No matter what we've tried, it's turned from gold to dross. I *hate* you!" she hissed at Fordyce.

"Why so woebegone, my chuck?" Fordyce's apparent puzzlement was all that was insulting as he lifted Pru's chin. Then, eyes narrowing, he said, "Surely you didn't think a mere boy could stand in my way? Or a pair of schoolgirls? Or a great oaf with aspirations above his station? How foolish. You're not well-

named, are you, Prudence? But, you'll learn. Oh yes, you'll
learn!"

He pinched her chin so viciously she gasped. Then he seized
Mabel's old dressing gown from the bed's foot rail, and tossed
it to his cousin.

"Here, put this on," he snapped, "and hurry up about it. You've
cost me enough time as it is."

And then somehow they were in the entry, with Mabel and the
girls scurrying into the parlor ahead of them, Phoebe's arm quivering under Fordyce's hard grip. Her eyes flew to the hook by
the door. The key was missing.

"Just one moment, please," she said as he forced her toward
the parlor. "I've a question or two before matters proceed further."

"Ask away," he said with assumed good humor. "If it's in my
power to answer them I will, as I'm of a mind to be generous at
the moment, having won my point."

"I'd like," she said on a low note, looking up at him determinedly, "proof of what you claim to know of my father's death."

"Isn't it a little late to think of that?"

"Nevertheless."

"My word as a gentleman," he returned genially, "a word
which those who await us'll take as proof enough. A gentleman's
word is, after all, his bond. Need I remind you that not only is
your father's solicitor present, but also a dear friend of mine who
happens to be a magistrate?"

"But not from this district," Phoebe protested desperately.

"D'you really think that'll matter? There's a constable waiting
in the kitchen as well. At least I presume he's there by now. He
merely had to see to your groom prior to coming to the house.
What's it to be, my dear," he murmured, "Mabel to the scaffold,
or Phoebe to the nuptial bed? You're certainly garbed for it!"

Phoebe pulled her green shawl more tightly about her, shivering.

"I'll pay you," she offered. "Just go away and leave us be."

"With what?"

"Papa's Watford hunters. They're infinitely valuable."

"And will be mine in just a few moments. You must think I've taken leave of my senses! Now, enough of this dilly-dallying." Fordyce spun her around, opened the parlor door and shoved her through.

She glanced about her, details assaulting her senses.

The pungent pine boughs, so festive in last night's candlelight, so futile now in their defiance of all Underhill had been, and always would be.

The kissing wreath, bedraggled and crooked and infinitely pathetic despite its bright red bows and lovers' knots. Had Oakwood really kissed her beneath it, not once, but twice? And sworn all would come right in the end? So much for promises!

The gifts for Mabel and the girls. Her new cloak, still draped across the table.

Mr. Broome and Hezekiah Hatch, standing by the windows as if on watch. The vicar, hovering in a corner. Mabel, cowering on her customary seat by the fire. Prissy and Pru on the hearth's other side, heads high, cheeks tear-stained. Alfie, bound to the chair in front of them, head lolling, a trickle of blood running down his temple.

Dear God in heaven—what had they done to the boy?

Squaring her shoulders, she whirled on her captor.

"Nothing shall occur until I've seen to Alfie," she snapped in a flash of rebellion. Time? She'd gain them time! "I don't know what you think you're about, but—"

"The sooner the ceremony's concluded, the sooner you may tend him," Fordyce interrupted. "After I've made you my wife in fact as well as word, naturally. Shouldn't take long. I'm anxious for my breakfast. Mr. Dorning, we're ready for your services. And Mr. Hatch's, to present me with my lovely bride."

The parlor door opened to reveal Mrs. Short toting an old wooden tray on which stood a steaming pot, a sugar boat and cream pitcher, and a plate of biscuits.

"Blast it, woman, we want that later, not now!" Fordyce snapped.

"I say, I could do with some coffee and a biscuit or two," Dorning protested as Mrs. Short, unperturbed by Fordyce's ill-temper, kicked the door closed behind her. "It's devilish early, don't you know? What's your rush?"

"Cup wouldn't strike me amiss either," Broome said, striding forward as Pru glanced jubilantly at Phoebe. "Had it all your way so far, Fordyce. Never spent such an uncomfortable night in my life! Blasted cottage was filthy. And not so much as a crumb upon awakening? Can't see what difference a few minutes'll make."

With a snarl Fordyce swung a clumsy right that sent tray and contents to the floor, pot and cups smashed, biscuits baptized by brown liquid. Mrs. Short collapsed on her knees, scrabbling among the remains as she bemoaned the destruction. Pru laid her head on Prissy's shoulder with a sad little cry as Prissy's arm crept around her waist.

"Oh, I say!" Dorning protested.

"Mite testy, are you?" Hatch cackled. "Told y'not to drink so heavy last night, Fordyce. Been making indentures this morning as well, I'd say."

"Damn and blast!" Broome spluttered, swiping at his breeches, which had received a baptism of their own. "Was that really necessary, Fordyce?"

"You spent the night in my bailiff's cottage?" Phoebe managed.

"Where else?" Broome shrugged. "Fordyce wanted us here before first light. It was that or the stables. One thing for certain: he isn't marrying you for your housekeeping skills, nor yet your home. I've seen poorhouses better appointed."

"Given you're not here at my invitation, I don't care in the least what you think of my housekeeping skills. Come to think of it, I rather imagine you've been trespassing." Phoebe swung on the crabbed solicitor. "Your opinion, Mr. Hatch: has Mr. Broome been trespassing?"

"Don't matter if he has or not," Hatch grinned. "You welcomed him to Underhill just a bit ago. Heard you m'self. Ain't trespassing now, and that's what counts."

"Enough!" Fordyce roared. "You," he said, pointing at Dorning, "pull out your prayer book and turn to the right page. Here's the license. You," pointing at Mrs. Short, "on your feet! Never mind the crockery. You can clean the mess up later. You, Hatch, over here on my beloved's other side. Broome, stand by my Cousin Mabel, if you please. She appears about to turn up her toes. Are we all ready? Good, then. Begin, blast it, Dorning! Let's get this over with."

Phoebe huddled in her bright green shawl, beyond thought or feeling. After a few moments Hezekiah Hatch shoved her hand in Fordyce's. After that, every so often Fordyce poked her in the ribs with his elbow, and she gave whatever response Dorning demanded of her. A ring was jammed on her finger, and then it was done.

Fordyce was turning her to face him, forcing her to look up. She shuddered at the expression in his eyes, a mixture of triumph and something else she desperately didn't want to identify, though she understood its significance all too well. So had her father looked at her mother and, after that poor woman's death, at Mabel—at least in the beginning. Later the look had changed. She wasn't sure which had been worse.

"And now," Fordyce said with soft menace, "a kiss for my bride."

"I think not."

Phoebe's head turned slowly.

Peter Oakwood. Standing beneath the kissing wreath. With a pistol in his hand. And, behind him, Lord Soames and Mr. Ware, similarly armed. And behind them, Mick and Joe Bodger toting rifles, and old Tom with a pitchfork, and Flossie with a skillet.

"Took yer long enough!" Mrs. Short snapped. "What'd yer do, stop t'milk the cows?"

Oakwood was uncocking his pistol and tucking it in his coat pocket. Then he was seizing the vicar's prayer book, extracting the special license.

"See here, what—"

"Stubble it, Clare," Soames ordered, following Oakwood into the room. "You're perilously close to losing the Chedleigh Minor living. My patience does have its limits, no matter how easygoing a chap I seem. Sorry for the sudden intrusion, ladies, but we didn't feel it wise to tarry longer. Uncle, I think you'd best see to Mrs. Parmenter. She appears about to faint."

"I wouldn't particularly mind following her example," Phoebe muttered, torn between fury and despair as she glared at Oakwood.

Damn them all! Quite obviously, they'd been lurking beyond the parlor door for some time. Why hadn't they intervened before her life was signed away? As things stood, they might as well have not bothered to come at all.

Desperately she forced her fists to unclench. There was precisely nothing she could do about her racing heart, or the fact that she had trouble catching her breath. That Oakwood was sending a bracing message with his traitorously soft hazel eyes didn't help in the least. Neither did the fact that, despite all appearances, she found herself wanting to tear across the worn carpet, throw herself in his arms, and sob out her despair.

"Now we've arrived," Soames said to the magistrate from Pilchester as Ware pocketed his pistol and joined her stepmother, "I believe Miss Parmenter can dispense with your presence. Mr. Broome, isn't it? Of Broome Manor? I'll handle matters from here on."

"Oh, I think not," Fordyce smirked, clearly sure of his ground. "You see, Broome's here at my invitation, and that's *Mrs. Fordyce* of whom you're speaking, and as I'm now master of Underhill—"

"You are?" Oakwood broke in. "How intriguing. And just what leads you to that conclusion?"

"As both the vicar and my wife can tell you," Fordyce gloated, "the vows've been said, duly witnessed, and sanctified by God's blessing. Now, I'll thank you to make yourselves scarce, as I've every intention of bedding the wench and then having my—"

"But, how can that be?" Soames broke in with a quick glance at Oakwood. "The banns aren't to be called until after the New Year."

"Special license. Oakwood's got it now."

"I'll see that, if you please." Soames pocketed his pistol and extended his hand.

Why, Phoebe wondered as she watched Oakwood pass the document to his lordship, did she have the feeling she was attending a theatrical performance, especially as she'd never been near a theatre in her life? And that the players were making most of it up as they went along, albeit rather skillfully?

"I do believe," Soames was saying, "that you'd be best served by asking your friend to remove himself, Fordyce. Mr. Hatch, you may stay or leave as you wish, but you may be certain I'll be speaking with you soon or late."

"Now, see here," Fordyce blustered, snaking his arm around Phoebe's waist as she cringed at his touch, "you're interrupting—"

"No," Oakwood thundered, *"you* see here!"

He flattened Fordyce with an efficient right against which better men than Mabel Parmenter's cousin had found no defense.

"Oh, dear," Soames grinned, "d'you think I'll have to charge you with assault, old fellow? Especially if Fordyce insists, which he's sure to?"

"No, and I want Hatch most particularly to remain," Oakwood returned grimly. "I've a use for him. Broome, however, would be best served by making himself scarce. You'll find your constable tied up in the stables, Broome. I doubt he's much the worse for wear beyond a touch of insult to his *amour-propre*. Crown should rectify matters."

Broome caught the coin flipped him by Oakwood, crammed it in his pocket. Then, warily eyeing first his lordship and then Oakwood, he scuttled from the room, pausing at the door to cast a nervous glance at Pru.

"My coat?" he pleaded.

Rolling her eyes to the ceiling, a grinning Pru followed Broome into the entry. Moments later she was back. Behind her the front door slammed as Fordyce groaned and sat, blearily staring about him and fingering his jaw.

"Well?" Alfie said, seeking out Oakwood's thick form through swollen lids. "Is it as we thought?"

"Hush, whipper-snapper. It's in his lordship's hands, now. Pru, fetch Alfie some snow for that temple. I have it on the best authority it's a sovereign remedy for such hurts. If you're feeling particularly charitable you might bring some for your other cousin as well, but I don't particularly insist upon it."

"I do believe I'll leave him go begging," Pru giggled.

"See here, what d'you think you're doing, issuing orders in my house?" Fordyce bristled as Pru, with a saucy grin, sped from the room.

"Showing a member of your family more care than you seem capable of."

Soames looked up from his place by the fire. "This is yours?" he said, indicating the special license, eyes narrowed, watching as Fordyce clumsily rose from the floor.

"Yes, it's mine. I'll thank you to return it to Mr. Dorning."

"And it's this document which you employed to wed Miss Parmenter?"

"It's the one I employed to marry Mrs. Fordyce."

"Interesting. Where'd you get it?"

"From a bishop."

"Which one? Because it's a forgery. Were you aware of this, Clare?"

"I, ah, I—"

"Marriage isn't valid," Soames continued, ripping the document first in two, then four, and tossing it on the grate as Pru slipped back into the parlor with a basin of snow. "You're married to no one, Fordyce. Neither're you, Miss Parmenter. You might as well take that ring off. It's meaningless."

Phoebe sagged into the nearest chair, gaze darting from Fordyce to Soames, then, in desperation, to Oakwood. "Oh, dear heaven," she murmured at the message in his eyes. Of a sudden the room seemed at once too hot and too cold, too bright and too dark, as if she were seeing and hearing everything from a great distance. And it was tilting alarmingly. Desperately she shook her head to clear it. Nothing seemed to help.

"You'll have to think again, Fordyce," Soames continued. "As for you, Clare, did you examine the license?"

"Thought never occurred to me," Dorning protested. "How could it? Provided by a gentleman and his solicitor, after all!"

"Ah—*you* provided the license," Soames said, turning on Hezekiah Hatch, who was easing his way toward the parlor door.

"Don't matter," Hatch cackled. "Doesn't exist any more. Right quick to burn it, y'were. Beware the grand gesture in the future, your lordship. Y'may come to regret it. Evidence is everything, and you've got none."

On those words he slipped from the parlor. Oakwood was after him in two steps, forcing him back to sit in a chair by the door, which Oakwood then blocked with his considerable bulk.

"Why did you agree to wed Philip Fordyce?" Soames said, overriding Hatch's grumbles as he turned to Phoebe.

Her eyes sought first his lordship's, then Oakwood's, as the parlor ceased its spinning. Then, trembling, she glanced quickly at her stepmother, huddled in Ware's protective embrace.

"Because," Soames continued, turning back to Fordyce, "I happen to know precisely how Portius Parmenter died, if that's it. From the lips of a witness. While not quite as initially reported, the discrepancy's hardly serious enough to reopen the case. An accident, pure and simple. Quite frankly, I'm far more interested in forged ecclesiastical documents and attempted blackmail."

"Now, see here, you've no cause to—"

"Oh, give it up," Hatch said. "Y'weren't quite as clever as y'thought y'were. Tale was a hum, and you've been caught out, and that's all there is to it. Wouldn't've bothered t'help if the pickings hadn't been so good. I'll be taking my leave now," he continued, rising creakily to his feet, "as there's no excuse for detaining me."

Oakwood's heavy hand descended on the old man's shoulder, holding him in place, then more or less gently returning him to the chair by the door.

"What's it to be, Fordyce?" Soames asked. "Do you make a peaceable departure, or do I institute some rather pointed inquiries?"

"There's no use my protesting your invasion of what is now legally my home?"

"None in the least, because it's not legally yours."

Fordyce reached for the pistol at his waist, apparently thought better of it as the Bodgers raised their rifles. He frowned, gaze flying from Mabel and Ware to the girls and Alfie, then to Soames, lastly to Phoebe and Oakwood. And then the starch seemed to melt from him, for all his posture remained elegantly languid.

"Wise man," Soames said. "Mick, Joe, take this, ah, gentleman to the bailiff's cottage, assist him with his packing, escort him to Pilchester and load him on the stage. There's one comes through at noon.

"Here." Soames tossed a thin purse to Fordyce, who caught it expertly. "This contains payment for your nag, and the wherewithal to reach Bristol and procure your passage on a ship that's outward bound. I care not in the least where you go, so long as it's far from England and your absence is permanent."

He tossed a second purse to Mick Bodger. "Stay with him until he's embarked and the ship's sailed, Mick. Otherwise he'll be back within a fortnight. And well done. Doubling back and watching from the spinny to make certain nothing untoward was going forward was a stroke of brilliance. I'm sure Lord—ah— Mr.—ah—that you'll be well rewarded when you return to Penwillow after seeing that coxcomb on his way."

"So that's how you arrived so inopportunely. My compliments," Fordyce said, pocketing the purse. "You're cleverer than I'd've dreamed."

With the bravado of a life-long gamester, he swept them all a graceful bow. Then he turned to Phoebe, still seated and watching him blank-faced. Oakwood was beside her on the instant.

With a wry smile Fordyce extended his hand. "My dear, temporary, and probably sole wife," he said, "won't you give me your hand in parting? Ah well, that's to be expected, I suppose. Still, it wouldn't've been so bad, you know. I kept telling you I'm a most peaceable man, but you refused to believe me. What was I to do?" Then, at her stony silence, he shrugged. "It was all a game, don't you see," he insisted, eyes sweeping the company, "and I lost, but ah, the rewards would've been grand had I won."

"Give him his ring, Phoebe," Oakwood growled.

She tugged it over her knuckles, held it out. Fordyce took it, twisted it this way and that, then slipped it over his watch fob and shrugged.

"Thank you, my dear," he said. "Only pot metal with a bit of gilt, but maybe I'll find a buyer for it."

And then Mick Bodger was prodding Fordyce with the tip of his rifle, and the three men disappeared through the door.

"It's over?" Mabel quavered, lifting her head from where she'd hidden it in Ware's neckcloth.

"Completely and permanently," the young earl said with a reassuring smile. "You've no more need to cower in corners, Mrs. Parmenter."

"Good," Mabel said with a brilliant smile, "for it was most uncomfortable living in such a fashion. I'm delighted you don't have to marry Cousin Philip after all," she burbled, turning to Phoebe. "I did caution you against him, you know, but you refused to listen, silly girl."

Then Mabel sprang to her feet, totally unconscious of her state of dishabille as she crossed to the table of gifts.

"What's all this?" she said. "Why, I do believe it's a new cloak! Oh, Justin," she dimpled, shaking out the deep green folds and swirling it across her shoulders, "you shouldn't've. But it's wonderful, truly wonderful. Thank you! I'll never be cold again."

She twirled in delight, posing first this way and then that.

"Except it's not yours, Mama," Pru said, attempting to retrieve the cloak. "It's Phoebe's."

"But whoever would give Phoebe such an expensive gift?" Mabel asked, maintaining a death grip on her new treasure. "You've the wrong of it, dear. It's mine, isn't it, Justin?"

"No, I'm afraid not," Ware said.

"It's *yours?*" Mabel spun incredulously to her stepdaughter. "Wherever did you get such an expensive garment? Have you been starving us all just so you could play the peacock?"

"I gave it to her," Oakwood snapped before the woman could betray herself further. "Her old one was ruined."

"Well, and so is mine," Mabel pouted. "I call it most unfair."

"But you've never liked green, Mama," Prissy protested. "You say it turns your complexion sallow."

"Enough of this," Ware snapped. "I'll buy you a cloak later, Mabel."

"Well, and so you should," Mabel said with a winsome smile. "I'm so fragile, you know, and really need a warm cloak if I'm not to catch my death. One with fur trim would be ideal, and a matching muff and toque. Toques're the latest stare. Much better than this cheap hooded thing. In royal blue, Justin, if you'd be so kind?"

"I do believe my poor uncle's going to be well repaid for his misplaced devotion," Soames murmured striding up to Oakwood as Mabel reluctantly relinquished the cloak. "She'll lead him precisely the sort of life that makes me avoid the ladies at all costs."

"There's a certain justice to it, that's certain," Oakwood murmured in response as Phoebe glanced from one to the other.

And then Oakwood peered down at her quizzically from his great height.

"You've got to forgive us," he said. "We were forced to permit Fordyce to go his length or there'd've been no way to send him packing this easily. You do remember I told you desperate men do foolish things?"

"Yes," Phoebe admitted reluctantly.

"We had to give him the opportunity to do something irretrievably foolish. Something provably illegal. I warned you of that."

"D'you have any notion what I suffered moments ago?" she demanded, eyes flashing.

"I've a fair idea. Had I not been certain we could pull the irons from the fire, I would've felt the same. Hearing you supposedly wed someone else is not the way I'd choose to spend an early Christmas Eve morning."

"Wouldn't you indeed? Fascinating!"

"You're angry," he sighed.

"A bit. Just a little bit, you understand! I think I've a right to be, don't you?"

"Things weren't supposed to go this far. I miscalculated badly last night, for I'd no notion Hatch or Dorning or Broome were at the cottage. I merely checked on Fordyce, and didn't think another thing about it."

"And that's supposed to make all right?"

"No, as only a portion of the problem's been solved," Oakwood said, hesitation in his deep voice. "As Mr. Hatch would tell you, there's another that remains, and it was the cause of the first."

"Papa's will. Yes, I know."

"I've a solution for that one as well. Fortunately it won't involve such stratagems as we were put to to rid you of your unwanted bridegroom. I know something of farming, you understand, and I've the reputation of being an honest, steadfast man, for all I enjoy the occasional joke. And unlike Fordyce, I don't pander to forgers or seek their services. When I do something, it's aboveboard, cards on the table, and no aces up my sleeve."

"See here, Oakwood," Dorning broke in, "if you're tending in the direction I think you are, it isn't to be thought of!"

"Stubble it, Clare," Ware and Soames chorused.

"He ain't, well, his parents, well—"

"I'm perfectly aware of Mr. Oakwood's situation," Phoebe returned gently, eyes locked on Oakwood's, head swimming, heart pounding, fury and insult forgotten. "It in no way lowers him in my estimation."

"I'm glad to hear that," Oakwood said with a sudden grin, "for I have it on the best authority that when an oak falls it makes a horrific crash, and I shouldn't care for it to be futile. Hark, Phoebe: the sound of an oak thundering to the forest floor." Peter Oakwood dropped to his knee, grasped her trembling fingers.

"Can you trust me never to hurt you?" he asked, hazel eyes boring into hers as the others watched and listened. "Or belittle you, or abuse you? Will you believe I'll love you all my life, probably more with each day that passes? Certainly that's what's been happening up to now and I find it's a great inconvenience, for it makes me want to kiss you each time I see you, and as things stand I haven't the right. This isn't the most graceful of offers, but would you? Marry me, I mean? I promise to make you laugh at least once a day, and thrice on holidays. And," he added with a grin at Alfie, "there'll be chicken on Sundays if you wish, and I promise you as much mistletoe as you can possibly use each Christmas."

Smiling so hard she thought her face would crack, Phoebe nodded, fingers gripping his desperately.

"When?" Oakwood demanded.

"Whenever you wish," she returned unsteadily.

"So you forgive me for the last hour?" Again, Phoebe nodded. "Immediately, then," Oakwood smiled tenderly. "You've need of a keeper, and so do I, as his lordship would be only too glad to inform you."

"See here," Hatch snapped, rising from his chair, "I don't know as I'll approve you, not base-born as you are, for Parmenters're gentry no matter how they've come down in the world, and if I don't then you'll be marrying a pauper."

"I'll see her hosed and shod, if that's what concerns you."

"More like it should worry you, y'dolt! She's worth nothing without Underhill."

"To me she is. She's worth everything. Will you trust me to take care of you," Oakwood asked, eyes still boring into Phoebe's, "and forget this horrible place? It's brought you nothing but sorrow and pain."

"So long as we can see to Mabel and the girls, for I truly shall be penniless."

"Don't worry about them," Ware threw in.

"Then yes, with all my heart," Phoebe beamed, hardly able to believe the change a few minutes had made.

"Oh, my dear girl," Oakwood murmured, "if only we'd not quite so may witnesses. I've a great longing to pluck every berry from yon wreath, you see."

Then crunching on the broken crockery, he strode over to where Clarence Dorning scowled by the chimney.

"I think you'll find this one's quite in order," he said, handing Dorning an oblong document. "We'd like to put it to immediate use, if you don't mind."

Doming glanced at it, eyes widening. "See here," he squeaked as he whirled to Soames, "d'you mean to tell me it's been *him* all along?"

Soames grinned, nodded. "Y'never were too bright, Clare, and always much too quick to leap to conclusions, especially the conclusions y'wanted to leap to."

"D'you have any notion whom you're agreeing to marry?" Dorning spluttered, stalking over to Phoebe and waving Oakwood's special license under her nose. "Why, your father was a saint by comparison! This man's a thorough rotter, a gamester, a rakehell steeped in all the evils of the world, the Antichrist—"

"I've always known his name isn't Peter Oakwood," Phoebe shrugged. "Beyond that, I believe I'm a better judge of his character than you are, Mr. Dorning."

"See here," Dorning insisted, whirling on Oakwood, "y'can't do this! Your father'll—"

"My father will kill the fatted calf, once he's done with congratulating me on acting sensibly for once in my life. Stubble it, Clare. There's a wedding service to read, and then I rather imagine you'll be wanting to return to your duties. After all, it's Christmas Eve. Must be a few things y'have to do in honor of the season."

On those words Piers Duchesne, Marquess of Stovall, garbed in the rough country tweeds of an itinerant landscaper—perhaps, of a nobleman more interested in his comfort than in setting a style—seized the hand of Miss Phoebe Parmenter, spinster and country heiress, garbed in her nightdress and a green shawl trimmed in red, and pulled her before the vicar of Chedleigh Minor.

"Get on with it, Clare," he ordered.

And so Clarence Dorning reluctantly got on with it, stumbling a bit over the words, and scowling at the dainty golden band Duchesne produced at the appropriate moment.

And then it was over, the band on her finger, with only the papers to sign.

"Piers Percival Charles Edward?" Phoebe said, gazing quizzically at her new husband as Pru darted in from Portius Parmenter's office toting ink pot and freshly mended pens. "And not a Peter in the lot? That's a deal of names for a simple landscaper. Who are you, really?"

"Your lord and master," Oakwood grinned. "Also purveyor of cloaks and mistletoe, and all other things rare and wonderful. I did promise you a Christmas you'd never forget, you know." He accepted a pen from Pru, dipped it in the pot and, blocking Phoebe's view with his back, signed with a flourish, sanded his signature, then covered his name and style with one large hand. "Sign first. Then you may have at me."

Frowning slightly, Phoebe accepted the pen from him and did her part. Oakwood removed his hand.

"Dear God!" she murmured, blanching.

Soames, with a humorous glance at old Hatch, who was dancing about on the fringes of the crowd in an effort to see precisely who it was his former crony's daughter had married, performed a deep bow.

"Lady Duchesne, let me be the first to wish you happy," he said.

About the Author

A French and English tutor when she's not writing, Ms. Ellis lives in Arizona with her husband of 35 years, a gifted artist and popular watercolor instructor. She loves to hear from readers, and can be reached at PO Box 24398, Tempe AZ 85285–4398. Please include a stamped, self-addressed envelope if you wish a response.

ROMANCES BY BEST-SELLING AUTHOR COLLEEN FAULKNER!

O'BRIAN'S BRIDE   (0-8217-4895-5, $4.99)

Elizabeth Lawrence left her pampered English childhood behind to journey to the far-off Colonies . . . and marry a man she'd never met. But her dreams turned to dust when an explosion killed her new husband at his powder mill, leaving her alone to run his business . . . and face a perilous life on the untamed frontier. After a desperate engagement to her husband's brother, yet another man, strong, sensual and secretive Michael Patrick O'Brian, enters her life and it will never be the same.

CAPTIVE   (0-8217-4683-1, $4.99)

Tess Morgan had journeyed across the sea to Maryland colony in search of a better life. Instead, the brave British innocent finds a battle-torn land . . . and passion in the arms of Raven, the gentle Lenape warrior who saves her from a savage fate. But Tess is bound by another. And Raven dares not trust this woman whose touch has enslaved him, yet whose blood vow to his people has set him on a path of rage and vengeance. Now, as cruel destiny forces her to become Raven's prisoner, Tess must make a choice: to fight for her freedom . . . or for the tender captor she has come to cherish with a love that will hold her forever.

Available wherever paperbacks are sold, or order direct from the Publisher. Send cover price plus 50¢ per copy for mailing and handling to Penguin USA, P.O. Box 999, c/o Dept. 17109, Bergenfield, NJ 07621. Residents of New York and Tennessee must include sales tax. DO NOT SEND CASH.